PRAISE FOR
JAMES GRIPPANDO
AND
BLACK HORIZON

"Fantastic. . . . Finely crafted dialogue
and a realistic yet nuanced hero
make this thriller a standout."
Publishers Weekly (*Starred Review*)

"With a story that's ripped from the recent
headlines (remember the 2010 BP oil spill?),
this is a solid legal thriller that should appeal
to the author's fans."
Booklist

"James Grippando is a master
of the legal thriller."
New York Times bestselling author
Robert K. Massie

"A briskly paced thriller. . . . The complex plot
points combined with the breezy narrative—
not to mention the Florida Keys setting—make
for a solid beach read that will no doubt
leave longtime fans looking forward to [more]
adventures of Jack Swyteck."
Houston Chronicle

"*Black Horizon* is timely, relentlessly paced,
and a thrill ride of the first order."
BookPage

By James Grippando

Coming Soon in Hardcover
Cane and Abe

And for Young Adults
Leapholes

* A Jack Swyteck Novel
+ Also featuring FBI agent Andie Henning

JAMES GRIPPANDO

BLACK HORIZON

HARPER

An Imprint of HarperCollins*Publishers*

HARPER

An Imprint of HarperCollins*Publishers*
195 Broadway
New York, New York 10007

Copyright © 2014 by James Grippando
Excerpt from *Cane and Abe* copyright © 2015 by James Grippando
Back cover author photo © Monica Hopkins Photography
ISBN 978-0-06-210990-3

First Harper premium printing: December 2014
First Harper hardcover printing: March 2014

HarperCollins ® and Harper ® are registered trademarks of Harper-Collins Publishers.

Printed in the United States of America

Visit Harper paperbacks on the World Wide Web at
www.harpercollins.com

10 9 8 7 6 5 4 3 2 1

For Tiffany, with love.
Thanks for twenty years of happy beginnings.

1

.

Two words, and life changes forever. Nothing new for a criminal defense lawyer. This time, however, Jack Swyteck wasn't waiting outside a jury room for a verdict of "not guilty." He was rehearsing his most important line.

I do.

Jack straightened the white boutonniere on his lapel and adjusted his bow tie in the bathroom mirror. His hand was shaking as he brushed the sleeve of his tuxedo jacket, shedding the raindrops that he'd carried indoors. He wasn't sure why he was so nervous. For a guy whose love life could have filled an entire volume of *Cupid's Rules of Love and War, Idiots' Edition*, he should never have expected a wedding without glitches.

"Plan A" would have been picture perfect: bride and groom standing barefoot on a sandy beach, a canopy of white sails and colorful orchids overhead, the turquoise waters of an underwater national park glistening in the background. Mid-September, however, was the height of Florida's hurricane season, and their Saturday-afternoon ceremony became a race against Mother Nature. They lost. Just as the mother of the bride was escorted to her seat, Key Largo was hit by a storm straight out of its name-sake movie starring Bogie and Bacall. Soaked guests ran to their cars through a wind-driven downpour. Band after band of torrential rain blew ashore, making it pointless to wait out a tropical storm that stretched from Miami to Havana. The ceremony was moved a few miles north, indoors, to Sparky's Tavern, an old gas station that had been converted into the last watering hole between the mainland and the Florida Keys. The proud owner was Theo Knight, a former gangbanger from Miami's ghetto who'd survived death row and then named his bar Sparky's—a double-barreled flip of the bird to Flor-ida's old electric chair, nicknamed "Old Sparky." Actually, it was a fitting place for the wedding. Jack had presented the DNA evidence to prove Theo innocent, and the down payment on Sparky's had come from Theo's "compensation" for having come so close to execution that they'd fed him a last meal and shaved his head and ankles to attach the elec-trodes.

"Ready, dude?" asked Theo. He was the best man.

"I do," said Jack. "I mean, yes."

Jack led the way from the men's room, down the hall and into the bar. On saxophone was Theo's great-uncle Cy, entertaining the waterlogged guests with his jazzy interpretation of the Pachelbel Canon. In his prime, Cyrus Knight had been a nightclub star in old Overtown Village, Miami's Little Harlem. The music calmed Jack, and it made him smile to see how quickly the friends of the bride and groom had transformed Sparky's into a worthy venue. The white canopy from the beach had been reconstructed beneath the vintage disco ball. Folding chairs covered the dance floor, bride's side and groom's side separated by a makeshift center aisle. Every chair was filled, not one of the seventy-odd guests having decided to bag the wedding to dry off at home.

Jack and Theo entered from the side, taking their places near a jukebox that hadn't worked since Reagan was president. Harry Swyteck shook his son's hand. At the height of his political career, back when Jack was just a newbie lawyer at the Freedom Institute, Harry had served two terms as Florida's governor, but it was his enduring office of notary public that empowered him to perform a wedding ceremony.

"Your grandmother is so proud," Harry said softly.

Many familiar faces were in the audience, but Jack's gaze was fixed on Abuela. There were tears in his grandmother's eyes—mostly joy, but surely some sadness that Jack's mother wasn't there. She'd died in childbirth, and it wasn't until Jack was a grown man that Abuela had found a way to leave Castro's Cuba. Abuela had made it her mission to give her gringo grandson, "half Hispanic, in blood only," a crash course in Cuban culture. A marriage outside the Church could bump him down to about a C-minus, but there was endless potential for extra credit upon delivery of great-grandchildren.

The music stopped, and Sparky's fell uncharacteristically still for a Saturday afternoon, only the patter of raindrops on the roof. All eyes turned toward the set of double doors in the rear that led to the billiard room. A golden retriever named Sam, the guide dog for groomsman Vincent Paulo, came down the aisle first. One paw at a time, his dark, reddish coat shining, Sam unfurled the runway, a long pink ribbon connecting his collar to a roll of white butcher paper that Theo had found in the storeroom. It would have been fun to pair up Sam with Max, the lovable dumb blond who thought he was Jack and Andie's first child, but the runway was impromptu, and Max would have freaked in the storm anyway. On cue, Uncle Cy began to play a jazz-laden, spirited version of "Here Comes the Bride."

The guests rose, the doors to the billiard room opened, and Andie appeared at the end of the aisle.

"Wow," Jack heard himself say, completely involuntarily.

Andie Henning was unlike any woman he had ever known, and not just because she worked undercover for the FBI. Jack loved that she wasn't afraid to cave-dive in Florida's aquifer, that in her training at the FBI Academy she'd nailed a perfect score on one of the toughest shooting ranges in the world. He loved the green eyes she got from her Anglo father and the raven-black hair from her Native American mother, a mix that made for such exotic beauty. *Radiant* was probably an overused word at weddings, but it fit. There was nothing like a beautiful woman and a long, white wedding dress in the neon glow of a Bud Light sign.

Andie walked down the aisle escorted by her

father, and they stopped at the front row. Her father kissed her on the cheek and went to his wife's side. The maid of honor carried the train of the dress as Andie climbed the single step onto a small stage where many a local band had played. Her run from the beach in the sudden downpour had left her bouquet battered and shaken, and the ivory bloom of a rose broke off and dropped to the floor. Jack quickly picked it up.

"Five-second rule," he whispered, and then he kissed it and tucked it into his pocket.

"So glad you didn't say, 'This bud's for you,'" Andie said through her teeth.

Jack tried not to laugh as she joined him beneath the canopy. The music stopped, and the guests settled into their chairs. Harry paused to punctuate the moment, then spoke in a strong voice that beamed with pride.

"Ladies and gentlemen, we are gathered here today to join Andrea Henning and John Swyteck—Andie and Jack—in matrimony. Marriage is a very important institution. One built on trust and love. We are here to celebrate their love for one another and have asked you as guests to share in this display of their love for each other."

Harry paused. Jack and Andie had asked him to dispense with the anachronistic verbiage from traditional wedding ceremonies, but like all politicians Harry loved to hear himself talk.

"If there is anyone here who can show just cause why these two should not wed," said Harry, "speak now or forever hold your peace."

The crack of a thunderbolt rattled the room. It

was a near miss—too near. The neon beer lights flickered, and the room went dark.

"*Ay, Dios mío!*" said Abuela, crossing herself.

Jack and Theo exchanged glances, the irony not lost; they were, after all, in *Sparky's*.

"I guess He prefers a candlelight ceremony," said Jack, glancing upward.

Andie squeezed Jack's hand. "You mean 'She.'"

Jack smiled. "Yes, dear. She."

2

The storm system was centered over the Florida Straits, midway between the hundred-mile swath of Gulf Stream current that separated Key West from Havana. Sustained winds of forty miles per hour were barely half those of a Category 1 hurricane, but they were strong enough to churn twenty-foot swells that could pitch and roll the most massive of oil rigs. And they were just strong enough to earn the storm a name.

"Come on, Rosa! Blow, bitch, blow!"

Rafael Lopez leaned over the safety rail and punched his loudmouthed crewmate in the chest, but it landed with little more force than the driven rain. The storm's name was Miguel. Rosa was Rafael's sister back in Havana.

"Shut it!" Rafael shouted into a howling wind.

His friend laughed it off. Rafael was in no mood for jokes. The night shift was just beginning, and he was dreading another twelve hours of horizontal rain that would slap him in the face and soak through his foul-weather gear. Under normal conditions, the rig's white industrial lighting would set the surrounding seas aglow, but tonight Rafael couldn't even see to the end of the platform.

"You two!" the drilling supervisor shouted at them. "Quit clowning around. It's dangerous out here."

No shit, thought Rafael.

Rafael and his Norwegian supervisor were part of a multinational crew of 167 oil workers who operated the largest exploratory rig in the world for a drilling consortium that included Cuba, China, Russia, and Venezuela. A Scottish company had pulled out, but its name for the rig stuck. The Scarborough 8 was specially built in response to official estimates that Cuba's North Basin held anywhere from 5 to 20 billion barrels of oil and 9.8 trillion cubic feet of natural gas. It was problem enough that those reserves lay beneath five thousand or more feet of ocean. "Ultradeep-water drilling" was the industry classification. An added problem was the long-standing U.S. policy toward Cuba that prohibited American companies from participating in any drilling south of the boundary between the exclusive economic zones of the United States and Cuba—roughly sixty miles from Key West. To sidestep Washington's fifty-year-old trade embargo against the Castro regime, the Scarborough 8 had been built at a shipyard in the Shandong Province of China with less than 10 percent of U.S. parts. At 36,000 gross tons, it was too big for the Panama Canal and had to be transported around the Cape of Good Hope on its maiden voyage across the globe. An Olympic soccer field couldn't match its astounding length and width. In fair weather, the submerged hull dipped thirty-five meters below the water surface, more than three times the draw of the *Queen Mary II*. In survival mode, facing the likes of Tropical Storm Miguel, the Scarborough 8 was engineered to rise up in the water, with just a nineteen-meter draft, which elevated the platform above rough seas.

Not high enough to suit Rafael.

The spray on his face tasted of the ocean, not of the falling rain. His gaze followed the string of lights that ran up the side of the derrick, a tapered mast of steel framework that was the oil industry's most recognizable symbol. Rafael was six months away from a degree in engineering, but on this rig he was a derrick monkey, one of several handsomely paid risk-takers whose job it was to support the team of drillers from a catwalk above the platform. His work station, the "monkey board," was a fifty-foot climb up the side of the derrick.

"Any chance we'll shut down tonight?" he shouted.

The supervisor chuckled and shook his head, as if to remind Rafael that the Norwegian engineers on the Scarborough 8 had all earned their drilling stripes in winters on the North Sea.

"It costs a half million euros a day to lease this rig from the Chinese. A little wind and rain are not going to shut us down."

It was more than "a little," even if the storm had weakened considerably since making landfall on a northwesterly path of destruction across Cuba. Management had counted on the island as a storm barrier that would keep the system from becoming a hurricane, making evacuation of the rig unnecessary. Rafael could only wonder if his tiny apartment in Havana had survived.

"Hi-ho, hi-ho," said the supervisor. "Off to work."

Rafael wiped his goggles clean and started up the ladder. The rungs were slippery, so he gripped extra tight. Forty pounds of wet gear—raincoat, boots, flashlight, radio, helmet, and more—didn't make it any easier. Below him, the day-shift workers disappeared into the dormitories, glad to take shelter. They'd return in twelve hours; the Scarborough 8 never slept.

Wind gusts intensified as Rafael climbed higher on the derrick. It was best not to think too much about the danger, but he'd checked the status board at dinnertime, and he couldn't erase the most current drilling data from his mind. The Scarborough 8 was in 5,600 feet of seawater, and the titanium drills had cut through 14,614 feet of layered rock beneath the ocean floor. Also on his mind—it was posted all over the rig, from the cafeteria to the cinema—was the fast-approaching deadline to find petroleum and gas in quantities that qualified as a "commercial discovery." Just five days remained on the consortium's forty-five-day lease of the only rig in the world that was both 90 percent free of American parts and big enough to tap Cuba's North Basin. Rumor had it that next in line was a Brazilian-Angolan-Vietnamese consortium, with a Spanish-Indian-Malaysian group behind them. A strike by any of them on the Scarborough 8 would earn the Cuban government half the profit.

A blast of wind rattled the derrick. Rafael stopped climbing, hitched his safety strap to the rail, and held tight. He was on his way to the monkey board, some twenty-five feet above the platform, more than a hundred feet above the raging ocean. His supervisor's voice crackled on his radio.

"You okay up there?"

Rafael turned his face away from the wind and rain to speak. "Couldn't be better."

The derrick rattled again, a deep vibration that started in his feet on the bottom rung of the ladder and coursed all the way up through his body. The radio crackled again with the voice of his supervisor.

"Stand by, Rafael."

It was hard for Rafael to tell in a raging storm, but something about that last jolt didn't feel like the wind. The follow-up from his supervisor only heightened his concerns.

"Rafael, come down!"

The lights on the derrick blinked off, then back on.

"What is going on?"

"Get down—*now*!"

Red-flashing emergency lights were activated, and an alarm sounded. The workers below were suddenly in "all hands" mode. Day-shift workers rushed from the dormitories, pulling on their gear as they raced through the rain toward the derrick. Rafael unhitched his safety harness and started down the ladder quickly, then stopped. Again he felt that strange rumble in the metal rungs.

Suddenly the rain seemed to reverse course and spray up from the platform, but Rafael knew it wasn't rain. It was the industrial "mud"—a mixture of clays, additives, and water—that in the normal course circulated through the drill pipe to clear away the cuttings and cool the equipment. Another alarm sounded. More lights flashed. Rafael held tight.

"Rafael, you—"

His earpiece crackled, and the voice of his supervisor broke off. Rafael pressed the receiver more firmly into his ear, but he couldn't hear anything but the driving wind, pounding rain, and pulsating alarms.

The sound that followed was like a sonic boom. It rocked the derrick and nearly knocked Rafael from the ladder. Fighting to keep his balance, he glanced down toward the platform. From his vantage point, high on the derrick and in the blurring rain, the chaos below was like a swift kick to an ant mound. Men were literally running for their lives, pulling on inflatable vests and scrambling toward the lifeboats at the platform's edge. The crew had trained for disaster at sea, but no amount of preparation could erase the sense of panic that attended a bona fide emergency.

Rafael felt another vibration beneath his feet, more powerful than the previous one. A wave of heat rose up from directly below him, a rush so intense that he could feel it through the soles of his work boots. Again the deck lights blinked on and off. The red and yellow flash of emergency beacons seemed to highlight the swirl of confusion below him. One man went overboard, and another followed. It wasn't clear if they had jumped or if they had been swept from the platform. Either way, Rafael knew they were caught up in a force more powerful than the storm. Another vibration, another intense wave of heat, and a blinding flash of light told him so.

Rafael closed his eyes and gripped the ladder with all his strength.

"Mother Mary," he said softly, "I'm a dead man."

3
·

"Technically, it would be *lunch* in bed," said Jack.

Andie had room service on the line. She rolled over, wiped the sleep from her eyes, and checked the clock on the nightstand. It was one o'clock in the afternoon.

"Never mind," she said into the phone, then hung up. Jack pulled her close beneath the sheets.

"Let's eat by the pool," she said.

"Let's stay in bed," said Jack.

"Don't you want to see me in my new Brazilian bikini?"

Seeing as how they were naked, it was hard to know the right answer. "Uh . . . yes?"

"Good one, Jack. You've got this husband thing down pat."

Andie popped out of bed first, and Jack followed. The honeymoon was at the Big Palm Island Resort in the lower Keys, about twenty-five miles up the chain of islands from Key West. Thatched-roof bungalows in a secluded tropical setting made it a favorite destination for newlyweds and couples who didn't care how much it cost to reexperience Life B.C. (before children, that is). Jack and Andie followed the sandy footpath through the scrub of sea grapes and hibiscus to the pool area. The tiki bar was open, but it was as quiet as the warm ocean breeze, until a shirtless baby boomer arrived with his much younger woman. The boomer pulled up a couple of bar stools and flagged the bartender, his accent pure Texas.

"Could you turn that up, pardner?"

He was pointing at the television. The bartender obliged.

It had been Jack's intention to spend his honeymoon on a news blackout, but the soothing sounds of the ocean were suddenly mere background for CNN. He tugged at Andie to join him for a walk on the beach, leaving the real world behind, but the story caught her attention:

"For many Americans, memories of the Deepwater Horizon oil spill, the biggest man-made environmental disaster in history, have not even begun to fade. Once again, millions of gallons of oil are spewing from a hole in the ocean floor, this time in some of the most pristine waters in the world. In a matter of just days, huge black slicks may be headed straight toward Florida's coastline."

Jack stepped closer to the bar, staring in disbelief at the ominous satellite images of the spill area on television. "You gotta be kidding me."

Andie shooshed him. The newscast continued:

"Critics point to lessons that should have been learned from the Deepwater Horizon catastrophe that devastated the Gulf Coast. But last night's deadly explosion of a massive oil rig in the Florida Straits presents an even bigger challenge. The oil company in charge of drilling, Petróleos de Venezuela, is owned by the Venezuelan government, which has done little to improve relations with the United States since the death of its very anti-American president, Hugo Chávez. The manufacturer of the $750 million, semi-submersible rig is Sinopec, the state-owned petroleum giant from China. The owner of the rig and the company in charge of cementing the well for periodic pressure tests is Gazprom Neft, the oil-producing arm of Russia's largest natural gas exporter. And even though the rig exploded just sixty-five miles from Key West, Florida, it was in Cuban waters northwest of Havana, and the entire operation is controlled by a mineral lease from the Cuban government under a production-sharing agreement with Cuba's state-owned oil company, Cubapetróleo, or 'Cupet,' as it is called."

"Well, ain't that just fine and dandy," said the Texan. He was on the opposite leg of the tiki hut's four-sided bar, but his voice carried clear across the bartender's work area to where Jack and Andie were seated.

"Why don't you shoosh *him*?" Jack whispered.

"He's not married to me," said Andie. "He's married to Miss Teenage U.S.A. over there."

Andie turned her attention back to CNN, but Jack noticed another couple approaching the tiki hut from the beach. The man's skin radiated the atomic glow of too much sun on the first day of vacation, but it was the woman who seemed angry. She split the pair of empty barstools beside Jack and slapped a rolled-up beach towel on the bar top.

"Excuse me," she said in a tone so sharp that the bartender dropped his pineapple. "Does your manager know about this?"

He gathered the fruit off the floor and went to her. "I'm sorry, ma'am. Know about what?"

She unrolled the beach towel. Inside was a black blob that, from Jack's angle, looked like a lump of wet coal.

"*This*," she said as she pushed the towel toward the bartender. "It's a tar ball. I found it on your beach."

The Texan walked over and took a look. "That's a tar ball, all right."

"See, I told you," she said to her sunburned mate.

"Marsha, I never said it wasn't a tar ball."

Marsha ignored him, turning her glare back to the bartender. "I want to see your manager."

"Right away, ma'am." The bartender went to the phone, no argument.

Jack and Andie exchanged glances, each wondering if the other wanted to hang around for the imminent bloodbath. The Texan dove right in.

"You know, ma'am, it's not unusual to find tar balls on Florida beaches. They fall off barges, ships, what have you, all the time."

"This didn't fall off a ship. Have you been watching the news?"

"Sure have," said the Texan. "But that Cuban spill just happened last night. Sixty-five miles from Key West means ninety-five miles from here. We wouldn't be getting tar balls already."

"Oh, really?" she said. "And who are you, some kind of tar ball expert?"

"Buddy Davis," he said with a tip of his baseball cap. "Worked in the oil industry for thirty-seven years. If you call countin' your money 'work,'" he added with a wink.

"No disrespect, Buddy," said Marsha. "This is my honeymoon, and it took us ten months to save up the fifty-percent deposit on a suite here. I am not staying if there's an oil slick on the way."

The point registered with Jack, even if Marsha's attitude left something to be desired. Andie, too, had been listening. "I feel the same way, Jack."

"Y'all on your honeymoon, too?" asked the Texan.

Andie was scheduled to start a new undercover assignment in two weeks, so Jack knew well enough to keep his mouth shut and let her respond in a way that was sure to shut down the personal questions from a total stranger.

"No, I work for an escort service," Andie said as she pressed herself against Jack, winking at the Texan, "if you call a week in paradise with a stud like this 'work.'"

Miss Teenage U.S.A. looked up from her iPhone. "Like, that's so random! I work for a service, too! Who are you with?"

"Babes R Us."

"Hmm. Don't know them."

"We really need to get out of this place," Marsha said to her husband.

The bartender returned with the resort manager, a smiling and cheerful man whose accent Jack pegged as Jamaican. The oil spill was obviously a resort-wide concern, so he addressed all three couples at the tiki bar as a group.

"I want to assure each and every one of our guests that—"

"Blah, blah, blah," said Marsha. "There's an oil slick on its way, my husband and I are checking out of this resort before it gets here, and we want our deposit back. Period."

Jack cringed. It was entirely possible that he and Andie would be asking for their deposit back, too, but Marsha's abrasive style made him reluctant to cast his lot with her.

The manager maintained his smile. "Let's all relax a moment, shall we? First of all, the oil slick is not on its way to Big Palm Island."

The Texan popped a gin-soaked olive into his mouth, chewing roundly. "What makes you say that?"

"Well, as you might expect, our number-one objective is to make sure that both our guests and our beautiful resort are protected. Our New York office has been in direct contact with scientists from the National Oceanic and Atmospheric Administration, and I am happy to tell you that they have assured us that geography is completely in our favor."

"Do you mean geology?" asked Jack.

"No, geography," said the manager. "The Gulf Stream flows right between northern Cuba and the Keys. Those currents are like a conveyor belt and will carry everything north, away from land and into the Atlantic. The only thing that could get the oil off that track is a minimum thirty-knot wind out of the southeast that blows continuously for days and days and days. And even with that kind of wind, it would still take the oil a week or more to reach land, which means that most of the oil would wither away before it got to the Keys. So even in the worst-case scenario, we wouldn't have a lot of black oil coming ashore. What we will have are tar balls, which are much less of a threat."

Marsha poked at the blackened beach towel. "Tar balls like this one, you mean?"

"Yes, but that one has nothing to do with the spill. We had the same situation after Deepwater Horizon in 2010. People all over the Florida Keys were freaking out, but a few tar balls on the beaches are an everyday occurrence on an island this close to a shipping lane. It doesn't mean we are feeling the effects of an environmental disaster."

Marsha shook her head. "I'm not buying it."

The manager was still smiling. "I understand, ma'am. Please enjoy a complimentary cocktail from our award-winning mixologist, and let's all stay in touch on this. I'll certainly let you know if anything changes. Have a very pleasant afternoon on Big Palm Island."

He started away. Marsha grabbed her husband by the arm and followed. Jack could still hear her hammering away for a refund as they walked all the way to the other side of the swimming pool, and the badgering persisted as they continued down the walkway and disappeared behind a leafy stand of bamboo.

The Texan looked at Jack and said, "That lady's right, you know."

"Right about what, exactly?"

"You didn't actually believe that NOAA-scientist bullshit, did you?"

"I was hoping the resort isn't just making it up."

The Texan chuckled. "Listen, pardner. The only kernel of truth is that this tar ball's got nothin' to do with the spill. But don't believe for one second that the slick ain't headed this way."

"How do you know that?"

He leaned closer, elbow on the bar top, narrowing his eyes. "I made a killin' in this business, son. Got friends all over the world with a keen eye on Cuba's North Basin. Those impact projections in that government report were based on the first exploratory wells drilled by a Spanish company called Repsol. Those were just fifty-five miles from Key West, but they turned up dry. So the Chinese, Russians, and Venezuelans moved farther west. Folks breathed a sigh of relief because the new drill site wasn't so close to Key West and the Florida Keys National Marine Sanctuary. But moving farther west actually put the Keys and the Florida coast more at risk."

He had Andie's attention, too. "How can that be?" she asked.

"It's a lot like the NOAA's hurricane prediction cone. If you move the eye of the storm—in this case, the source of the spill—fifty miles, or even twenty-five miles, to the west, it means a huge change in the impact area."

Over the years, Jack had seen enough hurricane predictions and the "cone of danger" to understand. "That makes sense."

" 'Course it makes sense," said the Texan, " 'cuz

it's true. My advice is to pack your bags and *git*. Unless you like the smell of petroleum blowing through your bungalow."

"Are you leaving?" asked Jack.

"Yup." He leaned even closer so that only Jack could hear, his eyes cutting toward his escort. "Which is just as well. Even with Viagra, a man needs a break every now and then. Get the picture, pardner?"

"I so wish I didn't," said Jack.

The Texan slapped Jack on the back, wished him luck, and led his escort away by the hand. Jack and Andie sat alone at the tiki bar with CNN. The bartender was rubbing the bar top furiously, trying to remove the black stain left by the "unrelated" tar ball. It wasn't coming off.

Andie breathed a heavy sigh and said, "This certainly puts a little rain on a bride's wedding day in perspective."

"We'll be all right," said Jack. "That guy's a blowhard."

"Thirty-seven years in the oil industry. Mr. *Exxon Valdez* seems to know what he's talking about."

"Maybe," said Jack. "I'll give Marsha the pit bull a few more minutes to chew on the manager's leg. Then I'll pay him a visit and get to the bottom of that NOAA report."

"I really don't know who to believe."

Jack glanced up at the television. "Spill Coverage" on CNN had moved to the next phase. The president of the International Drillers Association was in the hot seat.

"I think we're in for a lot of that," said Jack.

$$\frac{4}{\cdot}$$

Jack woke to the sound of honking geese.

He was half-awake, anyway. The room was still dark, and the windows were black as midnight in the Florida Keys, far from the glow of city lights. It was Monday morning, and he wasn't sure if an actual flock of geese had wrested him from sleep or if he was simply a slave to his internal alarm clock and workday habit.

He listened for it again, but the honking had stopped, and it must have been a dream. All Sunday night, the television news coverage had focused on the potential environmental impact of the Cuban spill, the screen flashing with images of past oil disasters and sludge-covered birds on despoiled beaches. Even with no sound, cable news was a poor choice for a lovemaking night-light. Jack settled his head into the pillow and slowly drifted back toward sleep.

Honk, honk.

He jackknifed in the bed, cursing those damn geese.

Geese? In the middle Keys? No way.

He reached for Andie, but her half of the mattress was empty. "Andie?"

Honk.

The noise was coming from the bathroom. Jack slid out of the bed and crossed the dark suite slowly, mindful of his toes and the hidden posts that seemed to jump out of nowhere in hotel rooms. He approached the crack of light beneath the closed bathroom door and tapped lightly. "Are you okay in there?"

"No," she said, breathless. "This has been going on since five a.m."

The first flock of geese.

He tried the doorknob, but it was locked. "Andie, let me in."

"I'm okay. Go back to sleep."

The honking gave way to something more guttural, a retching noise worthy of Ferris Bueller and his famous day off. "You don't sound okay."

"I'll be out in a minute."

Jack stepped back, not so sure. He thought of the grilled dolphin Andie had eaten for dinner last night. "Fresh as fresh can be," the waiter had told them. Maybe fresh enough to contain petroleum from the spill.

We need to get out of this place.

Jack sat at the foot of the bed, found the remote that was buried deep in the twisted down comforter, and switched on the TV. The same story dominated every channel. Jack stopped surfing to catch the tail end of an interview in progress with a retired rear admiral from the Coast Guard.

". . . is releasing at least as many barrels per hour

as the Deepwater Horizon spill of 2010," he said, "and there is no bilateral treaty between the United States and Cuba to coordinate a response. That's a recipe for disaster on top of disaster. Cuba has no deepwater submarines, no capability to deal with a spill of this magnitude. U.S. containment equipment, technology, chemical dispersants, and expert personnel are literally on the sidelines. They cannot focus on the spill where the need is greatest—at the faucet. U.S. ships cannot even get close enough to drill relief wells."

More honking from the bathroom. Jack hit the MUTE button. "Andie?"

"I'm okay," she said in a voice that faded.

Jack left the television on MUTE, but the image on the screen spoke for itself. It seemed counterintuitive, but Jack was strangely reminded of the aerial photographs of the islands in Biscayne Bay that the pop artist Cristo had famously wrapped in pink fabric in the 1980s. These satellite views were the antithesis of art—ugly black blobs floating on beautiful blue seas in the Florida Straits. Comparisons were already being made to the worst spills in the history of exploratory drilling. It made Jack feel like a bridezilla to consider anything less than the big global view of the disaster, but he could apologize to the world later. Keeping one eye on an oil slick was no way to spend a honeymoon.

"Andie, we're checking out today."

She didn't answer, but he'd said it loud enough to be heard. He grabbed their suitcases from the closet and started emptying dresser drawers. They'd packed light, and he moved quickly, so it didn't take long. It felt like the high-speed rewind of that cute joke his grandmother had told at the reception in honor of the newlyweds, about the first thing that honeymooners do when they get to their hotel room: "Open their drawers and put their things together."

Jack zipped up the suitcases and put them on the bed. The bathroom door opened. Andie's feet shuffled across the marble tile, but they didn't take her far. She leaned against the door frame, exhausted. She was wearing the resort's terry-cloth robe, but somewhere in the dash from the bed to the bathroom she'd lost one of the matching slippers. Her hair was up in a chip clip. The color was gone from her face.

Jack caught himself before telling his new bride how she looked. "Do you feel like you're getting better or worse?" he asked.

"It comes in waves."

"I bet it was that dolphin you ate last night," said Jack.

"It's not food poisoning," she said.

"I just heard on the news that fifty thousand barrels a day could be flowing from that spill. Commercial fishermen in the Keys go all the way out to the edge of Cuban waters if they have to. Yesterday morning's catch could have easily been contaminated."

"Jack, it's not the fish."

"How can you be so sure?"

"I had a hunch yesterday, so I asked the concierge to make a run to the drugstore and get me a kit."

"A kit?"

She dug into her pocket and showed him the blue test stick. "I'm pregnant," she said.

5

"Wow, I'm gonna be a dad."

It was about the tenth time Jack had uttered words to that effect since leaving Big Palm Island. They were in Jack's convertible, driving north toward the mainland on U.S. 1 with the top down. Andie looked much better. The sunshine and fresh air were working wonders on her morning sickness—for the moment, anyway.

"I'm glad you're happy."

"Of course I'm happy," said Jack. "Only one little concern."

"What?"

"How do I tell Abuela I didn't marry a virgin?"

"By my calculation you've got almost eight months to figure that out."

Jack had intended it as a joke, but the more he thought about it, the more he hoped that his grandmother simply wouldn't do the math.

The narrow highway stretched for miles before them. Not a building was in sight, the tropical sun glistening on clear and shallow waters on either side, the gulf to the west, the Atlantic to the east. The entirety of the aptly named Overseas Highway ran from Miami to Key West. It made driving seem like *the* way to get there, but at certain isolated segments along the way it was easy to imagine that Henry Flagler had just built the bridges and laid the railroad tracks that had originally connected the Keys, only to be blown away in the hurricane of 1935. The Seven Mile Bridge was particularly breathtaking, a concrete ribbon at odds with nature that somehow managed to maintain harmony with the surrounding natural beauty. For miles, the only sign of civilization was the traffic. Jack noted that virtually all of it was against them—heading south, toward Key West and the biggest news story on the planet. About every third vehicle was a satellite van.

"When should we alert the media?" Jack asked.

"What?"

Andie didn't get the joke, but Jack subscribed to the shotgun theory of humor, so rather than explain, he just moved on and hoped that the next pellet would hit the mark. "When can we start telling people you're pregnant?"

"Let's wait until I see a doctor."

"That makes sense. Let's go."

"You mean now?"

"Yeah. Tell her we decided on Jamaica as Plan B for our honeymoon and we need a doctor's okay to fly on an airplane."

"Pregnant women fly all the way up to the eighth month. I don't need a doctor's approval."

Jack thought about it, then realized that he'd seen many an expectant mother on airplanes. "I guess that's right. But maybe you shouldn't be visiting a foreign country."

"Jack, if you're going to be one of those neurotic pregnant husbands, I'm going to head off into the woods, pop out this baby on my own, and call you when she heads off to college."

"How do you know our baby's a girl?"

"I don't. Could be a boy."

"Or twins."

"Do you have twins in your family?" she asked.

"No. But you might. You've said yourself that knowing who your birth parents are doesn't mean knowing the whole family history. A set of twins somewhere along the genealogical line strikes me as something that an adopted child might not know about."

"I guess it's possible."

"Or triplets."

"Jack, the woods are looking really good to this she-wolf right now."

"Sorry."

Andie's cell rang, and Jack focused on the road as she took the call. The traffic ahead was stopped, so he braked to cut his speed.

"Jack, please." She was still on the phone, but apparently even the slightest motion in the car was more than her morning sickness could take.

"Sorry," said Jack. A long line of cars ahead of them was at a dead stop. It seemed odd that northbound traffic would be backed up, unless the authorities had road-blocked the entrance to the Keys, forcing southbound vehicles to turn around and head back toward Miami.

"Jack, *really*," said Andie.

He had barely touched the brake. He put the car in neutral and tried coasting to a stop. At least fifty cars were lined up ahead of them, and it was exactly as Jack had suspected. Florida Highway Patrol was shutting down the lower Keys and Key West. The only people getting through the roadblock were the media vans, cleanup convoys, and, presumably, residents. It was enough to erase any of Jack's lingering questions about leaving Big Palm Island. The last thing any sane ob-gyn would recommend was a beach vacation less than ninety miles from an oil spill. And even if those tar balls on the beach were "unrelated" to the spill, and even if the fresh dolphin filet wasn't contaminated, the hotel manager's comparison of the Gulf Stream to a "conveyor belt" was hardly soothing. Jack's house sat right alongside the road, so to speak, just another fifty miles to the north. His recollection was that it had taken almost three months to cap the Deepwater Horizon spill, and that was with the best equipment and most highly trained response teams in the world. Who knew how long it would take the Cubans to get this one under control? Fifty thousand barrels a day had to go somewhere.

"I need you to take me to Tamiami Airport," said Andie.

Her phone call was over, and Jack didn't have to ask if it had been work related. A flight out of Tamiami always meant one thing: a destination dictated by the FBI, unknown even to Andie, never to be known by Jack.

"Today?"

"Sorry, yes. The start date for my assignment has been moved up."

"But you cleared both the wedding and the honeymoon two months ago."

"That was then. The situation has changed."

The situation. That was as much as Jack would ever hear about one of Andie's undercover operations. This time, however, he'd seen enough Cantonese-language instructional CDs around the house to figure out that there was a China connection.

"Could this possibly have anything to do with the fact that the exploded oil rig is owned by the Chinese?"

He glanced in Andie's direction, but she was gazing out toward the ocean, showing him the back of her head, refusing even to acknowledge the question.

"That's what I thought you'd say."

Northbound traffic was suddenly moving again. Jack punched the gas to close the gap between him and the pickup truck ahead, but he'd accelerated too quickly. Andie suddenly didn't look so good. She reached into the backseat and grabbed the ice bucket they'd borrowed from the resort. Her head went down between her knees, and those rare birds—the September geese of the Florida Keys—were honking again. Jack reached over and laid his hand between her shoulder blades. Finally she sat up, her eyes closing as her head rolled back against the headrest.

"You might want to take that bucket with you."

"You might want to wear Kevlar," she said as her left fist catapulted across the console and nailed him squarely in the chest.

"Damn, girl! That hurt!"

"Good," she said, managing a little smile. "It was supposed to."

6
.

Jack parked along the road outside Tamiami Airport and watched from his open convertible as the jet cleared the runway and disappeared into the clouds.

The first leg of Andie's trip was under her actual credentials, a commercial flight to a destination that had nothing to do with her assignment. Leg two was where Andie Henning would vanish, and only after leg three or beyond would she settle into her new community under an assumed identity. The abrupt end to their honeymoon was a bummer, and even though Jack had married her with eyes open, the morning sickness had put an entirely different spin on her open-ended assignment.

Next time I see you, our baby could be kicking.

Jack drove away, not sure where he was headed. It wasn't easy for a sole practitioner to clear his calendar, but Jack had blocked out the entire week, and he didn't especially feel like going into the office. He called Theo, who was his usual sympathetic self.

"Bitch."

"It's her job," said Jack. "She's not a bitch."

"No, I meant *you*, bitch. Looks like we're a couple of honeymooners."

"I knew I shouldn't have called you."

"You totally called the right guy," said Theo. "We're going to Key West."

"To do what?"

"To stand up for the fish and birds and everything else that is about to be covered in oil."

"How very social-minded of you."

"Not really. Journalists are a bunch of drunks. Business is about to explode at my buddy's bar on Duval Street. He needs a hand."

"I hate to rain on your sudden conversion from nature lover to capitalist pig, but they're shutting down the Keys. You can't get to Key West."

"My buddy will get us through."

"How?"

"Dude, trust me."

The last time Jack had done so, his classic 1966 Mustang with pony interior was reduced to a heap of charred metal by some very pissed-off Colombians. But his packed suitcase was still in the trunk and he had nothing else to do. "I'll pick you up in twenty," he said.

Jack made it in half that time, but every extra minute and then some was lost on U.S. 1, which south of Sparky's had become a veritable parking lot. Florida Highway Patrol had moved the middle-Keys roadblock up to Key Largo, a pretty reliable indicator that the NOAA's projected zone of impact had expanded north to the upper Keys. Southbound traffic was backed up all the way to the mainland.

Theo spent the entire trip surfing the Web on his iPhone, giving Jack oil-spill updates in real time as they crept along in stop-and-go traffic.

"Get this," said Theo. "Says here that if American cleanup equipment isn't allowed into Cuban waters, it could take anywhere from fifty to seventy days for the right equipment to arrive from Africa or South America."

There was a new oil-spill tidbit every two minutes, and Jack had no idea how much of the Internet slosh was true. Ninety minutes into the trip, the FHP checkpoint was in sight. Theo had yet to contact his friend who owned the bar in Key West, so he tried calling one more time.

"He still doesn't answer," said Theo as he tucked away his phone.

"This guy's a friend of yours?"

"Friend of a friend."

"You dropped everything in Miami to help out a friend of a friend in Key West?"

"It's business. Word on the street is that Rick's looking to sell his café. I got a group of about five guys thinking about making an offer. Two of 'em actually have money. I'm the scout."

"Well, scout. How are we getting through the roadblock?"

Theo fell silent for a moment, thinking. Jack's gaze returned to the roadblock, where just about every other car was being turned away. They were in need of a plan, and from the expression on Theo's face, one had just come to him.

"Do you still have your room key from Big Palm Island?" asked Theo.

"Yeah, but—"

"Give it to me."

"*This* is your plan to get us through the road-block?"

"Just give me the key," said Theo.

Jack opened his wallet and handed him the plastic card. The convertible inched forward to the checkpoint, where a state trooper stopped them and approached the vehicle from the driver's side.

"Afternoon, fellas. We're turning away all sight-seers. What's your business in the Keys?"

Theo leaned over from the passenger seat and handed him the key. "We're staying at Big Palm Island Resort."

The trooper looked skeptical. "The two of you are staying on Big Palm Island—together?"

"Yes," said Theo. He reached across the console and slid his hand onto Jack's knee. Jack froze.

"Is there something wrong with that?" asked Theo.

"Well, uh, no," the trooper said, backpedaling. "Of course not."

"Because you're acting as if there is something wrong," said Theo, indignant.

"Nothing wrong at all," said the trooper. "I have lots of friends who are . . . well, I have a few friends who probably know some gay people."

"May I have our key, please?" asked Theo.

The trooper gave it to him.

"I'll have you know that this key is to the honeymoon suite at Big Palm Island Resort. Isn't that right, Jacky?"

Jack hesitated. "Technically, yes, that's true."

"So you two are on your honeymoon?" asked the trooper.

"Yes," said Theo.

"No," said Jack.

"It wasn't a trick question," said the trooper.

"I'm on my honeymoon," said Jack. "But he's not . . . I mean, *we're* not—this is not *our* honeymoon."

Theo folded his arms in pouty fashion, glaring at Jack. "So hurtful, Jack. You promised: no more double life. Officer, could you please let us through before my so-called partner ruins everything?"

The trooper hesitated.

"*Please*," said Theo.

"All right." The trooper stepped aside and waved them through. "Enjoy your honeymoon. But you may want to check out early if that oil comes this way."

"Thank you," said Theo as they pulled forward.

Jack massaged away an oncoming headache as he drove. "Theo, you just lied to a state trooper."

"I know."

"I'm going to kill you."

"No, you're not."

"I know," said Jack as they entered the Keys. "Bitch."

They reached the southernmost city in the continental United States at dinnertime and headed straight to Rick's Key West Café on Duval Street. The owner, Rick Cavas, was out. The hostess had "no idea" where Rick was or when he would return. Jack and Theo took an outside table and killed the waiting time with a plate of "*con fuego*" chicken wings and a cold pitcher of beer.

Overnight, Key West had become ground zero for the American response to the impending oil disaster—a quirky coincidence, since it was also mile marker zero of U.S. Highway 1. Duval Street, the main drag in the Key West tourist district, was known for its art galleries and antique shops housed in renovated Victorian-style buildings. But day trippers and cruise-ship passengers really flocked there for the offering of reef-diving excursions, deep-sea fishing charters, bicycle rentals, overpriced junk jewelry, and—the really big sellers—enough T-shirts to clothe a Third World country and an assortment of sex toys worthy of *Fifty Shades of Grey*. Crucial to the lively mix were dozens of open-air bars and cafés where local bands and musicians from all over the Caribbean created a mélange of rock, salsa, and calypso. Jack took note of the usual attractions, but they were clearly secondary to a much bigger phenomenon. Duval and its cross streets had become media central.

Every major news organization had pounced on the oil-spill story and literally staked out ground. Mallory Square, a public gathering spot on the wharf where musicians, jugglers, and portrait artists turned sunsets into a festival every day of the year, had been overtaken by a temporary but monstrous two-story shelter for reporters and crews. No national news show was without its own Duval Street café for live broadcasts, roundtable discussions, and immediate "man on the street" audience participation. Environmentalists marched down Duval, posters and banners in hand, fighting to save the ocean, shoreline, and wildlife. On every street corner stood a television reporter, microphone in hand, interviewing tourists, locals, and business owners. The must-get story of the day was the firsthand account from someone in the commercial fishing or tourist industries. It was the perfect mix of drama and journalism, personal and angry pleas to the U.S. government to do something to avert a potential death blow to the Florida economy.

They were about to order a second plate of wings when Theo got a text message.

"Rick says to meet him at the marina," he told Jack.

"He owns a bar *and* a boat?"

"He has a charter fishing business on the side."

"I want his life."

"No, you want *my* life. I own two bars and borrow your boat."

The marina was a short walk from the café, and even on overcrowded sidewalks, they got there in five minutes. It was a good thing they'd left the car behind, because the parking lot was transforming into a staging area for cleanup equipment. Volunteers filled sandbags by the shovelful. Teams of handymen assembled floating booms to contain the oil. Cases of dish soap—the waterfowl-cleanser of choice in the Deepwater Horizon spill—were being unloaded from the back of pickup trucks. A palpable sense of urgency coursed through the marina, at times bubbling up into disagreements over containment strategies or arguments over salvage priorities.

Rick stepped off the stern of his fishing boat and greeted them on the pier, giving Theo a bear hug and a friendly slap on the back. It seemed like a lot of love from a "friend of a friend," but then he gave Jack the same big hug and back slap. It was just Rick's style.

"Glad you came, boys."

Rick was almost Jack's height but he was packing at least another thirty pounds of muscle. Jack attributed the added bulk to wrestling with ninety-pound marlin or tuna on a daily basis. Clearly it wasn't all recreational "catch and release," as evidenced by the too-tight T-shirt that bore the stains of dried fish blood and the logo for "Rick's Deep Sea Fishing Adventure."

"You done for the day?" asked Theo.

"Yup. But there's a little group of us leaving at dawn to see if we can catch a glimpse of the spill. You guys want to come?"

"Sure," said Theo.

"Jack, you up for it?" asked Rick. "It's about three hours each way."

"Jack's in," said Theo. "Trust me, he's got nothin' to do."

"How close can we get?" asked Jack.

"How good is your Spanish?"

Jack knew it was a joke, but Theo laughed even harder than he should have, as if Jack needed to be reminded how many times his god-awful "Spanglish" and general lack of awareness for all things Hispanic had embarrassed his *abuela*.

"Better stay in U.S. waters," said Jack. "This half-Cuban boy has filled his quota for affronts to the Cuban people."

"Good, we're on, then," said Rick. "No way you guys will find a hotel tonight. You're welcome to sleep here on the boat, if you don't mind sharing the state cabin."

"No, we don't mind," said Theo. "We're on our—"

"Shut it," said Jack. "Just shut it."

7
.

They left the Key West marina at dawn, heading south-southwest at twenty knots.

The "little group" going out to see the spill, as Rick had advertised it, was more like a flotilla crossing the Florida Straits. Jack counted twenty-nine vessels, a mixed fleet of fully enclosed cruisers, charter dive boats, and fishing yachts like Rick's refurbished Hatteras forty-five-foot convertible.

Jack had seen countless sunsets on the water in his lifetime, but the only time he got anywhere near an "ocean" this early in the morning was when his seventy-five-pound golden retriever peed on the bedroom floor. He wondered how Max was doing. They'd boarded him for the honeymoon at Mitzi's Boot Camp, which, despite the name, was more like the doggy version of Big Palm Island. Andie always spoiled him, and this time she'd done everything but hire Max his own escort from Babes R Us.

Jack savored this rare morning at sea, watching Key West vanish on the eastern horizon as the glowing orange ball emerged from the Atlantic behind them. A warm southerly breeze foreshadowed another hot September day in the subtropics. Shorts, T-shirts, and sunglasses were the only gear required. An hour into the journey, the wind kicked up, and their pleasure cruise on gentle swells gave way to seas of eight to ten feet, with intermittent whitecaps that sent a geyser-like spray across the bow. Midway through the third hour, the chaise lounges on the beach were calling him back to Big Palm Island, tar balls or not.

"How deep is it here?" asked Jack. He was with Theo and Rick on the open flying bridge, above the main deck and forward of the rumble of twin inboard engines. Rick was in the captain's chair at the helm.

"Deep," said Rick, checking the instruments. "A mile, give or take a few hundred feet."

Jack tried to imagine a floating oil rig with a drill at such depths, the nautical equivalent of halfway to the Titanic—and that was before it even scratched the surface of the ocean floor. For a lawyer who couldn't pump gas without getting it on his shoes, it was hard to fathom.

"You're looking a little green," said Rick.

"I'm fine," Jack lied. He tightened his grip on the safety rail, bracing for the next whitecap. "How much farther?"

"Twenty minutes, maybe."

That's what you said twenty minutes ago.

Jack gazed far into the distance, knowing better than to focus on the chop around them or the pitch and roll of nearby boats. The lead boat, way ahead of them, seemed to be slowing down. Jack figured it was just wishful thinking on his part, but then Rick cut their speed as well.

"Are we getting close?" asked Jack.

"Only so far we can go before we hit Cuban waters," said Rick. He reduced his speed further, down to just a few knots. "Looks like everyone is stopped right at the boundary."

Jack rose from the bench seat and took a better look. The flying bridge was twenty feet above sea level, which extended visibility with the naked eye. Jack hadn't committed every boat in their group to memory, but it was plain to see that they had joined up with many more boats than the twenty-nine he'd counted out of Key West. One in particular stood out as much bigger than the rest.

"What's that ship at two o'clock?" asked Jack.

Rick aimed his binoculars in that direction. "That's CCA."

"What's CCA?"

"Clean Caribbean and Americas. It's an emergency-response cooperative out of Fort Lauderdale. I've watched their practice drills around Key West. As far as I know, they're the only guys in the country who are licensed by the U.S. government to help clean up a spill in Cuban waters."

"I was under the impression that no U.S. company could help," said Jack. "That's what all the news reports have said."

Rick kept the binoculars trained on the ship. "It's hard to know who's right. When they were doing practice drills in Key West, the guy from CCA said he had the only license for actual on-site cleanup. A handful of other companies are licensed to lend training and know-how to Cuba. But this is all new ground. I don't think anyone really knows what they can and can't do in an actual catastrophe."

"They can't be much help sitting around here like the rest of us," said Jack. "We still must be a long way from the actual blowout."

"A good five miles, I'd say. Let me get CCA on the radio. A guy named Bobby Timms is in charge of operations. He brought his whole crew by my bar after the training exercise, and I took good care of them. If he's aboard, he'll tell me what's up."

Rick put the engines in neutral, bringing the boat to a dead stop in the water. He tried the radio— "CCA, this is Rick's Café, do you copy?"—and after several attempts, a response came.

"This is CCA. Bobby here. Go ahead, Rick's Café. Over."

"That's my buddy," Rick told Jack and Theo, and then he keyed up the mic. "Bobby, it's Rick. Why is the cavalry on the sidelines like the rest of us rubberneckers? Over."

"Can't go in. License problem. Over."

"Why the problem? Over."

"OFAC tells us we can enter Cuban waters only if the drilling is being done by foreign oil companies that are members of CCA."

Rick went off-mic again. "OFAC is the Office of Foreign Assets Control."

"I know," said Jack, "I dealt with them when I went to Guantánamo. But I want to understand exactly what he's saying. Scarborough 8 was a consortium of companies from China, Russia, and Venezuela. Is that the problem?"

"Let me ask," said Rick. He keyed up the mic: "Lemme guess, Bobby: CCA has no member companies from China, Russia, or Venezuela. Over."

"Affirmative. Over."

Jack could hardly believe what he was hearing. "Member, schmember," he told Rick. "Tell him to go in, clean up that mess, and ask for forgiveness later."

Rick repeated the gist of Jack's message, without attribution.

"No can do," said CCA. "Have you seen what's out there? Over."

"Oil?"

"Besides oil. North latitude 23.374496 degrees, west longitude 82.492283 degrees. Check it out. Gotta go now. Over and out."

Rick found the coordinates on the map, then aimed his binoculars accordingly. "Can't see that far from this level. Let's go up."

Jack and Theo followed him up the side ladder to the fiberglass crow's nest atop the flying bridge, but there was only room for Rick and Jack. Theo hung back, a few rungs down. Standing another eight feet above the helm, almost thirty feet above sea level, made the sway of the boat more noticeable, and Jack had to work his sea legs to keep his balance.

Rick focused his binoculars on Cuban waters and froze. "Ho-lee shit."

Jack looked in the same direction. "Is that what I think it is?"

"You bet it is," said Rick.

Theo borrowed the binoculars, still on the ladder. "Looks like the whole damn Cuban navy."

Jack shook his head in disbelief, then happened to glance down at the water. Floating past their boat was a black, oily stain on the dark-blue sea. He hadn't noticed from the lower level of the flying bridge, but at this height he could see a long line of big black amoebas approaching from the southwest—headed toward the Florida Keys, just as the Texan at Big Palm Island had predicted.

"Well, isn't that just beautiful," said Jack.

8.

They docked at noon. Oil stains at the water-line ran the length of Rick's boat, so cleanup involved much more than simply hosing off salt water. An hour of scrubbing still didn't remove all the sludge. Jack was starving by the time they reached Rick's Café, but he got a surprise phone call just as lunch arrived. He stepped out onto the sidewalk on Duval Street to take it.

"I miss you," he told Andie.

"I was beginning to wonder," she said. "You and Theo seem to be having quite the honeymoon."

He pressed the phone more firmly to his ear, not sure he'd heard her right. "How did you even know I was with Theo?"

"The Bureau checks the Facebook pages of virtually everybody I know when I'm on assignment."

"Theo posted on Facebook that we're on a honeymoon?"

"Uh-huh. It's become a running joke around here."

"I really am going to kill him." Jack glanced back

inside the café toward their table. Theo had already finished his lunch and was starting on Jack's, but Andie said just the right thing to make everything else irrelevant.

"I saw a doctor," she said.

"How's the baby?"

"Everything's good. Due May 14."

"Wow! And how are you?"

"Perfect. They cleared me to stay with the assignment. Even after I'm showing."

"But you won't be showing for another two months, right? You'll be home by then, I would assume."

Andie didn't respond. Jack knew she couldn't reveal the length of her assignment any more than she could tell him where she was or what name she was using.

"Gotta keep this short," she said. "I'll call again when I can. I love you."

"Love you, too," he said, and the call was over.

Jack put his phone away and went back inside to their table. Before he could lay into Theo about their honeymoon on Facebook, Rick joined them.

"There's someone I want you to meet," said Rick. "You got a minute?"

It was clear he wasn't talking to Theo. "Sure," said Jack.

Rick signaled across the bar. A waitress stepped from behind the cash register and walked toward them, negotiating the crowded maze of tables and lunch patrons. Most of the servers at Rick's Café, men and women, were young and good-looking. This waitress was especially attractive, a long-

legged Latina with gorgeous dark hair and a face
you might see in an Abercrombie ad. But she didn't
smile—not when Rick introduced her, not after she
joined the men at the table.

"Bianca has worked with us for over a year now,"
said Rick. "She started right after coming here from
Cuba."

"Where in Cuba?" asked Jack.

"*Habana*," she said softly.

"My mother was born right near there, in Bejucal," said Jack.

She didn't answer, and there still was no smile.

"So," Jack asked, "are you one of the Cuban nationals who came here after Raúl Castro eased up
the restrictions on travel from Cuba?"

She lowered her eyes, then answered in good, but
not perfect, English. "No. I didn't believe that day
would ever come. My husband and me, we saved for
three years. We bought a spot on a boat."

"Bianca is an American citizen now," said Rick.
"I'm sure you know this, being a lawyer, but U.S.
immigration policy toward Cubans has always been
the same, both before and after the Cuban government started to let nationals travel off the island.
Any Cuban refugee who sets foot on American soil
can claim asylum."

The same policy allowed the Coast Guard to
turn back Cuban refugees who couldn't afford a
visa under the new law, jumped on an old-fashioned
raft, and weren't lucky enough to swim all the way
to U.S. shore. "I'm very familiar with wet foot/dry
foot," said Jack, and then he turned back to Bianca.
"Did your husband come with you?"

"No. I didn't want to leave Cuba without him, but we had money only for one. The plan was that Rafael would come later, after he saved more money to buy a spot on a boat."

"Why doesn't he come now? It's a lot easier under the new Cuban laws."

"Not so easy as people think," she said. "It can cost less to buy a spot on a smuggler's boat than to buy a travel visa from the government. My husband was saving money. Got a good job."

"Doing what?" asked Jack.

Bianca didn't answer. The response seemed to catch in her throat.

Rick said, "He was a derrick hand on the Scarborough 8. One of about two dozen Cubans who were allowed to work for the oil consortium."

"What did he do on the rig?" asked Jack.

Again Bianca was silent. Finally, she looked at Rick and said, "You tell."

"From what I understand," said Rick, "he worked the night shift on something called a 'monkey board.' It's a platform high up on the rig's derrick. I'm not an oil expert, but there are a ton of websites on offshore drilling. Basically a derrick hand's responsibility is to monitor the drill fluids and circulation systems, control the drill pipe in and out of the drilling hole, and keep the pipe steady when parts are attached or removed. He does all this from his platform."

Jack was almost afraid to ask the next question. "Sounds like it could be dangerous," he said.

"One of the most dangerous on the rig," said Rick. He glanced at Bianca, then confirmed Jack's suspicions: "Rafael is one of sixteen workers reported dead."

Bianca sobbed but said nothing.

"I'm sorry," said Jack. "Are you sure he's gone?"

"I picked up a BBC News broadcast out of Havana," Rick said. "There were a hundred sixty-seven workers on the rig from seventeen different countries. None of the workers was from the U.S., of course. Two of the fatalities were U.K. citizens. The BBC report that identified the U.K. workers also listed Rafael Lopez among the dead."

"Man, that's horrible," said Theo.

"It is," said Rick, but he was looking at Jack. "I was hoping a good lawyer could help."

"What can I do?"

"Again, I'm no oil expert, but I've done some quick homework on the Internet. The average payout to the widows of the eleven men killed in the 2010 BP Deepwater Horizon disaster was between eight and nine million dollars."

"Are you asking me to file a wrongful death suit on Bianca's behalf?"

"Yeah. It's a foregone conclusion that the Cubans, the Chinese, the Russians, and the Venezuelans won't give her ten pesos. Her only hope is to file a lawsuit in this country."

"I hear what you're saying," said Jack. "But it's not so clear cut."

"Why not?" asked Rick. "Bianca is an American citizen."

"That's true. But her husband was Cuban. The manufacturer of the rig is Chinese. And the consortium was drilling within the territorial waters of Cuba."

"So she has no rights in U.S. court?"

"I'm not saying that. But it's a definite hurdle."

"Do you think you can help her?"

"Of course Jack can help her," said Theo. "Compared to keeping me out of the electric chair, this has to be a piece of cake."

"We need to talk about this," said Jack. "First, the fact that an oil rig exploded does not make this an open-and-shut case. To win a wrongful death lawsuit we have to prove that the oil consortium's negligence or other wrongdoing caused the explosion."

Rick was unfazed. "BP coughed up twenty-three billion dollars. I find it hard to believe that the safety standards on Scarborough 8 were any better than they were on Deepwater Horizon."

"That's probably true," said Jack. "But in the Deepwater Horizon case, lawyers had court-issued subpoenas, and they used all the regular channels of discovery to get evidence and place the blame where it belonged. In this case, it's possible, maybe even likely, that no one will *ever* uncover the truth about what really caused the explosion. Suing the Chinese, the Russians, and the Venezuelans for negligent operation of an oil rig in Cuban waters is the legal equivalent of running headlong into a stone wall."

Theo grabbed the last french fry from Jack's plate. "Which is why they came to you, Jack. You're the world's foremost legal expert on banging his head into walls."

"Thanks so much," said Jack.

Bianca was no longer gazing down shyly at her hands on the table. She looked right into Jack's eyes. "Please, *Señor* Swyteck. I am new in this country and my husband is dead. Don't make me look all over Florida to find a lawyer who I can trust. Can you take my case?"

It was a double-barreled shot of pain for Jack. Not only was there a young widow at the table, but she was about to become the hunk of bloody red meat in the proverbial shark tank of lawyers who lived by the mantra *"Have you been injured?"*

Rick said, "I'm happy to help work out the business side of it, if that would make it easier for Bianca. But I'm sure your standard contingency arrangement will be fine."

Theo literally kicked Jack under the table, and then he said what Jack himself was only thinking: "You'd have to be a horse's ass to say no, Swyteck."

Jack knew that "standard contingency" in this situation could well mean pro bono, but he wanted to help. "All right. We'll work something out."

"*Gracias*," said Bianca.

"But fair warning," said Jack. "This stone wall I'm talking about could prevent us from gathering the evidence we need to prove a case in court."

"*Sí, claro.*"

"And even if we overcome all the hurdles and win, I want you to understand something very important."

"What?"

Jack paused, adjusting his tone to make sure that his words did not come across as insensitive. "Closure for you—and by that I mean the peace you might get from knowing what truly happened to your husband on that rig—is not something I can promise. I can't stress it enough: we will be filing a lawsuit in U.S. court against a Chinese, Russian, and Venezuelan oil consortium operating in Cuban waters. Transparency will not come easy."

"I understand."

Rick reached across the table and shook Jack's hand. "Thank you, counselor."

Jack glanced at Bianca. She wasn't crying, but it wouldn't have taken much to push her over the edge. "It's the very least I can do," said Jack.

9
.

Havana. The capital city that defined Cuba for revolutionaries and dissidents alike. For Josefina Fuentes, it was simply home.

"What a mess," she said under her breath, no one near enough to hear her.

Josefina was on Avenida Salvador Allende, just west of a ten-block neighborhood that was once the largest and most vibrant Chinatown in all of Latin America. A half-century of communism and racial assimilation had dulled the influence of thousands of Chinese immigrants who had risen from slave-like conditions in sugarcane fields to become shop owners and businessmen in pre-Castro Cuba. A few signs of Chinese culture remained, but on that Wednesday afternoon, Chinatown was no different from any other Havana neighborhood: the mark of Hurricane Miguel was everywhere.

Before heading out to sea and slamming into the Scarborough 8 as a tropical storm, Miguel had blown across Cuba as a Category 1 hurricane and dumped more than a foot of rain in twenty-four hours. It had taken two full days for floodwaters to subside. Block after block was littered with fallen palm fronds and tree limbs, blown-off roofing tiles and pieces of old buildings, and tons of other debris. The neighborhood cleanup strategy was to push the mess into huge piles along the curb. Some residents used shovels and rakes while others improvised with boards, poles, branches, or whatever else they could find. The odor of wet garbage hung in the hot air.

Josefina cut a winding path down the cluttered sidewalk, with occasional side steps into the street to find a clear passage. No need to check for traffic. Buses weren't running, and anyone fortunate enough to own a car, a truck, or a taxicab was also smart enough not to waste precious fuel after a major storm. Most of Havana was still without electricity, so the usual sounds of the city were absent. No music blaring from *las tiendas*. No pockets of conversation at the walk-up café windows along the sidewalk. No groups of old men arguing over games of dominoes at shaded tables. Even the government offices remained closed—with one major exception.

"Go to MINBAS," Josefina's friends had told her at lunch. "There is supposed to be an announcement at three o'clock."

And so, off Josefina had gone.

MINBAS was the Ministry of Basic Industry, which administered Cuba's energy program and offshore exploration. By Tuesday afternoon, the ministry had become the go-to destination for relatives and friends of Cuban workers on the Scarborough 8. All were desperate for details, having heard nothing from their government except that the rig had been evacuated. Misinformation was flying through Havana neighborhoods, and Josefina was not alone in fearing a major catastrophe. The forthcoming three p.m. announcement might turn out to be just another rumor, but word of mouth was all Josefina had to go on. The Internet was no help. Even in ideal weather conditions, Web access was sketchy, as the U.S. trade embargo prevented Cuba from linking up to the Web via a direct fiber-optic line to the states, leaving the island cyber-dependent on a single underwater line from Jamaica and on even less reliable satellites. The power outage had shut down all Internet cafés except those that were accessible by tourists in the most expensive hotels. The afternoon announcement from MINBAS was her only hope.

Josefina approached a group of women on the sidewalk. MINBAS occupied seven stories of an unremarkable office building that was built in the minimalist and drab architectural style of the former Soviet Union. The women were standing right outside the main entrance. Directly overhead, a huge banner the length of three city buses hung from the roofline, draping over the windows of the top three floors: CADA CUBANO, it read, UN EJÉRCITO (each Cuban, an army).

Josefina didn't know any of the women, but their worried expressions gave her something in common and made them seem approachable.

"Any news?" asked Josefina.

"*Nada*," the women told her. Nothing.

Josefina continued down the sidewalk outside the ministry, scanning the crowd but seeing no one she knew. It was apparent that not everyone waiting for the announcement from MINBAS was a friend or loved one of an oil-rig worker. Many had gathered to get information of any kind, or because they had nowhere else to go. Generators were scarce throughout the city, so the promised broadcast from the temporary audio system that the government had rigged up outside MINBAS was, for many, the only working radio in the neighborhood.

At three o'clock, the speakers crackled. Josefina's pulse quickened. Her friends, it seemed, had given her reliable information. An announcement was indeed coming.

"Good afternoon," said the speaker, but he was not from MINBAS. He introduced himself as the minister of foreign affairs. The crowd outside the building fell silent as the minister spoke in a tone befitting the most serious addresses by high-ranking members of the Communist Party.

"This morning, eleven ships, six aircraft, and two helicopters from the United States penetrated into the waters and airspace of Cuba in a flagrant violation of international law. Cuban naval ships maneuvered alongside the intruders to physically prevent the U.S. ships from going straight toward our coasts."

Josefina took a step closer to the loudspeaker, confused. It wasn't the kind of emergency that she had feared, but it sounded ominous enough.

"This is a hostile invasion," said the minister, "and it is being conducted under the guise of international assistance to relief efforts. The people of Cuba do not need the assistance of capitalist interests who lack all commitment to the environment. Unlike the United States and its demonstrated incompetent responses to past oil disasters in its own waters, Cuba has a long history of commitment to the environment. With the help of the International Maritime Organization, we have prepared for a possible spill emergency. The United States and the rest of the world must know that we have this situation completely under control."

Josefina struggled to contain her frustration. *Situation? Exactly what* is *the situation?*

"To be clear," said the minister, "this morning's transgression was not a genuine offer of assistance. This is driven by right-wing elements in Miami who wish to seize on any opportunity to invade Cuban waters and conduct terrorist activities. Our border troops have shown restraint, firing no weapons. However, like any other nation, Cuba cannot tolerate a flagrant violation of its frontiers or provocative acts against our country. It is well documented that on many past occasions intruders from the United States have entered our waters and violated our airspace to perpetrate terrorist actions against economic targets and helpless civilians. Some people have been assassinated in cold blood. The Revolutionary Government reiterates its firm determination to take every necessary action to prevent acts like this from happening. We therefore issue this final warning: Any ship coming from abroad which invades by force our sovereign waters is liable to be sunk, and any plane, brought down. We are a peaceful and patient people, but the patience also has limits. The responsibility for what happens will fall exclusively on those who encourage, plan, implement, or tolerate these piratical actions. Thank you and good afternoon."

Josefina stood silent. People around her exchanged empty glances, as perplexed and unfulfilled by the announcement as she was. There was nothing in the radio address about the dead, injured, or missing from the Scarborough 8.

A warm, salty droplet ran to the corner of her mouth, but she wasn't crying. It was a trickle of blood from her nose. She dabbed it away with her sleeve, repeating to herself the lesson she'd learned from this latest injury.

Keep your left up.

Josefina worked with a trainer at a boxing gym near the University of Havana. The Cuban boxing team was one of the most successful in modern Olympic history, but the government had refused to field a women's team for the sport's debut at the London games, deeming *el boxeo* "appropriate" only for men. Attitudes were changing, and Josefina was determined to be the first female Cuban Olympian to win gold in the ring. She was two years into it, and she had a lot of work to do. Her sparring session that morning had marked an all-time low. Never had she been clocked so squarely in the nose. It was the price a fighter paid for distractions from her personal life. She tilted her head back and pinched her nostrils shut for two minutes.

"Josefina!"

She turned and saw her trainer coming toward her. She gave her nose a final pinch, the way her trainer had taught her in the boxing ring, and the bleeding stopped.

"The three o'clock announcement wasn't much help," she said.

"I know, but I have another idea. Come with me." He grabbed her by the hand and led her away quickly.

"Where are we going?"

"To see a friend."

They were walking fast, almost jogging as they continued around the corner. "What kind of friend?"

Her trainer kept them moving forward. "The best kind. He has a homemade computer. If anyone can get uncensored Internet, he can. He even went to Festival Clic."

Festival Clic was Cuba's biggest social-media conference ever. Most young Cubans had heard of it, even though in a nation of eleven million only about a hundred people had actually been allowed to attend.

"This way," he said as he led her up a flight of stairs to a pink stucco building. The sign on the door said PELUQUERÍA UNISEX.

"Your friend is a hairstylist?"

"His wife is," he said, knocking.

The door opened about six inches, and a woman peered out from behind it. "We are not open today."

"I know. We're here to see Javier."

"What about?"

"A friend. It's important for her to find out what happened to the Cuban workers on the oil rig. Please, I know Javier can help."

"He's busy," she said, and the door started to close.

"Tell him it's Sicario."

That was enough to keep the door open, if only a couple of inches. Josefina was not surprised. Many times before, she'd seen her trainer get results with the mere mention of his name. Sicario meant "hit man," the nickname he'd earned as a light-heavyweight boxer for the Cuban Olympic Team.

"Wait right there," the woman said. She closed the door, but Josefina noted that she didn't lock it.

Several minutes passed, and Josefina handled her anticipation by watching the huge white clouds pass overhead. They were moving so fast, like time-lapse photography—which was ironic, since the wait for Javier's wife to return seemed endless. Finally, the door opened.

"Javier will see you," she said, and she led them to a back office. The man behind the desk did not look up, did not acknowledge them in any way. He kept to his work. Josefina had seen ham radios before— often enough, in fact, to recognize this one as a solid-state Jaguey. But it was the first one she'd seen powered by a twelve-volt car battery.

"Where's the computer?" asked Sicario.

"We sold it," the woman answered. "But the radio will get you the information you need. It will just take a few minutes, since it's not voice transmission. It's Morse code on CW through data transmission."

"Who is Javier's contact?" asked Sicario.

"He's been going back and forth for about a day now with a ham member in Canada. The man seems to know everything about the rig."

Javier continued to scribble notes onto a pad, de-coding. Josefina wasn't keeping track of time, but again the wait seemed without end. Finally, Javier switched off the radio and looked straight at Sicario. The tip of his index finger was resting on the paper, pointing ominously at the handwritten list of names.

"Sixteen workers are dead," he said. "I have their names here."

Josefina swallowed hard. "Any from Cuba?"

"Two," said Javier. "Who are you checking on?"

She couldn't find the strength to say his name, to have her worst fears confirmed. "My fiancé," she said.

Sicario stepped forward and took the pad from the desktop. Josefina looked away at first, then forced herself to watch her trainer read the list. The moment he lifted his eyes from the paper and looked at her, she knew. Slowly, he laid the list aside and came to her.

Her whole body trembled as her trainer held her tight. "I'm so sorry, Josefina."

"Oh, no!" she said, burying her face into his shoulder. "No, no! Please tell me no!"

Not even the arms of a former Olympian could stop her from shaking.

"I'm sorry," he whispered. "Rafael is gone."

10

Jack found the last remaining room in Key West at a bed-and-breakfast, at quadruple the normal September rate, and worked all night.

It was important to move quickly. Although no one but Bianca was in a position to bring a wrongful death suit in the United States, Jack knew that armies of lawyers were ginning up individual and class-action claims on behalf of Florida businesses and property owners. Bianca's injury was of an entirely different nature, and he didn't want it buried in the avalanche of litigation over lost profits and damaged beach homes.

Around ten o'clock Wednesday morning, Jack got a text message from the courier: *Done.* The wrongful death action on behalf of Bianca Lopez, a widow, was on file with the circuit court in Key West.

Jack was too tired to walk upstairs to his room. His B&B was one of many century-old Victorian-style houses built during the commercial shipping heyday of Key West, and he fell asleep in a rocking chair on the front porch. The manager woke him at half past noon.

"My apologies, Mr. Swyteck. I have your secretary from Miami on the line. She says it's urgent."

Jack took the cordless phone. Bonnie sounded out of breath, which was normal whenever there was a surprise development in a case. And a surprise it was: Jack needed to be at the Monroe County courthouse at two p.m. for a hearing on an emergency motion filed by the oil companies. Jack had expected a counterattack of some sort that was intended to send him a message that this was a war he should never have started. But this was ridiculously quick.

"How can this be?" said Jack. "Our process server hasn't even served our complaint yet."

"It's weird. I called the clerk of the court, and there's no motion on file either."

"Have you gotten anything from the opposing lawyers?"

"No. Like I said, nothing's been filed, so I don't even know who they are."

"Has our case been assigned to a judge?"

"Judge Carlyle. I called her chambers, but it went to voice mail."

"Who told you there's an emergency hearing?"

"Freddy Foman."

Jack sat up in the rocking chair. "Huh?"

"Surely you remember Freddy."

Freddy was hard to forget. He'd started law school with Jack, flunked out after one semester, enrolled in a night school that was barely accredited—and then he'd gone on to become one of the richest lawyers in Miami, mostly on the backs of dead and dying clients in asbestos litigation. He was a gregarious guy with a big personality and stature to match, carrying a rotund three hundred pounds almost his entire adult life. The last time Jack had seen him, however, he had dropped to fewer than two hundred. It wasn't the South Beach diet. Freddy's law partner had turned out to be a con man who was running a multimillion-dollar Ponzi scheme. Freddy knew nothing about it but was swept up in the indictment. During the course of a two-month criminal trial, Jack had witnessed the suppression of Freddy's appetite firsthand: Jack was the lawyer who'd won his acquittal.

"What does Freddy Foman have to do with Bianca's case?"

"I honestly don't know, Jack. He was getting ready to fly his plane to Key West and didn't have time to explain. He just said you need to be at the hearing and that he would meet you outside the courtroom. If I were you, I would go."

Jack couldn't remember a time when Bonnie had steered him wrong. He ran upstairs and put on the nicest clothes he had with him. Khakis and a long-sleeve shirt wouldn't have cut it in Miami, but the rules were different in Key West.

The Freeman Justice Center is the main courthouse for Key West, probably the only judicial center in the world that closes one full business day each October for a citywide Halloween celebration. It was one thirty by the time Jack entered the building. He dialed Freddy's cell for a fifth time before passing his iPhone through the metal detector. Again, the call went straight to voice mail.

Answer your damn phone, Freddy.

Jack counted at least three or four dozen lawyers in the hallway outside Judge Carlyle's chambers, and more were pouring out of the elevators. Bianca's lawsuit named multiple defendants—the manufacturer and owner of the Scarborough 8, the oil companies in the consortium, and about a half-dozen related entities that arguably did enough business in the United States to justify bringing Bianca's lawsuit in Florida. As a sole practitioner, Jack had been outnumbered in cases before, but this was insane.

No way can all these lawyers be defense counsel in my case.

"Swyteck, how you doin', my friend?"

Jack recognized Freddy's voice immediately. He turned and did a double take. Freddy had ballooned back up to well over three hundred pounds, and his size XXXL Hawaiian shirt looked like a circus tent covered with smiling dolphins and dancing hula girls.

"Freddy, what's this about a hearing in my oil case?"

"Not *your* case," he said, extending his arms widely. "*Our cases.* As of noon, there were about three thousand lawsuits filed against the consortium for property damage and lost business in Florida. Many more to come."

Jack suddenly felt like Rip Van Winkle, having slept through it all in a rocking chair on the front porch of his B&B.

"Who do you represent?" asked Jack.

"'Places of lodging' is the best description. Everything from trailer parks to Big Palm Island Resort."

"You don't say," said Jack, deciding not to bite on Big Palm. "What's the hearing about?"

"Money," said Freddy. "The biggest problem we will all face—including you—is collecting a judgment from Chinese and Venezuelan companies who were drilling in Cuban waters. So a group of us came up with the idea to ask the court to freeze some of the defendants' assets in the U.S. pending the outcome of our cases. The plan was to go after a supertanker filled with Venezuelan crude when it enters a U.S. port. One supertanker is worth about a hundred million bucks."

"Sounds like a tough argument," said Jack.

"Even tougher now. The oil companies somehow got wind of it, and they filed this emergency motion to stop us from going after any supertankers before trial."

"Why didn't I get notice of this?"

"Because these sneaky bastard defense lawyers didn't file the motion in your case. They don't want you here. You got the only client who's a widow. Everyone else here is complaining about property damage and lost business. Judges are human, and the oil companies know that if they are going to persuade a judge to protect their assets, they need to keep the widow out of the courtroom."

"What do you want me to do?"

"I want you to take the lead at the hearing."

"I haven't even seen the motion."

"We have smart lawyers on our side, too, Jack. We can prep you in thirty minutes."

"You should have given me more time."

"I had to get the Plaintiffs' Liaison Committee on board before talking to you. Everything's all set."

It wasn't an ideal situation, but Jack had gone into

court with less advance warning, sometimes in matters of life and death—literally.

"What do you say, Swyteck?"

Jack's gaze drifted toward the elevators, where more lawyers were pushing their way into the overcrowded hallway.

"Either way," said Jack, "it looks like my second honeymoon is officially over."

11

•

At two p.m. Jack was seated in the last row of the public gallery in Judge Carlyle's courtroom in the Freeman Justice Center.

As expected, the Cuban government and its state-owned oil company refused to participate in the hearing in any way, through legal counsel or otherwise, but more than a dozen attorneys for the Chinese, Venezuelan, and Russian oil companies were at the defense counsel's table. To their right, near the empty jury box, sat the Plaintiffs' Liaison Committee—six men and one woman, seven distinguished members of the plaintiffs' bar—and the not-so-distinguished Freddy Foman. Each had muscled his or her way to the forefront in the race to speak on behalf of all those who had filed lawsuits against the oil companies for property damage and loss of business. Jack had declined the invitation to join them, instinct having told him to keep Bianca's claim away from the pack of wolves. To Freddy's chagrin, Jack attended the hearing only as an observer.

"How many property claims you got?" asked the man beside Jack.

The question only confirmed that there were few bona fide "spectators" in the courtroom. Dozens of lawyers had lost round one in the power struggle to serve on the Plaintiffs' Liaison Committee, and they were crammed shoulder to shoulder in the fifteen rows of public seating along with Jack. A separate, reserved section of seating for the media was likewise filled beyond capacity. More members of the press had managed to plant themselves throughout the gallery between the elbows of lawyers. Jack was pretty sure that the guy next to him was a lawyer, not a reporter—but it wasn't always easy to tell.

"I'm just here to watch," said Jack.

"I picked up six hundred new clients this morning, including Big Palm Island Resort."

"Really? I heard that Freddy Foman has Big Palm."

"Freddy *had* Big Palm," he said with a wink.

The feeding frenzy had begun, triggering one thought for Jack: *Thank God I stayed out of this.*

"All rise!"

The crowd heeded the bailiff's command, and a chorus of fading conversations and foot shuffling echoed through the courtroom as Chief Judge Sandy Carlyle took her seat at the bench. Carlyle was a transplanted lawyer from Manhattan who'd retired to Florida, nearly died of boredom in her condo, and so ran for one of Key West's elected judgeships. With her typical "212" directness, she instructed everyone to take a seat and moved straight to the afternoon's business.

"I've read the briefs," said the judge. "The most directly impacted defendant appears to be Petróleos de Venezuela, the state-owned Venezuelan company that was in charge of the drilling on the Scarborough 8. The parties seem to be in agreement that Petróleos currently has a supertanker full of oil at the Port Arthur Refinery in Texas. It's my understanding that Petróleos seeks an order of this court that would prevent the plaintiffs from seizing any Venezuelan supertanker in U.S. waters until after there is a trial on the merits and a final judgment is entered in the plaintiffs' favor. Is that a fair summation, counsel?"

A distinguished Latin man with silver hair rose from his seat at the defense counsel's table and buttoned his suit coat. Despite the relaxed Key West dress code, he was a walking advertisement for Savile Row.

"Yes, that's fair, Your Honor."

"And you are . . . ?"

"Luis Candela on behalf of Petróleos de Venezuela."

Jack knew the name. Candela was a past president of the American Bar Association, the first Hispanic ever so elected. His Washington law firm specialized in mineral rights in Central and South America. He spoke with all the confidence of an authority on the subject.

"As the court is well aware, assets can be frozen before trial only in very limited circumstances, such as where the defendant is hiding assets in order to make himself judgment-proof. In this case, there is absolutely no danger that Petróleos will hide its supertankers. My client has long-term oil-supply contracts with refineries in the United States. It is absolutely critical to keep all of those supertankers moving freely in and out of U.S. ports to fulfill those contracts."

"That's a compelling point," said the judge.

"It's especially compelling here," said Candela, "where it is highly doubtful that the plaintiffs will prevail at trial."

"It's too early to be arguing about that," said the judge.

"This is a key point, Your Honor. After the *Exxon Valdez* spill in Alaska, Congress passed the Ocean Pollution Control Act. That act makes it unnecessary for anyone affected by an oil spill to prove that the oil company was at fault. The only issue is whether the oil spill caused damage and the dollar amount of those damages. But the act doesn't apply to spills in Cuban waters. Every single one of the plaintiffs in this courtroom must meet the strict requirements of international maritime law. They must prove to a jury exactly what each defendant did wrong. In other words, the plaintiffs here are a long, long way from collecting any money."

"That's an issue I've not yet focused on," said the judge, "but I understand your point."

"One last thing," said Candela. "It is important for the court to understand the history of over-reaching in situations like this one. For example, in the Deepwater Horizon spill of 2010, two of Mr. Foman's clients from south Florida were eventually convicted of fraud and had to give up their Bentley and waterfront McMansion on Lighthouse Point to serve a thirteen-year sentence in federal prison."

"I object," said Freddy, rising. "Mr. Candela is talking about two bad apples in a class action with over ten thousand members. Unbeknownst to me, they stole the identities of folks in Broward County and filed three million dollars in phony claims. I never even met those crooks."

"No need to explain," said the judge. "No one's motives are being impugned today. But I will say this, Mr. Foman: the issue before the court seems like a no-brainer. I can't imagine why any assets should be seized before one drop of oil has even reached the Florida Keys."

"Commercial fishing has already been impacted," said Freddy. "Tourism is tanking as we speak. As we saw in Deepwater Horizon, if people even think there's oil in the water, they won't eat your fish or stay at your beachfront hotel."

"People need to get their fears under control," the judge said. "Until there is actual damage, any effort to freeze the defendants' assets is premature."

"I respectfully disagree," said Freddy. "But if the question of prematurity is foremost in the court's mind, I would point out that there is one case before this court in which the injury has undeniably occurred."

Jack froze. *Freddy is going to drag me into this.*

"My colleague from Miami, Jack Swyteck, has filed a wrongful death suit on behalf of a widow of one of the workers on the rig. I would be more than willing to yield my time to Mr. Swyteck. I believe it would be beneficial for the court to hear from him."

Jack could hardly believe his ears. To his dismay, the judge took the bait.

"Yes, my law clerk brought that case to my attention this morning," said the judge. "Mr. Swyteck, are you in the courtroom?"

Reluctantly, Jack rose. Heads turned toward the back of the courtroom.

"Yes, Your Honor," said Jack.

"Sadly, your client has already lost her husband, which would seem to put you in a different circumstance. So let me ask you this: If I rule for the oil consortium with respect to the property claims, should my ruling also prevent your client from attempting to seize any of the defendants' assets before trial?"

Jack wasn't fully prepared to explain his position, but there was only one answer he could give. "My client should not be affected."

The judge waved him forward. "Come to the microphone, please. The court would like to hear more from you before ruling."

Jack hesitated. "If the court would indulge me, I would like to have a little time to prepare—"

"Mr. Swyteck, *come forward*. The court is being asked to decide whether Venezuelan supertankers can or cannot sail into U.S. ports without threat of being subject to seizure. I am not about to defer ruling so you can go back to Miami and think about it."

"Yes, Your Honor." As Jack squeezed out from the bench seat toward the aisle, the new lawyer for the Big Palm Island Resort handed him a Post-it.

"My legal gem," he said softly. "Use it."

Jack read it quickly to himself: *Mr. Candela is as*

slimy as the sludge in our ocean. A bolt of courtroom brilliance worthy of a law-school dropout.

"I'll pass it on to Freddy," Jack whispered. He walked down the center aisle, pushed through the swinging gate at the rail, and went to the podium.

"Jack Swyteck, counsel for Bianca Lopez," he said, adding the case number.

It could have been Jack's imagination, but reporters in the media section seemed to take even greater interest with Bianca's wrongful death suit front and center. The judge, too, seemed more energized, twisting her long strand of white pearls as she spoke.

"Mr. Swyteck, what is your response to Mr. Candela's point that anyone suing the oil consortium must come forward with affirmative proof that the consortium was at fault? That strikes me as a pretty tough row to hoe, given that this spill took place in Cuban waters."

Jack had two possible strategies: He could be brief and simply distance himself from Freddy and the others, or he could go on the offensive and try to score points. Choosing the latter, he laid his iPad atop the podium and opened his research file.

"Proving fault will not be a serious obstacle for Bianca Lopez," said Jack. "Already I've uncovered a damning report from the Center for Democracy in America, a Washington-based organization that sent a team of specialists to Cuba on an offshore drilling investigation. I would note that the CDA is not a right-wing anti-Castro organization. To the contrary, the stated goal of the CDA is to end the trade embargo and normalize relations between the United States and Cuba. Even with that agenda, the CDA made the following finding," said Jack, pulling up the report on his iPad. "I quote: 'A foreign diplomat provided the CDA delegation with one concerning evaluation. He said some of Cuba's partners see Cuba as something of a laboratory for gaining experience in deep water.' End quote."

Not a single reporter in the courtroom missed that jewel.

"A laboratory," said Jack, driving home the point, "conducting experiments in five thousand feet of water—without the necessary experience. I'm confident that we will be able to show that this 'laboratory' operated without proper safety and evacuation standards."

Candela jumped to his feet. Even in his unprepared state, Jack was too well armed to suit the oil consortium.

"Your Honor, this is highly improper."

"Yes, but highly interesting," said the judge.

"I have much more," said Jack.

"I think we've heard enough," said Candela.

"I have time," the judge said.

Reporters in the front row literally scooted to the edge of their seats.

Judge Carlyle settled back in her tall leather chair, making herself comfortable. "Continue, Mr. Swyteck."

Jack could feel the momentum, but Candela cut him off, his tone somewhere between nervous and conciliatory. "Your Honor, since there is only one wrongful death suit filed in the United States, I am sure that the consortium can come up with an arrangement to satisfy Mr. Swyteck that, in the unlikely event his client prevails at trial, there will be sufficient assets to satisfy a judgment. As for today, we would urge the court to focus solely on the property claims and enter an order that protects our supertankers and keeps business operating as usual."

The judge considered it. "Is that acceptable to you, Mr. Swyteck?"

"A ten-million-dollar bond posted in the next three business days is acceptable," said Jack.

"*Ten million?*" said Candela, incredulous.

"On the other hand," said Jack, turning back to his iPad, "there are good reasons for this court to allow me to seize a supertanker. The latest projections from the National Oceanic and Atmospheric Administration have oil landing on Florida's beaches within the next four to five days if the spill is not shut off at the faucet. My understanding is that the consortium is still waiting around for a capping stack from Scotland. Seizure of a Venezuelan supertanker might give Mr. Candela's client just enough incentive to get things under control before disaster strikes."

Candela quickly conferred with his co-counsel, urgent whispers flying back and forth at their table. The entire team appeared anxious to shut down Jack's pipeline to the press. Candela faced the judge and cleared his throat, the words not coming easy.

"Your Honor, a ten-million-dollar bond in the wrongful death suit will be fine."

"So ordered," said the judge. "I will defer ruling in the property claim cases."

"Defer ruling?" said Candela. "But our super-tankers—"

"The matter is deferred," the judge said firmly.

Candela shot a quick but angry glare at Jack. It was obvious that Jack's final point—his mere suggestion that the court had the power to push the consortium to expedite containment efforts—made it impossible for a judge who was *elected* by the citizens of Key West to side with a Venezuelan oil company.

"Judge," said Candela, "Venezuela is this country's fourth-largest supplier. The United States depends on Venezuelan crude for heating oil and—"

"That will do, Mr. Candela. We are adjourned."

The judge ended it with a bang of her gavel. The crowd rose upon the bailiff's command, the judge exited through the side door to her chambers, and the courtroom was immediately abuzz. Reporters leaned over the rail, calling Jack's name, peppering him with questions about a lawsuit that, until Freddy's ambush in open court, had managed to slide into the courthouse without notice.

"Who is Bianca Lopez?"

"Where does she live?"

"When can we talk to her, please?"

Jack did not respond. He grabbed his iPad and pushed through the crowd toward the rear exit, not so much as glancing in Freddy's direction on his way down the center aisle.

12
.

Andie took the Red Line into Washington, D.C., exited the Metro at the Judiciary Square Station, and walked three blocks to the J. Edgar Hoover Building. She was alone. And she was at that early stage of an assignment where she needed to remind herself every now and then that her name was Viola.

Viola, she thought, noting another wave of "morning" sickness, even though it was five o'clock in the afternoon. *How do you like that name, baby?*

Her meeting at FBI headquarters was in a windowless room below ground level. The entire undercover team had been summoned for an update on Operation Big Dredge. Three months before, when Andie had signed on to the operation, she was told that it was an investigation into organized crime and business cheats from south Florida to Guangdong who were making billions on the smuggling and sale of counterfeit goods. But that evening, at their first official meeting since Andie's deployment into the field, the team leader's welcome made it clear that "smuggling" and "counterfeiting" had never been the real targets of the investigation.

"Say good-bye to Big Dredge," he said to a roomful of agents, "and welcome to Operation Black Horizon."

Andie was seated in the front row of metal folding chairs as the lights dimmed and, with the hum of an electric motor, a projection screen descended from a slot in the ceiling. Andie had seen enough television news coverage about the spill to recognize the image immediately: the Scarborough 8 oil rig floating in blue waters—before the explosion.

Agent Anthony Douglas was a Gulf War veteran and former Marine officer, the quintessential team leader. He walked slowly up and down the aisle, as if inspecting his soldiers, as he spoke. "What I want to talk about this evening is this team's mission, which is, simply stated: How did we get from this," he said, pointing at the screen, "to this?"

With a click of the remote the rig was gone. The blue waters had turned black. Seas that had foamed with whitecaps were teeming with chemical dispersants. The sight was enough to make Andie nauseous.

Or maybe that's Viola again.

"As you probably have guessed by now, the education you received over the past two months—everything from improved proficiency in the Chinese language to sharpened insights into the Chinese Mafia—has nothing to do with counterfeit Gucci handbags. So-called Operation Big Dredge was a mere cover to ensure the secrecy of your preparation for a much more vital operation at the core of our national security. The explosion of the Scarborough 8 has only shortened the timeline and heightened the urgency of the real investigation. I assure you, however, that everything you have learned will be of use to you."

Another click of his remote brought the image of a shipyard onto the screen.

"From the day construction began in this shipyard in Yantai, Shandong Province, China, we have kept a close eye on the Scarborough 8. That scrutiny intensified when the world's largest oil rig—an engineering and technological monster built entirely in China with less than ten percent American-made parts—ended up just sixty miles from the city of Key West. Through means that I will not get into here, FBI tech agents and experts from U.S. Homeland Security were able to access the Chinese rig's computer system during drilling operations. We monitored the rig right up to the moment of the explosion. At this time I would like to introduce Special Agent Raj Gupta, who will briefly explain the technical aspects."

Andie found that sickening as well. *Oh, my God, Viola, you little stinker. If you make me vomit in the middle of this meeting* . . .

Special Agent Gupta walked to the front of the room and took the remote.

"Unfortunately, no one will ever be able to recover the exact software events leading to the Scarborough 8 disaster because, even on a state-of-the-art semi-submersible rig, there is no 'black box.' But here is what we do know."

The projected image on the screen was suddenly

a collection of circuits in a tangle of colored wires, which did absolutely nothing to alleviate Andie's nausea.

Ugh, spaghetti.

"Offshore oil rigs are made up of dozens of complex subsystems that use embedded software or are operated under software control. Each system is a potential point of failure. When the software is operating properly, alarms are routed to a central control station."

Gupta stopped and looked straight at Andie. "Are you okay, Henning?"

"Fine, thanks," she lied.

Where is the Big Palm Island ice bucket when a girl really needs it?

Gupta went to the next slide. "Industry standards for manageable alarm rates are one alarm per 'normal' ten-minute period with a maximum of five in any 'peak' five-minute period. During Tropical Storm Miguel, in the peak period immediately prior to the explosion, our monitoring systems detected almost *five hundred* alarms. It was impossible for the system and its operators to sift through this overload of alarms and prevent the explosion."

Andie pulled herself together to ask a question. "Are you saying the storm caused a computer malfunction?"

"Homeland Security does not believe it was the storm, per se, that caused the computer malfunction. We believe the system failed in the storm due to computer sabotage, unleashing a cascade effect that resulted in catastrophe."

"But sabotage usually involves advance planning," said Andie. "How would someone who sabotaged the alarm system know far enough ahead of time that the Scarborough 8 was going to be hit by a major tropical storm?"

"Excellent question, Henning," said Douglas.

Thank you. May I puke now?

Gupta replied, "As it turned out, the storm was the trigger event that overloaded the alarm system. But the same catastrophic failure could have been triggered by a major equipment failure or any number of events and conditions that rigs typically face in ultradeep water. We believe the sabotage rendered the system unable to deal with *any* significant emergency. In essence, the Scarborough 8 was a ticking time bomb that was doomed to explode the first time the rig faced an emergency situation that, if not for the sabotage, would have been manageable."

Agent Douglas thanked Gupta for his presentation and resumed his place in front of the team. "All of this raises an obvious question: Who was behind the sabotage?"

A photograph appeared on the projection screen. It was a grainy black-and-white headshot of a man, like a mug shot without the prison identification number. Andie didn't recognize the face, but it did elicit a gut reaction.

"He doesn't look Chinese Mafia," said Andie.

A steely gaze from Douglas swept across the entire team. "Not even close," he said.

13
.

Jack was back in Judge Carlyle's overcrowded courtroom on Thursday morning.

The supertanker hearing had been a complete victory for Jack, but it didn't take long for thousand-dollar-an-hour defense lawyers to mount a counterattack. This time, the consortium's sights were trained solely on Bianca Lopez. She was seated beside Jack at the mahogany table, leaving the plaintiff's counsel and his client outnumbered six-to-one by the defense team on the other side of the courtroom. Luis Candela seemed to hide a smirk of satisfaction as he addressed the court from the podium.

"Judge, this wrongful death lawsuit should be dismissed immediately, with sanctions entered against Mr. Swyteck for perpetrating a fraud on the court."

Candela had the full attention of a packed courtroom. Unlike the previous hearing, there was no overflow of property-claim lawyers to fill the gallery. Members of the media had replaced them, the courthouse beat having tripled overnight. The young and pretty Cuban-American widow's lawsuit against a foreign oil consortium had become the spill's David-versus-Goliath sideshow.

Judge Carlyle glanced in Jack's direction, then peered down from the bench at defense counsel. "Fraud is not an accusation I allow to be cast about loosely in my courtroom, Mr. Candela."

"There is no other way to characterize it, Your Honor. Mr. Swyteck's client, Bianca Lopez—this so-called widow—was not the wife of Rafael Lopez."

The judge's gaze swung back toward Jack, and this time he felt the full weight of her stare. Or maybe it was his sense that everyone else in the courtroom was looking at him, too.

Bianca dug her nails into Jack's arm and whispered, "That's just not true!"

"It's okay," he whispered back. "We'll have our chance to speak."

The judge leaned forward, but her stare shifted to Candela.

"Let me save Mr. Swyteck's breath," she said, her tone taking on an edge. "I've read the joint motion filed by the defendants. I fully understand your position: even if we assume that Bianca and Rafael Lopez were married at one time, that marriage was nullified under Cuban law. And I suppose that some jurists might find it creative to argue that Ms. Lopez abandoned her husband when she boarded a smuggler's boat without him and fled to the United States. But I'm not impressed."

"Judge, she has no legal status as a widow to support her wrongful death claim."

"I'm not buying it," said the judge.

"I expected that reaction," said Candela. "But as a matter of U.S. law, it is Mr. Swyteck's burden to prove that his client was in fact married to Rafael Lopez at the time of his death. Nullification issues aside, Mr. Swyteck can't even prove as a threshold matter that his client was *ever* married to Rafael Lopez."

Jack rose. "Your Honor, if I could interject. It's true that we can't simply call up the City Hall in Havana or search publicly available databases to get a copy of the marriage license. The Cuban government registers marriage licenses with international data banks only for tourists who are married in Cuba, not for Cuban citizens, since international registration would facilitate defection."

"Judge," said Candela, "I realize that the Cuban government has exercised its right not to participate in this hearing, but could I ask the court to instruct plaintiff's counsel to refrain from gratuitous attacks?"

"It's not gratuitous," said Jack. "I'm simply explaining the constraints under which my client is operating. And we have the added difficulty that, for the average citizen, the Internet is inaccessible in the home and prohibitively expensive at a café, so the marriage record is not obtainable online from any public records database."

The judge seemed puzzled. "If that's the case, then how *do* you intend to prove that Ms. Lopez was married?"

"We have hired a reputable service in Miami to retrieve the marriage license, but this process takes time."

"Reputable?" said Candela, scoffing. "Your Honor, these so-called record-service companies are all over Miami's Little Havana neighborhood. They operate outside the law, and they lead their clients to believe that they pull strings and even bribe Cuban officials to get copies of birth certificates, death certificates, marriage licenses, what have you. It's a money-making scam. They charge hundreds and even thousands of dollars, and most of the documents they produce are fake."

"Your Honor, the defendants can challenge the authenticity of the marriage record once it's produced."

"Or," said Candela, "the court could cut to the chase by allowing me to ask Ms. Lopez a few simple questions under oath today."

"Nice try," said Jack. "But ambushing a young widow by calling her to the witness stand without prior notice just two days after she files a lawsuit isn't the way things work in this courtroom."

"Judge, *please*. Mr. Swyteck's repeated slaps at the Cuban people have to stop."

"I wasn't slapping the Cuban people."

"You said '*in this country*.'"

"I said '*courtroom*.' I wasn't—"

"Enough," the judge said, as she banged her gavel.

Candela persisted. "Your Honor, if I could have just five minutes to cross-examine Mr. Swyteck's client, I'm confident that I can save us all a lot of time and establish beyond any doubt that she is not Rafael Lopez's widow."

"I object," said Jack. "No notice was given that any witnesses would be called at this hearing."

"The objection is well taken," the judge said. "Mr. Candela, we can schedule an evidentiary hearing for a later date. But if you claim to need only five minutes, I suspect that you must have some sort of smoking gun in your possession. This isn't a TV show, and I don't like surprises. Let's hear it."

"Judge, I'd rather wait."

"Let's *hear it*."

"Yes, Your Honor." Candela walked back to his table, and an assistant handed him two folders. With the judge's permission he approached the bench and handed one up. On his way back to the podium, he dropped the other folder on Jack's table.

Jack glanced at Bianca, but her expression told him that she had no idea what might be inside. Jack opened the folder as Candela addressed the court.

"Your Honor, the defense can prove that at the time of his death, Rafael Lopez was engaged to be married to a Cuban citizen. She lives in Havana. Her name is Josefina Fuentes."

Jack's eyes were drawn to the first line of the handwritten letter inside the folder: *Querida Josefina*.

"Exactly what do these letters purport to be?" the judge asked.

"These are love letters that Rafael wrote while on the rig and sent to his fiancée in Havana. For the court's convenience, translations are also in the folder."

The judge thumbed through her copies. "How did you get these?"

"All mail from the rig was monitored by the Cuban government. It could take weeks for the letters to be reviewed before being forwarded to the intended recipient. These last two letters from Rafael were still in the hands of the Cuban government at the time of the explosion."

Judge Carlyle put on her eyeglasses and read to herself. Jack, too, read in silence. He focused mostly on the translations, but his Spanish was good enough to understand Rafael's last written words: *Todo mi amor.*

All my love.

The judge looked up from the letter, her interest clearly piqued. "Let me ask a few questions of Mr Swyteck."

Jack rose. "Yes, Your Honor."

"Counselor, have you seen these letters before?"

"I have not," said Jack.

"Has your client seen them?"

Bianca looked up at him and shook her head.

"No, Judge," said Jack.

"I don't mean to put Ms. Lopez on the spot. Mr. Swyteck, perhaps you can help me get answers to some questions that come to my mind. Does this look like Rafael's handwriting?"

Jack conferred with his client briefly, then replied. "She can't say for sure it is."

"Then I assume she can't say for sure that it isn't," the judge said. "Is that right?"

"That's correct, Your Honor."

The judge took a moment, then continued. "Did Rafael write any letters like this to your client? More specifically, does she have copies of any such letters?"

Again, Bianca shook her head.

"No, Your Honor."

"Has your client had any communication with Rafael Lopez since she left Cuba?"

"No," Bianca told Jack, and he repeated it more loudly for the record.

The judge continued. "That seems odd. Even after the Cuban government eased the travel restrictions on Cuban nationals, there was no communication at all between you about Rafael coming to the United States?"

Bianca shook her head, and Jack verbalized it. "No, Your Honor."

"Hmmm."

Jack tried not to wince: *Hmmm.* No vowels. Technically not even a word. But it was one of the most potent messages a judge could send from the bench.

The judge scratched her head. "Does she have any wedding photographs or any such things to substantiate the fact that there was a ceremony or celebration?"

Jack had discussed this previously with Bianca, but he double-checked before answering in open court.

"Your Honor, my client came to this country as a refugee, before the technical lifting of the travel ban. She arrived literally with the clothes on her back. Her personal belongings were left behind in Cuba."

"I understand," said the judge. "One final question: Has Ms. Lopez held any kind of memorial service for Rafael since his death?"

Jack looked at his client, and the meeting of their eyes was the most awkward moment to date in their young lawyer-client relationship. Jack needed no elaboration from her.

"There has been nothing formal at this point," he told the judge.

"So your client has filed a multimillion-dollar lawsuit, but she has yet to conduct a memorial service. Do I have that right?"

"Well, I wouldn't put it like that, Your—"

The judge raised a hand, stopping him. It was clear that she wanted no answer. Equally clear— and more disturbing to Jack—was that the media was eating this up, and the judge was beginning to pander. The evening sound bite was in the can.

"I'm going to set this matter for a hearing," the judge said. "Mr. Swyteck, come prepared to convince me that your client was married to Rafael Lopez at the time of his death. Come very prepared. We're adjourned."

At the sharp crack of the gavel, Jack's client popped from her chair and stood beside him. Together, they watched Judge Carlyle disappear into her chambers. The paneled door closed with a thud, unleashing another volley of questions on top of questions from reporters who were standing on the public side of the rail. Jack ignored them.

"We need to talk," he told Bianca, "in private."

14

J ack needed a way out.

A gauntlet of reporters stood in the gallery, blocking the main exit at the rear of the courtroom. The bailiff allowed Jack and his client to escape through a side door that led to a vacant jury deliberation room. Jack closed the solid oak door and sat Bianca down at the end of a rectangular table that was long enough to accommodate twelve angry men (and women). Standing, he laid the handwritten letters before her.

"Is this Rafael's handwriting or not?" He was trying not to be too accusatory, but it was pointed, nonetheless.

"I told you: I can't be sure."

"Bianca, I need the truth."

She took a long look at the letter, studying it, as if wishing it weren't so. Her lower lip quivered with her reply. "It . . . it could be."

Jack drew a breath and stepped away. His thoughts made him pace—back and forth in front of an old portrait of James Monroe, the president for whom the entire county was named in recognition of old Key West and America's "manifest destiny."

Jack stopped and planted his palms atop the table. "Who is Josefina Fuentes?"

"I don't know."

"The truth, please."

"That is the truth. I've never heard of her."

Jack pulled up a chair and looked her straight in the eye. "I need you to be completely straight with me. If you have something to clear up, now is the time to do it, before this spirals out of control: Were you or were you not Rafael's wife when he died?"

"Yes!"

"How do you explain these letters?"

The response caught in her throat. "I—I know that . . ."

"You know what?"

"I know Rafael would never give up on us, on our marriage. These letters must be fakes."

"You just admitted that they could be his handwriting."

Bianca shifted uneasily. "You heard Mr. Candela in the courtroom. He said that all mail from the rig was screened and that he got these letters from the Cuban government. You can't put this past them. I defected. To the government, I am a *gusano*. All defectors to the United States are *gusanos*."

"Worms, I know. My grandmother is one, too."

"Just because they changed the travel laws after I left doesn't mean they forget the people who defected. They would do anything to hurt me. This woman—this Josefina—must be an impostor. She is working with the government to kill my lawsuit and punish me, the way all *gusanos* should be punished."

It sounded like paranoia, but Jack considered it. "That's not easy to prove."

"You don't believe me, do you?"

"I didn't say that. I said it would be hard to prove."

Bianca's face reddened. Jack saw a flurry of mixed emotions in her eyes, hurt and anger the most obvious.

"Why is everyone so mean to me?"

"You can't look at it that way," said Jack.

"How else can I look at it? Even the judge hates me!"

"Judge Carlyle got a little carried away. That sometimes happens when the media pays this much attention to a case. It's nothing personal against you."

"That judge thinks I am a cold witch. Didn't you hear the last question she asked?"

"We weren't prepared for it, but her question was a fair one. And at some point in the future, we are going to have to explain: Why no memorial service?"

"Why no service?" she asked, her voice rising. "I'll tell you *why*. Maybe I hope Rafael is still alive, okay? Did you ever think of that?"

Jack hadn't, and it embarrassed him.

Her voice grew louder. "I know, I'm stupid, right? Everyone tells me I have to let go. I know what happened to those men who died in Deepwater Horizon. They . . . how do you say? *Vaporizado*."

"Vaporized."

Her voice shook, huge tears streaming down her

cheeks. "I don't want to think about those things. You understand? I don't want to think about Rafael that way! So no memorial. Not yet. Is that a crime? Does that make me a bad wife?"

"No."

"A liar?"

"No," said Jack.

"Then why do you treat me like this?"

"Bianca, I'm your lawyer. I have to ask questions."

"*Bueno.* And I am human. Some questions I should not have to answer."

Jack wasn't sure if her distinction between lawyers and humans was intentional or a language thing. It didn't seem to matter.

She leaned in to the table, looking at him squarely in the face. "Why can't you understand how I feel? You should understand, no?"

"I'm trying."

She pushed away from the table. "I hate this!" she shouted. "I hate this lawsuit already!"

In tears she hurried to the door and flung it open. A mob of reporters was right outside the jury room. They surged forward, blocking the doorway, calling her name, making it impossible for her to leave.

"Get away!" she shouted.

Jack stepped between his client and the mob, slammed the door, and locked it.

Bianca fell more than leaned against the door-frame, emotionally overcome. Slowly, her back slid down the wall to the floor. She drew her knees to her chin and lowered her head, her body shaking with another wave of sadness.

Jack wanted to console her, but there wasn't much anyone could do. Something told him that this was Bianca's first good cry since the news about Rafael had reached Key West. He sat on the floor beside her.

"I'm sorry, Bianca. I am so, so sorry."

15
.

The drive back to Miami was five hours. Jack and Theo grabbed a mid-afternoon lunch in Little Havana.

"I swear, I can't win," said Jack.

They were at a picnic table outside a café on Eighth Street. *Calle Ocho* was once the heart of a small community of exiles, a place where old Cuban men could be found playing dominoes, smoking cigars, and speculating about the death of Castro and the end of communism. Some of the old men were still around, but anyone born after the Cuban Missile Crisis was more likely to be overheard talking about *béisbol* and their 401(k) than dictators and politics.

"What's the problem?" asked Theo.

Jack was staring down at the sandwich on his plate. "Whenever I order a Cuban *sin mostaza*, the waitress looks at me like I'm an idiot and says a traditional Cubano doesn't have mustard. But when I don't say 'without mustard,' it comes with mustard."

"What's wrong with mustard?"

"I don't like it on my Cuban sandwich."

"I can fix that." He grabbed half of Jack's sandwich and killed it in two bites.

Resigned, Jack pushed his plate, offering up the other half.

"You're welcome," Theo said, chewing.

Jack ordered a café con leche—*sin mostaza*—and took it to go.

It was a short walk around the corner to a tiny storefront office called Servicios de Andres. With traditional *tiendas* feeling the squeeze of El Walmart and La Target, service-oriented businesses were filling in the growing vacancies. The name on the plateglass window was ANDRES, but close inspection revealed faint traces of DULCES DE LANA, a neighborhood bakery.

Jack was right on time for their three o'clock appointment. The door was locked, so he pushed the bell. An old man let them in, and when the door closed, there was barely enough room for three men to stand without invading one another's personal space. Andres' desk was shoved all the way up against the far wall. Two-thirds of the floor had been overtaken by dozens of cardboard boxes stacked all the way to the ceiling. Andres apologized for the clutter.

"After thirty-eight years, my sister had to close her antique doll store. You want to buy an authentic Cuban *muñeca*?"

Theo pulled a handmade treasure from one of the boxes. "How much?"

Jack took the doll and put it back. "We're not here to buy dolls. Andres, I'm sorry about your sister's business, but I told my client I had a three o'clock appointment, so every second that goes by without a phone call from me is like Chinese water torture to her. What's up with the marriage license?"

Servicios de Andres didn't look like much from the outside—even less on the inside—but the word on the *calle* was that Andres ran the most reliable service in Miami for the retrieval of vital documents from Cuba. Certificates of birth, death, or marriage were the most commonly requested. Andres boasted a 90 percent success rate. He never explained how he did it, and he never spoke with his clients on the phone. Face-to-face dealings only. Paranoia to some, but most folks didn't second-guess an old man whose brother was tied to a tree in the Sierra Maestra Mountains and shot to death on the direct order of Fidel Castro.

"You sure you don't want to buy a doll?" asked Andres.

"I'm sure," said Jack.

"Then I'm afraid your trip here has been wasted time."

"Okay, okay. We'll buy a doll."

"Take this one," said Andres. "Very special."

"Fine." Jack gave him a twenty.

"It's two hundred dollars," said Andres.

"Two hundred!"

"It is an antique," said Theo. "And museum quality."

"What do think this is, *Pawn Stars*?"

"I love that show."

"One-ninety-five," said Andres. "Good price."

Jack had already paid five hundred dollars in advance. He hated shakedowns, but haggling wasn't worth the effort. He peeled off the rest of the money, nearly emptying his wallet. "Can I see the marriage license now, please?"

"I don't have the license," said Andres.

"But I just bought a doll."

"You bought a very nice doll."

"It *is* a nice doll," said Theo.

"As compared to what, your inflatable? Look, Andres. You seem like a good guy. Your reputation is solid. Don't play games with me."

"I'm being very fair with you, Mr. Swyteck. I'm losing money here, even with the doll."

"I paid you almost seven hundred bucks. How are you losing money?"

"Truly, I want to help Miss Bianca. I see her face on the TV and it makes me cry. But her lawsuit . . . it's not so popular with the Cuban government. I have worked every contact I have, every possible angle. I put in *way* more than seven hundred dollars. Not one person will help."

Jack read between the lines: no bribe was big enough to induce the usually reliable sources to produce a copy of Bianca's marriage license.

"So that's it? Brick wall, end of story?"

"I'm sorry. I wish I could do more. But keep the doll, please. No one leaves Andres empty-handed."

Jack thanked him. Theo walked out with the doll, and Jack followed. Spanish-speaking men selling limes and bottled water trailed them along the sidewalk, but Jack was thinking through the unhappy phone call he needed to make to Bianca. He was still deep in thought as they reached the car. Jack got behind the wheel, and Theo placed the doll on the dashboard, front and center.

"That's blocking my view," said Jack.

Theo bent it at the waist and put it back in a seated position. The doll's red shoes were facing them, heels out. Jack was about to push the doll aside when he noticed the handwriting on the sole of the right shoe. He took a closer look.

"Josefina Fuentes," he read aloud. Written on the other shoe was a street address in Havana.

Theo chuckled. "Looks like *la muñeca* is trying to tell you something, Jack."

It seemed like the stuff of amateur spy novels, but Jack had seen quirkier things from men of Andres' generation who truly believed that Cuban spies lurked around every corner of Little Havana.

"I guess that's worth the extra two hundred bucks," said Jack.

"So are we going to Cuba? We can hit the Copa."

"Copa Cabana?"

"*Sí.* Hottest spot north of—"

"I got it, I got it." Like it or not, Jack would have an old Barry Manilow song playing in his head for the rest of the night.

"Come on, let's do it," said Theo.

"We are not going to Cuba."

"Why not?"

Jack turned the key, and the ignition fired. "*I'm* going. Alone."

16

•

Jack flew to Havana through Nassau and landed at José Martí International Airport on Friday morning. The view across the runway, from his window seat, made him do a double take.

"Are those crop dusters?" Jack asked the passenger next to him.

Jack was pointing at six old open-cockpit biplanes lined up on the other runway. Any one of them looked barely capable of chasing down Cary Grant in *North by Northwest*.

"*Sí*. The spill," the man said, trying his best in English.

Jack had thought that American media reports were overblown, but he was seeing it with his own eyes. An oil disaster that rivaled Deepwater Horizon, and the Cubans were spreading chemical dispersants with crop dusters that dated back to the Second World War.

"God help us," said Jack.

The same embargo that prevented U.S. companies from drilling in the Cuban Basin and responding to the Scarborough 8 disaster also restricted the rights of American citizens to travel freely to Cuba. Under normal circumstances, it could have taken weeks or even months to plan Jack's trip—time enough for oil to smother the entire Florida coastline. As it was, Jack landed before the spill had even reached Key West. Two years earlier, as a volunteer defense lawyer for a detainee in Guantánamo, Jack had completed the approval process for a general license from the U.S. Department of the Treasury to travel to Cuba. The license had nothing to do with his legal work. Jack was entitled to it because Abuela's brother in Bejucal met the Treasury Department's definition of a "close family relative" in Cuba. To justify the trip, all Jack had to do was visit him.

After he visited Josefina Fuentes.

"A donde va?" asked the cabdriver. Where to?

The taxi was a midnight-blue 1957 Chevrolet Bel Air, chrome bumpers glistening in the morning sun. In Miami, it would have been an antique seen only in parades. In Cuba, classic Buicks, Fords, and Chevys were everywhere—part of the island's "frozen in time" charm to some, but a reminder that for over fifty years it was illegal to buy or sell an American car manufactured after the 1959 revolution.

Jack gave him the address. "I think it's near Chinatown."

A roll of the driver's eyes told Jack that he was offering directions to a man who knew the streets of Havana as well as any middle-aged Cuban cabbie who had never left the island of his birth. *Of course* he knew it was near Chinatown.

"How much?" Jack asked in Spanish. His last trip to Havana had taught him to get the price up front.

"Twenty-five CUC."

CUC, the Cuban peso convertible, was used mainly by tourists. It was distinct from the *peso cubano* or *moneda nacional*, the currency in which the average Cuban was paid a salary of about $150 a month. One CUC was roughly equal to one U.S. dollar. Under U.S. law, Jack could spend a maximum of $179 per day. He did the math and was glad he'd already eaten breakfast.

"*Bueno*," said Jack.

The twenty-minute ride into the city took Jack past a national park and the Havana Golf Club before the suburbs vanished and they hit urban traffic. One government building that Jack recognized from the photographs he'd studied was the towering Ministerio de Justicia. Seeing it from the cab served to remind him that even if Josefina wouldn't talk to him, the trip to Cuba might still be productive. Even for church weddings, the only legally recognized proof of marriage was the civil license, and Jack's to-do list included a visit to the Ministry of Justice, where he would personally follow up on the license that his experts in Miami had been unable to retrieve. Bianca had also given him the name of a friend who might have wedding photographs.

The buildings got older and the streets got rougher as they continued into the city center. The stop-and-go over potholes was enough to convince Jack that the shock absorbers on the vintage Chevy were original. The ride in the back was about as comfortable as settling down onto a toilet bowl with no seat.

"How much farther?" asked Jack.

The driver just smiled.

The cab had no A/C, so Jack watched the city blocks pass through an open window. The "Cuban influence" in Miami was undeniable, but to Jack, this piece of Cuba—*Habana Centro*—looked nothing like his hometown. Ornate nineteenth-century apartment buildings lined the wide Paseo de Martí, styles ranging from Moorish to neo-baroque. Most were crumbling, all needed paint, and many had dropped huge chunks of stucco and concrete from decades of neglect. Dogs yapped from balconies, and it was obvious that multiple families were living in each flat, but colored-glass windows and decorative *azulejos* (Moorish-style Spanish tiles) were signs of former wealth. The cab stopped on a narrow side street. Jack double-checked the number above the door, and it was definitely the address that Andres had written on the doll's foot. But the sign on the door, painted in crude letters, read ESCUELA DE BOXEO. Jack couldn't hide his confusion.

"A boxing gym?"

"*Sí.*"

Jack reached for his wallet. "How much of the twenty-five CUC do you get to keep?"

The driver shrugged. "*No bastante.*" Not enough.

Jack tipped him ten CUC, and the note caught his eye. It bore the image of an electric power plant and boasted of Cuba's *Revolución Energética*. The Energy Revolution.

"I'm curious," Jack tried to say in Spanish. "What do you think of the oil spill?"

Again, the driver gave him only a shrug and a

little smile. It was possible that Jack had mangled the question in Spanish, but more likely the driver didn't want to talk about it to an American. Jack dropped it, thanked him for the ride, and climbed out of the cab. The door creaked like a wounded animal as it closed, and the tailpipe belched blue-gray smoke as the driver pulled away.

Jack stepped onto the sidewalk across the street from the gym and took a minute to absorb the neighborhood. His gaze drifted toward a twelve-story landmark bearing the Gotham-like emblem of a large black bat atop the art deco tower. Any true Miamian who had ever enjoyed a Cuba Libre (rum and Coke) knew the story of the old Bacardi building, "donated" to the Cuban people when the family fled Cuba after the revolution.

"Hey, dude."

Jack froze, not sure he was hearing correctly. He turned, looked, and nearly fell over. "Theo?" he said, more an expression of shock than a question. "What the hell are you doing here?"

Theo removed his sunglasses. "What kind of welcome is that?"

Jack checked over his shoulder, more out of instinct than any real concern about confidentiality. "You can't travel to Cuba."

"Why not? *You* did."

"I'm legal. I have close family relatives here."

"Close family relatives my ass. There are card-carrying members of the Ku Klux Klan who speak better Spanish than you."

"How did you get here?"

"Same way thousands of Americans do every

year. Through Cancún. The Cubans are totally cool about it. They don't even stamp your passport at immigration."

"You're breaking the law, Theo."

"Actually, I've already *broken* the law. So we might as well make the most of it. After all, dude—we are still on our honeymoon."

"This isn't a joke. Don't you remember how crazy things got when Jay-Z and Beyoncé went to Cuba? If they hadn't been able to prove they had permission, they would have been prosecuted."

Theo laughed. "Maybe Jay-Z and me can rap about it. Come on, let's check out this gym."

It was a can't-beat-'em-join-'em situation, so Jack followed him across the street.

La Escuela de Boxeo was in an old building that in another century had served as the carriage house and horse stables for the wealthy residents on the Paseo. The stable doors had been bricked over, and the lone entrance was a metal door halfway down the block. A pair of young fighters exited as Jack approached, and they held the door open for him and Theo.

"*Gracias, chicas,*" said Theo.

Jack let the door close and said, "You just called them girls."

"Those were girls, dumbshit."

Jack had been so on-mission, wrapped up in his thoughts, that he hadn't noticed.

The sounds of the gym were at the end of the hallway, and the sweaty smell of hot, stale air welcomed them to the training area. Jack counted six rings and two windows, neither of which was open. It had to be ninety degrees inside.

Jack walked up to the old man behind the desk. He was absorbed in his copy of the *Granma*, the official newspaper of the Cuban Communist Party—the name "Granma" borrowed from the yacht that had carried Fidel Castro and his band of rebels to Cuba's shores in 1956, launching the revolution. Jack translated the above-the-fold headline to himself. The oil spill, front-page news across America, was apparently not as big a story as the 88 percent voter turnout in the election of delegates to the People's Power Municipal Assemblies.

"Josefina Fuentes?" asked Jack.

The old man looked up from his daily. With a jerk of his head he indicated a ring to Jack's right, where a young woman was sparring with a male fighter. Jack and Theo walked around the weights and mats on the floor and stood outside the ring. It was impossible not to admire the quick hands, sculpted arms, and amazing footwork.

Theo smiled at what he saw. "That girl is ripped."

Jack took a step closer to the ring. Theo followed, unable to tear his eyes away from her. They watched for several minutes until the sparring ended. Josefina went to the ropes, where her coach gave her pointers as he removed her headgear and unlaced her gloves. Josefina's trainer was beyond boxing age but looked as though he'd spent some serious time in the ring in his not-too-distant youth. He gave her a fist bump and moved to the next pair of fighters. Josefina was dripping with sweat as she walked toward the watercooler.

"Josefina?" Jack asked.

She stopped, removed her mouth guard, and

smiled. Her face was a little puffy from the workout, but she still qualified as an athletic Latin beauty.

"Do you speak English?" asked Jack.

"Yes. Who are you?"

"Jack Swyteck, from Miami. I'm the lawyer for Bianca Lopez. Rafael's husband." *wife,*

The ambush was necessary to gauge her reaction. If Jack had caught her off guard, she didn't show it.

"What took you so long?"

"Can we talk?"

Josefina glanced toward the next ring. Her trainer, though working with another fighter, was watching Josefina—like a hawk.

"Not now," she said. "And not here. My trainer misses nothing."

Jack understood. "You name the time and place."

She glanced again toward the next ring, then back at Jack. "Four o'clock. Heladería Coppelia."

"An ice cream parlor?"

"*The* ice cream parlor. El Vedado neighborhood. Packed with tourists."

Obviously she wanted no one she knew to see her talking to an American lawyer.

"Okay," said Jack. "It's a date."

17

Jack ordered strawberry and chocolate, a nod to the famous film *Fresa y Chocolate*, in which the main characters meet at the Heladería Coppelia in Havana. Theo did him one better and ordered one scoop in every flavor. To his disappointment, only two of the twenty-six *sabores* on the state-owned menu were available—*fresa y chocolate*.

The claim of "world's largest ice cream parlor" was debatable, but Coppelia was both a local landmark and a tourist magnet. The main pavilion was a modernist design, shaped like a flying saucer, and the park surrounding it occupied an entire city block that was within easy walking distance of Hotel Nacional de Cuba and other signature hotels in the relatively expensive Vedado district. Tourists could pay Western prices in CUC to avoid the long lines, but thirty minutes of people-watching and anticipation was part of the Coppelia experience. Jack paid in *moneda nacional*.

"For twenty-seven cents, I'm cool with two scoops," said Theo.

Jack wasn't really listening, his gaze having drifted toward a young Cuban mother. She was sharing ice cream with her toothless infant, one tiny spoonful after another. From the joyous expression on the baby's face, Jack guessed it was her first taste, though it was more of a multisensory experience, including an all-ten-fingers-in-the-mouth feel. A mother-daughter moment like this would have barely caught Jack's eye before the morning sickness. Now, it made him miss Andie more than ever.

"Where you want to sit?" asked Theo.

Most patrons seemed to prefer inside seating at the upstairs tables or downstairs stools—again, part of the Coppelia "experience." Jack figured that Josefina would rather be outdoors, away from the center of activity. They took a patio table beneath the shade of a towering banyan tree. Jack's ice cream was nearly melted when Theo spotted Josefina on one of the curvilinear paths that led to the elevated flying saucer.

"Damn, she's gorgeous," said Theo.

Jack signaled to catch her attention. As Josefina started toward them, Jack gave Theo an under-his-breath warning. "I don't know what the real deal was with Rafael, but if you hit on a woman who is mourning her dead fiancé, I'll bust you myself for violating the trade embargo."

They rose to greet her, and Josefina joined them at the table, Jack and Theo together on one side, Josefina on the other. It had been Jack's plan to ease into the conversation, but like a good fighter, Josefina went straight on the offensive.

"Rafael was my best friend since I was three. Did you know that?"

"No," Jack countered. "His wife didn't mention it."

"I'm not surprised," she said, looking off to the middle distance. "I don't think she ever really liked me, which is so unfair. If you asked her, she'd probably tell you that she doesn't even know who I am."

Jack didn't answer, but as he recalled, those had been almost Bianca's exact words.

"That's why Rafael couldn't even invite me to his wedding. I think Bianca felt threatened, which is stupid. All I ever did was help her."

Jack pushed his empty bowl of ice cream aside. "How did you help Bianca?"

Josefina sighed, as if not sure where to begin. "When a Cuban national defects to the United States, the way Bianca did, do you know what happens to family members who are left behind?"

"They go work on an oil rig?" asked Theo.

"Actually, the opposite," said Josefina. "Those jobs on the rig were excellent jobs. A man like Rafael, whose wife turned her back on Cuba, would be lucky to find work sweeping the street. No way could he get hired by the oil consortium."

"Then how did he get the job?"

"I helped him. And I helped Bianca."

A boy approached their table, breaking their conversation. He was handing out leaflets for the annual *Tras las Huellas del Che* (In Che's Footsteps), a chess tournament dedicated to the memory of Che Guevara. Jack gave him ten pesos to go away.

"How did you help him?" asked Jack.

Josefina paused, seeming to have some difficulty.

Then she looked Jack in the eye and said, "I became his fiancée."

"So you're saying that your engagement was a . . ." Jack stopped himself, not wanting to say "fraud."

"An arrangement," said Josefina.

Theo jumped in. "So you and Rafael never slept together?"

"Theo!"

"What? You think Bianca don't want to know the answer to that question?"

"It's okay," said Josefina. "I like a man who says what he thinks. The answer is no. Never. Look, the whole point was this: Rafael had to prove that he was a good Cuban who still loved his country. The only way he could do that was to show them he no longer loved his wife. He loved another woman in Cuba."

"But he was still really in love with Bianca?"

"Yes."

"And he still considered her his wife?"

"Yes. *Claro.*"

Jack had the letters with him, and it seemed like the time to lay them on the table, literally. "What about these letters that Rafael wrote to '*Josefina, mi amor*'?"

Josefina skimmed them. "I haven't seen these before."

"The lawyers for the oil consortium gave them to me in court. I'm told that the Cuban government reviewed all mail sent from the rig. These were still under review when Rafael died."

"That makes sense."

"I've read the letters," said Jack. "These sound like they were written to a woman he truly loved."

"That's because they were," said Josefina.

Jack took a moment, confused. "But you said the engagement was just an 'arrangement.'"

Josefina opened her exercise bag and removed a stack of letters—a dozen or more.

"What's this?" Jack asked.

"More letters from Rafael. Just like the ones you have."

Jack took a quick look. "They all are written to you."

"No. They are addressed to me. They are written to Bianca."

"I don't follow you," said Jack.

"That was the 'arrangement,'" said Josefina. "The whole reason Rafael wanted the job on the rig was so that he could earn enough money to buy his way out of Cuba and be with Bianca. He couldn't write letters to his wife saying, 'Dear Bianca, I can't wait to be with you again.' He couldn't have any contact with her at all."

"That is what Bianca told me: no contact with Rafael since she landed in Key West."

"Right," said Josefina. "That's the way it had to be."

"But there's still something I don't get," said Jack. "Instead of applying for a job, why didn't he just apply for a visa? Cubans can travel now. The law changed after Bianca got off the island."

"Change of laws on the books doesn't change the way a government thinks. A man whose wife defected to the United States before or after the law changed has zero chance of getting a travel visa. Especially a man like Rafael, who is college educated and studying to be an engineer in the oil industry. My government is paranoid about the brain drain— the flight of doctors and other professionals. They would never let Rafael leave Cuba if they thought he had any connection with his wife in the U.S."

"So Rafael sent the letters to you," said Jack.

"Yes. All these letters," she said, holding up the stack, "Rafael sent them to me. But in his heart, they are all written to Bianca."

Another boy with the Che Guevara leaflets approached. Word was apparently out on the street that Jack was an easy mark. It cost him another ten pesos to be left alone.

Jack recovered his train of thought. "I think I know the answer, but you tell me, Josefina: What were you supposed to do with all these letters?"

"It was my job to get them to Bianca."

"*Yer fired,*" said Theo, mimicking the Donald.

Josefina didn't understand the reference to American television, but she got Theo's drift. "I failed," she said. "I was afraid to pass them on."

"Afraid of what?"

"Getting caught. *Oye,*" she said. Listen. "I have it good here. A real shot at being an Olympian. *El Boxeo* is my life. If the government finds out I was pretending to be engaged to Rafael, that's the end for me. So I didn't pass along the letters."

"I can understand that," said Jack.

"Here," she said, handing them to Jack. "Please give these to Bianca. Tell her I am sorry. I have to get back to the gym now."

Jack took the letters. He and Theo rose to say good-bye.

"Maybe we'll see you around," said Theo.

Josefina slung her bag over her shoulder. "Maybe."

"We'll be at La Floridita tonight."

"Ah, *sí*, where the daiquiri was invented."

"That's what I hear," said Theo.

"Expensive tourist trap. Have one drink to say you did it, follow Ernest Hemingway's footsteps over to La Bodeguita del Medio, where he drank his mojitos, and then quit wasting your time and go to La Zorra y el Cuervo. Do you like Latin jazz?"

"Are you kidding me? I play the sax and own a jazz bar in Miami."

She seemed to approve. "You'll love La Zorra."

"Thanks. So . . . see you around nine thirty?"

Josefina hinted at a smile, noncommittal. "Have a safe trip home."

They watched her walk away, saying nothing until she reached the street corner a half block away.

"I think I got a date," said Theo.

Jack shot him a look of disbelief. "That's how you read that exchange?"

"How else would you read it?"

"Dude, we'll never see her again."

"Well, that's not true. She's your star witness, all the proof you need to show that Bianca is Rafael's widow."

Jack shook his head. "First of all, there is no law or treaty between the United States and Cuba that I can use to force a Cuban citizen to sit for a deposition or appear in an American courtroom."

"We don't have to force her. Maybe we can talk her into it."

"Yeah, right. She was afraid to pass on Rafael's

letters, but she's going to blow her Olympic dream and volunteer to testify under oath that her engagement to Rafael was a fraud, just so Bianca can get ten million dollars from the oil consortium in a lawsuit that was filed in Key West and that the Cuban government doesn't even recognize as legitimate."

Theo took a minute, seeming to process the boatload of information Jack had just delivered. "So you're saying this was a total waste of time?"

"Basically, we got nothing."

Theo reached for Jack's bowl and scooped out the final melted spoonful.

"Ice cream was good. That's something."

"Yeah, that's something." Jack gathered up the empty bowls, rising. There was more on his to-do list.

"Come on. Let's go collect some wedding photos."

18

·

It was Jack's first look at a Cuban farm. But it wasn't in the countryside. The taxi pulled away, leaving Jack and Theo at the street curb in southwest Havana. On the other side of a chain-link fence were two acres of green urban land.

"This is a first," said Jack. "A farm that backs up against the biggest hospital in a major city, with a tavern on one side and a bowling alley on the other. Can't say I've seen that before."

"Now you have. Let's go to the bar," said Theo.

"Business first."

Jack opened the gate, and Theo followed him down a sandy path that bisected the farm into two separate parcels. They passed a plot of beans, then a smaller plot of sweet potatoes. Marigolds were at the end of each row, which Jack knew from his *abuela* was an age-old Cuban bug repellent. To Jack's left, on the other side of the path, men were planting seedlings in neat rows. Their only tools were plastic water bottles with the bottoms cut off, which they plunged into the ground to create a perfect seedling hole. Skinny chickens in a variety of colored feathers roamed freely; a tattered patchwork of wire fencing along either side of the path was completely ineffective in keeping them out of the garden.

"I feel like any minute now I'm going to run into Eddie Albert, Eva Gabor, and Mr. Drucker," said Jack.

Theo caught the reference to the ancient TV show, adding his own geographically appropriate rendition of the theme song from *Green Acres*.

"*Verde* Acres is the place to be . . ."

Green was the operative word, the whole idea behind the rise of urban and suburban farms and gardens in Cuba. More than a hundred thousand small farms sprang up in the 1990s and on into the next decade, when the Ministry of Agriculture distributed use rights ("in usufruct") to an estimated three million hectares of unused state lands. It was the government's answer to the collapse of the Soviet Union and Cuba's loss of its source of pesticides, oil, and other staples of large-scale, state-run farming. People were starving. Of necessity, a *campesino*-style spirit and Cuban ingenuity took hold in the cities. Families grew what they ate, and their farming methods—no chemicals—caught the eye of environmentalists worldwide.

Bianca's old friend—the photographer at her wedding—was lucky enough to work on one of the oldest urban gardens in southwest Havana.

"Can you tell me where I can find Olga Mendez?" Jack asked one of the workers in Spanish.

The man rose from his stooped-over position, arching his back to iron out the kink. He wiped the sweat from his brow and pointed toward the tin-roofed bungalow at the back of the property. It was in the late-afternoon shadow of the hospital that stood directly behind the farm. Jack thanked him and continued down the path. A huge feral cat darted across Theo's shoe tops as they approached the front door.

"Now, that's what I call rodent control," said Theo.

Jack knocked on the door. A young woman answered. Her puzzled expression disappeared as soon as Jack mentioned Bianca. His client had obviously followed through and gotten word to Olga that Jack was on his way. Olga invited them inside, and Jack drew on his every facility with the Spanish language to answer a flurry of questions about Bianca. She led them to the kitchen, where several dozen empty beer bottles were lined up on the table.

"Guess we found the party house," said Theo.

Olga laughed, obviously understanding. "No, no. Is for our salsa," she said in English.

She opened the cupboard and showed them the finished product. Hundreds of recapped beer bottles were filled with a red sauce. She handed Jack one of the clear Corona bottles so he could see it.

"Is the best," she said. "All from *el jardín*. We sell at the market in *Habana* on Sundays."

"Very cool."

"If you need any help emptying the beer from the bottles, I'm available," said Theo.

She laughed again. "*Botellas* from *la taberna*."

There wasn't much in the kitchen, but they tried the sauce on a slice of sweet potato.

"Wow," said Jack. "There should be a law that requires mango in all salsa."

"And Cuban limes."

"Is sour orange," said Olga. "Like in *mojo*."

Jack wanted more, and the Cuban people were so generous that they'd give you every last bit of food in the cupboard, even if it meant their going hungry for the next two days. Jack kept it to a mere sample, cutting himself off and shutting down Theo, the human vacuum.

When the small talk was over, Olga brought out a handful of photographs and laid them on the table.

"These are all I have," she said.

Jack went through them, one by one. Olga narrated and identified everyone by name. Bianca looked like a girl, barely a woman. Rafael didn't look much older, and it saddened Jack to think of his life cut so short.

"This one is what you want," said Olga, saving the best for last.

Jack felt a rush of adrenaline, the way any lawyer would upon hitting pay dirt. It was a photograph of Bianca and Rafael outdoors, standing on the fourth step of a wide stone staircase. Rafael was dressed in a gray suit, blue shirt, and striped tie. Bianca wore a simple white dress and was holding a wedding bouquet. Mounted on the blue stucco wall behind them was a large brass plaque.

"*Ministerio de Justicia*," said Jack, reading it aloud.

"This was right after the ceremony, right outside *el ministerio*. See how happy they are?"

Jack's gaze locked onto the smiling newlyweds.

It wasn't a marriage certificate, but it was the next best thing.

"May I take this to Bianca?" he asked.

She nodded. "Yes. All of them. She should have them."

Jack thanked her, then took the conversation in a slightly different direction. "Did you stay in touch with Rafael after Bianca left the island?"

"Not really. Sometime he come by the market in *Habana* and say hello. He loved *la salsa*."

"When was the last time you saw him?"

"It makes one month."

"After he started working on the rig?"

"*Sí*. We talked about that. He work two weeks on the rig, two weeks off." Her expression saddened. "He was on this two weeks. *Que triste*."

Jack gave her a moment, then followed up. "Do you know anything about Rafael and a woman named Josefina?"

"How you mean?"

Jack tried to be delicate. "There's a rumor that Rafael was seeing a woman here in Havana named Josefina."

"No. Not Rafael. That's crazy."

"But . . . how do you know? You said you hardly saw him since Bianca left."

"He loves Bianca."

Jack glanced at the wedding photograph. "I'm sure he did. But they were apart for a long time."

"He still loved her as much as before. Maybe more."

Jack and Theo exchanged glances. The former prison inmate was about as jaded as they come about long-distance relationships, and some of it was wearing off on Jack. "That's a really nice sentiment," said Jack. "But can you tell me why you believe it's true?"

"He told me."

"When you saw him last?"

"*Sí.*"

"Rafael said he still loved Bianca?"

"Not in those words."

"What did he tell you?"

She drew a breath, then let it out. She breathed deep a second time, and Jack sensed a bit of a digression coming on.

"Did you know Rafael was student at *la universidad*? To be engineer?"

"Yes, Bianca told me."

"And you know what job he worked on the oil rig?"

"He was a derrick monkey."

"*Sí.* Such dangerous work for student of engineering. Is that not strange to you?"

"I was told that the pay is good, and he wanted the money."

"No. Not about money.

"How do you know that?"

"We talked. Rafael explained." She took another breath, as if the words were no longer coming with ease. "Have you ever been on an oil rig, Mr. Swyteck?"

"No."

"*Ni yo tampoco.* But Rafael tell me it is the highest point on the rig. If you climb to top, you are hundred meters above water."

"I'm sure it's pretty scary up there."

She shook her head. "Rafael not scared. He *wanted* to be up there."

"Why?"

"He told me why. He say, on a clear day . . ." She paused again, a lump coming to her throat. She pushed through it. "He say, on a clear day he can see all the way to Key West, Florida."

Her words went straight to Jack's heart, and her point became clear. "All the way to Bianca," said Jack.

She nodded slowly, sadly.

There was silence in the room. Jack's gaze returned to the wedding photograph on the table. He picked it up, gave it another good look, and then glanced at Olga. A tear ran down her cheek.

"*Gracias*," he said, more convinced than ever that his client had lost her husband.

19

·

Jack woke at four o'clock. The sun was streaming through the hotel window and hitting him in the eyes.

Sun? At four a.m.?

He checked his phone. It was four *p.m.* Saturday afternoon. His flight to Miami was leaving in two hours.

Idiot!

He tried to lift his head from the pillow, but it was too heavy.

Friday night had begun at La Zorra y el Cuervo (The Fox and the Crow). When the "fox" (Josefina) proved a no-show, Dr. Theo had prescribed all-night bar hopping. They made several stops in Old Havana, circled back to La Zorra, closed it down sometime after the live jazz stopped at three a.m., and then found more clubs. By the time they'd found their way back to the hotel, a new day had dawned on the diurnal half of Havana. Whether he was getting old was open to question, but Jack was admittedly too "mature" to be hitting local bars in foreign countries and drinking whatever firewater flowed from the well. The last thing Jack remembered was the sunrise over Havana Harbor. He'd slept through his last day in Cuba.

Gotta get up.

Jack sat up slowly in bed, massaged away the pain between his eyes, and moved to the edge of the mattress. The room spun for a moment as his toes brushed the carpet.

"Oh, my head."

There was a pounding on the door. Jack forced himself up and answered. It was Theo, his backpack over one shoulder.

"I'm on the six-thirty flight to Jamaica," said Theo. "You want to share a taxi?"

Jamaica? It took a second for Jack's brain to catch up. Jack had a nonstop to Miami. Felonious Theo, embargo buster, needed a more circuitous route back to the States.

"By 'share a taxi,' I assume you mean I pay and you ride."

"With no extra charge for the pleasure of my company."

"What a deal."

Jack switched on the TV to keep Theo occupied, found his overnight bag, and started packing. Cuba's state-run television had nothing about the spill, which was just as well, since Jack was feeling more polluted than the waves that marked the grave of the Scarborough 8. As he stepped out of the tiny bathroom with his Dopp kit in hand, he suddenly remembered all that he had forgotten to do.

"Shit! I was supposed to be at the Ministry of Justice this morning to look into Bianca's marriage license. I can't believe I slept in."

"Don't beat yourself up. They're not open on weekends anyway."

Jack breathed a heavy sigh. He should have known that. *Too much going on.* "Then I have to stay till Monday."

"No, you don't," said Theo. He removed an envelope from his backpack and dropped it on the bed. Jack opened it. Inside was a copy of the license.

It was in Spanish, so Jack went through it slowly, checking each entry against the information Bianca had given him: full name, date, and place of birth for *el contrayente* and *la contrayente*; parents' names, location of the ceremony, and the name of the civil officer performing the ceremony. The only entry that gave Jack pause was Rafael's *fecha de nacimiento*—not because his date of birth had been recorded incorrectly, but because of the sobering reminder that twenty-two years of age was way too young to die. All was in order, including the stamped certification of the Cuban *registrado del estado civil.*

"Thank you," said Jack. "But I'm curious. This trip was supposed to be step one in a process that I expected would take months, if we ever got the license at all. How'd you get it so fast?"

"Easy as egg pie."

Flan was more than "egg pie," but a lesson in Cuban desserts was for another date. "So you just went to the Ministry of Justice and they gave you a copy?"

"No, no, *nooo*," said Theo. He tossed Jack's wallet onto the bed.

Jack patted down his empty pockets to confirm that it was his. "How did you get my wallet?"

"You gave it to me last night."

"I didn't give you—"

"Give, take? It's a fine line after four a.m. Anyway, you don't want to know how much that marriage license cost you."

"Wonderful. So now the oil companies can add bribery to their list of reasons why the license should be kept out of evidence at trial."

"It's not a fake. That's a real certified copy. What difference does it make how we persuaded some Cuban paper pusher to do his job?"

"I just like doing things the right way."

"But you can use it in your case, right?"

"Probably. But the truth is, the license and the wedding photos only go so far. They prove Bianca got married, which logically should be enough. But Candela has raised enough of a stink to make our judge demand some form of additional proof that Bianca was still married to Rafael when he died."

"You need Josefina to testify," said Theo.

"We're not going to get Josefina."

"I'll work on her next time we come."

"*Next time?* Dude, I'm not bringing you to Cuba on business. Do you want to get us both indicted?"

"Hmmm. Let me think about that. No, just you."

Jack ignored him and tucked the license into his bag. "Let's hit the road before we miss our planes."

Checkout was reasonably quick, and there was no wait for a taxi at the valet stand. This time the ride was in a 1956 metallic-blue Buick with bright yellow bumpers. They left the hotel with time to spare, which was a good thing, because traffic was moving slowly out of central Havana. The driver tried a side street, but it was no better. He tried another route, but that didn't help, either. At each turn, Theo glanced out the rear window. Finally, they were back where they had started, in front of their hotel.

"We're being followed," Theo said to Jack.

"Very funny."

"We circled around the block, and that car behind us copied every move we made."

Jack glanced out the rear window. It was a vintage eighties Toyota with a big man behind the wheel and an even bigger guy in the passenger seat.

"They probably think our driver knows his way out of this jam," said Jack.

The gridlock broke, traffic was suddenly moving, and their taxi was approaching a confusing intersection of six separate streets.

"Make a sleft!" Theo told the driver.

"*Cómo?*"

"A sleft!" Theo shouted.

"*Cómo?*"

"A left," Jack said.

"No, a sleft!" said Theo. "Slight left."

"Havana is not the place to make up words in English, you moron."

Jack directed in Spanish, and at the last moment the driver managed to make a soft left turn. Jack checked behind them. Even with five choices at one intersection, the Toyota followed.

"Okay, now this is getting weird," said Jack.

"Change cabs right here," said Theo. "See if the Toyota stays with us."

Jack liked the idea. "Stop!" he told the driver.

The brakes screeched, and even with the driver practically standing on the pedal, the best a sixty-year-old taxi could do was coast to a stop. Jack paid the fare as Theo flagged another cab that was headed in the opposite direction. They jumped in the backseat, and the taxi started back toward the six-point intersection. The Toyota pulled a U-turn and caught up with them.

"Told you, dude," said Theo.

Jack handed up a fifty-peso note to the driver. "Lose that Toyota," he said in Spanish.

The taxi screeched to a halt so abruptly that Jack and Theo slammed into the front seat. The driver threw up his hands, refusing even to touch the wheel, let alone take the money.

"No, señor. Son Rusos."

Jack translated: "He says that—"

"I heard," said Theo. "They're Russian mob, and he just shit his pants."

"Well, that's not exactly what he—"

Theo yanked him by the elbow and flung open the door, barely giving Jack time to grab his carry-on. They flew from the taxi as if it were on fire and raced down the sidewalk. The Toyota was in pursuit, but on such a narrow and crowded street, it was an advantage to be on foot.

"Keep running!" Jack shouted.

It was an all-out sprint, bags flailing, as they dodged down an alley between two old apartment buildings. The opening was far too narrow for the Toyota to follow them, but Jack refused to slow down long enough to find out if the Russians were interested in a footrace. Theo was breathing loudly but managed to puff out a few words.

"Dude, I . . . got a . . . confession."

"What?" asked Jack, matching Theo stride for stride.

"Didn't get . . . the license . . . from no Ministry of Justice."

Jack would have strangled him if they weren't running for their lives. Instead, he pushed forward, throwing an occasional glance over his shoulder for anything Russian as they approached the new Cuban record for the fifty-meter dash.

20

·

They found a crowded restaurant in Habana Centro and lay low for an hour. They sat Mafia style, which Jack had learned from multiple viewings of *The Godfather*: rear table, back to the wall, so that no one could sneak up from behind, a side door nearby in case of emergency. Theo ordered chicken and rice. Jack was unable to eat, too much on his mind.

Another run to the airport would have been foolish. It wouldn't have taken a genius to figure out that Jack and Theo—bags packed, leaving their hotel in a taxi—were on the way to the airport. If those thugs were as scary as the cabdriver had let on, they were surely staking out the terminal, just waiting for Jack and Theo to show up for the one and only evening flight from José Martí International to Miami. Calling the police was also out of the question. Theo was in Cuba illegally, and Jack was pretty sure that Bianca's lawsuit against the oil consortium had knocked her lawyer right off the short list for Comrade of the Year.

"You pissed at me?" It was the third time Theo had asked, but for the first time Jack chose to respond.

"It was stupid of you to shop the black market."

"Dude, the only way to get the marriage license was to grease someone's palm. Even I don't have the balls to fly over here illegally, walk into the Ministry of Justice, and buy off the *registrador*. The only sensible thing was to hire a facilitator. How was I to know that the one I found was Russian Mafiya?"

"Russians have deep roots in Cuba."

"The man named a price and I paid him. Cash. It's the way everything gets done in this country. Why should I even think that would blow up in my face?"

Jack took the edge off his tone, cutting him slack. "I'll give you this much: you would have to put two and two together to see it coming."

"I suck at math," said Theo. "Who do you think these guys are?"

"Probably not Mafiya. My guess is bodyguards for high-level Russian oil executives."

"I still don't get it."

"One of the companies in the oil consortium is Russian. The whole lot of them are trying to stop me from proving that Bianca was Rafael's wife. Luis Candela makes his arguments in court, but technically his only client is the Venezuelan company. I guess the Russians have their own style."

"Kind of extreme, don't ya think? A Russian oil company sending out a couple of goons to kill us just to get a marriage certificate back?"

"More likely they were just trying to scare us by

following us to the airport. But who knows? Did you get a good look at them?"

"Pretty good."

"Even if they're not Mafiya, they're thugs. Just for grins, they'd grab us by the ankles and hang us off the roof of an apartment building until the marriage certificate falls out of our pockets. Their job is to keep us from leaving the island with the documentation we need. Whatever it takes."

"So the guy who sold me a copy of the marriage certificate works for the oil consortium?"

"I wouldn't go that far," said Jack. "Bianca's lawsuit is getting press worldwide. My guess is that he follows the news outside Cuba enough to know that Bianca's marriage status is a hot-button issue in the case. He sold you the license, but he was also smart enough to figure out that the consortium would appreciate a heads-up about a guy from Miami who just bought a copy of the license on the black market. He made a few phone calls, and the oil consortium probably rewarded him handsomely for his efforts."

Theo swallowed another mouthful of rice. "How was I supposed to see that coming?"

Jack was hard-pressed to fault him. "It doesn't matter. The question now is: What do we do?"

"We're less than three blocks from the boxing gym. I say we go there."

"Forget Josefina."

"She's our best angle. We can't go to the airport, we can't go back to the hotel, we can't call the cops. We need to hide the way only a local can hide us."

There was some logic to that, but Jack needed to

be persuaded. "Okay, make your case: What makes you think Josefina will help us?"

"The Russian connection is a game changer."

"It doesn't change anything from Josefina's perspective. She has no interest in sticking her neck out for an American lawyer and putting her boxing career at risk."

"Asking her to testify in court against the oil consortium is too much. But all we're asking for is a place to hide until it's safe to make another run to the airport."

"I still don't see an upside for her."

"Then you're blind. Josefina wants to know the truth about what happened to Rafael. And if two Russian thugs tailed us to the airport, then someone wants Bianca's lawsuit to go away really bad. And if they want it bad enough to threaten and intimidate us, it isn't just about money. Someone has a secret to hide about what happened on that rig. They don't want an American lawyer poking around trying to find the real cause of the explosion."

"I can't disagree with that," said Jack.

"Everything you just agreed with is on Josefina's need-to-know list."

"Curiosity isn't reason enough for her to help us."

"It isn't curiosity, dude. It's love."

"Shut up. Josefina is not in love with you."

"Not me. Rafael."

"Now you're just making things up. Their engagement was a sham."

"Says her," said Theo. "But it doesn't add up. She told us that she was willing to pretend to be Rafael's wife, but she was afraid to pass on his love letters to

Bianca. Bullshit. It's not that risky to send a few letters to Miami. Josefina wasn't worried about saving her own ass from the big bad Cuban government."

"Then what was it?"

Theo smiled, but it was mostly out of disbelief. "You really don't see it, do you?"

"No, I don't."

"Look, this is the situation. I got no doubt that Rafael was just pretending to be engaged. But Josefina? Nope. Not pretending. Or at least she wished it wasn't pretend. That girl was in love with Rafael. Probably has been since high school. That's why she didn't pass on his letters to his wife."

"How do you come up with that?"

"I'm a bartender, dude. Got myself an honorary degree in pop psychology and screwed-up relationships. These things I know."

Jack paused, but not because he thought Theo was off base. "Your theory actually makes some sense."

"Yes, it does," said Theo. "And when you spell it out for Josefina, she is going to help us."

"When *I* spell it out?"

"You're Bianca's lawyer, dude. Not me."

"That I am," said Jack. "That I am."

21

.

"Think whatever you want to think," said Josefina.

Jack heard a denial without heart, which spoke volumes about Josefina's feelings for Rafael. Or maybe it meant nothing. Jack drew his own conclusion: Theo had nailed it; Josefina had found love on a one-way street.

Right or wrong, Jack had her cooperation.

"I know a place you can stay," said Josefina. "Two days, no more. No one will find you."

The neighborhood behind La Escuela de Boxeo was mostly government buildings, all closed for the weekend. Burned-out bulbs made the streetlamps useless, and there was not even a porch light or glowing residential window to brighten the deserted streets. Overcast skies made the night even blacker. Josefina led the way with Theo at her side. The sidewalk was just wide enough for two abreast, but they were off the curb and walking in the street anyway.

"Stay off the sidewalk," she told Jack. "Buildings are really bad on this street. Last week a poor old man ended up in the hospital when a chunk fell off and landed on his head."

Jack minded the warning, careful not to fall into the gaping holes in the pavement. The shallow ones were ankle deep; the only "pot" these holes brought to Jack's mind was on a soup-kitchen order of magnitude. After a nine-block walk, they reached a more lively area, a mixture of the local bar scene and century-old apartment buildings. Jack had no map, but the smug bourgeois mansion blocks left him guessing that they were near the University of Havana, where the Paris École des Beaux-Arts was once the major influence on the prized school of architecture. It required serious imagination to see the mansions in their original glory, as most had transformed into overcrowded apartment buildings, too many families in too little space.

Josefina led them up an outdoor staircase to a second-story apartment. The staircase and the door were a post-revolution addition—an ad hoc point of access to what had once been an upstairs bedroom in a nineteenth-century estate. She stopped outside the door to give Jack and Theo a little more information.

"My friend Vivien lives here."

"Alone?" asked Jack.

Josefina shot him a "stupid question" expression. "With her mother, two aunts, and five cousins. But lucky for you they are all in Cienfuegos for a wedding this weekend."

Josefina retrieved a key from beneath a clay pot beside the door, but before she could insert it in the lock, the door opened.

"Vivien?" she said, obviously startled to see her friend.

Josefina stepped inside, leaving Jack and Theo on the other side of the threshold, but the door was open as the women spoke to each other in Spanish. Jack caught most of it. Vivien's family was in Cienfuegos, but Vivien wasn't traveling until Saturday morning. The upshot was that Jack and Theo were invited inside, but Josefina needed to stay until the Americans proved their trustworthiness. It was far from clear that Jack and Theo had a place to stay for the night.

Theo turned away from the doorway so that the women wouldn't overhear him. "Jackpot," he whispered, eyebrows dancing. He was obviously referring to the fact that Josefina's friend was as hot as she was.

Jack stepped closer, his tone stern. "First of all, you are with a married man. Second of all—"

"You can come in," said Josefina, interrupting. "But be gentlemen."

"Absolutely," said Theo, entering. "Tonight we are *caballos.*"

"*Caballeros*, moron," said Jack. *Caballos* are horses."

Theo kept his voice low so that only Jack could hear. "Hey, if the condom fits . . ."

"Knock it off," said Jack. "Right now."

Vivien closed the door and offered them a seat on a lumpy couch. Jack inferred from the old wind-up alarm clock on the end table that it also served as someone's bed. A small lamp on the same table was the only light in the room, and a quick glance around the apartment confirmed that it had once been a single room in a splendid mansion. Makeshift walls of unpainted plywood butted up awkwardly against the original baseboards, crown molding, and coffered ceiling, subdividing a much larger room into smaller spaces, creating the feel of a construction site.

Vivien pulled up a pair of wooden chairs that didn't match, one for her and the other for Josefina.

"Please," said Jack, offering his spot on the couch.

"No, *gracias*," said Vivien. Her body language made it clear that she wasn't just being polite. She preferred a seat closer to the door—just in case. The Americans had a ways to go before earning her trust, even if Josefina did vouch for them.

"Do you speak any English?" asked Jack.

"Some," said Vivien.

"She's being modest," said Josefina. "She speaks very well, and she writes it fluently. Vivien is a contributor to *Cuba Times*."

"What is that?" asked Jack.

"An English-language Internet newspaper about Cuba."

"Does it have anything to do with *Granma*?"

"Very different from *Granma*," said Vivien. "We are not propaganda. We are an independent voice."

"The Cuban government is okay with that?"

"Well, we are only on the Internet. No print."

"Then how does the average Cuban read you?"

"Internet cafés are not just for tourists anymore. Five American dollars an hour is pretty expensive for a Cuban worker, but Havana has at least a dozen public cafés now."

"A dozen? In a city of how many million? And of the people who can afford a quarter of their monthly salary for an hour of Internet, how many read English?"

Vivien shifted uneasily, her tone taking on a tinge of embarrassment, a hint of sincere sadness. "We have very few readers who live in Cuba. I wish that weren't so, but it is."

"Sorry," said Jack. "I wasn't suggesting that your work is not important."

"It's okay. Someday it will be different. Maybe soon."

"Have you done any stories on the oil spill?"

"Not me. But *Cuba Times, sí.*"

"How about the lawsuit filed by Bianca Lopez against the oil consortium? Has *Cuba Times* written about that?"

"Of course."

"Against it, I presume?" said Jack.

Vivien smiled a little. "Typical American."

"What do you mean?"

"I just told you that *Cuba Times* is an independent voice. But your question presumes that no one in Cuba ever says what she thinks."

"I wasn't trying to insult you," said Jack.

"I'm not insulted. It's my chance to educate you. Do you know who the biggest critic of *Cuba Times* is in your country?"

"No idea," said Jack.

"We wrote a story on him. He is a rich old man in Connecticut who owns www.sex_for_pesos.com. He arranges trips for men who want to fly over for a weekend and have cheap sex with Cuban girls."

Jack glanced cautiously at Theo, keeping him in check, but the big guy simply shook his head.

"Not even remotely my style, dude."

That was reassuring. "Sounds like good investigative journalism," said Jack. "But from the Cuban government's standpoint, my lawsuit against the oil consortium is probably way more offensive than 'sex for pesos.' I'm shocked that you're allowed to report anything about it that isn't critical, even if *Cuba Times* is available only in English over the Internet."

"It's not a question of what the government allows," said Vivien. "The website is hosted out of Nicaragua. When I write I use . . . how do you say, *seudónimo*?"

"Pseudonym," said Josefina, translating.

"Ah, now I understand," said Jack.

Theo rose. "You got anything to drink, Viv?"

"Vivien," she said, correcting him. "Not really."

"I saw a bar on the way over here. I'll pick something up."

"Theo, we're in *hiding*. That's the whole point of this."

"Josefina will come with me. Come on, let's go kick some Russian ass."

Josefina hesitated.

"Go ahead," Vivien told her. "I'm enjoying my talk with Mr. Swyteck."

It was mutual, so Jack didn't press the "hiding" point with Theo. "Just be smart, okay?"

Theo agreed, Josefina assured him that they would be quick, and they left together.

"Your friend likes Josefina, no?"

Jack smiled. "Not too subtle, is he?"

"He's very good-looking. Who knows?"

"A bit of a long shot. Geography the least of it. Josefina must be heartbroken about Rafael."

Vivien paused, showing some caution. "You understand that I know, right?"

Jack didn't know for certain, and he reminded himself that he wasn't just talking to Josefina's friend. Vivien was a journalist. "Know what?"

"It was not a real engagement. Don't worry. I would never write that."

Jack studied her expression.

"If I was going to write it," she said, "it would have already been in *Cuba Times*."

That much Jack could believe. He pushed a little deeper. "But even if they weren't engaged, Josefina must be upset."

"Yes, very. Rafael was a good friend."

"More than a friend, it seems to me. I get the feeling that Josefina was really in love with him."

Vivien made a face. "Josefina and Rafael? In love? Ick. They were like brother and sister. Friends since they were little kids. Grosses me out just to think about anything romantic between them."

"So I'm wrong about that?"

"*Totally* wrong. That would be like Ross doing it with his sister Monica."

The somewhat dated pop-culture reference surprised Jack at first, but *Friends* and other syndicated American sitcoms were staples of Cuban television. And it made the point.

But if Josefina wasn't in love with Rafael, why didn't she forward his letters to Bianca? It was not a question that Jack felt comfortable asking a reporter for *Cuba Times*.

Jack heard footsteps on the outside staircase, and then the door opened.

"We're back," said Theo. He had two six-packs of beer. Josefina was holding a steaming paper bag of food. It smelled like empanadas.

"Did you two have an interesting talk while we were gone?" asked Josefina.

Jack glanced at Vivien, then back at Josefina. His question about the letters that Josefina had never forwarded came back to mind, along with the unconvincing denial that he'd gotten from Josefina when he'd tested Theo's theory about her unrequited romantic interest in Rafael. A firm *no* would have left him less confused. Or maybe it was Vivien and *Friends* who had confused him. Or the "independent" *Cuba Times*.

Which one of you is trying to mislead me?

"Yes," said Jack, locking eyes with Josefina. "Our talk was very interesting."

22
.

The beer was gone by ten o'clock. Jack was tired, Vivien was leaving for Cienfuegos at six a.m., and Josefina needed to be at the boxing gym by seven. Theo was just getting started, his vocal rendition of Woody Herman's "Sidewalks of Cuba" leaving them in stitches. Theo followed Josefina to the door. "I'll see you again tomorrow, then?"

Josefina smiled. "Maybe."

The plan was for Vivien to spend the night at Josefina's apartment Jack and Theo would stay at Vivien's, with the understanding that they would be gone no later than Sunday at dark, when the family returned. Fifty dollars cash in advance made the arrangement satisfactory. The ladies said good night, and Theo closed the door.

"That was a fun night," said Theo.

Jack went to the couch, no answer.

"I say that was fun. Right, Swyteck?"

Jack still didn't answer.

Theo hopped onto the couch beside him. Jack scooted away, creating space.

"You're such a tight-ass," said Theo.

Jack fidgeted with his shiny new wedding ring. "I was just thinking about Andie. Not exactly the way I planned to spend our honeymoon."

"Now, don't go feeling all guilty for having a beer with a couple of *señoritas*. For all you know, Andie is out sucking face right now with a twenty-five-year-old hottie as part of her new undercover role."

"Thank you, Theo. That makes me feel so much better."

"You're welcome." Theo stretched his legs out onto the coffee table, hands clasped behind his head. "You know, I really like Josefina."

"Too bad, because I can't imagine someone more geographically undesirable."

"I still got tomorrow. And tomorrow night."

Jack's mouth opened, but his words were on a few-second delay. "No, uh-uh. You are not bringing her back here."

"She lives with her brother, dude. You gotta give me a shot."

"You have no shot."

"I think she likes me."

"Three hours ago you thought the love of her life was Rafael. According to Vivien, they were more like brother and sister. Your radar is suspect."

"Okay, so I misread her feelings about a dead man I've never met. I'm rarely wrong about how a chick feels about me."

"Then get a hotel room."

"That won't work."

"Why not?"

"I asked her, just in a kidding-around kind of way when we were out. She laughed, but then, totally serious, she told me it's illegal. A foreigner can't book a room with a Cuban national. It's an anti-prostitution law. If she got caught, Josefina would be labeled a *jinetera*. Boom. No more boxing team."

"Theo, that law hasn't been on the books since Raúl Castro's first year in office. She was blowing you off. Anyway, this is not my problem."

"Aw, come on, dude. I'm not saying for sure it's gonna happen, but if it does, just get a hotel room and let us stay here."

"We're in hiding. I'm not going to hunt for a hotel."

"There are tons of little places to stay right in this neighborhood."

"Forget it."

"I'll even pay for your room."

"No. It's not happening."

Theo swatted him with a sofa cushion. "You shit-head. You can't be with Andie, so you're busting my balls."

"Do you think I'm that petty?"

"Yeah, it's a proven fact: a married man feels better about having sex with the same woman for the rest of his life when his single friends aren't getting any. Only most men don't actually sabotage their buddies after just one week of marriage."

It was a blow too low. From a screwed-up honeymoon to being hunted down by Russian thugs, Jack had reached his limit. And he knew exactly how to deal with his anger.

"Theo," he said in a calm but firm voice. "There is absolutely no way on earth that Josefina is going to sleep with you. I guarantee it."

"Care to put a little wager on it?"

"Save your money," said Jack. "When you and Josefina went out to buy beer, Vivien asked some very pointed questions about you."

A look of concern came over Theo. "What did you tell her?"

"I told her that you were a great guy."

"And?"

"I told her the truth according to Theo Knight: you and I just spent the most wonderful honeymoon together in Key West."

Theo's expression fell. "Say what?"

"You heard me."

"Dude, tell me you didn't really do that."

Jack raised his hand, displaying the band of gold. "Payback's a bitch, ain't it, Theo?"

Jack woke in the middle of the night. A sliver of moonlight shone through a crack in the window shade, the only light in the room. The streets outside Vivien's apartment had finally gone quiet, the neighborhood bars having closed.

It had taken an hour of tossing and turning on the lumpy couch for Jack to fall asleep. Theo had won the coin toss and got the bedroom. Jack listened in the darkness, but he heard nothing, not even the hum of a refrigerator. He waited for his eyes to adjust, wondering what had woken him.

A gun barrel against his forehead was his answer.

"Do not move," the man said.

Jack froze. The intruder was standing behind him. Jack could see only the shiny nickel plating of a revolver and the fist—a huge hand—that held it steady. Jack wished he knew enough about guns to tell if it was Russian made.

"Do what I say, and you live. One mistake, and you die. Nod if you understand."

The accent was hard to discern. It sounded like he had cotton in his mouth to disguise his voice. Hispanic, maybe, but Jack was listening for hints of Russian. *Rusos* had been the cabdriver's take; but, then again, Jack didn't know for certain that those thugs had been Russian.

Cabdriver could have been paranoid.

He pressed the barrel more firmly against Jack's forehead, then spoke again through the thick cotton. "I said: Nod if you understand."

Jack nodded.

"Excelente," he said.

Definitely not Russian.

"We are going out that door, and you are going down the stairs in front of me. You get a bullet in the back if you screw up. Got it?"

Jack nodded without hesitation this time.

"You learn fast, Swyteck."

It chilled Jack to hear the man use his name. *Not good.*

"Get up now," the man told him.

Jack rose. The barrel of the gun slid across his eyebrow and around the side of his head, coming to rest at the base of his skull. Theo was suddenly at the top of Jack's list of worries—whether he was okay, whether the intruder even knew he was in the bedroom, whether Theo was waiting in the wings and about to do something heroic or stupid.

"Look, if it's money you want, I—"

"Shut up," he said. "I know what you're trying to do, but it won't work. Your friend Theo can't hear you."

Jack's heart sank. "What did you do to—"

Jack dropped to his knees. With a mere squeeze to the back of Jack's neck, the gunman had put him there.

"I wanted this to be easy," he said, his thick voice hissing into Jack's ear. "But I guess you like the hard way. Facedown, on your belly."

The thought of Theo dead or unconscious in the next room was enough to make the room spin. Jack hoped it was the latter as the pressure of a gun barrel directed him toward the floor.

"Arms out, like on the cross," the man said.

Flashes of resistance and escape raced through his mind, but Jack wasn't even close to a plan of action. He extended his arms out on the floor, hands level with his shoulders.

"Let's talk about this," said Jack.

"Let's not."

A needle pierced his skin, and Jack recoiled at the cold pressure of fluid entering his body through a syringe.

"Back to sleep," the man said. "Then we'll take a little ride."

23
·

Jack's eyes blinked open, but only for an instant. The light was unbearable. He waited a minute and tried again, squinting this time, giving his pupils a chance to adjust to the brightness. Slowly, the strange room came into focus.

He was on his back. A bed was right beside him, but he was lying on the floor. Not the smooth Cuban tile he remembered from Vivien's apartment. This was rough, unfinished concrete. A bare bulb hung by a wire from the ceiling, the assault to his eyes making it impossible to open them fully. He tried to sit up but could only go so far. Both his wrists and ankles were chained to the metal bedframe, and there was enough slack to move no more than a foot in any direction—left, right, or upright. The chains rattled as he lowered himself back to the floor.

Whoa, head rush.

That simple up-and-down motion stirred the fog in his brain, reminding him how the ordeal had started: the gun to his head, the jab of the needle, the slow loss of consciousness. Many hours had passed since then, he was sure of it. The bladder doesn't lie.

Man, I gotta go.

"Jack, you awake?"

The familiar voice made his pulse quicken. Theo was in the bed. "Thank God you're okay."

Theo extended his hands over the edge of the mattress, showing Jack the cuffs. "You call this okay?"

"Better than what I feared. How did you end up here?"

"Fucking weird. I mean, I've gone to bed in one apartment and woken up in another one before. And being handcuffed to a bed is nothin' new. But this is the first time I went to bed in one place, woke up handcuffed someplace else, and got no memory of any of it. Three beers never make me pass out like that."

It had actually been more like seven or eight, Theo having downed more than anyone, but the point was still valid. "It wasn't the beer," said Jack.

There was a knock on the door, which seemed odd. The door had an opening at knee level, like a mail slot, and a hand emerged, holding a smartphone.

"Do I hear talking?"

The voice was mechanical, like Siri on the iPhone, so it was impossible know if it was the same man who had put the gun to Jack's head. One man or two, one thing was clear:

The guy doesn't want us to know his voice.

The phone withdrew through the slot, then re-appeared. "No talking," Siri said, "unless I allow it. Turn around and face the wall."

Jack rolled on his side, his back to the door. Theo did the same. Jack heard the door open, and he lay motionless as the click of leather heels on concrete drew closer.

"I need a bathroom," said Jack.

It took a moment, and he could hear the man typing on his smartphone. Then came the mechanical response: "Okay. But from now on, it's every six hours. I am not getting up every time you have to piss."

Jack was suddenly reminded of his golden retriever.

"I need to go, too," said Theo.

More finger-clicking on the smartphone, then Siri: "One at a time. Swyteck, you're first."

Jack suddenly felt a blindfold over his eyes. It was strange how, even though he was already chained to a bed, total blackout made him feel so much more like a hostage. Jack heard the lock at his ankles click open, then the lock at the bedframe. His wrists remained shackled.

"Get up."

Jack rose slowly, wary of a trick, half-expecting the chain on his handcuffs to tighten and jerk him back to the floor. It didn't happen, but the probe of a gun into his spine dispelled any sense of relief.

Jack felt the man's hand on Jack's shoulder. "I'll direct you," the Siri voice said. "Just keep putting one foot in front of the other until I say stop."

Jack started walking, each step calculated to be as close to two feet in length as Jack could measure. He counted. Ten steps, then a left turn. Another five steps and he stopped on command.

"Stairway," the Siri voice said. "Twelve steps up."

Jack's mind went to work. A floor of rough concrete. A room with no windows. Stairway. *Holding us in the basement.*

Jack climbed. A heightened sense of aural awareness came with sight deprivation, and he noted the unique sound of each creaking step. They stopped at twelve. Right turn. Five steps, stop. The blindfold came off. Jack was looking into a bathroom.

"You got two minutes," said Siri.

Jack hesitated, hoping he would leave and close the door, but doing everything at gunpoint seemed to be the order of the day. Hopefully, a bullet in the back while peeing wasn't this guy's idea of death with dignity. He got another minute to wash his hands and face. His stubble cried out for a shave, but there was no offer of a razor. Just as well. The bathroom had no mirror, and he probably would have hacked himself bloody.

As soon as Jack dried his hands and face in the towel, the blindfold was back in place. The return walk to the basement stairs, however, was longer than expected. Nine steps instead of five. The blindfold came off again, and Jack found himself in a different room. It had windows, but they were darkened by storm shutters on the outside. An old card table, a small lamp, and a folding chair were the only furniture. The voice was still Siri:

"Sit and face the wall at all times."

Jack took the only chair available, keeping his eyes forward. Behind him, his captor closed the door. In the silence, Jack heard him punch out a number on his phone. Jack could hear him talking, but he couldn't hear what he was saying. It wasn't even easy to discern the language he was speaking. But it sounded like Spanish.

Okay, he's not working alone.

Jack heard him cross the room, still speaking into his phone. Jack kept his eyes forward as the man approached from behind and laid a notepad and a pen on the table in front of Jack. The man ended his call. A moment later, Jack felt a gun at his temple. The man thumb-typed a message into his phone, and audible instructions from Siri followed.

"Write down exactly what I say."

Jack swallowed hard and picked up the pen. He knew he was about to write his own ransom note.

Or his obituary.

24.

Andie was looking for her car. Actually, Viola's car.

The approved budget for Operation Black Horizon included a vehicle, but typical FBI snafus had delayed delivery. Andie's instructions were to pick up a white Ford Taurus with Virginia license plates anytime after eight p.m. on day three of Operation Black Horizon. It would be parked on Twenty-third Terrace, a quiet residential street in an old section of Alexandria. The keys would be under the driver's seat.

Andie followed the sidewalk from the Metro station, walking alone in the suburban quiet. A nearly continuous row of parked cars lined the curbs on either side of the street, precious few spaces open. A rush of wind stirred the leaves overhead. A few fluttered in the cool night air and fell in Andie's path, but it was still a bit too early for northern Virginia's red maple trees to surrender to autumn. Halfway down the block, she cast a casual glance over her shoulder. She thought she'd heard footsteps behind her, but no one was in sight. Up ahead, the sidewalk darkened in the shadow of older, larger trees. Gnarly old roots had caused entire sections of weathered concrete to buckle over the years. Low-hanging limbs blocked the light of the streetlamps, allowing Andie to see only a few cars ahead of her, making her search for the Taurus more difficult.

Would it have killed them to drop it off at my apartment?

Again she heard footsteps. She walked faster, and the click of heels behind her seemed to match her pace. She stepped off the sidewalk and down off the curb, as if she were going to cross the street. The sound of the footsteps behind her changed right along with her own, from heels on concrete to heels on asphalt. She returned to the sidewalk and heard the clicking heels behind her do the same. She kept walking, almost certain that she was being followed. All doubt was removed when the white Taurus came into view. A man was leaning against the car that was parked directly in front of it, waiting. And she could still hear the footsteps approaching from behind her.

A double-team.

Andie stopped and checked her phone. It was exactly the thing she had warned countless young women never to do—stop to read text messages on a dark street, oblivious to all surrounding danger—but she was only playing dumb. Her phone was set on the front-facing camera mode, the narcissist's dream for photographing her own face. By angling the lens over her shoulder, Andie could use it like a mirror, no need to turn around to see what was coming behind her.

The mysterious footsteps emerged from the darkness, the image came into view on Andie's screen, and her fears dissolved into confusion. She recognized the face. It was one of the agents from the Virginia field office—her undercover handler.

"Walk with me," he said as he passed.

Andie put away her phone and matched his casual stride, her confusion growing. Her undercover protocol called for meetings with her FBI handler at specified times. This was not one of those times.

"What are you doing here?"

"From the standpoint of maintaining the integrity of the operation, headquarters thought it was preferable to sending an agent to the apartment and pulling you."

"What do you mean, 'pulling' me?"

"Family emergency. That's all I know," he said.

Two words no one ever wanted to hear, but it didn't quite ring true for Andie. She had gone into undercover work with the full understanding that no "family emergency" was reason enough to get pulled from an assignment.

"Where are we headed?" she asked.

"Just ahead. To that blue car parked right in front of your Taurus."

The one with the man standing beside it. "Who's the guy?" she asked.

"Secret Service agent."

"Secret Service?"

"Yeah," he said. "You're going to the White House."

Family emergency, huh?
"Okay," she said. "This should be interesting."

Jack was alone in the basement, chained to the metal bedframe. He wasn't sure if it was day or night. Assuming that his captor had been true to his promise of a bathroom break every six hours, however, Jack calculated the passage of twelve interminable hours since his first break. It had been somewhere between six and twelve hours since his graduation from the concrete floor to the prison-thin mattress—since Theo had last gone upstairs at gunpoint, yet to return.

Jack was getting seriously worried.

He heard the door open at the top of the stairway. The mechanical voice of Siri told him what to do: "Face the wall."

Jack turned his back to the stairs and waited, listening to the approaching footsteps. Jack couldn't see him, but he sensed his captor was right behind him.

"Where is Theo?" Jack asked, more a demand than a question.

The man laid a paper bag on the floor in front of Jack. Jack heard the click of typing on his smartphone, and then the mechanical response: "Don't worry about your friend."

Jack was trying to figure out the smartphone technology. He assumed it was some kind of medical app for mutes. "There's no reason to hurt him," said Jack.

His captor stepped closer, still standing behind him, his shadow hovering over Jack. The mechanical response followed: "Shut up, before I stick another needle in your ass."

It was the most bizarre thing Jack had ever heard through Siri.

The man reached over him, and Jack feared another syringe was coming. But he was just reaching for the paper bag. As he reached, the man's sleeve rode up over his wrist, exposing an eye—a tattoo above the right thumb. Jack averted his gaze so as not to convey that he'd taken note of it.

The eye disappeared into the paper bag, and the man handed Jack a sandwich. The chains around his wrists had only enough slack for him to rise up on his elbows to eat. It was his first meal in captivity, and it was edible only because Jack was starving. The minced meat was unidentifiable. Maybe pork.

His captor typed another message, then played it on his phone: "I'll be back for your next bathroom break. If all goes according to plan, it might be your last."

The two very different interpretations of those words were not lost on Jack. He chewed slowly, not sure which meaning to take, as his captor turned and walked away.

25

Andie's White House meeting was in the West Wing. It was relatively quiet at nine o'clock on a Sunday night, especially with the president and his family staying at Camp David for the weekend. A stoic Marine in dress uniform escorted Andie to the office of the chief of staff. Andie had never met Jim Murphy before, but he was that rare breed inside the Beltway whose forte was cutting government waste. The president often alluded to the fact that it was a young Jim Murphy who had rooted out the five-hundred-dollar hammers in the Pentagon budget while at the Government Accounting Office.

The other man in the chief of staff's office was family. Harry Swyteck rose and embraced his daughter-in-law.

"Everything is going to be okay," he told her.

Harry Swyteck was Florida's most distinguished senior statesman. After two terms as governor of the fifth most populous state in the nation, he'd received serious consideration as a vice-presidential candidate. He got out the vote, even if he wasn't on the ballot, and he continued to have strong White House connections. Tonight, he needed them more than ever.

Andie took a step back, looking him squarely in the eye. "What is the 'family emergency'?"

"Jack has been kidnapped. But he is going to be okay."

Andie had delivered such news to the families of victims, and her own reaction on the receiving end was no different from what she had seen in others: little else registered after the word *kidnapped*, and promises that "everything is going to be okay" counted for very little.

The white-haired chief of staff stepped out from behind his desk and offered similar words of concern and support. At his direction, they moved to a small seating area by the window, Andie and Harry on the camelback couch, and the chief of staff facing them in a striped armchair. Harry did most of the talking for the next five minutes, explaining the "family emergency."

"Right after lunch today Theo showed up at my house. He said he and Jack were kidnapped in Havana."

"Jack went to Cuba?"

"Yes. Anyway, on Saturday night they were sleeping at an apartment in central Havana."

"An apartment? Who does Jack know with an apartment in Havana?"

"Theo said the young woman who lived there was named Vivien. He didn't know her last name."

"Doesn't know her name?"

"She was a friend of another woman named Josefina. Anyway, Theo says that the four of them had a few beers at the apartment and—"

"Stop!" said Andie. "Jack I trust. Theo, uh-uh. Are you about to tell me that Theo got my husband kidnapped by a couple of hookers in Havana?"

"No, no!" said Harry, suddenly aware of how this must have sounded. "That's not where this is going at all. This was investigative work for the lawsuit Jack filed against the oil consortium."

"I've seen the news reports," said Andie.

"Then you know that the oil companies say that Jack's client wasn't married to the Cuban oil worker who was killed in the explosion. Jack was in Havana trying to prove them wrong. He and Theo rented an apartment, totally on the up and up."

Andie needed to catch her breath. "That's much better than what it was starting to sound like, but you do understand that the kidnapping is not our only problem here?"

"What do you mean?" said Harry.

The chief of staff interjected. "I think what Andie is alluding to is that at some point we will have to deal with the fact that if Jack was doing investigative work in Cuba, that's a violation of the trade embargo, even if Jack is of Cuban descent."

"Which is a minor problem compared to the kidnapping," said Andie.

"Hell, yes, it's minor," said Harry, obviously annoyed.

"Harry, listen to what I'm saying," said Andie. "I'm sure what you meant to say is that Jack was in Cuba visiting relatives. When you speak to anyone in law enforcement about the kidnapping, I know you will make that clear. Nothing more needs to be said about this issue. Then we can focus all our energy on getting Jack back safely, which is what we all want."

Harry paused, digesting her advice. "Understood," he said.

The chief of staff steered him back to the immediate problem. "Harry, tell her about the note."

"Right," said Harry. "The kidnapper broke into the apartment, drugged them, and took them back to a basement somewhere in Havana. When he released Theo this morning, he gave him a ransom note and told him to deliver it to me. The note is in Jack's handwriting."

"A common practice," said Andie. "Proof to the family that the victim is still alive. Was it checked for prints?"

"Yes, I called the FBI immediately. Jack's prints were on it. Others couldn't be identified."

"Okay, good that the FBI is on it. But did the note have any kind of warning not to contact law enforcement?"

"Quite the opposite," said Harry. "That's why I'm here tonight."

"I don't understand."

"The ransom note lays out just one condition for Jack's release: if I deliver the note to the White House, Jack will be released, unharmed. The note even specifies the proof of delivery: an independent news organization must run a photograph of me meeting with the White House chief of staff."

Andie considered it. "It's actually not uncommon for kidnappers to ask to speak to the president or to have a message delivered to the White House. Usually it's an act of desperation, or someone with a screw loose. Or both."

"This may be different," said Harry. "The kidnapper knows that Jack is the son of a former governor with political connections. Since the note mentions the White House chief of staff by name, he probably got Jack to tell him who my closest personal contact is in the White House. Jim and I go back twenty-five years."

Murphy said, "I lean toward Andie's first impression. I think it's a nut-job."

"What does he want the White House to do?" asked Andie.

"Pay him money."

"But the note says he will release Jack if Harry delivers the note to the White House. So pay him money for what?"

Harry and the chief exchanged glances, and Harry answered. "He claims to know the 'real story' behind the Cuban oil spill. Obviously he thinks that's the kind of information that the White House would be willing to pay for."

"Obviously he doesn't know my reputation for fiscal responsibility," said Murphy.

"Jim's the kind of guy who once saw a GAO pen on the counter at a bank and brought it back," Harry said for Andie's benefit.

"Can I see the note?" asked Andie.

The chief of staff rose and retrieved the copy from his desk. Andie read it carefully, in its entirety, focusing in particular on the final two lines:

Scarborough 8 was sabotage. I know who did it.

Pay my price and you will know too.

The note had no signature, at least not in the conventional sense. Instead there was a number sequence: *3/6/11/17/9/42.*

"What do the numbers mean?" asked Andie.

"We don't know," said Harry.

"Is anyone looking into it?"

"Yes, of course," said the chief of staff. "But getting back to your original point about a nut-job, the numbers could be utterly meaningless."

"Meaningless? Really?"

"Granted, I'm not one to dismiss numbers easily," said Murphy. "Heck, I can't even walk into a White House banquet without trying to guess exactly how many people are in the room. But I call it as I see it."

Harry took a deep breath. "Jim, with all due respect, I think you're too quick to dismiss this as the work of a lunatic."

"I'm not trying to minimize the danger to your son," he said. "My point is that anyone who sends a letter like this to the White House has zero credibility in my eyes. The minute the Scarborough 8 went up in flames, the crazies started coming out of the woodwork. Two days ago we got a letter saying that the Cuban government will allow the United States to assist in the cleanup only if Bill Gates wires a hundred million dollars to a Swiss bank account and the Castro brothers are awarded the Nobel Peace Prize. It was 'signed,'" he said, making air quotes, "by Fidel Castro."

"That's not the same thing," said Harry.

"I don't see any difference."

"Andie, what do you think?" asked Harry.

Andie paused, thinking. Rather than discredit the kidnapper, the note's reference to sabotage actually enhanced his credibility, at least in Andie's eyes. Her entire undercover operation was premised on the theory that the cause of the explosion and spill was sabotage. It was possible that the kidnapper was a nut-job—but only if he had made one very lucky guess about causation. Unfortunately, she was sworn to secrecy about Operation Black Horizon, and it didn't matter that she was sitting in the White House with the chief of staff and her father-in-law.

"Mr. Murphy, may I use your phone?"

"Of course."

"Who you calling?" asked Harry.

"Headquarters," said Andie. "I need permission to tell you what I think."

26
.

Monday morning brought cloudless blue skies. From a window seat at twenty-two thousand feet, Jack had an unimpeded view of the black stain on the Florida Straits.

Jack's kidnapper had held true to his word. A White House–issued photograph of Harry Swyteck in the West Wing with the president's chief of staff had done the trick. Within hours, it was all over the World Wide Web. The only news story running with the photograph was of a former governor conveying to the administration his "grave concerns" about the oil spill's potential impact on his beloved state. Jack wasn't sure if it was the FBI or the White House that wanted to keep his kidnapping out of the media. Either way, the photograph was enough to satisfy Jack's captor that the ransom note had been delivered.

It's heading straight for the Keys.

Jack could not turn his gaze away from the window. While in Cuba, even before the kidnapping, Jack had lost track of the spill's movement.

The last reliable reports Jack had seen were Thursday's OAS projections, which three days later were coming true: The spill was on a northeasterly track, with Florida directly in its sights. Key West, it seemed, might actually dodge the bullet. But to Jack's untrained eye, it looked as though the upper Keys and the southeast coast of mainland Florida needed to prepare for the unthinkable. Viewed from an airplane, the problem was obvious. The front line of U.S. containment efforts began at the outer reach of Cuban waters. By that point the disaster had already fanned out from the source and spread across the surface in a black cone of unmanageable breadth. The early warnings of the experts that Jack had watched on television from his honeymoon suite at Big Palm Island were coming true. Chemical dispersants were less effective on oil after it was a full day or more from the source of the spill. Treatment within hours, near the faucet, was crucial to the relief effort.

Sabotage. The word had been echoing in Jack's brain ever since his kidnapper had forced him to write his own ransom note: *Scarborough 8 was sabotage.* Jack had come face-to-face with evil before, from convicted killers on death row to accused terrorists at Guantánamo Bay, but it was hard for him to construct even a loose psychological profile of the beast behind this work.

"It's all a big conspiracy, you know," said the old man seated next to him.

"Excuse me?" said Jack.

He gestured toward the window. "The spill. It's a White House conspiracy with Big Oil."

Jack should have simply nodded and turned away, but the old man seemed so sincere that Jack stayed with the conversation. "Why do you say that?"

"Just look at the facts. We have a president who took millions of dollars in campaign contributions from Big Oil. The oil companies are all licking their chops to drill for oil in Cuban waters, but the president can't get Congress to end the trade embargo without his entire party committing political suicide in Florida. Along comes a convenient oil disaster that the White House can point to and say, 'See, if we allowed U.S. oil companies to drill in Cuba, we wouldn't be at the mercy of the Cuban government and a consortium of Chinese, Russians, and Venezuelans.' Smells like a conspiracy to me."

"So you're saying that the White House conspired with the oil companies to blow up the Scarborough 8?"

The man shrugged, not with confusion, but as if the answer were obvious. "Look at what they did to the World Trade Center on nine-eleven."

It was a sensational theory straight out of the "infotainment mill"—enough to make Jack wonder, albeit only for a moment, if there wasn't at least one advantage to sanitized Cuban television.

The oil spill disappeared from view, and Jack closed his eyes to rest. Before long, the overhead speakers crackled with the flight attendant's announcement of their preparation for landing. It was a slow and gradual descent, and touchdown was just before noon. Law enforcement was waiting for Jack as he entered the international terminal. Two FBI agents escorted him through immigration and led him to a windowless room in which, over the years, several of Jack's clients had been poked, probed, and otherwise examined. A psychiatrist was on hand for his counseling needs, as in any kidnapping case. There was only one person Jack wanted to talk to.

"Is my wife here?"

The supervisory agent spoke for the FBI. Agent Linton was a tall ex-Marine type with a hint of a Jamaican accent. "Henning wanted to fly down, but it was the Bureau's judgment that stepping that far out of her role could jeopardize the operation."

Jack was disappointed but not surprised.

"She did ask me to give you this letter," Linton added.

Jack took it and read it to himself. It gave him the assurances he'd wanted—that she was doing fine, and that he shouldn't worry about her or the baby. The final paragraph made him smile—how sorry she was about the honeymoon, and how she was going to make it up to him. When he was finished, Agent Linton steered him toward a chair.

"We have some questions, of course," said Linton.

"No problem," said Jack.

The agents sat on one side of a small rectangular table, with Jack on the other. He told them everything, from the suspected Russians who had followed him and Theo on their way to the airport on Saturday afternoon, to his ultimate release on Sunday morning. Eventually the focus turned exclusively to the kidnapper. Jack told them about the eye tattoo just below his wrist. But even more than distinguishing physical characteristics, the FBI seemed interested in evidence of his technical expertise. Jack gave the question careful consideration before answering.

"I can't say that he comes across as some kind of computer genius," said Jack. "But he did use what seemed like a medical app for mutes to speak to me. It disguised his voice. Whenever he wanted to say something to me, he typed it into his phone. Then I'd hear Siri's voice."

"Smart," said the agent. "Did he use that to construct the ransom note?"

"Yes. It was highly scripted. He was on the phone beforehand. I think he was speaking Spanish."

"That certainly narrows down the list of suspects, seeing as how you were kidnapped in Cuba."

"My point is that I think someone was telling him what needed to be in my note."

"So you think he was taking directions from someone on the phone?"

"Possibly," said Jack. "On the other hand, I've met at least half a dozen death row inmates who have had absolutely delightful conversations on the telephone even though no one was on the line."

Linton didn't crack a smile. "Did your kidnapper seem delusional to you?"

"No more than he seemed like a computer expert."

"The two aren't mutually exclusive."

"Agreed. But I'm curious: why are you so focused on his computer savvy?"

The agent hesitated. "I'm sorry, but we can't get into that with you."

"Why not?"

"Information on that subject is shared only on

a need-to-know basis. There's no need for you to know."

Jack was undeterred. "*Sabotage* is a word that has been playing in my head ever since I was ordered at gunpoint to write it into the ransom note. Could it be that the FBI suspects computer sabotage as the cause of the explosion?"

"Sorry, Mr. Swyteck. Can't discuss it."

Jack wasn't one to sensationalize, but the words of that old man on the airplane were suddenly replaying in his head—the theory that Jack had dismissed as entertainment news babble: "*It's a White House conspiracy with Big Oil.*"

"I'm seeing a pattern here," said Jack. "First came the strict order to keep the kidnapping out of the news. Now you won't even share information with me—the victim."

"Those barriers are sometimes necessary in a criminal investigation."

"Sometimes," said Jack. "But I'm starting to wonder if the firewalls are being put up by the FBI, strictly for reasons related to law enforcement. Or by the White House, for some other reasons."

More silence.

There was a knock on the door. The agents seemed surprised, even annoyed, but when the door opened, the intrusion was more than welcome. Harry Swyteck was just off a plane from Washington. He rushed straight to Jack, who could feel the sense of relief in his father's long embrace. Pools of emotion welled in the older man's eyes, and at Harry's request, the agents stepped out into the hall to give him a minute alone with his son.

"I can hardly explain it," said Harry. "It was painful enough to hear you were held at gunpoint somewhere in Havana. But when Andie told me she was pregnant, all I could think of was you growing up without your mother. The thought of your child coming into this world without a father was . . ."

Harry stopped, unable to finish.

"It's okay," said Jack. "It's all okay now."

Harry took a breath, composing himself as he took a seat at the table. Jack sat across from him.

"Does the FBI have any leads on who did it?" asked Harry.

"They're not telling me anything."

"What?"

"I'm getting the line that information barriers are a necessary part of the investigation."

"That's true to a point. I agreed to keep the kidnapping out of the press so that we wouldn't get five thousand bogus tips an hour from a bunch of crank callers looking for their fifteen minutes of fame. But keeping you and me in the dark was not part of the deal."

"That's not what the FBI is telling me."

"Well, that's bullshit. We have a right to know."

"That's how I see it," said Jack.

"I'll straighten this out with Jim Murphy right now."

Harry had the chief of staff on speed dial, and Murphy took the call immediately. For the first two minutes, Harry did all the talking. It made Jack smile to himself to see his old man get his back up and fight for his son, laying out the "information" problem in blunt terms. The Swyteck family ties had been up and down over the years, and at times Jack had been less than proud of the governor's politics. Ironically, on the heels of what could have been a family tragedy, this was a high point.

"Jim, you and I have been friends for a long time," said Harry, "but let's take that out of this. Someone put a gun to Jack's head, chained him to the floor in a basement, and threatened to kill him. He has a right to know who did this to him. I'm going to put you on speaker so Jack can hear, and I'm hopeful that you will have something to say to him."

Harry laid the phone on the table, halfway between the two of them. Jack waited, but there was silence.

"Go ahead," said Harry. "We're listening."

Another moment passed, and finally the chief of staff replied. "I can't tell you who the target of the FBI investigation is. But rest assured, the demand in Jack's ransom note is being given serious credibility."

"You need to do much better than that," said Harry.

There was a long pause. Harry leaned closer to the phone, and Jack sensed that his father was ready to play his trump card.

"Jim, are you alone?" asked Harry.

"Yes, I am."

"Good. I didn't want to have to mention this, but maybe you've forgotten a certain phone conversation that you and I had about six years ago. It was right after you determined that Ohio was an even bigger swing state in the election than Florida. I'm paraphrasing, but as I recall, I was asked to state publicly that I had no idea if my name was on the short list of possible VP candidates, but even if it was offered to me, I would decline. Am I jogging your memory at all?"

"Yes, of course."

"You may also recall that I was more than just a good soldier who did what was asked of him. All the way up until the first Tuesday after the first Monday in November, I traveled up and down the state, campaigning my heart out for the ticket. The president ended up winning Florida by, I believe, eighteen thousand votes."

Jack was dumbstruck, but moved. It was the first he'd heard that his father had truly *wanted* to be on the ticket. And now he was calling in whatever capital he'd earned—for his son.

"Seventeen thousand nine hundred sixty-one," said the chief of staff. Murphy was truly a numbers guy.

"In a state of twelve million registered voters," said Harry.

"Okay, Harry. Your point is made. Here's what I can tell you: We have figured out the significance of the string of numbers that the kidnapper used to sign the note."

Jack didn't have the numbers memorized, but he'd combed through every line of the note with the agents, and a copy was still on the table. He checked the kidnapper's "signature" once again: *3/6/11/17/9/42.* Jack leaned over the cell phone on the table between him and his father and said, "The FBI asked me a ton of questions about the kidnapper's technical savvy. I'm guessing this is some kind of computer code."

There was silence, which didn't sit well with Harry. "Jack makes a fair observation. What do you think, Jim?"

The chief of staff breathed so deeply that Jack could hear the crackle on the speaker. "You're asking for an awful lot," he said.

"I've never asked for anything before," said Harry.

There was a faint chuckle, and then the voice on the line turned very serious. "Don't ask me how, but Homeland Security was able to ascertain the sequence of alarms that signaled in the final minute of the emergency on the rig. A computer malfunction caused the alarm to get stuck in a loop, making it impossible for the system to respond to the emergency at hand."

"And these numbers in the ransom note?" asked Jack.

"Those numbers match the alarm sequence perfectly. It's the exact pattern of the loop that ran over and over again, until the explosion."

Jack and his father exchanged glances, silenced until the chills disappeared. "So my kidnapper is the real deal," said Jack.

"Yes," said the chief of staff. "It would appear that he's for real."

27

On Tuesday morning, Jack and his client were back in the Key West courthouse.

Judge Carlyle's courtroom wasn't the zoo it had been the previous week, which was not to say that the battle over property damage and lost profits had abated. An estimated ten thousand barrels of spilled crude was creeping ever closer to Key West, the leading edge of it just twenty-five miles from shore. Calculators across Florida were overheating as Freddy Foman and his band of lawyers computed the potential losses. But Monday's hearing was about Bianca and Rafael, exclusively. Jack needed a knockout punch for the oil consortium's argument that his client was not Rafael's widow.

"Mr. Swyteck, what evidence do you have for me this morning?"

Judge Carlyle was cordial enough, but her pointed words and harsh demeanor at the previous hearing were seared into Jack's memory: *Mr. Swyteck, come prepared to convince me that your client was married to Rafael Lopez at the time of his death. Come very prepared.*

There was no upside to waiting any longer. Jack's evidence was as strong as it was ever going to be. Josefina—Rafael's phony fiancée—would never be a witness in a U.S. court. Without her, a simple "hearsay" objection from the defense would prevent Jack from recounting her story. Rules of evidence aside, Jack couldn't in good conscience betray her trust. Josefina had helped Rafael secure a coveted job on an oil rig by pretending to be his fiancée. She'd committed a crime—a fraud on the Cuban government—and by outing her, Jack could have landed her in a Cuban jail.

Throwing Josefina under the *autobús* simply wasn't an option. Jack needed a different attack.

"Your Honor, I have two items of proof," he said. "A certificate of marriage from the Cuban Ministry of Justice. And a photograph of Rafael and Bianca standing outside the Ministry of Justice after their wedding ceremony."

The judge waved him forward to the bench. Jack handed up the originals and, on the way back to the podium, provided copies to opposing counsel.

"Any objection from the defense?" the judge asked.

Candela rose. The six other lawyers on his team remained in their Naugahyde chairs behind the defense table.

"No objection," said Candela. "But this evidence misses the point. We don't dispute that Bianca Lopez was at some time in the irrelevant past married to the decedent. Our point is that she was no longer the lawful wife of Rafael Lopez at the time of his death on the oil rig. The letters from Rafael

Lopez to his fiancée, Josefina Fuentes, are proof of that."

Jack glanced toward Bianca, who appeared ready to jump from her seat and tell opposing counsel exactly what she thought of him and those letters. A subtle gesture from Jack assured her that all was under control.

"Judge, this is painful and demeaning to my client," said Jack. "But let me respond this way: even if Rafael was 'engaged' to another woman at the time of his death, he was still lawfully married to Bianca. At trial, any rift in their marriage may figure into the calculation of damages suffered by my client in terms of the loss of affections of her husband. But it doesn't bar her from bringing this lawsuit as Rafael's widow. The only bar at this stage would be an official divorce decree, which the defendants have not produced."

The judge rocked back in her chair, eyes cast toward the ceiling, thinking before she spoke. "I tend to agree with Mr. Swyteck on this point."

"I strongly *disagree*," said Candela, rising once again. "Those letters call the marriage into serious question. Dismissal of the case may not be in order. But until Mr. Swyteck produces some evidence to rebut those letters and satisfy the court that his client is the widow of Rafael Lopez, at the very least, no discovery should be allowed. The defendants should not be required to respond to these allegations in any way."

"Are you asking me to stay this case?"

"Yes, Judge. The plaintiff is seeking an eight-figure recovery from one of the largest oil consortium's in the world. The court should at least require Mr. Swyteck to demonstrate that his client has the capacity to bring this lawsuit. He has *nothing* to rebut these letters."

"Well, we do have *something*," said Jack.

The judge raised an eyebrow. "Are you challenging the letters, Mr. Swyteck?"

Jack hesitated. He had hoped that it wouldn't come to this—that the photographs and certificate of marriage would get the job done. But he'd prepared for the worst. Plan B wasn't without risk, but it was one worth taking.

"Your Honor, at this point I'm prepared to cast enough doubt over those alleged love letters to demonstrate that Bianca Lopez should have her day in court. If the court will permit, I have one witness I would like to call at this time."

"I object," said Candela.

"What a surprise," said the judge. "But let's hear who he is first, shall we?"

"Francis McGregor, retired, United States Coast Guard," said Jack. "Captain McGregor served on various Coast Guard cutters in the Florida Straits over a thirty-year career. He also holds an advanced degree in mathematics and taught nautical science courses at the Coast Guard Academy in New London, Connecticut. Since retirement, the captain has worked extensively for the oil industry. Specifically, eleven different oil companies have retained him to rebut claims by drilling opponents that a proposed rig would be visible from shore and hurt tourism. In fact, six of Mr. Candela's other oil clients have retained him for that very purpose."

"Does the defense stand on its objection?" the judge asked.

"I don't question the captain's qualifications," said Candela. "But I can't see any conceivable relevance of his testimony."

One of the moments from Cuba that had stayed with Jack was his talk with Olga, and her explanation of how she knew that Rafael was still in love with Bianca. *He said he could see the Key West shore from up high on the derrick.* It had triggered a thought in Jack's mind—one that made him go back and look more closely at the love letter Rafael had written to Josefina. But the less said about his visit to Cuba, the better.

"This is a five-minute witness," said Jack. "The relevance will be immediately apparent."

"Oh, I just love it when a lawyer puts his credibility on the line. Five minutes, relevance immediately apparent. You're on, Counselor. But for your sake, I hope you weren't thinking of putting one over on me. Bailiff, start the clock."

"But the witness hasn't even been sworn."

"Tick tock, Mr. Swyteck."

Jack turned sharply and signaled to the first row of public seating. Theo raced out of the courtroom to get the witness. Thirty seconds later, Captain McGregor was rushing down the center aisle. He was sworn, seated, and ready to testify in record time.

"Four minutes," said the judge. "And counting."

"Captain McGregor, I asked you to make some calculations for the court based on your review of a letter that defense introduced into evidence at the last court hearing," said Jack, handing the judge a courtesy copy. "Have you made those calculations?"

"Yes, I have."

"This is a letter that Rafael Lopez allegedly wrote to a woman named Josefina Fuentes in Cuba. As translated, the letter states, in part: 'I miss you, my love. I think of you every day. On clear days I climb the derrick, as high as I can climb. From there, I see the shore you walk on. We are *that* close. I swear I can see you. This makes me smile, but it makes it even harder to be apart."

Jack put the letter aside. "I want to focus on one sentence in particular, where the letter states that from the highest point on the derrick, quote: '*I can see the shore you walk on.*'" Jack paused, allowing the judge to focus on the language. "Captain Mc-Gregor, is that possible?"

"No."

"Why not?"

"Simple mathematics."

"Simple for you, maybe. Make it simple enough for a C student in geometry who was smart enough to become a lawyer."

"There's no trick," said the captain. "Any career cutterman who's read Nathaniel Bowditch's *American Practical Navigator* could probably tell you the formula in his sleep: visible distance in nautical miles is equal to 1.17 multiplied by the square root of the height, in feet."

"How does that formula apply here?"

"Let's calculate the height first. The Scarborough 8 was a floating rig, so the platform height could vary. So I took the maximum elevation of the platform, which was a hundred fifty feet above the waterline."

"Where did you get that information?"

"It's publicly available. The derrick rose another hundred and eighteen feet above the platform. Just to be safe, I based my calculation on the overgenerous assumption that a derrick monkey could climb to a height of three hundred feet above sea level. Applying the formula, Rafael's maximum visibility would be about twenty miles."

Jack laid out the coordinates of the drilling site, which were not in dispute. "So if the Scarborough 8 was drilling a distance of seventy miles from the Cuban shore . . ."

"Absolutely no way Rafael could see it."

"What if he had binoculars?"

"Binoculars would make objects at a distance of twenty miles appear closer, but it wouldn't enable him to see anything more than twenty miles away. Binoculars don't change the curvature of the earth. It was simply impossible to see Cuba from that rig at that drilling site, if you accept the premise that the earth is round and not flat."

The judge smirked. "It may be the one and only point of agreement in this case, but I think we can all accept that the earth is not flat."

Jack stepped away from the podium. "No further questions, Captain."

"Nicely done," said the judge. "Twenty seconds to spare."

"I aim to please, Your Honor."

He would have loved to say more, to come right out and tell the court that the letters, though addressed to Josefina, were in fact written to Bianca, and that the shoreline within sight from the rig was Key West, not Cuba. But he didn't have to prove that much. He needed only to raise doubts in the court's mind. He returned to his seat, enough said.

"Any cross examination, Mr. Candela?"

"No, just outrage. Mr. Swyteck's obvious implication is that Rafael Lopez did not write these letters to Josefina Fuentes. Again he is attacking a sovereign party that is unrepresented in this courtroom, accusing the Cuban government of fabricating these letters to undermine his lawsuit."

The judge looked straight at Jack. "Are you making that accusation, Mr. Swyteck?"

It wasn't the argument Jack had intended to make, but Candela was inadvertently doing a better job of discrediting the letters than had the captain. But Jack had to be careful. He knew that Rafael had in fact written the letters. He couldn't make an argument that he knew to be false.

Jack rose. "Your Honor, all I'm prepared to say at this juncture is that something is just not right about these letters."

Candela couldn't let it go, couldn't stop digging his own grave. "Judge, Mr. Swyteck should be required to come forward with actual proof that these letters are fakes created by the Cuban government. His insinuation is not evidence."

The judge groaned, but Jack read it as a sign that opposing counsel had done the work for him: the letters were imbued with the requisite stink.

"I've made up my mind," the judge said. "Mr. Swyteck has produced a marriage certificate. Mr.

Candela, if you want to challenge Ms. Lopez's capacity to bring this lawsuit, show me a divorce decree."

"We're working on that, Your Honor."

Jack did a double take. "What?"

"We are in contact with the Cuban Ministry of Justice."

The judge banged her gavel. "I've heard enough promises of what might be coming. Until the defense can show me a divorce decree, this case is moving forward. That's my ruling. We're adjourned."

"All rise!"

The lawyers, Jack's client, and a handful of reporters in public seating rose as the judge stepped down from the bench. Jack cast a sideways glance at Bianca, who seemed even more concerned than ever.

"How can they be working on a divorce decree?" Bianca asked, her voice a mere whisper in an otherwise silent courtroom.

Jack waited for the judge to exit to her chambers. The side door closed with a thud, breaking the silent show of respect for the judge. The crowd started toward the rear exit, but Bianca had taken hold of Jack's arm, her nails digging through the sleeve of his jacket.

"Mr. Candela said they're working with the Cuban Ministry of Justice," said Bianca, her voice filled with concern. "What does that mean?"

Jack glanced across the courtroom at opposing counsel. Not a single lawyer on the defense team appeared disappointed by the judge's ruling.

"It means the battle is a long way from over," Jack told her.

28

.

Spill. It was the buzzword of the hour outside the courthouse. Never before had Jack walked the streets of Key West and felt more tension than humidity in the autumn air.

"Looks like that black blob of shit is coming right at us," said Theo. He was scrolling through the latest news on his iPhone. Jack assumed he was paraphrasing the headlines.

"When?" asked Bianca. They were a couple of blocks from the courthouse, waiting in line at a little shop called Glazed Donuts. Theo was torn between the flavors of the day: blood orange or Key lime. He ordered a dozen of each, then checked the "spill update" on his phone again.

"It's moving slower than they thought it would," said Theo. "But it's coming. Two more days, they say."

The blood orange was just too tempting, and before they left the shop, Jack and Bianca were as hooked as Theo on the sugar fix. They were walking three abreast on the sidewalk, Bianca in the middle, doughnuts in hand, as they passed directly beneath a sleeping cat that was perched on the sprawling limb of an old oak. An open-air shuttle bus stopped at the corner, and there was nothing like glazed doughnuts to make walking seem like a bad idea.

"Come on," said Jack, as he nudged Theo and Bianca aboard. "My father is being interviewed from Southernmost Point at nine thirty. Live."

"Cool," said Theo. "Let's all shoot him a moon and see how he copes."

"Shoot him a moon?" asked Bianca. "That means what?"

"It means—"

"It means you should ignore Theo Knight," said Jack.

The shuttle took them south on Whitehead, past the old Naval Air Station at the Truman Annex, where President Truman had built his "winter White House." Since the opening of a new air station on Boca Chica Key, most of the annex had been converted into a residential development and public green space, only a small part of it reserved for military use. But the grounds occupied the prime southwest corner of the key—in the direct path of Cuban oil from Scarborough 8, carried by the same warm currents that had deposited thousands of refugees on the annex shores during the 1980 Mariel boatlift. A tall hibiscus hedge blocked most of Jack's view from the street, but he guessed that preparations and activities behind the closed gates were at a level not seen since the Second World War.

The shuttle let them off two blocks from Southernmost Point. A sea of pedestrians—tourists, members of the media, and curious locals—made it impossible for vehicles to get any closer. The usual vendors of conch shells and trinkets lined the sidewalks, but the overflow of visitors was all about oil and ground zero. Jack cut a zigzagged path down the crowded street.

Southernmost Point was one of the most visited and photographed sites on Key West, even if the island's true southernmost point was inside the Truman Annex, on Navy property and inaccessible to civilians. Jack had seen it before, but the inscription on the big concrete buoy—an old sewer junction painted in green, red, black, and yellow stripes—was particularly poignant, given the nature of the impending disaster. Directly above the words "Southernmost Point, Continental United States" was the inscription:

Conch Republic
90 Miles from Cuba

A protestor covered in black oil stood beside the buoy with a homemade sign of her own: LESS THAN FIFTY MILES FROM CUBAN OIL. A long line of more protestors squeezed past her, their bodies likewise covered with oil. They brandished poster-sized photographs of dead animals on an oil-drenched beach—porpoises, manatees, giant sea turtles, and birds of all kinds.

"*Stop the drilling, stop the killing,*" was their chant.

Jack walked to a grassy area adjacent to the buoy that had been cordoned off with yellow police tape. It was for "media only." The famous marker and the steady line of protestors made Southernmost Point coveted space for TV morning shows and endless hours of "spill coverage."

The *Action News* interview of Harry Swyteck was already under way. The former governor and Rhea Sonnet, the attractive brunette co-host of *Ronaldo & Rhea*, were seated in matching director's chairs, their backs to the turquoise water. Behind them, cleanup crews prepared for the worst, maneuvering huge oil-containment booms into position. The police tape kept Jack and the other onlookers at a distance from the makeshift set, but the interview was broadcast in real time over a concert-quality loudspeaker.

"What are they talking about?" asked Theo.

"How the U.S. government needs to get American expertise to the source of the spill."

Theo asked another question, but Jack blew him off, his focus on the interview. The *Action News* reporter continued her line of questioning.

"Governor, right now the Cuban navy is standing between the source of the spill and U.S. cleanup capabilities. What can be done about that?"

"This is a major crisis. If dispersants aren't applied close to the source, uncontained oil can't be dispersed, burnt, or skimmed. That means all of our standard response technologies, like containment booms, are ineffective once the oil drifts out of Cuban waters. We have to break the standoff. Our responders and equipment need to get through."

The wind was kicking up, and the reporter fought to keep her hair out of her face. "Do you mean military action?"

"No, of course not. Diplomatic channels."

"*Action News* has heard unconfirmed reports that the Cuban government will roll back the naval blockade and allow U.S. cleanup efforts in Cuban waters only if the U.S. agrees to end the fifty-year trade embargo against Cuba. Do you care to comment on that?"

"I hope that's not true. But that's an issue for the White House, not a retired governor."

Another gust from the ocean, and Rhea struggled to keep the windward side of her oversprayed hair from flapping in the breeze like a loose jib.

"Fair enough," she said. "Since it has been more than a decade since you left the Governor's Mansion, let's refresh our viewers on where you stood on some of the key issues raised by the current crisis. You opposed offshore drilling, am I right?"

"Yes. And so did the overwhelming majority of Floridians, who elected me to two terms in office."

"You were also a firm supporter of the U.S. trade embargo against Cuba."

"That is true."

"Looking back on it now, do you find it surprising that voters back then didn't see the linkage between the two issues?"

Jack was standing fifty feet away from the interview, but even at that distance he could see the discomfort in his father's body language.

"Linkage?" said Harry. "I don't see any linkage."

"Really?" she said. "Let me share with you a quote that was issued this morning by a senior official in Cuba's diplomatic corps. He states: 'When Cuba decided to drill offshore in the Gulf of Mexico in the mid-1990s, the first letters sent by Cuba's government to invite foreign concerns to participate went exclusively to U.S. energy companies. They declined interest, due to the embargo, and Cuba looked for partners elsewhere.' Your reaction, sir?"

Again Harry hesitated, seemingly tongue-tied. "I . . . I don't know anything about that."

"You were governor during that time period, correct?"

"Yes, but—"

"The implication seems obvious, does it not? But for the embargo, we would now have U.S. oil companies with two decades of deepwater drilling experience in the Cuban basin. Instead, we have an underexperienced Chinese, Russian, and Venezuelan consortium spilling oil on Florida's beaches."

"Well . . . that's . . . uh."

Jack cringed. It was the kind of spit-in-your-eye remark that called for sharp response, and one obvious comeback was that the Deepwater Horizon disaster had managed to become the most expensive man-made disaster in history without any involvement at all from Chinese, Russian, or Venezuelan companies. But Harry was still fumbling for words.

Shit, Dad. She's killing you.

"Look, I—we . . . um."

"Governor, wouldn't you admit that this is a case of twenty-first-century technology and environmental policy bumping up against Cold War ideology?"

Harry paused, then finally managed a sentence: "As a nation, the appropriate thing is to deal with the problem at hand, not point fingers."

Jack allowed his gaze to drift toward the shoreline, away from the journalistic carnage on the makeshift set. While his father had held his own and done Jack proud at the White House with the chief of staff and at the airport with the FBI, there was nothing like a live media ambush to expose the vulnerability of a retired politician who was no longer in the day-to-day fray. Governor Swyteck in his prime would not have been so easily pushed around, and it was a painful reality check for Jack: his dad was getting older, if not old.

"The guv ain't gonna like that tape," said Theo.

Mercifully, the segment ended. The reporter thanked the governor, cut to a commercial, and then stepped out of the ocean breeze to fix her hair.

Jack wondered if he should quietly slip away, if the best thing would have been to let his father think he'd missed the interview. But Harry spotted him in the crowd and waved him over. A police officer let Jack pass under the tape. The governor met him halfway between the morning-show crew and the spectators.

"Pretty awful, wasn't it?" Harry said impishly.

"Oh, I didn't think it was so bad."

Harry smiled. "Liar."

"Okay, you've done better."

"It's been a rough week," Harry said, his smile fading. "Really rough."

Jack felt a wave of guilt—and a splash of insight. Guilt about the stress and anxiety his trip-to-Cuba troubles had caused; insight into the fact that he and Andie knew virtually nothing about the never-ending job of parenting. "I'm sorry about that, Dad."

Harry blinked awkwardly, as if he had something in his eye—both eyes.

"Are you okay?" asked Jack.

"Like I said, rough week. Can you do me a favor?"

"Sure."

"First, keep smiling."

Jack rolled his eyes. "Okay."

"I'm serious. The media are swarming all over the place. It's very important to keep smiling." Harry dug his car keys from his pocket and handed them to Jack.

"You want me to move your car?" asked Jack.

"No." Again Harry blinked hard, this time even more awkwardly.

"Dad, are you sure you're okay?"

Harry took a breath. "You and I are going to smile our way right past the cameras, the reporters, and everyone else between here and my car."

"Then what?"

"Then," said Harry, taking another breath. "Then I want you to drive me to the emergency room."

29

___
.

Jack was desperate for information.

The largest hospital in Key West was Lower Keys Medical Center, at the opposite end of the island from Southernmost Point, but still fewer than five miles away. Even in traffic, it had taken Jack less than fifteen minutes to get his father into the ER. A doctor evaluated him immediately. Jack hadn't heard a thing since they'd whisked his father away in a wheelchair to radiology for a CT scan.

Stroke was the unspoken fear.

"Any word yet?" Jack asked the desk attendant.

"Not yet."

"It's been two hours."

"We're totally jammed. Lots of injuries with people preparing for the oil spill. Three hernias and two ruptured discs already this morning. They shouldn't make those sandbags so heavy."

Jack returned to the waiting room. A woman with a vomit bucket in her lap had taken his chair by the window. Whatever ailment she had, Jack didn't want it. He moved to the other end of the room, closer to the homeless guy with infected needle marks on his arms.

"Got any coin, dude?"

The homeless guy had his hand out. Jack gave him a buck and turned his attention to more spill coverage on the TV. Jack caught a glimpse of what cleanup crews were doing with those heavy sand-bags on the beaches.

"A whole dollar, huh?" said the homeless guy. "That don't buy much dish soap for all those birdies about to be covered in oil."

Jack ignored him, but it triggered a weird chain of thought. Freddy Foman popped into his brain, along with countless other lawyers who, at the first sight of oil, would point to the birds and file for bil-lions of dollars in "lost profit" claims on behalf of anyone with his hand out.

The sliding door opened. A nurse rolled Harry into the waiting room in a wheelchair. Jack popped up from his seat and went to him.

"What's the word?"

"I'm fine," said Harry. "Just stress."

Just stress. "People die from stress."

"I'm not dying."

"Why are you still in a wheelchair?"

The nurse answered for him. "Anyone who gets any kind of diagnostic testing on the brain or head leaves in a wheelchair. It's hospital policy."

A policy born of lawsuits filed by the likes of Freddy Foman, no doubt. "So you're fine, really?" asked Jack.

"Really," said Harry. "Just needed to adjust my blood-pressure medication."

Jack felt relief. Stroke and Alzheimer's had been

among the parade of horribles coursing through his brain in the previous two hours. He just hoped his father was being completely straight with him.

"Can you drive me back to the hotel?" asked Harry.

"Sure. I'll bring the car around."

The nurse wheeled Harry across the waiting room as Jack walked ahead to the exit. A pleasant morning had turned into a hot afternoon. Jack was crossing the car port just outside the ER when his phone rang. It was Bianca. He talked while continuing to the parking lot.

"I had lunch with Theo," she said. "He says Josefina gave you more letters that Rafael wrote to me. Why didn't you tell me? I would love to see them."

Jack didn't answer right away. Before the court hearing, he had shared the good news with her—that he had brought back the wedding photographs and the marriage certificate. He hadn't shared the bad news about the letters.

"I'm sorry, Bianca. I don't have the letters anymore."

"What happened?"

Jack measured his response. His kidnapping was not public information, and he was under strict orders from the FBI not to say anything about it to anyone—his client included—until law enforcement could investigate the kidnapper's claim of sabotage on the Scarborough 8.

"My bag was stolen," said Jack.

"Where?"

"In Havana."

"Did they catch the guy?"

"No."

"How did it happen?"

Jack didn't want to make things up, but the truth was that the letters had been the only things missing from his bag when his kidnapper released him.

"There's not much I can tell you," said Jack. "The FBI is involved."

There was silence on the line. Bianca was young and new to America, but she wasn't stupid.

"Over stolen luggage? What can the FBI do about a little crime like that in Havana?"

Jack found his father's Cadillac baking in the sun. Oven-like heat poured from within as he opened the door and climbed behind the wheel. Black interior in Florida made no sense to Jack. He broke a sweat in just the few seconds it took him to turn the key and power on the AC.

"It's complicated," said Jack. "I'll try to explain later. Right now I'm at the hospital."

"Hospital? Why?"

"That's another story."

"Stop it!" she said. It was the first time she had raised her voice at Jack.

"I hear your frustration," said Jack.

"This is not fair! I asked Theo lots of questions at lunch, but he says almost nothing. And now you say everything is 'complicated' or 'another story.' Why the secrets? Why are you not telling everything to me about Havana? This is my case. *My* life."

Jack let the car idle in park but put the air on MAX, all vents aimed at his face. It wasn't just the heat that had him sweating.

"Okay, Bianca. You're right. I can't be specific, but

your case is going through a few changes. At first, I was looking at human error or maybe a technical failure on the Scarborough 8 that caused an explosion. Rafael's death may involve more than that. We are seriously looking at sabotage."

"You mean someone did this on purpose? Who?"

"We don't know. The FBI asked me not to even mention the word *sabotage*, and you can't, either. If this goes public, it could compromise the investigation. That doesn't help law enforcement, and in the long run, it doesn't help your case. Right now, the important point is this: if it was sabotage, we are up against some ruthless people. We all need to be aware of that. And we should be a little extra careful."

"How do you mean?"

"I don't want to scare you. The FBI is not advising that we all go out and hire bodyguards. Just don't be afraid to call me or Theo anytime, for any reason."

"Like, for what?"

"For—"

A loud slap to the rear window sent Jack's heart into his throat. The passenger-side door flew open. Harry Swyteck got in.

"Damn, Jack. How long does it take to bring a car around?"

Jack covered his phone. "Sorry. I needed to take this call."

"Never been chased out of a hospital before."

"What?"

"I gave some homeless guy a buck to help clean up the birds, and he went running all over the waiting room, shouting at the top of his lungs about what a cheapskate I am."

There but for the grace of God . . .

Jack went back to his phone call. "Bianca, I'm going to stay the night in Key West. Let's meet for breakfast and talk tomorrow morning before I head back to Miami. Say nine-thirty?"

"Okay. Oh, and, Jack. One more thing."

"What?"

"Thank you."

It took him aback. A simple expression of gratitude wasn't something he often heard from clients, not even when he was winning.

"You're welcome, Bianca."

30

.

Bianca spent the rest of the afternoon running errands. She was home before five. Her Tuesday shift at Rick's Key West Café was six p.m. to two a.m. She put the groceries away in short order and jumped in the shower.

"Come on, come on," she said into the showerhead. She and another waitress shared a 2/2 mobile home that hadn't been "mobile" in decades. If more than two people in the trailer park were showering or flushing the toilet at the same time, forget about it. The property manager had promised to fix the water pressure—and the oven, and the roof, and about thirty other things on the punch list. Maybe she'd ask Jack to sue him. Violation of constitutional rights: *Life, liberty, and a decent shower.*

She went stingy on the shampoo, knowing that it would have taken a good twenty minutes of this drizzle to rinse out a full lather. At least the water was hot. She closed her eyes and let soapy rivulets run down her face and body.

Bianca knew there was something her lawyer

wasn't telling her. Something important. A meeting tomorrow morning was a good idea. It would be her chance to ask the right questions and push Jack for real answers. She liked Jack. He meant well. She knew he wasn't trying to freak her out, but she needed to lay down some rules. First among them: never, ever color the most important part of a conversation with *"I don't mean to scare you but . . ."*

Bianca froze. She heard a noise.

Just the pipes, she told herself.

She heard it again. Definitely not the familiar rumble of mobile-home plumbing. It sounded like the front door. She turned off the water, peeled back the edge of the shower curtain, and listened.

"Carolina, is that you?"

Her roommate worked the four-to-midnight shift at Sloppy Joe's. It would have been odd for her to come home at this hour, even on a normal Monday, and with the media and cleanup crews flooding into Key West for the oil spill, no way would her boss have sent her home early.

Bianca stood silent, dripping wet, waiting for a reply. There was none. The trailer carried sound like a tin can, even noises as far away as the front door. She was pretty sure that she'd heard something. She had *definitely* heard something.

Stop it. Stop scaring the crap out of yourself.

She checked her hair for residue. Getting out all the shampoo was impossible with this water pressure, but it would have to do. She toweled off, wrapped her hair in a makeshift turban, and stepped from the shower. Her robe was on a hook beside the foggy mirror. She slipped it on and started toward the bathroom door. The fan was broken, and the window didn't open, so she needed to open the door a crack, just enough to clear some of the shower steam. But as she reached for the knob, something made her stop. Again, she listened.

Not a sound on the other side of the door.

"Carolina?" she said, keeping the door closed.

More silence. An uneasy silence. The decrepit old trailer was never *that* quiet. Something didn't feel right, and she wasn't sure what to do about it, but Jack's words were suddenly replaying in her head:

"Don't be afraid to call me or Theo anytime, for any reason."

She checked the tray by the sink, where she kept her makeup and phone charger. Her phone wasn't there. She'd left it on the dresser in the bedroom.

"Damn it!"

Tears came, and she suddenly found herself sitting on the bathroom floor, knees drawn up to her chin, arms wrapped tightly around her shins. For five days she'd pretended that a lawsuit could give her a reason to get up in the morning, could help her make sense of what had happened to Rafael. Now, afraid to open the bathroom door, unable to get up off the floor, crying seemed like the only thing to do.

Get up and get your phone. Now.

Bianca drew a breath, wiped her tears into her terrycloth sleeve, and pushed herself up from the cold linoleum. Her hand was shaking as she reached for the knob, but she took a deep breath and opened the door.

It slammed open, knocking her backward, and

the rest was a blur. A man wearing a rubber Halloween mask pushed his way on top of her. In a split second she was turned around, facedown on the linoleum. Her attacker was sitting on her kidneys, his huge hand covering her mouth before she could scream.

"Don't fight."

He was speaking Spanish, but it was thick and slurred. It made her think of the way Jack had described his attacker: *Like he had cotton in his mouth.*

"Don't hurt me," she said. She was pinned beneath him, unable to move. Fighting was not an option. The hand over her mouth and the crushing weight of his rock-solid body in the small of her back made it difficult just to breathe.

"I'm going to take my hand away now," he said, still speaking Spanish. "Scream and you die. Look into my eyes and you die. Understand?"

A part of her wanted to die, the part that dreaded what was about to happen, but she was too frightened to resist. She nodded.

His hand slipped away from her mouth. "I have something for you," he said.

Bianca cringed, and the sound she uttered was completely involuntary.

"Quiet!"

Bianca struggled to get control of her herself. She prayed for her roommate to walk through the front door, home early from work, but she knew that wasn't going to happen. She prayed for strength.

"I thought you'd want these," the man said.

Her head was cocked sideways, her right cheek pressed to the linoleum, and a stack of papers suddenly landed just a few inches away from the tip of her nose.

He grabbed her by the wet hair, lifting her head up from the floor. "Read."

The light was still on, but it took a moment for her eyes to adjust. Slowly, the handwriting came into focus. She recognized it, and she didn't have to read beyond the salutation to realize what she was seeing.

Querida Josefina, it read. Dear Josefina.

"Your lawyer left these in Cuba," he said. "I want you to give them to him."

It was all too bizarre, and Bianca was barely able to comprehend. She had no doubt that these were the missing letters from Rafael, and she could only assume that this man was the thief Jack had told her about. But she had no idea how or why he had come all the way from Cuba to give the letters to her.

"Will you do that for me, Bianca?"

She hesitated—not out of resistance, but because she was trying to make sense of it.

He jerked her head back harder, yanking on her hair. *"Will you?"*

She nodded quickly.

"Good," he said, pushing her face into the floor.

She lay still, hoping it was over. Hope evaporated as she felt him lean forward, felt his breath on the back of her neck.

"I have something else for you," he said in a harsh whisper, chilled by the thickness of his words from the cotton or whatever it was in his mouth.

His hand was suddenly right in front of her face. He cocked his thumb and a six-inch blade popped from his fist. The shiny steel switchblade glistened in the bathroom light. Slowly, it came toward her. Bianca closed her eyes tightly, bracing herself. She felt the pointed tip of the blade on her upper lip. She tried to pull away, but his left hand held her head in place, pressed to the floor. It felt like a needle puncturing her lip, more terrifying than painful. A trickle of blood entered her mouth, warm and salty.

"Taste it," he whispered, breathing onto the back of her neck. "Taste the blood of a Cuban whore."

31

•

O n Wednesday, Jack went for a morning run along the waterfront. He didn't get far.

Oil.

It was coming ashore. Not in quantities large enough for Jack to see birds floundering and beaches blackened. But to the south, toward Truman Annex, disaster relief was under way. Cleanup crews were moving into position, ready to rake and scrub the shoreline, workers on the frontline wearing protective hazmat suits. Coast Guard vessels and volunteer shrimp boats tended to the offshore booms and skimmers. Helicopters—both media and relief teams—buzzed overhead to assess the impact.

Jack stopped at the police barricade.

"Beach is closed," the cop told him.

"How bad is it?"

"Not as bad as it will be. Much worse on Ballast Key."

Ballast was privately owned, the *real* "southernmost point" in the continental United States.

Onlookers continued to gather at the barricade,

some squeezing in beside him, others pushing forward from behind. Oil was the star, and anyone with a smartphone was the paparazzi. An old woman beside Jack was holding back tears. "Never thought I'd live to see this," she said in a voice that quaked. "And this is what they call a glancing blow."

"That's what I heard, too," said Jack. "It's headed more toward the middle keys."

"I grew up snorkeling in Marathon. Say good-bye for good to Pickle Reef, Alligator Reef. All of it."

The cop urged everyone to go home, but few listened.

Jack's cell rang. It was Rick, Bianca's boss. Jack stepped away from the barricade and found a quiet spot beneath a palm tree.

"Don't mean to stick my nose where it don't belong," said Rick, "but did everything go okay at the court hearing yesterday?"

"Fine," said Jack, seeing no need to say more.

"I only ask because Bianca didn't show up for work last night."

"She didn't?"

"Nope. Didn't answer her cell, either."

Jack was getting concerned. "Have you tried her this morning?"

"I just did. Still no answer. I was hoping that she was having a meeting with you or something."

His concern was turning to worry. He checked his watch. A little after eight. "Actually, we were supposed to meet for breakfast at nine-thirty. Let me call her."

Jack hung up and speed-dialed Bianca. No answer. He tucked his iPhone back into the arm clip, thinking. *Missed work. Didn't answer her cell.* If not for what had just happened to him in Cuba, Jack might have blown it off as no big deal, just a confused young woman in need of some time to herself. But his own advice to his client was coming back to him: *We all need to be a little more careful.*

Jack hurried to the sidewalk and ran two blocks back to his hotel. The taxi stand at the valet was without taxis. Jack asked the attendant to call one, but the guy made a face, as if Jack were visiting from another planet.

"Streets are closed. Emergency vehicles only."

Jack plugged Bianca's address into his iPhone. Mastic Mobile Home Park was less than a half mile to the north, and the map showed him the way. It was an easy run up mostly residential streets. As Jack drew closer, he ran with a growing sense of urgency, flying past a bank, the Ocean Breeze Inn. His heart was pounding as he reached the entrance to the mobile home park. His GPS wasn't precise enough to lead him to Bianca's front door. The lot numbers, hand painted on conch shells and fish-shaped mailboxes, guided him in the right direction. He knocked on her front door.

No one answered. He dialed her cell again, but it went to her voice mail. He knocked harder on the metal door.

It opened. A young woman wiped sleep from her eyes.

"Are you Bianca's roommate?"

"Yeah," she said, grumbling. "Who are you?"

"Jack, her lawyer. Is she here?"

"No idea. I assume she is. I got home at three and went straight to sleep, until you woke me up."

"Can you check?"

"Are you serious?"

"Yes. I'm sorry to trouble you, but it's important that I talk to her, and she's not answering her phone."

She breathed a heavy sigh, as if Jack had just asked her to singlehandedly clean up the oil spill. "Okay, I'll check."

Jack waited outside the open door—until he heard the scream.

Jack raced inside and through the trailer's tiny living room. Bianca's roommate was standing in the narrow hallway outside Bianca's bathroom. One hand covered her mouth. With the other, she pointed. Jack stopped in the doorway and looked inside the bathroom.

No Bianca, but something was smeared across the mirror over the sink.

"Is that blood?" she asked.

Jack ran to Bianca's bedroom. "Bianca!"

He checked inside the closet, beneath the covers, under the bed. Still no Bianca. He rushed back to the bathroom. Bianca's roommate was still in the hallway, but as far away from the bathroom as she could stand, her back pressed to the wall, her whole body shaking.

"Please don't tell me that's blood."

Cautiously, Jack entered the bathroom and stepped closer to the mirror. It wasn't a splatter or random smear. It was a message—written in blood. Just two words:

DROP IT.

"Drop what?" she asked.

Jack dialed 911. "The case," he said.

32

.

Jack knocked on one trailer door after another.

Not a single one of Bianca's neighbors had seen or heard anything. By the time the first responder arrived from the sheriff's department, Jack had hit every mobile home in the entire park, and he'd rounded up a dozen volunteers to help search for clues of any nature. The most important thing, he kept telling himself, was to move fast and remain determined to find Bianca alive.

"Are you the person who called nine-one-one?" the deputy asked.

Jack confirmed that he was. Two more squad cars pulled up. The first responder debriefed Jack quickly, and two deputies went inside. A ring of yellow police tape encircled the lot, and a third deputy escorted Jack outside the perimeter, where he took Jack's formal statement. In five minutes, Bianca's trailer and the area around it was an active crime scene. The main gravel road through the park was blocked off by squad cars from the Monroe County Sheriff's Department, orange and yellow beacons swirling. Uniformed deputies, crime-scene investigators, and a pair of seasoned detectives were entering and leaving at the direction of the deputy posted at the perimeter.

Jack spotted Bianca's boss rushing toward him. He had a stack of papers with him. Rick's Key West Café kept photo IDs on file for all its employees, and Jack had asked Rick to print flyers with Bianca's picture.

"How's this?" asked Rick, breathing heavily from the run.

"Perfect," said Jack. "Keep making color copies all morning. Get as many people as you can to pass them out all over town."

"You got it."

"And let's get it going viral on Facebook and whatever social media we can. Bianca's roommate should be able to help with that."

"I know some Facebook junkies, too," said Rick.

A media van pulled up, and Jack seized the opportunity. He took a flyer from Rick and went straight to the reporter and her cameraman.

"Her name is Bianca Lopez and she's gone missing," said Jack. "We need help getting her photo on the air as quickly as possible."

Two more media vans pulled up, and Jack was on a roll. He hit all three—*wham, bam, wham*. He had people all over town distributing flyers and getting the word out. He had Bianca's roommate working social media. He had the FBI on alert for a possible kidnapping. He felt real positive energy—for about forty-five minutes.

And then it started to fade.

He was still waiting on an update from the FBI. One by one, squad cars were leaving the trailer park, and Jack was close enough to hear the radio calls. Their redeployment was all about the oil spill; they weren't going out to look for Bianca. It was the same with the media. Based on the conversations Jack had overheard on the grounds, most of the reporters were pretty annoyed about being pulled from the spill to cover a missing cocktail waitress. Neighbors watched the crime scene with some interest, but they, too, seemed distracted by the helicopters in the air and other trappings of the bigger story around them.

Jack ducked under the police tape and went to the lead detective, Sam Holiday.

"Excuse me," said Jack, "but exactly what is being done to find Bianca Lopez?"

Holiday was tapping out an e-mail on his smartphone, never looking at Jack. "Everything possible."

"Look, I know there's an oil spill, and I understand you're busy. But a young woman has gone missing."

"We're on it," said Holiday.

"It honestly doesn't look that way."

Finally, Holiday looked up from his phone, peering out over the top of his reading glasses. "We're on it," he said coolly. "Now, if you would, sir: please step back. You're on my crime scene."

Jack didn't move immediately, but finally he turned and walked slowly to a place just outside the perimeter. The detective was in charge, local enforcement was overwhelmed, and Jack didn't have time to turn Sam Holiday into his best friend in law enforcement. This was a bad situation within a bad situation. Oil-containment buoys on the ocean, barricades along the shoreline, and a crime scene at the mobile-home park. Key West, Swyteck style, was concentric circles of disaster.

Jack's iPhone vibrated with an incoming call. He checked the number, raised his eyes to the heavens, and said, "Thank you." It was Andie.

"You must have ESP," said Jack.

"No, CNN. They broke away from spill coverage to do two minutes on it. I'm so sorry, Jack."

Jack gripped the phone, alarmed. "Do you mean 'sorry' as in Bianca's no longer with us? Because the last I heard, she'd gone missing. Nothing more than that."

"No, that's the status I have, too. The CNN piece was all about the active search."

"Not sure how *active* it is. If it's not about the spill, law enforcement has it on the back burner down here. No one has seen or heard from Bianca in over eighteen hours, and we're losing precious time."

"That's a problem."

"Ya think?" he said, facetious.

"I'll call the field office right now."

"Agent Linton interviewed me at the airport when I got back from Cuba."

"He's a good point person. I'll make sure he calls you."

"You're the best. Thanks. So when can I see you? We have a honeymoon to finish."

"Soon, I hope."

A follow-up for something more specific would have been normal, but nothing was normal about marriage and undercover work.

"I have an ultrasound at eight weeks. We'll see the little heartbeat."

"And his enormous penis."

"That's at sixteen weeks. And anyway, I'm feeling it's a girl."

"Can't wait."

"I'll call you before then. But I'm following up with the field office right now, so Linton or someone else should get back to you about Bianca right away."

"Thanks. Love you."

"Me, too."

Jack hung up, feeling better on a lot of levels.

"Hey, Swyteck!"

Detective Holiday was fast coming toward him. Jack wasn't sure how to read the expression on the detective's face, but there was plenty of urgency in his voice.

"They found your client," he said.

33

.

For the second time in as many days, Jack was in the emergency room. The good news was that "found your client" meant found *alive*. Bianca was in the hands of the Monroe County Sheriff's Office Crimes Against Persons Unit, and a victim's advocate pulled Jack aside the moment he arrived.

"She denies any sexual assault," said the counselor, "and thankfully the physical examination backs her up on that. Only physical injury appears to be a cut lip. Just one stitch required."

Charlene Simmons worked out of Marathon, serving victims of violent crimes from Key West to Key Largo. She'd seen it all—rape, abuse, stalking, domestic violence, sex trafficking, adults, adolescents, children, straight, gay, male, female. Two decades of experience didn't make it routine. Jack could see the compassion in her eyes.

"That's good news."

"Yes," she said. "But the fear and threat of sexual assault can be almost as traumatizing as the real thing."

"I understand."

"Bianca asked to see you alone. But you need to be very sensitive. Be a good listener. Don't ask questions that might bring on shame or embarrassment, but don't shut her down if she needs to open up. I'll be right outside the door if you need me."

"Okay, got it."

Jack took a deep breath. He wasn't without experience in talking to victims, but this was going to be a tough one. Guilt was kicking in. The FBI had convinced him that, even under the new travel rules for Cuban nationals, the violence against him in Havana was unlikely to follow him back to the states. But his instincts were rarely wrong.

Should have hired a bodyguard.

Jack opened the door and went inside. Bianca was seated on the edge of an examination table, shoulders slumped. The room was noticeably colder than the hallway, and Bianca was wrapped in a hospital blanket. Jack closed the door quietly and walked toward the table. There was a chair in the room, but he stood facing her, waiting for her to look up. She didn't.

"Hi," she said softly.

"Hi."

Her gaze was still cast toward the floor. She looked exhausted. "Thanks for coming," she said.

"No problem. Can I get you anything? Water? Soda?"

"No."

The fluorescent light hummed overhead. Through the door, the usual noises of the ER were audible but muffled. The examination room was otherwise silent.

"They numbed my lip," she said. "Do I talk funny?"

It seemed like such a kid thing to say. *She's so young*. And yet she'd seen so much.

"Don't worry about it," he said.

She raised her eyes for an instant, then looked away. "Do you want to know what happened?"

"Only if you want to tell me."

Her hand began to shake. Jack sensed she was about to cry. He reached toward her, but she withdrew.

"He called me a whore," she said, her voice shaking. "When he cut me, he said, 'Taste the blood of a Cuban whore.'"

"I'm sorry," said Jack. He hesitated to ask what happened next, but he was mindful of the counselor's advice not to shut her down if she felt the need to talk.

"I don't remember much after that," she said. "He injected me with something."

It was sounding like Jack's kidnapping, but again he just let her keep talking.

"When I woke up, it was daylight. I was in the passenger seat of my car. I have no idea how I got there. I wasn't even sure where I was at first."

"How'd you get to the ER?"

"I couldn't find the car keys, so I walked. The car was parked in the Winn-Dixie lot, which is, *quizás*, two blocks from the hospital. I got here about an hour ago, I'd say."

"The hospital is one of the first places I checked when we knew you were missing. You must have walked into the ER right after I called."

"Sorry. They asked if I had any family they should notify, and I said no. I should have asked them to call you."

"It's okay. You saw the doctor, the counselor. That's more important. Let me ask you this, though. Do you have any idea why he left you where he did? Anything special about that place?"

"No. The cops told me I was lucky. They don't think the guy was stealing my car and just taking me for a ride. He took me with something very specific in his mind, but for some reason, he chickened out. Maybe he saw the police roadblocks for the oil spill and decided it was too risky, so he pulled into the parking lot and left me. Thank God he didn't . . ."

She didn't need to finish the thought for Jack. "Thank God," he said.

Bianca pointed toward a plastic bag on the counter. "Look in there."

Jack opened the bag. It held her wallet, her shoes, and other personal effects. And some papers. It took Jack only a moment to recognize them as the letters Josefina had given him.

"He gave those to me," said Bianca.

Jack felt chills. Of course he had suspected a direct link between his kidnapping and Bianca's disappearance. But he wasn't sure it had been the very same attacker—until now.

"Have you shown these to the police?"

"No."

"Why not?"

"Because he said I should give them to you. Only you."

"Okay. Then you absolutely did the right thing,

Bianca. But we need to let the FBI know about it. If this guy is trying to get back to Cuba, we may have a shot at catching him."

"Whatever you say."

Jack reached for his phone. "Thanks to my wife, I have a direct contact at the FBI now. Agent Linton, and he's completely dedicated to your case. I'm going to call him right now. There's nothing to worry about. I'll handle it."

Bianca seemed to have heard him, but she was staring blankly at the wall, her response distant. "He also told me to give you a message."

Jack stopped, not yet dialing. "A message?"

"He said the price is ten million. Whatever that means."

Jack knew exactly what it meant: ten million dollars was the price to be paid by the U.S. government for the names of the Scarborough 8 saboteurs.

"Did he say anything else?"

"That I should drop my case."

Jack didn't immediately follow the logic, but he could sort it out later. First thing was to get the FBI swarming on all available routes back to Cuba. He dialed Agent Linton and gave him the news. Linton had news for him, too.

"Interesting thing about the blood on the mirror," said Linton.

"What?"

"Sometimes the perpetrator's blood can be mixed in with the victim's. You just never know. So I ran a sample through CODIS and some other data banks. You know what CODIS is, right?"

The Combined DNA Index System (CODIS) is

an FBI-funded computer system that stores DNA in searchable profiles for identification purposes. It was how Jack got Theo released from death row.

"Yeah, I'm familiar with it."

"Anyway, I got nothing out of CODIS. But I got a hit in the weirdest place."

"Where?"

"The World Anti-Doping Agency. They hold about eighty thousand samples from Olympic hopefuls all over the world. We came up with a hundred-percent match to a female athlete. A boxer in Cuba. Her name is Josefina Fuentes. Ever heard of her?"

Jack went cold. For a moment, he couldn't even speak.

"Jack, you know her?"

Jack's mind was awhirl. Rafael's letters. The cut to Bianca's lip. Josefina's blood on the bathroom mirror—no doubt collected by Bianca's attacker in some unspeakable manner and brought over from Cuba in a vial.

Taste the blood of a Cuban whore.

"Yes," Jack said in disbelief. "I do know her."

34

J ack needed space. Literally.

The oil mess, the attack on Bianca, his father a ticking time bomb of stress—it was a ball of confusion, but one thing was clear: Jack wasn't leaving Key West anytime soon. A colleague in Miami linked him up with a Key West lawyer who had extra office space. Jack and Theo walked to White-head Street to check it out.

"We should go back to Cuba," said Theo.

"Bad idea," said Jack.

They were down the street from the courthouse, a few blocks from the cleanup on the southern shore. The Green Parrot bar was bustling with a lunch crowd, and Theo continued to plead his case as they walked through the sidewalk seating area.

"If Josefina isn't dead, she's obviously been hurt by this sick son of a bitch. I want to find out what happened."

"We need to stay right here with Bianca."

"But we dragged Josefina into this, Jack."

"The oil consortium dragged her into it. They put Rafael's letters in evidence."

"Then I'll go to Cuba, and you can stay here and fight the consortium. You *are* going to keep fighting, right? Don't let that bastard push you around and make Bianca drop her case."

They stopped at the curb, then continued through the crosswalk. "I actually don't think he meant drop the case."

"The message said 'Drop it.'"

"But if you think this through, he's not saying that he's on the oil consortium's side and that he's helping them win the lawsuit. Truth is, he probably couldn't give a shit about the lawsuit one way or the other. The only thing he wants is for the U.S. government to pay him for naming the men who brought down the Scarborough 8. So the last thing he wants is for me to make sabotage the centerpiece of Bianca's case, trying to expose in a high-profile trial the very information that he thinks will put money in his pocket. He needs to keep the sabotage dialogue between himself and the U.S. government."

"Ten million dollars sounds pretty ridiculous to me."

"He's already demonstrated that he's a credible source. I'm not saying he'll get ten million, but if he knows who's behind an environmental disaster that outdoes Deepwater Horizon, he could be negotiating for real money."

"Not if he killed Josefina."

They stopped at a white picket fence, where a

weathered wooden sign on the gate read LAW OFFICE OF ALEJANDRO CORTINAS.

"Let's talk about this later," said Jack. "I can't keep practicing law out of a hotel room. Let me nail down some kind of arrangement with Cortinas, and we'll go from there."

Whitehead Street near the courthouse was to the Key West bar what Wall Street was to white-shoe law firms. The Cortinas firm was in an old wood-frame house, two stories, and built in the Victorian style. Its traditional front porch and balconies spared none of the gingerbread details that defined the very best of the island's nineteenth-century architecture. Cortinas had been there since 1970, but the building had seen continuous use as a law office since 1828, when the first federal court opened in the territory and a newly established newspaper called the *Register* announced the arrival of a vessel from middle Florida with "an assorted cargo, and seven lawyers." For the next fifty years, frequent wrecks on the coral reefs drew talented maritime lawyers from around the country who laid the foundation for a rich and distinguished legal tradition in Key West. Depending on the source, Alejandro Cortinas might or might not be called "distinguished." Nobody disputed that he was rich.

Cortinas greeted them on the porch and showed them inside. They chatted and got acquainted during a ten-minute tour that took them upstairs to Cortinas' office, then down a back staircase to the much smaller office that was available to Jack.

"You can also use the main conference room," said Cortinas.

It was down the hall, behind double-paneled doors, and Cortinas led them there. An even older lawyer was seated at the long mahogany table, and Jack couldn't help thinking that they both looked like antiques. Cortinas made the introduction.

"Jack, I want you to meet Victor Garcia-Peña, founding member of the Key West Cuban-American Lawyers Association."

"*Con mucho gusto*," said Jack as they shook hands. "You probably wouldn't guess this about a guy named Swyteck, but my mother was born in Cuba."

"So I've been told."

"Victor has something he'd like to discuss with you," said Cortinas. "Can we all sit for a few minutes?"

"Sure," said Jack.

Victor sat at the head of the table. Cortinas was on one side, to his left. Jack and Theo sat opposite Cortinas, to Victor's right. Victor pulled a handful of cigars from his pocket and offered them around the table. Cortinas and Theo took one.

"You don't smoke cigars?" asked Victor.

"I really don't," said Jack.

"What the hell kind of Cuban are you?" he said, laughing.

"That's what his *abuela* wants to know," said Theo. More laughter.

Over the years, Jack had learned to let such jokes go, to avoid the mood-killer explanation that he'd been raised a gringo after his Cuban mother died in childbirth.

The cigars were lit, and before long, Jack might as well have been smoking one.

"On a more serious note," said Victor, "I want to talk to you about your Cuban oil case."

The "Cuban oil case" wasn't the way Jack referred to Bianca's wrongful death action, but he knew what Victor meant. "Sure. There are things I can talk to you about, and, naturally, things I can't."

"Understood," said Victor. He drew heavily on his cigar, the smoke pouring from his lips as he spoke. "Let me just say that I find the list of defendants named in your lawsuit to be incomplete. Have you thought about suing the Cuban government?"

From another lawyer, the question might have taken Jack by surprise. But not from Victor. His uncle had been killed in the 1961 Bay of Pigs invasion, which stood as the worst blunder of the Kennedy administration. Not a single Democrat had earned Victor's support since.

"The consortium operated under a production-sharing agreement with the state-owned oil company," said Jack, "Cubapetróleo. So, yeah, I did think about naming Cupet. But what's the point? Cuba never responds to any lawsuits filed in U.S. courts, and actually collecting a judgment against a Cuban sovereign entity is pie in the sky."

Victor smiled thinly. "You have much to learn."

Cortinas jumped into the conversation. "Victor was involved in the Brothers to the Rescue wrongful death lawsuits in the 1990s."

"This was back when your father was governor," said Victor. "You were probably still in law school."

"I was in jail," said Theo.

Jack kicked him in the ankle. "I remember Brothers to the Rescue," said Jack. "They flew private planes out of Miami to look for rafters who might be crossing the Florida Straits."

"Exactly," said Victor, his expression turning very serious. "Until the twenty-fourth of February 1996. That's when a Cuban Air Force MiG shot down two little Cessna 337s flown by the Brothers. One was flying nine nautical miles outside Cuban territorial airspace, and the other was ten miles out. Four men from Miami were killed. Two were very young men in their twenties. Two others married with kids. A lot of people told me don't waste your time suing the Republic of Cuba. Well, guess what? *Not* suing would have been a 187 million-dollar mistake."

Theo coughed on his cigar. "That's a lot of *moneda nacional.*"

"We were able to recover about half the judgment," said Victor.

"I don't see how you got anywhere near that much," said Jack. "My understanding is that most judgments against Cuba go uncollected."

"Most," said Victor. "But in the early sixties, the U.S. government froze Cuban assets worth hundreds of millions of dollars. We were able to tap into that fund."

"I can see that in the case of a Cuban MiG shooting Cessnas out of the sky," said Jack. "But an oil rig disaster is something else entirely."

"Not as I see it," said Victor. "Under the Anti-Terrorism and Effective Death Penalty Act of 1996, you have to prove four things. First, the foreign state is a 'state sponsor of terrorism' as designated by the U.S. State Department. Cuba is so designated."

Theo did a double take. "Cuba is a designated state sponsor of terrorism?"

"Four countries are on the list," said Victor. "Iran, Syria, Sudan, and Cuba."

"I had no idea," said Theo. "Did you know that, Jack?"

"Honestly, I did not."

Victor exchanged a quick glance with Cortinas, then shook his head. "I hate to sound like a broken record, but what the hell kind of Cuban are you, Jack?"

Theo reached for the ashtray, flicking his ashes. "I think we've already established that, counselor."

Jack kicked him again.

Victor continued. "The second thing you'd have to prove is that Rafael's injury took place outside the territorial boundaries of the Cuban state. I think we win on this, since the rig was beyond twelve miles of the Cuban shore. Third, the plaintiff has to be a U.S. national, which Bianca is. We might have some arguments over the fact that Rafael was a Cuban national, but I still think we win in a wrongful death action brought by Bianca."

"What's the fourth element?" asked Jack.

"This is where things get interesting," said Victor. "Basically, we have to prove that the Cuban government murdered Rafael."

"Murdered him?"

"'Unjustified killing' is the statutory language. Manslaughter would probably cut it. But not mere negligence."

Jack shifted in his chair, as if a straighter spine might help make his point. "I don't mean to sound glib, but I'll be lucky to prove that the oil companies were negligent. I can't prove the Cuban government murdered Rafael. There's no evidence of that. I don't even have colorable *theory*."

"I do," said Victor. "Have you read carefully the statement the Cuban government issued when it sent warships to seal off the spill site and refused any assistance from the United States?"

"I've seen the English translation."

"You don't read Spanish?"

"Well, you know . . . menus and such are easy. A speech would be tough."

Theo leaned back in his chair, out of Jack's peripheral vision. "*Not really Cuban*," he whispered to the other men.

Jack didn't even bother kicking him this time.

Victor continued. "The warning issued to the United States was filled with accusations that the relief operation is really a hostile invasion driven by right-wing elements in Miami, that the Revolutionary Government cannot tolerate a flagrant violation of its frontiers or provocative acts against its people, and that the Cuban military will take all necessary action to prevent intruders from committing acts of terrorism and piracy."

"I think we all hope they back off from that," said Jack.

"Here's my point," said Victor. "The language in this latest warning is taken almost verbatim from the statement issued by the Ministry of Justice after the Brothers to the Rescue planes were shot down in '96."

Jack considered Victor's point. "So from the

Cuban government's standpoint, the U.S. relief efforts are every bit the threat to national sovereignty that the Brothers to the Rescue flights were. Is that what you're saying?"

Victor struck a match and gave his cigar a booster light. "I'm saying much more than that. To me, this proves that the entire Scarborough 8 disaster was a well-choreographed plan by the Cuban government."

"The Cuban government is playing politics with the cleanup efforts," said Jack. "Is that your point?"

"No. Let me be clear. This is the biggest threat Cuba has presented to the United States since the Cuban Missile Crisis. That does not happen by accident. My point is that the Cuban government *caused* the explosion on the rig."

Jack paused, considering his response. "I mean no disrespect, and, without question, there has been political maneuvering on both sides since the explosion. But the idea that Cuba sent the Scarborough 8 into the Florida Straits intending to blow it up? You lost me there."

"You underestimate the Revolutionary Government."

"Oil is Cuba's ticket to economic independence. I've been reading up on this. The average Cuban makes twenty bucks a month. Every dollar matters in Cuba, and the government is planning to spend nine billion of them to become a serious player in the petroleum market. They wouldn't blow up the only shovel that can bring up the oil. Scarborough 8 was the *only* ultradeep-water rig in the world that was built to comply with the U.S. trade embargo."

"My point exactly," said Victor. "Cuba *would* blow up that rig if they could use the threat of environmental disaster to force the U.S. to end the embargo. That's the quid pro quo on the table: lift the embargo, and the U.S. can stop the spill at its source."

"The White House can't just lift the embargo. It's not an executive order. It takes an act of Congress to repeal it."

"And this oil disaster is exactly what the Cuban government needs to bring the U.S. Congress to its knees."

"A TV reporter raised that very point with my father. My dad's pretty plugged in politically. Trust me: it's just a rumor."

"It's *not* a rumor!" he said, pounding his fist. "Cuba has been fighting to end the embargo for over fifty years. If blowing up the Scarborough 8 helps them do that, so be it. If the embargo ends, there will be dozens of deepwater rigs that can drill in Cuban waters."

Jack didn't respond.

The cigars were burning low. Victor crushed out his nub in the ashtray. "Open your eyes, Jack. That's the politics of Big Oil—Cuban style. If you want to prove it in court, I'm more than happy to help." Victor slid his business card across the table. "All you have to do is call me."

Jack took his card.

"It's been a pleasure meeting you, gentlemen," said Victor.

The men rose and shook hands.

"I'll see you out," said Cortinas. He led the old

lawyer away from the table and into the hallway, leaving Jack and Theo alone in the conference room.

"You gonna call him?" asked Theo.

"Nope."

"So what *are* you going to do?" asked Theo.

"Whatever it takes to get Bianca as much money as I can, as fast as I can, from the oil consortium," Jack said. "Before this spirals out of control. And before anybody else gets hurt."

35

The lower Keys stretched more east-west than north-south, so Jack and Theo left the oil behind them on the drive from Key West. Jack knew they'd reached Marathon when they passed an ambulance from the Turtle Hospital—literally, a hospital for turtles; it wasn't just a name. The middle Keys also had a hospital for wild birds, and with an oil spill approaching, both facilities were preparing for environmental disaster. Jack was looking for pier number eight at Boot Key Harbor, which was due east of a capsized ship that Hurricane Georges had swept into the mangroves. He had to shade his eyes from the setting sun to see it.

"Ever had a settlement conference on a yacht before?" asked Theo.

They were crossing a gravel parking lot toward a long wooden pier at the west end of the marina. Their destination was one of the bigger boats at the deep end of the marina.

"Nope. Lots of 'firsts' in this case, starting with first client abducted."

"You have a short memory, dude."

Jack quickly conceded. "Well, then it has to be the first time my client and I have been abducted in the same case."

"Aren't you forgetting a little incident involving a TV weatherman, two prostitutes, and the mayor's daughter at the Hotel Bambi on Biscayne Boulevard?"

Jack would have liked to forget. "How about this: first case where I was kidnapped and my client was abducted on different days by the same guy?"

They stepped onto the pier as Theo searched his memory. "I do believe that's a first."

Boot Key Harbor is the best protected anchorage in all of the Keys, with plenty of marinas and thatch-roofed joints to reprovision, like the Chiki Tiki Bar and Grill. For those unfazed by the U.S. trade embargo, it was generally regarded as the best place to wait out the weather for crossing to Cuba. For lawyers who wanted to talk settlement, it was "meeting halfway," a rough midpoint between Key West, where Jack was staying, and downtown Miami, the oil consortium's first choice. It also solved the logistical problem of roadblocks, which prevented all but cleanup crews and emergency vehicles from entering the Keys. Jack couldn't leave the Keys with any assurance of getting back in, and by boat was the best way for the oil consortium's lawyers to enter the Keys.

"I'll do the talking," said Jack.

"Got it, chief," said Theo.

"You're here only as a witness, in case this blows up and somewhere down the line they accuse me of saying some outrageous thing I never said."

"I won't say a word," said Theo.

Luis Candela stood at the end of the pier. The sun had dipped into the Gulf behind him, and the lead lawyer for the oil consortium was a silhouette against the burnt-orange sky. A gentle breeze blew across the mooring field, setting off a chorus of metallic pings, the sound of taut halyards slapping against the barren masts of the few remaining sailboats. Most boaters had taken heed of the NOAA warning and moved their expensive hobby out of the oil's projected path, but still some motorboats and yachts slept silently in their slips, blissfully unaware of what was to come. Candela had just stepped off the bow of a forty-six-foot Hatteras Convertible named *Drill, Baby, Drill.*

Candela greeted them cordially and invited them aboard. The meeting was inside the salon, behind the closed cabin doors of highly polished teak. Candela's partner, a woman from the New York office, was seated on the couch. Jack had expected a much stronger showing of legal muscle—lawyers for the Chinese, the Russians, and any insurance companies on the hook. But it was just Candela and his partner.

"We're authorized to speak on behalf of all defendants," said Candela.

Jack and Theo took the matching club chairs, facing an old ship's wheel that someone with very little imagination and even less decorating skill had converted into a glass-covered coffee table.

"So here we all are," said Theo. "Another exciting legal episode of *David Versus Goliath.*"

Jack shot him a look that said *Shut it.*

Candela almost seemed to appreciate the ice-breaker. "I'm sure you're expecting the same old song and dance," he said. "This is where Big Oil is supposed to reach into its deep pockets, pull out a big fat check, and tell you to take it or leave it. And it would be my job to warn you that you'd better take it, because my client will spend ten times that amount in legal fees to make sure Goliath gets the *W* this time."

"I'm not here for the usual dance," said Jack. "There are good reasons for you to settle this case. Quickly."

"That's why I motored all the way down here on my boat."

"It's going to take well into seven figures to make this case go away," said Jack.

"I came here with that full understanding," said Candela.

"Are you making an offer?"

"That was my intention. *Was*," he added, shaking his head. "Then everything changed—just in the last hour, as we were pulling into the marina."

"Why?"

Candela peered out the window, catching the last flicker of daylight on the horizon. "It's a diverse group, this consortium," he said in a distant, philosophical tone. "Venezuelans, Russians, Chinese, Cubans. The American media portrays us as one big boogeyman. Truth is, we're not always of one mind, and each member has very little control over what the other ones do. But the defendants all agree on this much: we refuse to be blackmailed."

"I have no idea what you're talking about."

"Blackmail," said Theo, as if to clarify. "Like the time I had those photographs of you and—"

"I *know* what blackmail is," said Jack. "I'm telling the man it has nothing to do with this case."

"Let me spell it out for you," said Candela. "Today at two p.m. you met with Victor Garcia-Peña. At two-thirty, you called me and set up a settlement conference. At five p.m. Garcia-Peña went on Spanish talk radio, laying out his so-called evidence that the Cuban government blew up the Scarborough 8 and is responsible for the 'unjustified killing' of Rafael Lopez and fifteen other oil workers."

"You're linking things that aren't linked."

"It's simple logic."

"I don't see it," said Jack.

"God is love, love is blind, Stevie Wonder is God," said Theo. "That kind of logic."

"Stay out of this," said Jack. He moved forward in his chair, tightening his gaze on Candela. "Victor Garcia-Peña does not speak for me and my client. Period."

"Put that aside for a moment," said Candela. "Are you or are you not planning to tell a jury that the Scarborough 8 was sabotaged?"

"Sabotaged by the Cuban government?"

"By *anyone*," said Candela.

Jack wasn't ready to play his hand and tell Candela about the FBI investigation. But he chose not to lie.

"Here's how I see it," said Jack. "Safety is the number-one priority on an oil rig. If sabotage sank the Scarborough 8, you should have had security measures in place to prevent it. I don't have to prove who did it or why."

"No, of course you don't," he said with a mirthless chuckle. "All you need to do is send Garcia-Peña on a media tour to point the finger at the Cubans."

"That makes no sense. What does that get me?"

"It gets the exile community good and worked up. It's no secret that Key West juries are heavily Cuban-American. That's your strategy, isn't it? Take away any shot my client has at a fair trial and leave the consortium no choice but to settle for some extortionate amount."

"Maybe your mind works that way, but mine sure doesn't. I didn't even know Victor was on the radio."

"So you admit that you met with him before you called me," said Candela.

"Yes, but—were you spying on me?"

"That's none of your business," said Candela.

"The hell it isn't."

"I could make it our business," said Theo.

Candela bristled. "Is he threatening me?"

"Absolutely."

"Not!" said Jack. "I mean it, Theo. Stay out of this."

"Dude, it's time to cut through the shit. We're being called blackmailers because an old Cuban man went on Spanish talk radio? Really? Victor Garcia-Peña, who blows smoke even when his cigar isn't lit? I mean, *really*?"

"Theo, stop," said Jack.

"I'm just gettin' started."

"I got it from here," Jack said firmly. "I'm serious."

Theo settled back in his chair, quiet, but even his

silence made it clear that no one but Jack could have shut him down.

"What Theo is trying to say is this," said Jack. "Your allegations of blackmail are exactly like your claim that Bianca wasn't married to Rafael. Ripped from page one of the official handbook of bullshit accusations."

"I don't need to listen to this," said Candela.

"Listen good," said Jack. "You thought those letters from Rafael to Josefina would prove that Bianca was a fraud. It turns out that the fraud was Rafael's supposed engagement to Josefina. The judge figured that much out when she ruled that Bianca's case could go forward. I'm sure you figured it out, too. Two days later, Josefina's blood was found smeared on Bianca's bathroom mirror."

"What?"

"A message in blood," said Theo. "'Drop it.' As in 'drop the case.'"

Jack still wasn't sure if "drop it" meant drop the lawsuit or drop the claim of sabotage. But it didn't matter for present purposes. Candela looked genuinely stunned.

"I know absolutely nothing about anything you just said."

"It will be on the news tonight," said Jack.

"Or your client can fill you in," said Theo.

"That was completely uncalled for," said Candela.

"Was it?" asked Jack, his eyes narrowing. "I'm told it's a very diverse group, the consortium. Venezuelans, Russians, Chinese, Cubans. And one member has very little control over what the other members do."

"This discussion is over," said Candela. He went to the door and opened it. "Time for Shrek and Donkey to leave."

"That's it!" said Theo as he sprang from his chair. Jack grabbed him by the arm, half restraining him, half calming him.

"Forget it, Theo. Let's go."

Theo swallowed his anger. Jack led the way. Candela stood in the doorway, stopping them, one more thing to say.

"My client is not going to settle this case. Not now. Not on the eve of trial. Not ever."

"Not a problem," said Jack, meeting his stare. "Not for me. Not for Bianca. Not for the fifteen other widows your ego keeps you from thinking about."

Candela was the first to blink. He moved aside, allowing Jack to pass from the salon to the deck. Theo was two steps behind.

"Come on, Donkey."

Jack hiked over the boat's side rail and stepped onto the pier. Theo followed. Weathered wood planks creaked beneath the weight of each footfall as a cool breeze brushed the moonlit waves in the harbor.

"Donkey," Theo said under his breath, hands buried in his pockets. "Who you callin' Donkey?"

Jack was deep in thought, trying to imagine what he would tell Bianca. Candela was no bluffer, and Jack wondered if his client had the stomach for the long, hard fight.

"I'm not Donkey," said Theo, trailing a step behind. "*You're* Donkey."

Jack worried about Josefina, too, barely aware of Theo's single-minded stream of consciousness all the way back to shore.

"Honkey Donkey," Theo said in a deep Super Fly voice. "Got a nice ring to it."

36

·

It was long after dark when Jack returned to Key West, but the shoreline was aglow. Generators rumbled in the night, pumping out enough power for cleanup crews to work around the clock. One portable lighting tree after another stretched along the southeast coast, each tower connected to the next by a temporary power line, the sagging wires a string of sad smiles above the black gunk that glistened beneath yellow sodium lighting.

"I wish they would let us help," said Bianca.

Jack and Theo had caught up with her outside the Truman Annex, where the media and a crowd of onlookers had gathered to watch the emergency response teams from behind police barricades. It wasn't Bianca's night off at the café, but Rick had sent all but a skeleton crew to volunteer for the relief effort.

"Was it the Coast Guard that turned you away?" asked Jack.

"Yes," she said. "Anyone who touches the oil has to be trained. Four hours minimum. Volunteers, too. It's a law."

"Probably HAZWOPER," said Jack.

"Has a *what*?" asked Theo.

"Hazardous Waste Operations and Emergency Response," said Jack. "An oil spill brings out the ultimate alphabet soup of state and federal agencies. I'm sure OSHA is part of it, too, if it involves worker-safety training."

A police officer directed them back onto the sidewalk to allow a Coast Guard van to pass in the crowded street.

"So let's get trained," said Theo. "Where do we go?"

"Fort Lauderdale," said Bianca.

"That can't be right," said Theo.

"That's what the Coast Guard lady told me," said Bianca. "It's the closest place."

"They're being smart," said Jack. "No one needs a bunch of amateurs trained on the fly, getting oil all over their bodies, posing for pictures on the beach, and trampling every bird nest and turtle egg between here and Islamorada."

"The lady said we could volunteer for other things," said Bianca. "Unloading supplies, getting food and bottled water out to the crews, that kind of thing."

"Let's do it," said Theo.

The staging area for volunteers was at the high school gymnasium a few blocks north, an easy walk. They checked in at the information table, got a RELIEF TEAM hat and T-shirt, and signed a release that disclosed every conceivable injury and disease that a disaster relief worker could face—and then some.

"What the heck is leptospirosis?" asked Theo.

The woman at the registration table answered in a Haitian accent. "Symptoms are a lot like dengue fever. You get it by drinking water that has animal urine in it."

Theo glanced at Jack, eyebrow raised. "If that's what we're volunteering for, I say we go back and take our chances with the oil."

"No worries," the woman said. "We actually borrowed a form release from the Port-au-Prince earthquake."

Only then did Jack notice the HAITI RELIEF message in Creole on her cap. It was another sign of the international wave of volunteerism that was flooding into Key West from Global Green, the Oiled Wildlife Care Network, the National Audubon Society, and many others.

A fleet of supply trucks was parked outside the gymnasium, with new deliveries every few minutes. Teams of volunteers unloaded everything from hazmat suits to sunscreen and toilet paper. Around ten o'clock, Bianca started to fade. Staying busy was good for her psyche, Jack knew, with all she had been through. But there were physical limits. It wasn't just the stress of the attack. It was also the lingering effects of the injection of barbiturates. A four-hour nap in the afternoon had helped, but it wasn't enough. Theo was still working when Jack left to walk Bianca home.

"Theo likes to say you're not really Cuban," said Bianca.

They were on a quiet stretch of Whitehead Street, walking away from the gym. Bianca's trailer was still a crime scene, and she didn't ever want to go back there, anyway. Another waitress at Rick's Café had offered to put her up at her place.

"Theo says a lot of things," said Jack.

"Can I ask a personal question, if you don't mind?"

"Sure."

"How old was your mother when she came from Cuba?"

"Just a teenager. She was one of the fourteen thousand kids who came here without their parents under the Pedro Pan program. You've heard of Pedro Pan?"

"Yes, in school. The CIA operation."

"I've always thought of it as a humanitarian operation run by the Catholic Church. It was for families who opposed the Cuban revolution and didn't want their kids to grow up in a Communist country. Parents sent their children to live in America with friends or relatives, hoping to join up with them later."

"We learned in school that it was CIA propaganda to make the Cuban people afraid that the Revolutionary Government would take their children and send them to Soviet labor camps."

Jack looked off to the distant glow of emergency cleanup lights visible above the tree line. *And people wonder why we can't agree on what to do about an oil spill.*

"Did your *abuela* make it over before your mother died?"

"No. It took her forty years to get out of Cuba. I was a grown man. The last time they saw each other was when Abuela put her sixteen-year-old daughter on a plane and kissed her good-bye."

"That's sad," said Bianca. She stopped. They were outside the trailer park. "Makes me think of when I got on the boat and said good-bye to Rafael."

Jack nodded. It surprised him that he had not yet drawn that comparison—at least not consciously.

Bianca turned to face him more directly. "Do you ever wonder if your *abuela* wishes she hadn't sent her daughter away?"

Jack caught his breath, not sure how to respond. It was a little like asking Jack if he wished he had never been born.

"I'm sorry," said Bianca. "That wasn't a proper question."

"It's okay," said Jack. "It didn't come from a bad place. I understand your feelings."

She looked away. Jack suddenly felt the need to answer.

"I'm sure, in her darkest moments, Abuela told herself that her daughter would still be alive if she had stayed in Cuba. But a mother isn't to blame for trying to make a better life for her child. And a young woman isn't to blame if she gets on a boat hoping to find something better for her husband and the family they want to build. This is not your fault. None of it, Bianca, is your fault in the least."

Her eyes brightened a bit. It wasn't profound or all that wise, but Jack sensed that his words had actually helped her. She rose up on her toes and gave Jack a peck on the cheek.

"I think you will be a good papa."

She stepped away quickly and hurried up the

walkway to the trailer door. She opened it, then turned and waved goodnight. Jack returned the gesture, smiling on the inside as she disappeared behind the screen door.

So many things were unknown and uncertain, and having a pregnant wife away on an undercover assignment didn't make life any easier. But that brief moment brought him a little clarity. It was the first time anyone had ever said that to him.

And it was one of the nicest things Jack had ever heard.

37

·

Jack woke early the next morning. Five thirty-three a.m. Much earlier than planned. It was a bizarre dream. Josefina was there. Rafael was there. And Jack walked into the room.

"What am I doing here?" he asked.

The letters Rafael had written to Josefina, for Bianca, were stacked in a neat pile on the table, directly in front of an empty chair.

"Abuela got her wish," said Josefina.

Jack looked more closely at the empty chair. It had his mother's name on it—Anna.

"What wish?" asked Jack.

"You were never born."

The phone rang on the nightstand. He hoped it was Andie. Jack sat up in the bed, collected his breath, and answered. It was Abuela, which was almost too weird.

"Jack, *mi vida!*"

Mi vida—literally, "my life"—was what she always called him. She was almost shouting with excitement. "I so proud of you! I just hear on the radio this morning."

"Heard what?"

"You sue Fidel!"

Jack forced his eyes open wider. He knew he was no longer dreaming, but he was not yet fully awake. "No, you heard wrong. I'm not suing Fidel Castro."

"But the man on the radio. That what he say."

"First of all, Fidel is no longer president."

"Then you sue the brother?"

"No. I'm not suing Fidel, Raúl, or any other Cubans. I'm suing the oil consortium."

"But . . . the radio."

"Abuela, you may find this hard to believe. Shocking, even. But just because it's on Cuban talk radio at five-thirty in the morning doesn't mean it's true."

Abuela was a loyal listener of the shrinking number of talk radio stations that catered to Miami's hard-line exile community. Even WQBA had been reformatted for a more moderate pan-Hispanic message.

"All rumors?"

"Yes. Just rumors."

Jack could hear the deep sigh of disappointment over the line. "Abuela, I'm going back to sleep now. I'll call you tonight."

"Okay. But not on the *eh-smart* phone you bought me. El *eh-smart* phone *es estúpido*. It no work. The screen all black."

"Abuela, when is the last time you charged your smartphone?"

"Charge?"

Jack shook his head. "I'll call you on the landline. *Te quiero.*"

Jack was too engaged now to fall back asleep. He climbed out of bed and went to his laptop. Up-to-the-minute images of the spill appeared on his homepage. As bad as things had looked outside the Truman Annex just hours earlier, Key West was not in line for a direct hit. If the latest NOAA projections were correct, however, Jack's meeting on Candela's yacht had marked the last oil-free sunset in Boot Key Harbor for many nights to come.

Jack read the lead article about sludge on the reefs, then skimmed a companion story about benzene and other carcinogens already being released into the atmosphere by the natural evaporation of oil from the surface, which paled in comparison to the soot and other particles thrown off by the controlled burns that were part of the cleanup effort. It was making Jack sick just to read about it, but then he took the truly toxic plunge: his e-mail.

Jack had cleared most of his calendar for the honeymoon that was not to be, but there was still a ton of catching up to do. The wifi connection at the hundred-year-old bed-and-breakfast wasn't exactly state of the art, but it was plenty fast to e-file pleadings with the courthouse. It was almost nine by the time he went downstairs in hopes of finding an amazing breakfast to make up for the too-short mattress in this overpriced B&B. Agent Linton, the direct FBI contact that Andie had established for Jack, was waiting in the lobby for him. Another FBI agent was with him. Linton, the ex-Marine with the Jamaican accent, spoke first.

"Join us for coffee, Jack?"

If it was a question, Linton's delivery invited only one answer.

"Sure," said Jack. "But why the ambush?"

"No ambush."

"I know Andie raised hell with the field office about the need to communicate better with Bianca and me as victims. But that doesn't mean you have to track me down in person. A phone call every now and then would be just fine."

"It's no problem, Jack. We know where you are."

His tone wasn't entirely cordial. It could have been the accent, but Jack took it as a message: *We know where you are, Swyteck—at all times.*

They stepped outside and went to a white wicker seating arrangement at the far end of the front porch. The agents took the love seat. Jack got the rocking chair. A waitress brought them a fresh pot of coffee with three cups. She placed the tray on the table between Jack and the FBI, where a whirring paddle fan directly overhead was immediately blowing the coffee cold. She gave the dangling chain a tug, cutting the fan speed in half, and then left the men alone to talk.

Linton rose and put the fan back on high. "Sorry, guys. I know it seems odd to complain about smog in Key West, but my asthma doesn't lie."

"I just read about that," said Jack. "We're downwind from the spill. It's not actual smoke from the burns. In fact, the water is so rough in the Gulf Stream right now, I hear that the burn efforts aren't going that well. It's a chemical reaction in the atmosphere. 'Secondary aerosol compounds' is how they put it."

"Whatever it is, my lungs feel like I'm back in middle school in New Jersey in need of my inhaler. Pardon me if I make this quick."

"Quick is good," said Jack. "Any leads on who attacked my client?"

"No," said Linton.

"On what happened to Josefina?"

"No."

"Any new thoughts about the message left on Bianca's mirror?"

"No."

"I've heard nothing more from my kidnapper about who was behind the sabotage. Have you heard anything?"

"Can't discuss that."

"What can you tell me about the sabotage investigation?"

"Not a thing."

Jack reached for the coffeepot and filled his cup. "Well, that *was* quick."

"Sorry. I'm not trying to be a prick." He coughed, then drew a deep breath. "Sabotage is actually in the general ballpark of what I wanted to talk about."

He coughed a little deeper, then took some water. If compounds were in the air, Jack wasn't feeling the effects. But Linton was struggling.

"Are you okay?" asked Jack.

"Yeah," he said, wheezing. "Now, about the sabotage."

"So you can tell me something?"

"Not what you want to hear," said Linton. "There's no delicate way to put this, Jack. You need to shut it down."

"Shut what down?"

"All your talk about sabotage."

"It's what Bianca's case is about."

"That's the concern."

"Whose concern?"

"The FBI's."

"It's a civil lawsuit. How is that the FBI's concern?"

"There is an active criminal investigation into the possibility of sabotage on the Scarborough 8."

"So?"

"Pursuing a sabotage theory in the context of a civil lawsuit could be detrimental to the criminal investigation."

Linton signaled to the waitress and asked for some Claritin. She didn't have any. When she was gone, Jack followed up.

"I don't see how my lawsuit hurts your investigation. I see it as complementary."

"It's a multijurisdictional effort to determine who was behind the sabotage. I can't give you specifics about the targets of the investigation, but suffice it to say that your theory doesn't jibe with ours."

"Are you talking about Victor Garcia-Peña and his radio campaign against the Cuban government? Because that's not my theory."

Linton covered his nose and mouth with a napkin, drawing deep breaths of crudely filtered air. Oddly, he was simultaneously ticking off Jack and earning his sympathy.

"What *is* your theory, Jack?"

"Discovery hasn't even started yet. But, as I told Mr. Candela yesterday, I don't have to prove who did it. All I have to do is persuade a jury that the oil consortium failed to implement adequate security measures to prevent disaster and keep its oil workers safe."

"So your plan is to poke around in depositions until something about sabotage turns up? Sorry. Can't let you do that."

"What do you mean you can't *let* me? That's up to Judge Carlyle."

"I have the unpleasant job of giving you two choices. One, back off the sabotage theory. Or, two, the U.S. Attorney for the Southern District of Florida will intervene in your case and ask the judge to stay the entire action until the criminal investigation has run its course."

"Which could be years."

"I can't really say."

Jack smelled a bluff. "Let me get this straight: the United States government is willing to confirm publicly, in a Key West courtroom, that there is an active criminal investigation into sabotage on the Scarborough 8?"

Linton showed discomfort, and it wasn't just the air quality. "The answer to your question is yes. But only if you're unpatriotic enough to force us to do so."

Jack flashed a sardonic smile. "So the 'patriotic' thing would be for me to put my client's best interest aside and abandon the sabotage theory. Is that your point?"

"I'm just saying."

"That makes no sense," Jack said, and then he suddenly realized what was going on. "Have you spoken recently to Mr. Candela?"

Linton coughed twice, his breathing a little shallower. It wasn't all about the smog effect. "I have never personally spoken to Mr. Candela."

"I wouldn't think so. You're just the messenger. I'm sure his client has the ear of someone in Washington who is more keenly aware that Venezuela is this country's fourth-largest supplier of oil."

"This isn't politics. It's a national security issue."

Jack rose. "I'll be sure to pass that along to Bianca Lopez."

Linton rose too. "So do we have an understanding?"

"What do you think?"

"I think you're making a huge mistake."

Jack shook the agent's hand, remaining cordial. "It wouldn't be the first time."

"I would imagine you'll be hearing directly from the U.S. Attorney's office."

"Can't wait to hear how excited he is about siding with the Cubans, Russians, Chinese, and Venezuelans against a grieving young widow."

Linton sneezed into his fist. Jack was glad the obligatory handshake was already behind them.

"I'll give you the rest of the day to change your mind," said Linton. "If you're smart, you'll drop it."

Drop it. The FBI and Bianca's attacker were sending the same message.

"I hear you loud and clear," said Jack as the agents stepped away.

38

Jack spent the next two hours on the telephone with an expert at MIT on the computerized security and alarm systems that were used on engineering marvels like the Scarborough 8. He wasn't about to "drop" the sabotage theory. Not by a long shot. But he did need to distance himself from Victor Garcia-Peña. That was his next phone call, which was short and to the point.

"It has to stop, Victor. No more public innuendo that you are connected to me or my client, or that you have inside knowledge about the case strategy."

Victor totally got Jack's message. And Jack got Victor's. He was no longer welcome at the law offices of Alejandro Cortinas, and by noon Jack was searching for a new Key West outpost. Actually, he was looking for more than office space. The phone call to the MIT security expert was priced at a thousand dollars an hour. Jack needed well-heeled co-counsel to help front costs, which would mount quickly, and which he would never recover if he didn't win.

Jack called a law school classmate who practiced in New York. Jack and Cassie Hahn had spent their first year at Yale in the same study group. They'd also spent a few late-night study breaks in the same bed, but that was ancient history. What mattered was that Cassie's law firm had earned multimillion-dollar verdicts against multinational corporations for failure to protect their workers abroad. Cassie's bio listed her as lead counsel in victories against a construction company in Colombia whose chief engineer was kidnapped by FARC, and a mining conglomerate in Kazakhstan whose director of development was beheaded by "religious" radicals.

"I've been reading about your case in the *American Lawyer*, Jack. Congrats."

"Thanks, but I haven't won yet."

"Could be big," said Cassie.

"Could be a disaster."

"No pun intended, I'm sure."

Jack was having lunch at Goldman's, a local bagel and sandwich shop with Key West flavor. It had the best pastrami on rye south of Miami Beach and enough atmosphere to transport even a former New Yorker back to Amsterdam Avenue and brunch with Bubbie. It was also tucked away next to the Winn-Dixie on the northeast corner of the island, as far away as possible from the crowds around the emergency responders to the southwest. Jack found enough privacy to talk at a table by the window.

"So how can I help you, Jack?"

"I have a hypothetical problem."

"Ah, love hypotheticals. And would I be correct in assuming that this problem is so hypothetical that I will have to surrender my license, an ovary, and my firstborn child if I breathe a word to anyone about our conversation."

"You can keep the ovary."

"Thank you. Go ahead. I'm listening."

"This case started out like the international version of the wrongful death lawsuits filed after the Deepwater Horizon spill. There are major issues about what laws apply, but basically it boiled down to whether the oil consortium protected its workers from the usual occupational hazards."

"That's what I've read."

"Here's my hypothesis: What if it wasn't the 'usual' occupational hazard?"

"How *unusual* might it be?"

"Sabotage."

She paused, but it didn't seem to shock her. "I've seen the reports on the news. What is it, something like two hundred organizations have claimed responsibility?"

"Not that many. But a lot. None of them credible."

"How do you know *none* is credible?"

"I don't know for sure. But hunting down terrorists is not my job. The FBI and Homeland Security are involved in an investigation. Call it sabotage, call it terrorism. It doesn't matter. I need to prove the oil consortium should have protected its workers from an explosion that was not an accident. It was an intentional act."

"Actually, it does matter, Jack. It's one thing if this was a pissed-off employee acting on his own— purely an act of sabotage with no 'terrorist' implications. But if it was an act of 'terrorism' as defined under federal law, you have an entirely different case on your hands."

"Okay, smarty pants. How?"

"Let's put the oil consortium aside. Maybe they did everything they possibly could to protect their workers. Maybe they installed a state-of-the-art computer security system."

"They did," said Jack.

"There you go," said Cassie. "Maybe the breach of security wasn't the fault of the oil consortium. Maybe the culprit was the company who manufactured the security system."

"I've thought of that," said Jack. "That may well bear out in discovery. If it does, I'll add them as a defendant."

"Well, hold on," said Cassie. "That's where the terrorism/sabotage distinction becomes important."

"I don't understand."

"Most lawyers wouldn't," said Cassie. "It's a pretty obscure point of law. It's called the SAFETY Act. It was part of the Homeland Security Act passed after nine-eleven. The idea was to encourage companies to create technology that detects and prevents acts of terrorism."

"How does that apply here?"

"The way Congress chose to encourage companies to create antiterrorism technology was to put serious limits on their potential liability in the event something goes wrong."

"How serious?" asked Jack.

"Very," said Cassie. "Only one lawsuit can be filed. It covers all the property damage, all the personal injuries—everything the technology company might be sued for. The company's liability is capped at the amount of insurance coverage required by Homeland Security."

Jack thought of Freddy Foman and his team of lawyers. "My client, the fishermen, the hotels, the waterfront property owners, the boaters, the dive shops, the people who get sick cleaning up the sludge on the beach—we're all lumped together in one claim under the SAFETY Act?"

"Yes, if it was an act of terrorism, *and* if the technology on the Scarborough 8 was registered with Homeland Security as qualified antiterrorism technology. 'QATT' for short."

"This is a big deal," said Jack. "The payouts in the Deepwater Horizon disaster were in the billions. That must be way more than the insurance coverage required by Homeland Security for QATT."

"Way, way more," said Cassie. "Any disaster on that scale covered by the Safety Act would leave a lot of folks walking away empty-handed."

"How do I find out if the security technology on the Scarborough 8 was QATT?"

"As I see it, you have a couple choices. Do it yourself. Or let the smartest girl in your study group help you."

"Thank you, Cassie."

"Don't thank me. Pay me."

"Okay," he said with a chuckle. "We'll talk about a fee split."

"You bet we will," she said.

39

At three o'clock sharp, Jack met with an eager young real estate agent outside an old red-brick building on Simonton Street. Hunter Collins was dressed smartly in a white blouse, red scarf, and matching skirt. Simple gold jewelry finished a look that was conservative by Key West standards, but it was stylish and hinted at success. She reminded Jack of Elizabeth Taylor in *Cat on a Hot Tin Roof*, but he shook off the thought. Now that Andie was expecting, his cultural references needed serious updating if Dad hoped to be considered cool beyond their child's sixth birthday.

"This is the only office space available that meets your specifications and is truly within walking distance of the courthouse," she said as she unlocked the glass door.

"Has anyone ever told you that you look like Alexis Kiley?"

"Who? No. But people do say I look like a young Elizabeth Taylor."

"Really? Hmm. Yeah, I guess I see that."

Hunter went inside, and Jack followed.

The space appeared to have been vacant for some time, not a stick of furniture anywhere, just a broom in the corner and a wastebasket. The echo of their footfalls on the oak floor harked back to an era when coffered ceilings and walls of solid plaster were de rigueur.

"Lots of charm and character," she said. "The street level is two thousand square feet, and there's an option to expand to the second floor."

Jack stopped and looked around, confused. "This is not at all what I'm looking for."

Hunter Alexis Taylor looked as though she might cry. "It's not?"

"I'm sorry," said Jack. "There must have been some miscommunication. I need at most two hundred square feet, furnished, leased week to week. It's a very short-term thing for me, my investigator, and possibly a lawyer from New York from time to time. I'm not doing a build-out."

"But Ms. Hahn was very specific," she said, pulling up her message pad on the iPad. "She wanted space for eight lawyers, six paralegals, four personal assistants, two IT specialists, and two conference rooms."

"*That's* what Cassie told you?"

"Yes. With room to expand when your case goes to trial. It must be a big case."

"Getting bigger all the time," said Jack. "Excuse me a second, would you?"

Jack stepped outside and dialed Cassie's number. A little help was a godsend; a team of eight New York lawyers, a nightmare. After six rings the call went to voice mail. Just as Jack finished the short message—"Call me"—the line beeped with an incoming call. It was Andie, which changed his mood immediately.

"Hey, how are you, love?"

"Missing you."

"How's the morning sickness?"

"Didn't have it today. Or yesterday. Maybe I'm over it."

"Fingers crossed."

"I'm very sorry to hear about what happened to Bianca."

"Thanks," he said as he found a shady spot on the sidewalk. "She's pretty shook up, but she's tough."

"I confirmed that Agent Linton will be her victim liaison, too, so he should be in contact with both of you. There are things he's not at liberty to discuss, even with victims, but he promised to keep you informed to the extent possible."

"I just met with him this morning."

"So I heard."

An open-air trolley rolled by on Fleming Street, the tour guide's voice blaring over the loudspeaker: *"And coming up on our right, tucked behind these buildings, is Nancy Forrester's Secret Garden . . ."* It was theater of the absurd, not a single tourist on the trolley, the oil disaster already working its black magic. Jack plugged one ear to block out the noise.

"What did you hear?"

"That you totally ticked him off."

"Linton was out of line."

"I got a message from him. He asked if I could help bring you around to see things his way."

"Really? Did he tell you that the FBI wants to dictate the strategy of Bianca's case?"

"He didn't put it in those words. But I understand that he wants you to back off the allegations of sabotage."

It surprised Jack that she was pushing it this far, given their understanding that working the law was his job, enforcing the law was hers. "Andie, you and I shouldn't be discussing this."

"That's the reason I called. As far as I'm concerned, that is totally between him and you. And I told Linton exactly that."

"That's how you left it—it's between him and me?"

"Yes. I wanted you to know that."

Jack walked to the curb and back, as if moving his feet across the sidewalk would help him sort this out. "I'm not sure what to say."

"I thought you'd be happy."

"Happy? Really?"

"Is there something else I should have said?"

"You should have told him that it's between me and my client, and that it's none of the FBI's damn business whether sabotage is in or out of Bianca's case."

"Jack, first of all, don't get testy with me."

"Sorry."

"Second, I can't do that."

"Why not?"

"It works both ways. I can't tell you how to handle your cases for your clients. And I can't tell the FBI how to deal with you as a lawyer."

"But you're the one who told Linton to call me in

the first place, remember? When I came back from Cuba, you were madder than I was about the Bureau keeping me in the dark."

"I intervened on your behalf because you were the victim of a crime. That's totally different. I'm not going to get involved when you're just another attorney butting heads with the FBI."

"Butting heads? So you agree with Linton? I'm interfering with an FBI investigation?"

"I didn't say that. My point is—you know what, Jack? Can we just agree not to talk about this anymore?"

Jack breathed in and out. It wasn't the first conflict between Jack the lawyer and Andie the FBI agent, but it was their first since the wedding. Jack hadn't deluded himself into thinking that marriage would fix everything, but he had at least hoped that a lifelong commitment would make it *feel* more solvable. It felt the same, every bit as difficult.

"Good idea," he said. "It's best to let it go."

The next ten seconds of silence on the line felt much longer. "When will I see you?" asked Jack.

"Maybe soon," said Andie, her tone softer. "At the very latest, we will do the first ultrasound together. I want you there for it."

"I wouldn't miss it for anything. I love you."

"Me, too. Bye, Jack."

The moment he hung up, Hunter rushed outside, nearly pouncing on him before he could put his phone away. She was talking on her cell, and then handed it to Jack.

"It's Ms. Hahn," said Hunter. "I think we have this straightened out, but she wants to talk to you."

Jack took Hunter's phone. "Cassie, about this lease."

"Forget that," she said. "I have an answer for you on the Scarborough 8 technology. The entire computerized alarm system was registered under the SAFETY Act as qualified antiterrorism technology. And guess who the manufacturer is."

"The Chinese?"

"Far from it. Barton-Hammill."

"The defense contractor?"

"The *biggest* defense contractor. Actually a foreign subsidiary of Barton-Hammill. It was their way around the trade embargo against Cuba."

"Or the security system was part of the ten percent U.S. parts that are allowed under the embargo."

"Whatever," said Cassie. "Don't you see what's going on here? If the Scarborough 8 exploded because the alarm system failed, Barton-Hammill is your principal defendant."

Jack followed her train of thought completely. "But if the technology failed and the rig exploded because of an act of terrorism, the SAFETY Act applies. Barton-Hammill's liability for every conceivable claim would be capped at the limits of its insurance policy. A few million dollars."

"You got it," said Cassie.

Jack was pacing the sidewalk, the picture coming clearer in his mind. "That's what this pressure from the FBI is about. If I run with the sabotage theory in Bianca's case, I might prove that the failure of Barton-Hammill's technology and the oil disaster it caused had nothing to do with an act of terrorism."

"And if you proved that," said Cassie, "Barton-

Hammill would have no protection under the SAFETY Act."

Yet another trolley passed, not a single passenger aboard. No tourists.

"Barton-Hammill would be to this oil disaster what BP was to Deepwater Horizon: the deepest pocket in the courtroom."

"Bingo," said Cassie. "To be blunt about it, the Pentagon's biggest defense contractor would be totally on the hook for the worst oil disaster in history."

"And the FBI is running interference for them," said Jack, "keeping the sabotage investigation under its thumb."

"Now do you understand why we need office space for eight lawyers? This is going to go nuclear."

Jack glanced at Hunter. She was pecking furiously at her virtual keyboard, filling in the terms of the lease on her iPad.

"When do you get here?"

"As soon as I can," said Cassie. "Flights in or out of Key West are not easy to come by right now."

"Tell me about it," said Jack. "Thanks, Cassie. Thanks a million."

"I think you mean a billion."

"We shall see," said Jack.

40
.

His flight on Bahamasair left Miami International Airport at four p.m. The flight attendant invited him and the other passengers to sit back, relax, and enjoy the fifty-minute flight to Nassau.

Relax. The operative word. Mission accomplished.

The most important part of the trailer-park "meeting" with Bianca could not have gone better. Perfect execution, actually. His every word mattered, and it was vitally important that she live to pass them on, in detail, to Swyteck, along with the letters from Rafael. Bianca had been sufficiently frightened, at times petrified. But she'd never really lost her head—never screamed, kicked, clawed, or done anything totally stupid. Predicting how a woman will react when threatened was always difficult. Every person was different, and even the same woman might react aggressively under one set of circumstances, passively under another. Any level of resistance from Bianca could have put the outcome—life or death—in question. Luckily, she was the compliant type. Not weak, just not one to put up a physical fight.

Bianca Lopez was no Josefina Fuentes.

He poured himself a scotch. It was well deserved.

He'd handled the one and only glitch beautifully. It had always been his plan to release Bianca so that she could deliver his message, but he could not ignore the risk that she might see through his disguise to some extent. The benzodiazepine injection was his safety net. Without it, Bianca would have lain awake until her roommate's return from work. For hours, Bianca would have played the attack over and over in her mind, combing through every detail, trying to figure out who he was. Rendering her unconscious for a few hours had been his answer to that problem. He'd played it safe, medically speaking, administering less than half the dosage he'd given Swyteck and his buddy. But it was still too much. Bianca barely had a pulse. Her breathing was too shallow. After several minutes of slow but steady decline, the possibility of losing her had become all too real. He'd found her keys, put Bianca in her car, and started toward the hospital. The impromptu plan was simply to pull her car up to the ER entrance and leave her there, if necessary. Halfway to the hospital, however, Bianca's pulse and breathing returned to normal. She was still unconscious, but it was too dangerous to take her back to her trailer. He parked her car in a lot near the hospital and left her there.

There had been no way of knowing how quickly the police would find Bianca. It might have taken three minutes. Or she could have sat there all night. He knew, however, that as soon as they revived Bianca and learned of her attack, the roadblocks out of the keys would be traps waiting to be sprung. At Miami International Airport, baggage checkers, gate attendants, TSA personnel, immigration authorities, and a host of federal agents would be on alert for any suspicious character traveling alone to the islands and possibly on to Havana. Neither Swyteck, prior to his release, nor Bianca, before hers, had managed a good look at his face, but the safe thing was to assume that law enforcement would have at least a minimal physical description: over six feet tall, two hundred pounds, dark eyes, solid build, strong as a bull. Of course the authorities would be smart enough to monitor the circuitous routes to Havana through Cancún, Kingston, or Nassau.

The upshot was that it had been best to wait a day for things to cool off. His business with the bank in Nassau could wait that long. He needed a place to put ten million dollars, but he didn't need it yesterday. Time was on his side. The closer the oil got to Florida, the more pressure the government would feel to pay an informant.

To the spill, he told himself in a silent toast, raising his glass of scotch, but it was empty already.

He ordered another from the flight attendant and drank more slowly, listening to two guys from Nashville in the seats in front of him. He sized them up in ten seconds. Clowns like them were all over Cuba. Two married guys flying Miami to Nassau, leaving their wives at home to go fishing in the Bahamas—

"I'll be out on a boat, honey. You can't reach me by cell"—
only to hop another plane to Havana and roll with
the *jineteras*. Their conversation turned to the spill.

"Honestly, who gives a shit about a little oil in the
Gulf Stream? Nothin' but a bunch of homos in Key
West, anyway. A month from now it'll all be in New-
foundland or Iceland or some other who-the-fuck-
cares country."

The man may have a point.

He emptied the rest of his second scotch from the
minibottle and checked the specs. Fifty milliliters.
It had taken just one bottle that size to get his message across on the bathroom mirror. One bottle of
Josefina's precious blood.

Drop it.

His point, he assumed, had been made. He didn't
need the likes of Jack Swyteck poking around for
evidence in a lawsuit, stirring up the media, trying
to find out what had really happened on the Scarborough 8. That was valuable information. Ten
million dollars, payable by the United States government. Maybe he was asking too much. Maybe
not enough. He could really name his price. Only
he knew the cause. Only he.

He squeezed the empty bottle in his hand.

And all pretenders will pay in blood.

41
.

Jack hated to turn on the television. The footage on the five o'clock news was worse than the so-called experts had predicted. The middle Keys were awash in Cuban crude. Overnight, Boot Key Harbor had transformed into *Black* Boot Key.

"Perfect," said Theo, shaking his head. "Sir, how would you like your Florida snapper tonight? Grilled, fried, regular, or unleaded?"

They were downstairs at Jack's B&B, watching television in what was originally the smoking room in the Victorian mansion of a nineteenth-century treasure hunter. *Action News* was reporting live from Marathon, where pristine waters and priceless coastline bore the unmistakable scars of a massive spill. Oil-covered pelicans floundering in black goop. Manatees washing up dead on the beach. Coral rocks along the shoreline resembling giant lumps of coal. Cleanup crews worked frantically to protect the tangled and sensitive root system of the mangroves, as their booms and vacuum hoses battled huge black blobs floating on the oil-stained surface.

The young reporter on the scene was wearing a white hazmat suit and protective gloves, but somehow her hair and makeup still looked perfect. Jack turned up the volume for her report on "Keys outrage" over Washington's inability to convince the Cuban government to allow U.S. vessels to enter Cuban waters so that American cleanup crews and technology could get to the spill at its source. "Until that happens," she reported, "the United States has no way of knowing how much oil is actually gushing from the mile-deep well, no way of knowing if the proper emergency response is in place, no way of knowing how much longer the spigot will remain open . . ."

Theo pushed himself up from the couch and headed to the door.

"Where you going?" asked Jack.

"Work," said Theo. "I'm sure Rick can use an extra bartender at the café. Gonna be a lot of down and depressed citizens of the Conch Republic drowning their sorrows tonight. And with this much shit hitting the middle Keys, it's obvious we ain't leaving Key West anytime soon. I can use a little extra dough."

"Okay. Catch ya later." Jack watched a little more news, channel surfing. His phone rang, and he checked the incoming number.

Speaking of disasters, he thought, but he took the call.

"Agent Linton, what can I do for you?"

"We're running out of time, Jack."

It sounded as if Linton was shouting via Bluetooth from the driver's seat of his car. Jack would probably need to talk louder than normal to be heard, so he stepped outside to the front porch, where his voice wouldn't carry all the way up to the rooftop widow's walk of the old B&B.

"Time for what?" asked Jack.

"To rethink the direction of your lawsuit. I promised to give you until the end of the day to back off the sabotage angle. Guess what? It's the end of the day. I wanted to take one last shot before I tell the U.S. Attorney that there's no choice but for the government to intervene and ask the judge to put your case on hold."

"Intervene on what grounds?"

"National security."

Jack walked to the porch bannister, looking out onto the street. "Oh, well, national security. Why didn't you say that in the first place? I'm glad you brought it up, because that changes . . . not a damn thing."

"I had a feeling that would be your response."

"Thanks for calling."

"One more thing, Jack. We haven't forgotten about that trip you and Theo Knight took to Cuba last week. Totally illegal. I understand that you're of Cuban descent, but visiting relatives was not the purpose of your trip. And Theo Knight is just a blatant violation of the trade embargo. I didn't bring this up before. That was out of professional courtesy to your wife, since she's an FBI agent and all."

"Am I supposed to thank you for that?"

"Thanking me would be premature. You see, Andie told me this morning that she wants you treated fairly as a victim of a kidnapping. But the way I deal with Jack Swyteck, attorney at law, is strictly up to me. So I'm taking her at her word. No more favors because you're married to the FBI. You got it?"

"Are you actually threatening to prosecute me for violating the embargo?"

"We can start with prosecution. From there I was thinking that we might move on to suspension from the practice of law. Maybe disbarment."

"This is outrageous."

"Make no mistake, Jack. The investigation into sabotage on the Scarborough 8 is a matter of national security on the highest level. It's absolutely critical that the criminal investigation proceed without interference and public distraction from your civil lawsuit. So here's the deal: you can either find your way onto the bus, or you can be under it. Your choice. I'll give you until tomorrow at noon. Have a good night."

The call ended with a click, which triggered a replay of Linton's buzzwords, if only in Jack's mind: *national security*.

Jack was so angry he could barely think. He went back inside to watch the news, gathering images from every south Florida station. It was all about the local disaster. A few angry residents called it a national disgrace. Not a word about national security.

Until he switched to cable news.

Printed in bold letters in the banner at the bottom of the screen were the very same words that Agent Linton had just uttered in his threat, and they were even in quotation marks: "A MATTER OF

NATIONAL SECURITY ON THE HIGHEST LEVEL."

Jack's phone rang. It was Theo. He ignored the call and focused on the news coverage.

"Shocking rhetoric out of Washington about the Cuban oil disaster," the anchorman reported. "Minutes ago, thirteen congressional leaders gathered in the rotunda on Capitol Hill to condemn what they call an egregious breach of our national security."

Jack's phone rang a second time. Theo again. *Give it a rest, dude.*

"Speaking for the group," the anchorman continued, "was senior senator from Utah Robert Orville. Here's what he had to say."

The scene shifted to inside the Capitol, where a man stood before a bouquet of microphones, flanked by other men in suits. The clip picked up somewhere in the midst of his impassioned plea:

"We are calling for a special investigative committee to convene immediately," said the senator, "and to invoke all of its powers to get to the bottom of what caused this unspeakable disaster. Security on U.S. oil rigs is tighter than ever since the Deepwater Horizon disaster, making them difficult targets for terrorists. The same cannot be said of the Chinese oil rig in Cuban waters."

A reporter in the galley interrupted. "Senator, are you saying that the Scarborough 8 explosion was the work of terrorists, such as al-Qaeda?"

"Nothing has been brought to my attention that would link this act to any specific terrorist group," he said. "But it's essential that this inquiry consider all possibilities. And I do mean *all*. For example, we do know that certain left-wing elements fully expected that offshore drilling would stop after the Deepwater Horizon. It has continued to grow, both in sensitive areas off the Florida coast and in the Arctic Sea above Alaska."

"Excuse me, Senator," the reporter followed up. "Are you suggesting that the Cuban consortium's oil rig was the target of antidrilling left-wing extremists who are trying to create negative sentiment against offshore oil production?"

He raised his hands, as if to absolve himself. "I'm not making any accusations. Like I said, it's important to consider all possible angles. Thank you very much," he said as he stepped away from the podium.

Jack could hardly believe what he was hearing. Two decades wasn't really that long, but things that passed for reasoned political discussion in modern-day Washington would have been dismissed as lunacy when Jack's father had run for governor. Linton's words echoed in his mind:

This is not about politics. It's about national security.

Jack accessed the Web on his iPhone and instantly put those words to the test. His suspicion was quickly borne out. A search of "Senator Robert Orville" and "Barton-Hammill" pulled up over five hundred hits. A political action committee funded by defense contractor Barton-Hammill was Senator Orville's largest political donor.

Surprise, surprise.

Jack thought about calling his father for some political insights, but he resisted the impulse. Jack had made a promise to himself and to his stepmother after the trip to the emergency room, and he'd assiduously avoided putting any more stress on his old man. He made a quick call to Cassie in New York. She'd seen the same news from the Capitol, and she'd already made the same link between the senator and the defense contractor.

"Remember what I told you," said Cassie. "It has to be shown that it was an act of terrorism if Barton-Hammill is going to be protected from civil lawsuits."

"Senator Orville seems to be pushing toward environmental terrorism. Is that an 'act of terrorism' under the SAFETY Act?"

"Absolutely. Terrorism is not limited to religious radicals, if that's what you're asking."

"So if Barton-Hammill's technology was compromised by environmental terrorists, they would be shielded from liability to the same extent as they would if the terrorists were al-Qaeda or the Taliban, or whoever."

"That's exactly right."

"So environmental terrorism is a twofer," said Jack. "The senator discredits 'left-wing radicals' who oppose offshore drilling, *and* he protects Barton-Hammill, his biggest campaign donor, from any lawsuits."

"Only if we let him get away with it."

Theo rushed into the room, huffing and puffing. It looked as though he'd run all the way back from Rick's Café, and the expression on his face said: *"Urgent!"*

"Dude, why don't you answer your phone?"

Jack put Cassie on hold. "Sorry. I didn't know it was important."

"I just got a call," he said, catching his breath. "We definitely need to go back to Cuba."

"Theo, I told you—"

"No, listen to me!" he said, his expression deadly serious. "The call. It was Josefina."

42
.

New York. The Big Apple could not have been more different from Big Palm Island, but Andie would have taken it as a solid second choice for her honeymoon. If Jack were there.

"Canal Street, please," she told the taxi driver.

The rocky phone conversation with Jack had left a sickening feeling inside her, and it had nothing to do with the pregnancy—or maybe it had everything to do with it. These clashes were inevitable. An undercover FBI agent married to the son of a former governor—a lawyer who'd defended the worst of the worst on death row, didn't trust the government, and couldn't seem to keep his cases out of the media. Some might thrive on the conflict and say, "It must be karma," but Andie didn't. Jack didn't either. She saw no solution. Maybe Jack was banking on the erroneous assumption on his part that Andie would pop out a baby, chuck her career, and become a stay-at-home mom. Sort of the special appendix that appeared only in the man's version of *What to Expect When You're Expecting*.

Not gonna happen.

"Where on Canal Street, lady?"

"Anywhere between Mercer and Broadway is fine."

The driver smiled in the rearview mirror. "Gonna buy a new handbag, I bet. Gucci? Louis Vuitton?"

"Maybe," said Andie.

The driver seemed determined to strike up a conversation. "Just this morning I picked up a woman from California who got herself a Chanel bag for twenty bucks. So she bought another one for her sister. Finally she buys two more for her mother and her girlfriend, and the guy throws in a Hermès scarf for nothing. Incredible deal."

"Yes, it is," said Andie. *Unless you're Chanel, Hermès, or Louis Vuitton.*

Andie had seen the statistics as part of her undercover training. Counterfeit goods accounted for 7 percent of total world trade. Canal Street was like a New York outlet for the uncontested leader in knockoffs, China, which racked up $24 billion in sales annually. In a good year, Andie's counterparts over in Customs seized maybe $250 million in counterfeit goods. Originally, Andie had been led to believe that the goal of the operation was to slow down the counterfeiting pipeline. As it turned out, Operation Black Horizon had only one very specific connection to fake merchandise.

His name was Dawut Noori.

"Here you are, lady," the driver said as they pulled up to the curb. "Eleven-fifty."

Andie dug the cash from her purse—a fake Prada, which was part of an ensemble that included Moss

Lipow sunglasses and a classic Salvatore Ferragamo trench with three-quarter sleeves, all knockoffs. Tethering her to reality, a bottle of prenatal vitamins was right beside her wallet. The mere thought of folic acid used to worsen her morning sickness. Day three with no nausea, and she was counting her blessings.

She thanked the cabbie and got out on Canal Street. Literally, on the street; the sidewalk was too congested. Vendor after vendor displayed counterfeit merchandise on blankets, and hovering tourists were all too eager to buy it.

"Handbags," a man said coolly.

"Rolex, Cartier," said another.

"Heat!" someone shouted. In an instant, the handbags and watches were swallowed up by the blankets. A couple of beat cops from the Fifth Precinct passed, and the peddlers stood by their bundles of concealed merchandise, no sweat. It was just another round of cat and mouse in the NYPD Canal Street initiative, the mice fully aware that no one got busted for mere possession of such small quantities, and that 85 percent of vendors stupid enough to be caught in the act of selling got off on a misdemeanor anyway.

Andie kept walking. Sidewalk hustlers were small players, and she was after bigger fish. On the other side of Broadway, where the lines blurred between Chinatown and Little Italy, she found an electronics store called N.Y.C. Gadets. Legend had it that it was supposed to be "N.Y.C. Gadgets," but the sign maker had misspelled it, and the name stuck.

To call the storefront window a "display" would

have done violence to the term. It was little more than a repository for overflowing inventory, cameras stacked on top of computers on top of cell phones. The clutter continued inside the store, which was packed with electronics, every brand and product imaginable. Shelves were crammed, and narrow aisles were made even narrower by countless boxes of flat-screen televisions lined up on the floor, one after the other. Six months hence, it would have been impossible for a much more pregnant Andie to turn sideways anywhere in the store.

The man behind the counter was on the telephone, yelling so loudly that Andie wondered if he actually needed a phone. He spoke entirely in Chinese, except for the occasional English language reference to "N.Y.C. Gadets," which made the nonsensical name even more absurd. Andie browsed in the camera section until his call ended. She approached and handed him a business card that bore her undercover name.

"I have a six o'clock appointment with Long Wu," she said.

"I get him," he said in a heavy Chinese accent. "One minute. Maybe two. Call it one and one half." *Wuh ahn wuh hoff.* He laughed at his own joke and walked away, taking Andie's card with him.

Andie waited at the counter. A minute later, two young women emerged from the back room with their newly acquired knockoffs wrapped in green plastic garbage bags. They at least had to get out of the store before bragging to the world about trademark infringement. The funny man who liked fractions signaled to her from the rear of the store.

"Come, come," he said.

Andie went, stepping carefully around the clutter of merchandise on the floor, the aisle getting ever narrower toward the back. The man pulled away the curtain and directed her inside. It was the same passageway that the previous buyers had used, but ingress and egress were no longer just a matter of passing through a curtain. Andie wasn't posing as the occasional buyer. She was pretending to purchase in bulk—a mass shipment direct from Guangdong. Precautions were necessary for such transactions. The funny man pulled a secure metal door shut, and Andie heard it lock from the outside.

It was enough to make even a seasoned undercover agent a teeny bit nervous.

The backroom was like a warehouse. The ceiling had been removed, along with the floor above it, so that what had once been a cramped storage area with a separate apartment above was now a single two-story room. Electronics and appliances were nowhere to be found, which explained the overflow of legitimate merchandise—"gadets"—in the storefront window. Floor-to-ceiling pallets were laden with every conceivable form of fake designer clothing, accessories, and other merchandise. It almost made Andie wish that her assignment had something to do with knockoffs.

Stay focused.

A side door opened. An old man entered and locked the door behind him. A younger and much bigger man—more brawn than Theo—was at his side. A trained bodyguard was part of a dealer's "necessary precautions" in bulk transactions.

The old man and his bodyguard walked slowly toward Andie, their footfalls barely making a sound on the concrete floor, then stopped. The old man bowed. The bodyguard didn't acknowledge her in any way. Andie, nonetheless, returned the old man's greeting.

"My apologies for Dawut Noori," the dealer said.

Dawut Noori. The bodyguard's face, more Central Asian than Chinese, had matched that in the photograph in the FBI dossier. Now Andie had a name to go with it. She was standing three feet away from the man who was the central target of Operation Black Horizon.

"Does he speak English?" asked Andie, even though the intelligence report had already told her that he did.

"Yes, yes. But don't take rudeness personal. He very, very angry young man."

"It's okay," said Andie.

"He no bow, he no smile, he no talk to nobody."

"It's really okay," said Andie, casting a quick glance in Noori's direction.

He'll talk. The angry young man will definitely talk to me.

43

Jack called Agent Linton and told him that Theo had spoken to Josefina.

"I want to take Mr. Knight's statement," said Linton.

"I'll meet you at the satellite office at seven o'clock," said Jack. "And bring an assistant U.S. attorney with you—someone who has the wisdom to appreciate the level of cooperation Theo and I have demonstrated and the authority to drop all charges for the alleged violation of the trade embargo. See ya."

Jack hung up before Linton could cry foul. Jack didn't enjoy playing games, but it was the FBI that had made their relationship all about self-interest and negotiation.

"Let's go," he told Theo.

The Key West satellite for the FBI's Miami Division was on Simonton Street, just a short walk from Jack's B&B. Jack and Theo arrived a few minutes early. Linton did not keep them waiting. He escorted them back to a conference room. Jack immediately recognized the government lawyer waiting at the table. Sylvia Gonzalez was not an AUSA. She was from the Justice Department's National Security Division in Washington. Some years earlier, Jack had gone head-to-head with her while representing one of the detainees at Guantánamo Naval Base. There was history between them. Ugly history.

"So we meet again," said Jack.

"I promised that we would," said Gonzalez.

Jack's Gitmo case was both unusual and tragic. His client, a nineteen-year-old American of Somali descent, stood accused of murdering a teenage girl in Miami. His defense was his alibi: Jack's client couldn't possibly have killed the girl because, at the time of the murder, he was en route to Guantánamo, held by the CIA at an undisclosed "black site," and the subject of "heightened interrogation" for suspected terrorist activities. There was just one problem: the U.S. government refused to acknowledge the very existence of the alleged "black site." It had been Gonzalez's job to make sure the CIA kept its secrets, even if it meant depriving Jack's client of an alibi in a capital case.

Round One with Gonzalez had been Jack's introduction to courtroom warfare over matters of "national security."

"What brings you to Key West?" asked Jack.

"I just got here," she said. "I'm presenting the Justice Department's argument to stay your lawsuit until the conclusion of the FBI investigation into sabotage on the Scarborough 8."

"That's the national-security issue I explained to you," said Linton.

"Which is a reach," said Jack, "especially in front of a state court judge in Key West, Florida."

"That's for Judge Carlyle to decide," said Gonzalez.

"When?" asked Jack.

"As soon as we can schedule a hearing. You'll be the first to know. For now, let's talk about Josefina Fuentes. What is Mr. Knight proffering?"

"The number she called from and everything she told him, which may help you identify the man who attacked my client, put Josefina's blood on the mirror, kidnapped me, and claims to know who sabotaged the Scarborough 8."

"You should be eager to share that information with law enforcement."

"Unfortunately, Theo can't share any of it without at least a tacit admission that he traveled to Cuba in violation of the embargo. So we need immunity."

"I'll give it to him," said Gonzalez. "But not you."

Theo jumped in. "Then no deal."

"We'll take it," said Jack.

"No way, Jack."

Jack ignored him and went to his iPhone. "Sylvia, I'm e-mailing you a draft immunity letter right now. It's pretty standard. Take a minute, review it, and send a reply e-mail confirming our deal. Theo and I will be right back."

Jack pulled Theo away from the table and took him into the hallway. Theo spoke before Jack could say a word.

"They want to prosecute both of us," said Theo. "I'm not doing a deal that doesn't include you."

"Don't worry about me. You're a slam-dunk

conviction under the embargo, since you're not of Cuban descent. I am. To convict me of a crime they have to prove I didn't visit relatives. What are they going to do? Track down the whole Cuban side of my family and interview them? They have no case against me. Take the deal and tell them what Josefina said."

Theo considered it, then acquiesced. "All right, if you say so."

"I say so."

Jack's phone chimed with an e-mail alert. Gonzalez confirmed their immunity deal for Theo. Jack and Theo went back into the room and returned to the table. Gonzalez began the questioning with some preliminaries. Theo gave her all the details, including the incoming number. Linton made a quick call to the tech division to get them on it while Gonzalez continued the interview.

"Mr. Knight, how do you know it was actually Josefina who called?"

"I was pretty sure from the sound of her voice, but I still asked, 'How do I know it's you?' She said, ''Cuz it *is* me. Burnt Sugar.'"

"Burnt Sugar?"

"When I was in Cuba I told her that her boxing name should be 'Burnt Sugar.'"

"I like it," said Jack.

Gonzalez continued. "You're saying that only Josefina would remember that conversation?"

"Yeah," said Theo. "It was just the two of us. We went out to buy beer."

Gonzalez nodded, seemingly satisfied. "Tell me all you remember about the call."

"I knew about the blood on Bianca's mirror, so the first thing I asked was if she was okay. She said she was fine."

"Was she attacked?"

"She said she couldn't answer any questions. She was calling to give me a message."

"What's the message?"

Jack intervened. "Think carefully, Theo. Be as precise as you can."

Theo worked through it in his head, then answered. "She said to tell Jack that the exchange will go through her."

Gonzalez looked puzzled. "What does that mean?"

"That's what I asked," said Theo. "She had no idea."

"What else did she say?"

Theo shrugged. "Nothing. She hung up."

Gonzalez shot an angry look at Jack. "I gave Mr. Knight immunity for *that*? How does any of this advance the FBI's sabotage investigation?"

"It's the missing piece," said Jack. "We have a guy who claims to know who sabotaged the Scarborough 8, and he wants to be paid for his information. But he never specified how the money is going to be delivered, or how he is going to tell us what he knows. Now you know: he's using Josefina."

"Are you saying she's working with him?"

"No," said Jack. "He's *using* her. The exchange of money for information is being done through someone he controls."

"How do you know he controls her?"

"I don't mean to tell the FBI how to do its job, but the blood on Bianca's mirror is probably Exhibit A."

The prosecutor and FBI agent huddled on their side of the table, exchanging whispers in private. They seemed to be in agreement on their plan of action.

"Mr. Knight, you're free to go," said Gonzalez. "Mr. Swyteck, it is the government's position that this phone call from Josefina Fuentes underscores the need to put your lawsuit on hold until the FBI completes its criminal investigation into sabotage on the Scarborough 8. Will you agree to that?"

"If you can demonstrate in court that a genuine national security issue is involved, I'll accept the judge's decision to stay Bianca's case. But I won't agree to anything just because you invoke the words *national security*."

Gonzalez tucked her notes into her briefcase. "Then we'll see you in court tomorrow."

Jack rose and shook her hand. "Yes, you will."

44

.

Andie got a hotel room for the night in lower Manhattan. She had authorization to stay in New York another two days. And thanks to her trip to Canal Street, she had enough designer handbags, even if they were fakes, to be named an honorary Kardashian.

A deal with Long Wu for a container shipment of counterfeit goods was a long way from consummated. The next step in the charade was for Andie to send samples of "N.Y.C. Gadets" merchandise back to her people to assess the quality of the knockoffs. But that was all a sideshow to the real goals of Operation Black Horizon. It mattered only that she had made contact with Long Wu's bodyguard, and that another meeting was scheduled for Friday.

Phase I of her assignment—find Dawut Noori—was officially completed. The dossier had identified his last known contacts in eastern Virginia and the D.C. area. The FBI knew he was involved in counterfeits, and that the road would eventually lead to New York, but Andie's work in Virginia had streamlined the search to Long Wu on Canal Street.

At nine p.m., Andie checked in with her handler for Phase II of the assignment.

"Nice work," Agent Wolfe told her.

Wolfe wasn't even his real name. Unlike her handler in Virginia for Phase I, Andie had never met her Phase II handler in New York. It was that kind of operation.

"Intelligence was spot-on about Noori," said Andie. "Even Long Wu says he's an angry young man."

"With good reason," said Wolfe.

"Is that a tease?" asked Andie. "Or have I earned need-to-know status?"

"You've earned it," said Wolfe.

Andie was gathering intelligence piecemeal. She knew from Phase I that Noori was a Uighur, part of the Muslim population in a western region of China known as Xinjiang. Most of his family was from Kashgar, a historic village along the centuries-old Silk Road.

"Noori spent seven years as a detainee in Guantánamo. One of seventeen Uighurs rounded up in Afghanistan in 2002."

"I'm embarrassed," said Andie. "Not a single person I talked to mentioned that."

"Nothing for you to be embarrassed about. It was the CIA who lost track of him. And I wouldn't expect anyone to mention his time at Gitmo. No one knows."

"Psychologically scarred? He just doesn't talk about it?"

"It's more practical than that. The Uighurs were among the first detainees that the federal courts ordered us to release. They couldn't be sent back to China, because of the way the Chinese government has cracked down on the Uighurs. No town in America was waiting with open arms to welcome former enemy combatants, and we had a devil of a time finding a place for them to relocate. When we did manage to place them, it was in their own self-interest not to mention the fact that they were Guantánamo detainees. Some of them have adjusted quite well. Others . . ."

"Are very angry young men," said Andie, "like Noori."

"Angry is an understatement."

"What's next?"

"Pressure on the subject. Beijing has informed the White House that they believe the Scarborough 8 explosion is the work of Uighur terrorists. Noori is chief among them. It's payback for seven years of detention and interrogation."

The news didn't surprise Andie. Even though she was being fed information on a "need to know" basis, her "need to find out" personality had deduced as much.

"Something strikes me as odd about that," said Andie. "Probably a hundred terrorist organizations have tried to bolster their status by claiming to be the brains and the muscle behind the Scarborough 8 disaster."

"All of them bogus, of course."

"Which makes my point," said Andie. "The Uighur militants are not among those taking credit.

Why would any terrorist organization plan and pull off something of this magnitude and not claim responsibility?"

"That's an excellent question."

"Is that your way of saying you don't have an answer?"

"That's my way of saying that it's your job to find out. Welcome to Phase II of Operation Black Horizon, Agent Henning. Call me in twenty-four hours."

Andie put her phone away and sat on the bed, which was covered with handbags from Canal Street. She grabbed one and held it close to her stomach.

"Viola," she said, making her wish aloud. "Mommy has a very hard job, so don't you dare embarrass me."

She closed her eyes and pressed the handbag even tighter against her. "Promise me that this is the closest you ever get to a knockoff Tory Burch."

45
.

Jack was in court on Friday morning. Cassie was at his side, his new co-counsel.

The notice of the emergency hearing had come late Thursday evening. Cassie arrived in Key West before midnight, flown in by private jet on her law firm's dime. At the government's request, the hearing was in Judge Carlyle's chambers, closed to the public. Not even Bianca was allowed to attend, and the client representatives from the oil consortium were likewise excluded. It was strictly "attorneys only." Three different teams of lawyers were seated at a rectangular table that extended forward from the front edge of Judge Carlyle's oversized antique desk. Jack and Cassie were seated on one of the long sides of the table, to the judge's left; Luis Candela and his team were on the other, to the judge's right; and in the middle, directly facing the judge, were Sylvia Gonzalez and another Justice Department lawyer from the National Security Division on behalf of the government. Bianca's wrongful death lawsuit had taken on a whole new look since the

Freddy Foman circus and the sea of lawyers pressing property claims against the oil consortium. Such were the restrictions of "national security."

"So here we all are," said Judge Carlyle, rocking back in her leather chair. "From oil disaster one week, to national security the next. Just another day in the life of a Key West trial judge. I should have listened to my husband. What lawyer in her right mind comes out of retirement to do this?"

Gonzalez spoke first. "Your Honor, the Justice Department would not have proceeded on an emergency basis if it were not truly a matter of national security."

"If it is a matter of national security, why aren't you in federal court in Washington, D.C.?"

"This is not technically a national security motion under the Patriot Act. We are seeking relief under this court's inherent authority to control its own docket."

"Your Honor, if I could translate," said Jack. "The government can't meet the requirements under federal law. Instead, the plan is to shout 'national security' loud enough and often enough to bamboozle a state court judge into making a mistake, knowing that the judge's chambers are so close to the disaster that she can practically smell the oil."

The judge almost smiled. "I'm not sure I agree with everything Mr. Swyteck just said, but it does seem odd. Anyway, I've read the government's papers and understand fully what you are asking me to do. You want Mr. Swyteck's case shut down until the completion of a criminal investigation into possible sabotage. What's less clear to me is the basis for the government's assertion that this implicates national security interests."

"In a nutshell, here's the situation," said Gonzalez. "First, we have an anonymous but credible source who claims that the Scarborough 8 was sabotaged, and he also claims to be able to tell us who did it."

"How do you know he's credible?"

"The computerized security system failed on the rig immediately prior to the explosion. He was able to provide to us in writing the exact sequence of that alarm malfunction."

Jack spoke up. "That's accurate, Your Honor. The sequence was spelled out in a note that he forced me to write."

"Which leads to my second point," said Gonzalez. "Not only is he credible, but he's dangerous. He kidnapped Mr. Swyteck in Havana and forced him to write the note I just described. He attacked Bianca Lopez. He smeared the blood of Josefina Fuentes on a bathroom mirror."

The judge glanced at Jack. "Any disagreement so far, Mr. Swyteck?"

"That's accurate as well," said Jack.

"Third," said Gonzalez. "This dangerous man is now in active negotiation with the government as to how he will furnish his information about the sabotage and how he expects to be paid. Through a phone call last night, it was made clear that the point person in this exchange will be Josefina Fuentes. That name should be familiar to the court, since she is the Cuban woman referenced in the love letters from Rafael Lopez."

The judge leaned back in her chair, thinking. "All very interesting, Ms. Gonzalez. But not every active criminal investigation presents a national security interest."

Gonzalez removed several thin file folders from her briefcase. "Your Honor, I have for the court's consideration an affidavit from Vernon Daniels, Federal Bureau of Investigation. Mr. Daniels is the associate executive assistant director of the FBI's National Security Branch in Washington, D.C., where he oversees the Counterterrorism Division."

"Associate executive assistant—good grief, when there are that many adjectives in a job description, I know you should be in a Washington courtroom."

Bamboozle, thought Jack. *Wake up and smell the oil, Judge.*

"Let's see the affidavit," said the judge.

Gonzalez rose, handed the judge a copy, and shared courtesy copies with the other lawyers. Jack opened the file and flipped through the affidavit quickly. Aside from the introductory paragraphs that set forth the background and qualifications of the witness, the entire substance of the affidavit was blacked out.

"Judge, my copy is completely redacted," said Jack.

"So is mine," said the consortium lawyer.

"As is mine," the judge said. "Ms. Gonzalez, is this some kind of joke?"

"No, Your Honor. As I said, this is a matter of national security and—"

"And what?" the judge said. "The court is supposed to take your word for it? Did you think you were just going to walk into my chambers and have me rubber-stamp your assertion of national security based on an affidavit that I can't even read?"

"Well, Your Honor, we had hoped that—"

"Hope *what*?" the judge said. "That I had a golf game scheduled for nine-thirty and would give you anything you wanted just to get out of here on time? I laughed off Mr. Swyteck's remark about bamboozling the Key West judge, but I'm beginning to think he's exactly right. This is ridiculous."

"I'm sorry, Your Honor."

"You should be. I need an unredacted version of this affidavit, nothing blacked out."

"I will check with the National Security Division, Your Honor. That may be possible."

"*May* be? You'd better make it happen, if the government wants any relief from this court."

"Understood," said Gonzalez. "However, we would request that the full affidavit be for the court's eyes only."

"I object," said Jack. "How can I respond if I can't see the affidavit?"

"Mr. Swyteck has a point," the judge said.

"But that's just not acceptable," she said, which was exactly the *wrong* thing to say.

"*I'll* decide what's unacceptable," Judge Carlyle said. "I want the unredacted affidavit delivered to my chambers no later than noon. To ensure that no national security leaks occur, Mr. Swyteck will review that affidavit in the jury room, and access to that room will be restricted by my bailiff." The judge flashed a phony smile, her tone taking on a bitterly sarcastic edge. "I certainly hope that is acceptable to the National Security Division of the Department of Justice, and to the FBI's associate assistant executive supervisory chief head part-time director of whatever."

"To be honest—" Gonzalez started to say, but the judge shut her down.

"That's my ruling," the judge said, her glare like a laser.

Jack was never one to miss an opportunity to capitalize on the court's ire for opposing counsel. "Judge, we would also request the opportunity to cross-examine the affiant."

"That's absolutely unacceptable," said Gonzalez, repeating her error.

"There you go again," the judge said, chiding her.

Jack pushed. "Your Honor, the government is asking to stay my client's case indefinitely. That is a huge setback. The FBI's criminal investigation could go on for years. Evidence will be lost, witnesses will disappear, and memories will fade. We should have the right to cross-examine the government's one and only witness before the court takes this step."

"But—"

"No 'buts,'" the judge said. "We'll reconvene at four p.m. That should be plenty of time for the government to get its witness here from Washington. We're adjourned."

"Thank you, Judge." Jack pushed away from the table quickly, knowing better than to hang around after a favorable ruling and give the other side a chance to change the judge's mind. In less than thirty seconds he and Cassie were out the door, down the hallway, and waiting at the elevators.

"That was unbelievable," said Cassie.

"Pure luck," said Jack.

The elevator doors parted, and they stepped inside. "Let's hope your luck continues when you cross-examine the associate executive assistant schmuck," said Cassie.

Jack hit the lobby button. The doors had nearly closed when Gonzalez thrust her hand into the gap, forcing the doors to reopen. "Swyteck, I need a word with you."

Jack had seen Gonzalez angry before, but not like this. A crowbar could not have pried her fingers away from the elevator door she was holding. Jack told Cassie he'd catch up with her downstairs, stepped out into the hallway, and let the elevator go.

Gonzalez spoke low so as not to be overheard by anyone, but harshly. "This four o'clock hearing cannot happen."

"It's going to happen," said Jack.

"No," she said, wagging her finger as she spoke. "You are going to notify Judge Carlyle that your client has agreed to stay her case pending the outcome of the FBI investigation."

Jack took a step back from the wagging finger. "This has nothing to do with national security, does it?"

"That's *all* this is about," she said.

"I'm on to you, Sylvia. The more you protest, the more I smell a cover-up. I'm fully aware that the computer technology behind the faulty alarm system on the Scarborough 8 was developed and manufactured by Barton-Hammill. This is about protecting the Pentagon's number-one contractor from civil lawsuits that could tally in the billions. That's not a national security issue."

"You are talking way out of school."

"I'm not agreeing to stay Bianca's case. In fact, Cassie and I have talked about this. We are going to prove sabotage. And after we settle with the oil consortium, we are coming after Barton-Hammill."

"That will be very difficult for you to do when you're behind bars."

"Are you seriously still threatening to prosecute me over a trip to Cuba?"

"It's the law. Up to ten years in prison, two-hundred-fifty-thousand-dollar fine."

"No one has ever been put in jail for traveling to Cuba, and no one has ever been fined anywhere near the maximum."

"There's always a first time. And even if you get off with a small fine, it's still a felony. I'm betting that somewhere along the line you lied to a U.S. official about the purpose of your trip, so tack on additional felony charges under Title Eighteen as well. The Florida Bar may have something to say about a convicted felon practicing law."

"Are you really this desperate?"

"I granted immunity to Mr. Knight, not to you. So back off Barton—" She stopped midsentence, catching her gaffe, then continued. "Do the right thing on the national security issue," she said, correcting herself, "or you will be prosecuted."

"Nice try," said Jack. "But my answer is twofold.

First, any lawyer who would sell out his client to save his own skin should be disbarred. Second," he said as he pushed the call button, "go to hell."

The elevator opened. Jack entered, then turned and faced the government lawyer in the hallway, their eyes locking until the doors closed. Then he rode down to the lobby alone.

46

Andie had a lunch meeting with Long Wu outside of Chinatown. She hadn't specifically asked him to bring Noori, but she knew he would. Some said Long Wu didn't go anywhere without his bodyguard. Andie had a different take: the aging Long Wu was training his handpicked successor to his multimillion-dollar underground business.

"How you like merchandise?" asked Long Wu.

"First rate," said Andie. "All of it."

They were sharing a table near the window at a restaurant called Spice Market in the Meat Packing District in lower Manhattan. The old brick warehouse made for a cavernous dining area, which designers had warmed up with valuable period antiques from Rajastan, South India, Burma, and Malaysia. Raw timber beams were part of the original warehouse, offset by teak floors from a Bombay palace and an ambient color scheme of violet, indigo, ocher, and deep red. Embroidered silk curtains, wood-screen room dividers with elaborate carvings, and pretty young waitresses in traditional

Southeast Asia dress completed the transformation. Andie was seated on a Thai porcelain garden stool on one side of the rosewood tea table. Opposite her, the low-slung Colonial-style sofa with appointed white leather was just the right size for Long Wu, but Noori looked like a grown-up on dollhouse furniture, his knees higher than the tabletop.

"There's just one problem," said Andie.

Long Wu dropped his dumpling. "Problem? What problem?"

The waitress poured more tea for Noori. His hands made the teacup look miniature, too, but the waitress seemed to fancy the oversized young man with the rugged good looks, if her demure smile was any indication. Andie waited until the server left them alone at the table, then continued.

"I have to be very direct with you," said Andie, her gaze fixed on Long Wu. "My people are concerned."

"Why concerned? No need be concerned. Highest-quality goods. Delivery guaranteed. Good price."

"I'm sure all that is true," said Andie. "But you have to understand. The people I represent do not sell knockoffs out of a hovel on Canal Street. My clients are reputable boutiques, and even department stores in some of the most prestigious malls in America."

"Yes, understood. High quantity get you volume price."

"Price is not the issue. It's . . ."

"What?"

Andie's hesitation was no undercover act. She had truly been struggling over the best way to elicit the necessary information, and she wasn't absolutely certain that dropping a bomb on Long Wu and seeing where the dust settled would be the best approach. But she went with it.

"They are concerned about doing business with anyone who may have terrorist connections."

"What?"

The response was from Long Wu, but Andie was gauging Noori's reaction. She pressed the point. "Noori? Any idea what I'm talking about?"

His face reddened, but not with embarrassment. Noori's hand wrapped around the teacup so tightly that Andie thought he might crush it.

Long Wu answered for him. "Noori is not terrorist."

"It is our practice to investigate new suppliers very thoroughly," said Andie. "We know that Noori was a detainee at Guantánamo."

"I know, too," said Long Wu. "Also know he not terrorist."

"That's good for you. But how can you give me the same level of comfort?"

"I'll tell you how," said Noori. "You learn the facts."

He speaks. And with conviction. "Okay," said Andie. "Tell me the facts."

"I am a Uighur. Do you know anything about Uighurs?"

"I know they are Chinese Muslims."

"We are Central Asian. Twenty million Uighurs live in western Xinjiang province of China, but we are Turkic-speaking. My name, Dawut Noori, is not Chinese. I understand almost nothing Long Wu says, unless he speaks English. He speaks Cantonese, like most Han Chinese from Guangdong. In China, Long Wu and I would not be friends."

Long Wu smiled. "It work well for me here. People hear I have Uighur bodyguard from Gitmo, they no mess. Even Chinese Mafia scared."

"So you use the Uighur connection to your advantage," said Andie.

"Prejudice makes it easy to do that," said Noori. "This may be a surprise to you and most Americans, but not all Uighurs are terrorists."

"Not all Uighurs have spent time at Gitmo."

"Okay, but let me tell you how *I* ended up there. When the planes crashed into the World Trade Center, I was eighteen years old and living in Xinjiang. Right after those attacks, the Chinese government cracked down big time on the Uighurs. They said me, my brother, all the young men at our mosque were affiliated with al-Qaeda. None of it true."

"Why would they say it?" asked Andie.

"For decades Uighurs have wanted freedom and independence from China. To get it, we need support from the whole world. The Chinese government is not stupid. They know no one in the world will support Uighurs who share a border with Afghanistan and support al-Qaeda."

"So you're saying they made false accusations to discredit your movement," said Andie.

"More than accusations. They arrested me and three of my friends."

"For what?"

"For *nothing*. They put us in the back of a truck

with about a dozen other men. For the next twenty hours, we ride blindfolded. Finally, the truck stops. The soldiers order us out at gunpoint. We are in the middle of the Afghan desert. I think we are going to be executed. But no. They give us guns. No ammunition, just guns. And the truck drives away."

"What did you do?"

"We start walking. I don't know anyone except my friends, but I do know that two of the men in our group are not Uighurs. We walk all day. Finally, we stop to sleep. American troops wake us up."

"They think you're al-Qaeda?"

"Yes. Because the two men who are not Uighurs—they *are* al-Qaeda. And when we go back to the American interrogation camp, they tell the Americans we are *all* al-Qaeda. I guess you will tell anything if you are waterboarded."

"From there, I presume, you were sent to Guantánamo."

"Where I stayed for the next seven years," said Noori.

Andie studied his expression. If Noori's story wasn't true, he had been telling it to himself for so long—night after night in detention, perhaps—that he had come to believe it himself. It was that convincing.

"Finally, a judge in Washington ordered us released. All the Uighurs. Problem was, sending us back to China would have been a death sentence. Some of us were allowed to stay in the U.S. In Virginia."

Where my assignment started.

Long Wu joined in. "This is what Chinese government do. Disgrace Uighurs. Turn world against Noori. Like Scarborough 8."

Andie tried not to seem too interested, but her heart was pounding with excitement. "The oil spill?" asked Andie. "What do the Uighurs have to do with Scarborough 8?"

"Nothing," said Noori. "But the rig is Chinese. So of course the Chinese government will blame Uighur militants for blowing it up. Make the world hate Uighurs so they can continue the oppression."

Andie paused. The Chinese government was in fact making that very accusation, at least according to her contacts in Operation Black Horizon. But she had to tread carefully.

"I have not heard that," said Andie.

"You will," said Noori. "I get information from family and friends in Xinjiang. They say the Chinese government is working very hard to convince the Americans that it was the Uighurs. It's more convincing if the Americans make the accusation. The Chinese government is suckering the White House again, same as it did when it got the U.S. to ship me off to Guantánamo."

Long Wu put down his chopsticks. "Okay. We way off track. Back to business. You smart woman. You tell your people Noori not terrorist. Is all B.S. We talk again tomorrow. Deal?"

Andie drew a breath, struggling to process the information and remain in role. She would indeed tell her people.

"Okay," she said. "Deal."

47
.

At four p.m. Jack and Cassie were back in court. The Justice Department lawyers were at the mahogany table to Jack's left, closer to the empty jury box. Lawyers for the oil consortium filled the first row of public seating, essentially spectators—in fact, the *only* spectators. In a city that was gripped by an ongoing oil disaster, Judge Carlyle's court-room was eerily quiet, closed to the media and the public.

Judge Carlyle adjusted the gooseneck micro-phone, her voice reverberating in the empty court-room. "The noon deadline to deliver an unredacted version of the affidavit has come and gone. My clerk advises that the government failed to produce one. Is that correct?"

Jack rose. "Your Honor, we didn't get one either. It's our position that the government's request to stay our case should be denied for lack of evidence."

"Let's hear from the government first," said the judge.

Jack yielded, and Gonzalez went to the podium.

"First, I apologize to the court," she said. "Try as we did, the witness was unfortunately unavailable. However, we have a new witness who is prepared to testify. Dr. Richard Cooper. He is the executive vice president and director of research and development for Barton-Hammill Companies."

"Judge, I object," said Jack.

"On what grounds?"

"First off, I don't know how hard the government actually tried to bring in the witness from the FBI's National Security Branch, so I'm not going to comment on that."

"You just did."

Busted. "That aside, what I'm sensing here is the ol' switcheroo. Ms. Gonzalez is afraid that if she brings in a witness from the FBI, this court might compel that witness to answer questions that the FBI would rather not have answered. So the last-minute substitution is a Barton-Hammill employee, a private citizen who is suddenly the government's star witness on national security."

"I understand your point. Objection overruled. Ms. Gonzalez, proceed."

"Thank you," said Gonzalez. "But first, there are so many reasons to grant the government this protection. National security is a broad concept that includes environmental security, economic security, and—"

"Ms. Gonzalez, call your witness."

"The United States of America calls Dr. Richard Cooper."

The deputy unlocked the doors in the back of the closed courtroom and brought Dr. Cooper down the center aisle. Cooper was a man of impressive physical stature who beamed with confidence as he swore the familiar oath and took a seat. Jack had seen many men shrink in a witness stand. Cooper wasn't one of them.

"Good afternoon, Doctor," said Gonzalez. "Could you please introduce yourself?"

Jack listened and took a few notes over the next few minutes, as Gonzalez elicited Cooper's impressive credentials. Military service in the Gulf War. Ph.D. from Cal-Poly in computer engineering. Assistant director, Defense Advanced Research Projects Agency at the Department of Defense. And on it went. More telling than his résumé, however, was his demeanor. He looked entirely comfortable as a witness, conveying the distinct impression that this was not his first courtroom proceeding involving issues of national security. He radiated a certain vibe, and it wouldn't have surprised Jack in the least to hear that Cooper made most of his "business" phone calls using top military-level cell-encryption methods.

"Dr. Cooper, are you familiar with the computerized alarm system on the Scarborough 8?"

"Yes, I am. The technology behind the system was developed by a multidisciplinary team at Barton-Hammill. At the time, I was the head of that team."

"Broadly speaking, what was the function of that alarm system?"

"The goal of any such alarm system is to prevent an oil disaster. Ours was a state-of-the-art system designed to monitor every critical function on the rig. Most pertinent to the issues before this court today, it was designed to be highly resistant to un-authorized misuse and manipulation."

"Such as computer hacking by terrorists?"

"That would be one form of unauthorized use and manipulation."

Gonzalez turned the page in her outline and continued. "Now, it is my understanding that Barton-Hammill is a U.S. corporation. How did an-titerrorism technology from a U.S. corporation end up in a Chinese rig operating in Cuban waters?"

Cooper looked up at the judge, as if to convey the importance of his answer. "A request to share that technology came to Barton-Hammill—to me, specifically—from the National Security Branch of the FBI."

"What was the basis for that request?"

"As I stated earlier, the goal of the alarm system is to prevent an oil disaster. It was in everyone's best interest for state-of-the-art technology to be on a rig that was engaged in ultradeep-water drilling just sixty miles away from the United States."

"Dr. Cooper, as we all know, there is a trade em-bargo against Cuba. Did that present any kind of obstacle to the use of your technology on the Scar-borough 8?"

"It did indeed. Barton-Hammill had to file a re-quest with the Department of the Treasury for an exemption to the embargo. As the leader of the team that invented the technology, I signed that request."

"What was the basis for that requested exemption?"

"National security," he said. "Specifically, envi-ronmental security."

"Thank you, Doctor. No further questions."

Gonzalez stepped away from the podium, looking quite smug as she returned to her seat.

The judge's gaze swept the courtroom and came to rest on Jack. "Any cross-examination, Mr. Swyteck?"

Jack rose, puzzled. *Is that it?* He glanced at his co-counsel, but Cassie seemed equally underwhelmed by Cooper's testimony. She cupped her hand to her mouth and whispered a word that Jack never used, but he totally took her meaning.

"Lame-ola."

"Judge, I'll be brief," said Jack. He moved into position, standing directly in front of the witness, and began.

"Dr. Cooper, just so we're clear: the threat to our national security that you identified is an oil spill from the Scarborough 8."

"That's correct."

"You are aware that the Scarborough 8 is now on the ocean floor in the Cuban Basin, aren't you?"

"I am indeed."

"Oil from the Scarborough 8 spill has washed up in the Florida Keys as high as Marathon. You know that, right?"

"Yes. It may extend even higher by now."

"And while some members of the Conch Republic may dispute the point, the Florida Keys are within the territorial borders of the United States and share the same national security interests."

"Objection," said Gonzalez.

"I'll rephrase," said Jack. "Dr. Cooper, would it be fair to say that the only national security interest you've identified is one that has already been breached?"

"Technically speaking, yes."

"I don't mean to be pedantic, but, 'technically speaking,' a court order that shuts down my client's wrongful death lawsuit against the oil consortium isn't going to undo that breach, is it?"

"Objection," said Gonzalez.

"Sustained," said the judge. "I think your point is made, Mr. Swyteck."

"I think so, too, Your Honor. That's all I have."

It made Jack a little uncomfortable to cut short his cross-examination, but he saw no need for more. Gonzalez requested no redirect, so the judge excused the witness, and the courtroom fell silent as the deputy escorted him down the aisle and out the door.

Jack returned to his seat beside Cassie and whispered, "Am I missing something?"

"No," she whispered back. "Slam dunk."

The judge jotted down a few notes, then looked up.

"I'm prepared to rule," she said. "Ms. Gonzalez, many of my reservations have already been stated. I don't like lawyers who expect me to be pro-government just because I was once a prosecutor. I don't like lawyers who submit affidavits with more holes than Swiss cheese. I don't like lawyers who miss deadlines and switch witnesses without the court's permission."

Cassie whispered, "I think she's going to hold Gonzalez in contempt."

"Mr. Swyteck, I understand your point that the threat posed by the Scarborough 8 has already come to pass. But it's the job of our government to find out whether this disastrous oil spill was caused by an act of terrorism. It stands to reason that any such investigation must focus on whether this was an isolated act, or if further acts of environmental terrorism threaten our national security."

"Judge, this witness has provided no evidence as to the nature of the investigation, the scope of the investigation, or the target of the investigation."

"I think it's fairly implied. The government's motion is granted. Ms. Lopez's wrongful death action filed in this court against the defendants named in this lawsuit is stayed until the completion of the FBI's criminal investigation into possible sabotage on the Scarborough 8."

It ended with a crack of the gavel, and the judge hurried toward the side exit to her chambers.

"All rise!"

Jack tried to show no reaction, nothing to give Gonzalez the satisfaction. Cassie whispered, but she was almost breathless. "This was fixed."

"Quiet," said Jack.

"I mean it," she whispered, but with urgency. "Between nine a.m. and four p.m. somebody got to that judge."

"Later," he said beneath his breath.

The heavy side door closed with a thud, and the judge disappeared into her chambers. Gonzalez immediately crossed the courtroom to Jack's table for a parting shot.

"Justice prevails," she said.

"It isn't over," said Jack.

"You're right. But rest easy. I won't be asking a

grand jury to indict you for violation of the embargo." She paused, then added, "This week."

Gonzalez turned and headed for the exit.

"What an obnoxious bitch," said Cassie, but it was only for Jack's ears.

"Let it go," said Jack. He packed up his computer, grabbed his trial bag, and headed for the exit. Cassie was all but latched onto his arm in pit bull fashion.

"How can you say, 'Let it go'?"

"Judge Carlyle just did us a huge favor," said Jack. He pushed the double doors and stepped into the hallway, still walking.

"What are you talking about? Our client just got screwed."

"Far from it," said Jack.

"You're in denial. This judge was bought off. She'll be driving around Key West in a new Mercedes before Thanksgiving."

Cassie stopped short, a moment of panic triggered by the car allusion and the mere implication of an expensive lease. "Shit, I need to call Hunter at the real estate agency and cancel that office lease before the landlord signs it." She dug her phone from her purse and found an alcove by the window where she could get reception. Jack waited by the drinking fountain in the hallway.

"Swyteck, you got a minute?"

It was Luis Candela, lead counsel for the oil consortium. Jack said, "You were unusually quiet in the courtroom, Luis."

"I was in listening mode. I hope you were, too. Hope you listened really well to what the judge was telling you."

"I did," said Jack. "I heard her say that the case against the oil consortium can't move forward in Key West, Florida. I didn't hear her say anything about a case against a certain other defendant in another forum."

"You heard right," said Candela. "Bianca is your client, but if she were mine, I'd take a cue from the judge. I'd tell Bianca that there are dozens of multinational and jurisdictional reasons why the claims against the oil consortium will fail, that the U.S. laws that left BP on the hook for Deepwater Horizon don't apply here. I'd tell her that even if you win, it'll be ten years before you collect a judgment—*if* you collect at all. I'd tell her that unless she wants to go down in flames like Freddy Foman and his gang of plaintiff lawyers, she would do well to file a new lawsuit against Barton-Hammill in federal court."

It was exactly the cue Jack had taken. "Appreciate that insight, Luis. Just a little puzzled as to why you're sharing it with me."

"From day one, my law firm has been working every conceivable connection at the Justice Department, trying to convince them to shut down all civil lawsuits pending a criminal investigation into possible terrorist activity. I got nowhere. But the minute Barton-Hammill entered the picture as the manufacturer of the alarm system, the National Security Division sent in the wolves to tear your case apart. Why do you think that is, Jack?"

"I have my theories."

"As do I. So to answer your question, why am I sharing this with you? Because deep down, I believe in fairness."

"Really? Fairness?"

Candela smiled thinly as he started away, then stopped. "Oh, and there is one other reason," he said, his expression turning very serious. "Because Barton-Hammill is the only company at fault here. But you don't have to take that from me. Follow Judge Carlyle's lead."

Jack watched one very contented lawyer for the oil consortium walk away. It was still possible that Jack was right, that Judge Carlyle had reached out and done his client a favor by pushing her case into federal court, no impropriety about it. But Cassie's view was gaining traction in Jack's mind, seemingly affirmed by Candela's gratuitous insight. Someone *had* lined the judge's pockets and bought himself a favor—someone named Barton-Hammill.

48
·

Friday night in Havana. Mojitos poured from icy glass pitchers garnished with mint leaves. Latin rhythms pulsed from the shops and cafés on Calle Obispo in Habana Vieja. Josefina was in her usual place: La Escuela de Boxeo.

Boxing was her life's passion. Training was her discipline. For five years, she'd kept her eye on the prize. Most men had told her that she was wasting her time, that Cuba's refusal to send a women's boxing team to the London Olympics in 2012 confirmed that *el boxeo* would remain a "man's sport" in her country as long as an old man was president. Josefina had bet against the naysayers. She'd earned the trust of a trainer. Not just any trainer, but El Sicario, a boxing legend. She'd worked through injuries. She'd dragged herself out of bed and come into the gym with fever. She'd forced herself into the ring for "just one more round" when she was too tired to wipe her own blood from her nose. She had never missed a practice.

Until the attack.

"That's it, that's it, that's it!" Sicario shouted. *Eso es!*

Josefina was hammering away at the hundred-pound punching bag, blurry left-right combinations that would send all but world-class opponents to the canvas. Her trainer held the hanging leather bag in place, absorbing enough of the blows to make Josefina feel the resistance she would get from top competition. Sweat poured down her face. Down her neck. Her back. She felt the salty sting of her own perspiration in the wound between her shoulder blades. It was an inch-long vertical incision. Where the knife had cut her.

Ignore it.

She kept punching, fighting through the fatigue.

"Keep your left up!" shouted Sicario.

Josefina tried to focus, but the cut was on her mind, the sting too much of a reminder of the tip of that blade. Ironically, there had been no need for a knife. Maybe her attackers had brought a weapon for their own protection, in case something went wrong, but it was completely unnecessary as an instrument of control. They already controlled her. Very few people could physically overpower her, but anyone who knew the truth about her and Rafael had the power to control her absolutely.

"Again, again!"

What she'd told Jack Swyteck at Heladería Coppelia was completely true. Rafael could never have been accepted to study engineering at the university, and he could never have landed a coveted job on the Scarborough 8—not with a wife who had defected to Florida. A new fiancé named Josefina gave the Cuban government a false assurance that

Rafael would not become part of the "brain drain," yet another young professional who got education and training at the expense of the Cuban people and then bolted to greener pastures. Her fear, however, was not that someone like Swyteck would expose her complicity. *Anyone* who turned against her, who betrayed the trust of friendship and threatened to turn her in to the Cuban authorities, had Josefina Fuentes in the palm of his hand. She had no choice but to obey.

And it was killing her.

"Good. Two hundred sit-ups," said Sicario. "Gloves on, quick combination on each up count."

Josefina dropped to the mat on the floor, silently counting off the stomach crunches, but she soon lost track. Memories were always a distraction, and bad memories were the worst.

There had been two attackers. Only one had done the talking. Josefina had followed the directions to the letter. Don't call Swyteck, since his phone might be tapped. Call his friend Theo. Tell him that the exchange was going through you, with instructions to follow. Josefina knew that the chances of a happy ending were not good, but she saw no way out.

"We're done," said Sicario, as he untied the laces on her gloves. "Good work. Shower."

He left her alone, and Josefina took a seat on the bench. She pulled off her gloves and bent over to unlace her shoes. She loosened the left one and was starting on the right when she froze. Another pair of feet had come into view, and she recognized the shoes. Her old friend Vivien owned only two pairs.

Old friend.

Josefina straightened up but remained on the bench, her back resting against the wall. Vivien sat beside her.

"It's time to make another phone call," said Vivien.

Josefina said nothing. Acquiescence. No choice but to obey.

"Don't be angry," said Vivien. "This is going to make us all rich."

"I don't want to be rich," said Josefina.

"Fine," said Vivien. "Then just do as you're told, and don't make trouble. Be a good Burnt Sugar."

49

Key West was raving mad—even more than usual. Jack and Theo ran straight into the frenzy at the north end of Duval Street.

More than a week had passed since Jack's last visit to Mallory Square. In the immediate aftermath of the Scarborough 8 explosion, Key West's most famous wharf had turned into media central for "spill watch." Much of the media had drifted up to the middle Keys, along with the most damaging effects of the oil spill. The traditional carnival-like atmosphere at sunset, however, had yet to return. Although the people had retaken Mallory Square, they didn't feel like singing, juggling, or painting their kids' faces. They were pissed, and they wanted the world to know it. The wharf was jammed with angry protestors, and the overflow had clogged Duval Street all the way back to Rick's Café. Some carried sandwich boards, while others painted their messages right onto their half-naked bodies. Theo got caught up in the mood, and before Jack knew it, he was leading a chorus of drunks, thrusting his fist into the air, and shouting nonsense.

"*B-P must pay! B-P must pay! B-P must—*"

Jack pulled him away. "Theo, what the hell does BP have to do with this?"

"Nothing."

"Then why are you shouting that?"

"What am I supposed to shout, *Cubapetróleo y Petróleos de Venezuela* must pay? No wonder you don't get rap, dude."

Jack kept walking, pushing farther into the crowd. The handful of protestors that had first appeared outside the Truman Annex a week earlier had grown into a veritable Keys rebellion. The television media had left behind scaffolding and elevated camera platforms, which organizers (in the loosest sense of the word) had transformed into a makeshift stage for activists to make their plea. A handheld microphone passed from one speaker to the next, open to anyone with a grievance. An impromptu moderator stepped forward to limit each speaker to a few minutes, tops. One man read a poem he had written about the reefs back in middle school and cried. Another found countless ways to inject the f-bomb into a single rambling sentence.

I'm effing tired of this effing oil effing up our effing island and our effing government doing not an effing thing to effing . . .

The loudest applause was for a seventy-five-year-old woman who gripped the microphone tightly with both hands and said nothing. For a solid thirty seconds, she let out one long, primal scream.

Jack was about to move on, but the moderator

caught his attention with the announcement of a "special guest" who was "one of the world's leading authorities on climate change."

"Climate change?" asked Jack.

The moderator continued with the buildup, heaping one accolade after another on "a courageous man" who had come "all the way from Los Angeles in a show of solidarity to launch an appropriate response to irresponsible congressional leaders who have cast reckless accusations against so-called environmental terrorists for the Scarborough 8 disaster."

A chorus of boos came from the crowd, not for the speaker, but for the congressional leaders. In truth, Jack had been so focused on the national security hearing that he'd lost track of the accusations led by the senator from Utah—the ones that shifted the blame from Barton-Hammill to left-wing radicals who opposed offshore drilling. Jack watched with interest as the microphone passed to the speaker from Los Angeles—"Please welcome Dr. Allen Crenshaw"—whom the crowd received with enthusiastic applause.

"Thank you, thank you," said the gray-haired and ponytailed Dr. Crenshaw. "We have many folks with something to say, so let me get right to the heart of the matter.

"Ever since the discovery of huge oil reserves in Cuban waters, U.S. oil companies have been pushing the U.S. government to lift the trade embargo against Cuba so they could have one more way to line their pockets and profit from offshore drilling at the expense of the environment. Now, Big

Oil is not stupid. They have pushed this agenda secretly, behind the scenes. They know that Cuban-American groups would boycott their brands if Big Oil came out publicly against the embargo against Cuba. Am I right, Victor?"

Jack did a double take—*Victor?*—as his gaze shifted to stage right. Victor Garcia-Peña, ultraconservative from Florida, was in the wings, smiling at the environmentalist from southern California.

The speaker continued. "The White House refused to change its policy toward Cuba. Chinese, Venezuelan, and Russian companies moved in. So Big Oil upped the pressure on the White House. They warned the U.S. that foreign oil consortiums aren't safe. The only safe solution, Big Oil said, was to end the embargo and allow U.S. companies to drill. Now there's an oxymoron for you: 'safe offshore drilling.'"

That drew scattered laughter and applause from the crowd.

"Let me wrap this up," the speaker said. "When I heard the senator from Utah blame environmentalists for the explosion of the Scarborough 8, one thought came to my mind. Big Oil didn't get invited to the dance. To get into the dance, Big Oil warned us that drilling by anyone else but U.S. companies would mean environmental catastrophe. Now look around us. Could it be that Big Oil made its own warnings come true?"

The crowd erupted. Jack cringed.

Theo was into it. *"B-P must—"*

Jack ended Theo's renewed chant with an elbow to his solar plexus.

The speaker's voice rose, channeling the crowd's energy. "Let me assure you, Key West: there will be justice! My friend, Victor—come on out here, Victor. My friend Victor Garcia-Peña and I will be bringing Big Oil to justice!"

Center stage, the two men laced their fingers together in unity, and Jack could hardly believe his eyes as Victor and his newfound friend on the left raised their arms triumphantly. The crowd cheered even louder. Jack was feeling nauseous. He started walking toward Duval Street. Theo was right behind him, slapping high fives with strangers in the crowd, leading a new chant.

"Big-O must go! Big-O must go!"

Jack turned around sharply, glaring at Theo. "Shut up!"

"You shut up."

"Shut up and stop acting like an idiot!"

Jack walked away. Theo followed him through the crowd.

"What the hell's the matter with you?"

Jack kept walking until they were beyond the crowd's rough perimeter.

"I'll tell you exactly what's the matter with me, Theo. My client is way too young to be a widow and has to live the rest of her life knowing that her husband was incinerated on that rig. Today I had to tell her that her case against the consortium can't move forward. Judge Carlyle may think she's doing us a favor by pushing us into federal court, but it won't be a picnic filing a new lawsuit against the biggest defense contractor the Pentagon has ever known—who, by the way, has the U.S. Justice Department on its side. It's going to be one national security roadblock after another. I don't know if I'm ever going to recover a dime for her. And now, you watch what happens: Monday morning, Victor Garcia-Peña and Johnny Greenpeace, or whatever his name is, will file a hundred-million-dollar lawsuit against Big Oil. Freddy Foman and his band of thieves will probably join with them. And that bullshit lawsuit will probably get to trial before Bianca gets another day in court. *That's* what's the matter with me."

Jack turned and started down Duval Street. Theo caught up at the corner.

"Jack, dude. I'm sorry, man."

Jack kept walking. "It's okay. Not your fault."

Theo's phone rang. He checked the number, grabbed Jack by the shoulder and yanked him to a halt. "Dude, it says 'out of area.'"

"So do a lot of calls."

"Including the last one I got from Josefina in Cuba," said Theo.

The ringing continued. Jack grabbed his own phone and opened a "record" app. "Put it on speaker so I can listen and record it."

Theo did so, then answered, trusting his instincts about the caller's identity. "Josefina?"

"*Sí*. I need to be quick, so just listen. Tell Jack that the first piece is free. New Providence Bank and Trust Company, 200 Marlborough Street, Nassau, Bahamas. Ask for Mr. Jeffries. Jack is authorized to access safe-deposit box A-36. All he needs is a passport. Keep the FBI out of this."

The line clicked. Josefina was gone.

"Did you get it?" asked Theo.

"Yeah."

"First piece is free," said Theo. "First piece of what?"

"The answer to the ten-million-dollar question," said Jack. "Who blew up the Scarborough 8?"

50

At seven o'clock Andie was off to meet her new boyfriend on Second Avenue. She probably would never tell Jack, but if ever she had to, it was better than an undercover husband.

The Black Horizon team had been pleased with Andie's report on "N.Y.C. Gadets," save for one detail. An undercover agent locked inside a storage room with Long Wu was one thing. Locked up with a target as dangerous as Noori was quite another. It was decided that, going forward, she shouldn't work alone. Enter the boyfriend/business partner.

Hope my new beau likes pregnant women.

Andie was walking across the East Village to the designated meeting spot at Astor Place. She cut over on Ninth Street and immediately saw why this nineteenth-century immigrant neighborhood had become a mecca for artists, musicians, students, and writers. More recent gentrification had priced many of the free spirits out of the market, but it was hard not to feel the draw of the new cafés, bars, and boutiques. One shop, in particular, caught her eye. Dinosaur Hill.

Girlfriends had warned her not to venture into the baby stores until the third month, that anything could happen early in a pregnancy, and that it was wise to be patient and not open the door to added heartbreak. But there she was, a mother-to-be, with thoughts of Operation Black Horizon and fossilized dinosaurs—petroleum—almost perpetually on her mind. How could she not go inside? The woman who greeted her at the door was part artist, part salesperson, and eager to help.

"Looking for anything in particular?" she asked.

"Something for my baby," said Andie. "I'm planning ahead."

The saleswoman pointed out enough handmade wonderments and toys to make Andie think about having more than one child—colorful blocks, hand puppets from Burma, kaleidoscopes, marionettes from around the world, stained-glass fairies, wooden dollhouses. It was fun, but out of nowhere Andie needed to run to the bathroom. The saleswoman pointed her to the back of the store. Andie was back shortly.

"False alarm," said Andie.

"How far along are you?"

She turned sideways and pulled back her coat. "Seven weeks. Can you tell?"

"Not yet. But get used to the bathroom urges."

Andie browsed and ended up buying a fluffy pink rabbit, which came with a verbal assurance that she could bring it back for a blue one if baby Viola turned out to be a Victor. She tucked it into her fake designer handbag and walked another two blocks. New boyfriend Dennis was waiting at the subway entrance on the corner.

"You're late," he said.

"Which you're not allowed to point out, since we're dating this time, not married."

He smiled, as did Andie. Dennis was actually Special Agent Michael Brunelli of the New York field office, and the last time they'd worked together was during the Wall Street meltdown. They'd posed as husband and wife, a joint mission to prove that "too big to fail" didn't mean "too big to jail." It had been Andie's job to tap the most lucrative sources of information about banking fraud: the wives and girlfriends of investment bankers.

"You hungry?" asked Andie. "There's a Ukrainian restaurant on Second Avenue I've been wanting to try."

"*Ukrainian?*" he said, making a face. "Damn. They told me I had to let you eat whatever you wanted to eat, but this may require combat pay."

Andie led the way, their small talk a comfortable continuation of the banter that had carried them through the Wall Street investigation, which had dragged on for weeks. His undercover experience was extensive, mostly organized-crime investigations, and Andie actually enjoyed listening to his stories. And if his principal role in Operation Black Horizon was to match up, muscle for muscle, against Noori, the Bureau couldn't have made a better choice.

"I read your Spice Market report," he said. "Most of it made sense."

"Most of it?"

He picked up their pace, gaining some separation from the group of college students behind them.

"Are you actually buying the idea that the Chinese government blew up its own rig?"

It was Andie's job to test the FBI's theory that Uighur militants were behind the Scarborough 8 disaster. After hearing Noori's story of how he'd gotten from Xinjiang to Afghanistan to Guantánamo, she'd thought his accusations against the Chinese government were worth mentioning in her report.

"It's at least plausible that the Chinese government is making the Uighurs their scapegoat in order to turn world opinion against them."

"No way. Not possible."

"Eye-roll alert," said Andie. "You know I can't take any man seriously who states his opinions as if they were fact. *No way. Not possible.*"

"Fair enough. This is somewhere between fact and opinion. It's politics. The politics of petroleum."

"What does that mean, exactly?"

He seemed glad that she'd asked. "Who do you think is the world's biggest consumer of Iranian oil?"

"We're bringing Iran into this?"

"Just answer the question."

"I'll go out on a limb and say China."

"Correct-o," he said. "And with the United States calling for economic sanctions against Iran, how do you think the White House feels about China buying up all that Iranian oil?"

"Wild guess on my part, but I'll say they'd like to see it dry up."

"Correct-o, again. So here's the deal. China— you reduce your consumption of Iranian oil. And if you do, look at what you get in return: all the oil you want from the Cuban basin, with no competition from U.S. oil companies."

They stopped at the red light. A cyclist zoomed past them, making Andie glad she'd heeded the red light. "You're saying that the White House keeps up the trade embargo against Cuba as part of a deal with the Chinese?"

"That's what I'm saying."

"What proof do you have of that?"

"None whatsoever. But how else do you explain the continuation of a fifty-year-old embargo that is a proven failure while the Chinese poke around for oil in our backyard?"

Andie had heard crazier things since the explosion of the Scarborough 8.

The traffic light changed, and they crossed at a tree-lined stretch of Second Avenue near Stuyvesant Square. The wind picked up as they turned north, and Andie noticed a hint of autumn color in the rustling leaves. "Can we be completely serious for a second?" she asked.

"Sure."

"If Uighur militants did this, why haven't they claimed responsibility? This was so spectacular that practically every terrorist organization on the planet has tried to pin its name on it."

"Maybe they don't want to turn public opinion against themselves."

"If that's the case, it makes no sense to blow up the rig at all. The Uighurs want independence from China. How does blowing up the Scarborough 8 advance their cause?"

"Maybe we need a better understanding of what their cause is."

Andie stopped. Her partner took several more steps before realizing that he was walking without her. He circled back.

"What did I say?" he asked.

Andie's thoughts were still jelling. "You had the same reaction I did: we need to understand the Uighurs' cause better. But hearing you say it made my mind work in the opposite direction."

"Gee, thanks. Nice to know that the chemistry we established on Wall Street is still alive and well."

"Stay with me," said Andie. "I think the explosion of the Scarborough 8 had nothing to do with the cause of Uighur militants, their desire for independence, or their grievances with the Chinese government."

"Then why did they do it?"

Andie recalled the look in Noori's eye as he told of being captured in the Afghan desert, flown to Gitmo, and held without evidence for seven years. "This wasn't a terrorist act against a Chinese oil rig by a group of militants."

"Then what was it?"

"It was one man's personal act of retaliation and revenge against the United States for seven years of detention as an enemy combatant."

Andie's partner was silent. She resumed their walk, moving quickly against the chilly breeze, but she got less than half a block before stopping short.

"Another brainstorm?" he asked.

"No," said Andie. "Something far more urgent."

"What?"

"I need a bathroom."

51

Jack and Theo reached Nassau by mid-morning. Two seats on a Friday-night flight out of Key West were impossible to snag at the last minute, even without an oil spill, but Bianca's boss had managed to get them out by boat. Plenty of wealthy yacht owners had relied on optimistic projections that the Gulf Stream would carry the spill away from the Keys, or that most of the oil would evaporate before making landfall. The procrastinators were now paying top dollar to get their boats out of the impact area. Bianca stayed behind to run the café. Jack and Theo played first mate to Rick on the overnight delivery of a seventy-foot Johnson, which around two a.m. became prime fodder for the worst of Theo's bartender jokes. "Hey, Swyteck, how do I make my Johnson seventy feet long? Fold it in half." *Ahr, ahr, ahr.* Anything to stay awake as they cut through the waves in the blackest of nights.

At a cruising speed of twenty-two knots, it was about a twelve-hour trip to Nassau. Jack and Theo split the last eight hours into four-hour shifts, so they were reasonably rested and ready to go upon docking. Rick, the all-night captain, stayed on the boat to sleep.

A Bahamian immigration officer cleared them at the marina.

"Purpose of your visit, gentlemen?" he asked.

Jack paused. *To find out who blew up the Scarborough 8?* "A little business, a little pleasure," Jack said.

"Enjoy your stay."

The final leg of the journey was a ten-minute cab ride to the north end of the island. The driver dropped them on Marlborough Street, where they found themselves standing on a sunbaked sidewalk in front of a strip mall.

"Not what I expected," said Theo.

The bank with the impressive name—New Providence Bank and Trust Company—was little more than a storefront window tucked between a manicurist salon and a convenience store. Jack double-checked the address, but they were definitely in the right place. Seeing it, however, made Jack understand why he had been told to "keep the FBI out of this." It had all the markings of a bank that could shut down its Bahamian operations overnight and flee to the Cayman Islands at the first sign of law enforcement.

"Banks run the gamut in the Caribbean," said Jack. "From the big boys, like BNP Paribas, to . . . well, this."

Jack was no expert on offshore havens, but he had as much experience with Bahamian banks as any Miami criminal defense lawyer. While the Bahamas had shown enough cooperation with international tax regulators to improve their official status to "gray" in the eyes of the Organisation for Economic Co-operation and Development, bank secrecy continued to be a pillar of the Bahamian financial-services sector. There were more than four hundred bank and trust companies within the eighty square miles of New Providence alone. It didn't take a team of OECD officials to see that this particular hovel in a Nassau strip mall was among the island's darker shades of gray.

Jack and Theo walked past the manicure salon, the noxious chemical odor worse than oil-spill dispersants, and entered the bank. Inside were none of the usual trappings of private wealth management—no leather couches, expensive artwork, or rich wood paneling. The walls were basic beige, with commercial carpeting and simple furnishings to match. Two women were busy at computer terminals, separated by a simple workstation divider. In a separate office in the back, behind a glass wall, a Bahamian man dressed in casual slacks and a short-sleeve dress shirt was seated behind a metal desk, talking on the telephone.

One of the women rose to greet them. "Can I help you, sir?"

"Yes, I'm here to access a safe-deposit box," said Jack.

She glanced at Theo, then back at Jack. "We allow only one customer at a time in our secured area. Will that be you?"

"Yes. It is box A-36."

"May I see your passport, please?"

"I was told to ask for Mr. Jeffries," said Jack.

"He's a bit tied up at the moment. If I could have your passport, I'll get his attention without delay."

Jack handed it over, and she went to Jeffries' office. The next sixty seconds were tense, as Jack realized that the phone call from Josefina might well have been a runaround.

"What if your name's not on the access list?" asked Theo.

"Then we burned through seven hundred gallons of fuel for nothing."

"Well, not for nothing," said Theo. "They have casinos here. And a totally awesome waterslide."

Jack might normally have rolled his eyes and ignored Theo, but the waterslide made him think of his expectant wife and smile. "You could be one cool Uncle Theo."

The woman returned with Jack's passport and, to his relief, a pleasant smile. "Come with me, please," she said.

She escorted Jack to a locked door and, with nine beeps of the key pad, entered the passcode. The door opened to a small room. The only furniture was a small table and one chair. While the front area had borne little resemblance to a bank, the walls in this secured room had a thicker, more substantial appearance. The steel door looked bulletproof. She told Jack to wait at the table, and she entered another room that was behind a second locked steel door. Two minutes later, she reappeared with a metal box—safe-deposit box number A-36.

"Just press the button by the door when you're finished," she said, and then she left Jack alone. He stared down at the box.

With good reason, Jack had decided to heed Josefina's instructions and keep the FBI out of this. Nonetheless, he approached the opening of the box like a CSI detective. He'd brought latex gloves with him (with the oil cleanup, they were everywhere in Key West). Jack saw no security camera in the room, and a bank such as this did not earn its clientele by spying on them, so he pulled on the gloves without concern of being watched. He slid the metal top off the box and peered inside. He saw only papers. Actually, there was just one paper, which he removed.

It was a computer-generated bank record for the New Providence Bank and Trust Company, but not from this branch. It was a Parliament Street address, in the heart of Nassau's financial district. The only entry on the record was a cash deposit of fifty thousand dollars. The date of the deposit was the fifth of September, which hardly seemed like coincidence.

Three weeks before the Scarborough 8 disaster.

Jack checked the "Account Holder" line. It read: "NR050527." It was a numbered account.

No surprise.

Jack photographed the bank record with his iPhone, sealed the paper in a plastic bag, and tucked it into his coat pocket. He closed the box and pushed the call button for the bank employee. She came quickly, returned the box to its sleeve in the other room, and then let him out. Jack thanked her and headed straight for the exit, eager to get away cleanly and quickly with the bank record. Theo followed him out the door and down the sidewalk.

"Well?" asked Theo.

They were still walking as Jack showed him the

photo of the bank record on his phone. Theo studied it.

"Fifty thousand dollars?" he said, so surprised that he stopped walking. "Somebody blew up an oil rig for a measly fifty thousand dollars?"

They were a half block away from the bank, just beyond the odor of the manicure salon. "The amount of this deposit isn't important," said Jack. "For all we know, there are five hundred accounts like this all over the Caribbean."

"That would be . . ." Theo gave up on the math, too many zeroes to carry. "A shitload of money."

"The key is to find out who the account holder is. All we have is a number."

"I guess that's what Josefina meant when she said the first piece is free. We get the deposit record."

"But we don't get the name of the account holder."

Theo glanced toward the bank. "Why don't we go back and ask?"

Jack scoffed. "Offshore banks don't just give out that information because you ask."

"Maybe this one does."

"Trust me. They don't."

"You don't know till you try."

"It's a stupid idea. Forget it."

Theo nodded, but it was an acknowledgment of their disagreement, not acquiescence. "I'm gonna take a shot."

"You don't understand, Theo. Bank secrecy is the law in this country. You're asking them to commit a crime."

"I'm not putting a gun to their head."

"No, but if they get the impression that you're

making a veiled threat or even hinting at a bribe, that would be real trouble."

"I'll ask *nicely.*"

Jack laid his hand over his coat pocket, referencing the bank record. "The smart move is to take this and get it checked for fingerprints. I don't see any upside to going back inside the bank and asking questions that we shouldn't be asking."

"Then you wait here."

Theo started down the sidewalk. Jack went after him. "Theo, don't go back in that bank."

Theo didn't answer.

"Theo, *don't.*"

Theo yanked open the door and stopped. "Dude, it's totally okay. Just admit it. You brought me on this trip for the same reason you married Andie Henning: there needs to be at least one set of balls in the equation."

"*What?*"

"Now, let me do my job." The door closed and Theo disappeared inside.

"*Damn it,*" Jack said under his breath. He waited outside for a minute, but the waft of chemicals from the busy salon next door was making him dizzy. Or maybe it was the thought of Theo inside the bank, winging it. Jack didn't want any part of a half-baked plan, but he didn't want Theo in charge, either.

One set of balls?

He sucked it up, went inside, and found Theo speaking to the manager in the office behind the glass wall.

"Good timing," said Theo. "Jack, this is Mr. Leonard Jeffries."

Jack shook his hand. "Very nice to meet you, Mr. Jeffries. I apologize for any inconvenience."

"No inconvenience at all," said Jeffries.

"We'll be going now, right, Theo?"

Jeffries looked confused. "So you don't want the account holder information?"

Jack returned the confused expression. "Excuse me?"

"As I was explaining to your partner—"

"Partner?" said Jack, recalling Theo's running honeymoon joke. "No, we're not married."

"*Law* partner," said Theo. "I told the man we're law partners."

"Ah, right." *Impersonating an attorney now. Great.*

"As I was saying," said Jeffries. "As the lawyer for Bianca Lopez, you have access to all account information."

More confusion. "How did you know I was her lawyer?"

"Well, how else would you have been granted access to the safe-deposit box? It's all the same account. That information was input through our Internet banking system."

"By whom?"

"Perhaps it was your client. I can't say for sure. Anyone who knows the user ID and enters all three passwords in the correct sequence can update the account information."

Jack was trying to play it cool, but he was trying to catch up, too. "This may sound like a dumb question, but are you saying that Bianca Lopez is the account holder?"

Jeffries hesitated. "Mr. Swyteck, I deal frequently

with attorneys. You seem considerably less informed about the pertinent details than most. No offense, but may I see your bar membership card, please?"

Jack dug it from his wallet. Jeffries went to his computer and compared Jack's Florida Bar number to the data on file. He seemed satisfied, at least in the sense that he had done enough to cover his ass. But he was more guarded in his remarks.

"Thank you," said Jeffries as he returned the card to Jack. "To answer your question, Ms. Lopez is the named beneficiary under the account."

Jack felt a chill, inferring the answer to his next question, but asking it anyway. "So the account holder would be?"

"Her late husband," said Jeffries. "Rafael Lopez, of course."

"Yes," said Jack, still not quite believing. "Of course."

52

Jack's first phone call was to his client, who listened without saying a word, seemingly numb, as Jack laid out his findings. Finally, she spoke in a voice that shook.

"I don't understand any of this, Jack. Honestly, I don't."

Jack had put a few more questions to Jeffries before leaving the bank, but the added pressure of interrogation only made the banker more uncomfortable. Before long, Jeffries had completely shut down and asked them to leave. Jack and Theo cabbed it back to the marina and called Bianca from the yacht. Captain Rick had retired to sleep in the stateroom upon docking, and there was still no sign of him, so it was just the two of them on the skydeck seating salon behind the helm station. Jack's iPhone lay flat on the polished teak table. Even with 360-degree windows and unobstructed views of blue skies and the marina, cell reception was less than ideal in the islands, and Bianca's voice crackled over the speaker.

"This makes no sense," she said. "How could Rafael go to the Bahamas to open a bank account if he couldn't leave Cuba and come to me in Key West?"

"That's the key," said Jack. "The last thing Jeffries told me before asking us to leave the bank was that access to an account can be changed online, once the account is open. But to open an account in the first place, the customer has to appear in person at the bank."

"Then he should be able to tell you that it wasn't Rafael who opened the account. Did you show him a photo?"

"I did," said Jack. "I pulled one off the Web from the news coverage of your case. That's when Jeffries asked us to leave."

"So he knows the bank screwed up," said Bianca.

"That's possible," said Jack. "Somebody pretended to be Rafael and opened a bank account in his name. And now the bank is retreating into its cocoon, refusing to say another word."

"Why would someone pretend to be Rafael?"

"I can only guess," said Jack, "but it may be a good one. Whoever blew up the rig needed someone to blame. Rafael was a derrick monkey, very likely to die in the explosion. What better person to blame than someone who wouldn't live to deny it?"

There was no response. "Bianca, are you okay?"

"Yes," she said, but the crack in her voice belied it. "What do we do next, Jack?"

"One option is to go to the FBI."

"They haven't been very helpful," she said.

"No, they haven't," said Jack. "And we need to be very careful. The push to shut down your case is driven by the National Security Division. Offshore banking and national security go hand in hand."

He could hear Bianca's sigh over the speaker. "This is all . . . I don't know what. I can't deal with this anymore."

"I know. We'll talk more when I get back."

"Okay. I trust you. Whatever you say, I'll do."

It was nice to earn that level of trust, but Jack had heard the same words from clients who ended up in the electric chair or on the lethal-injection table. He said good-bye to Bianca and hung up. Theo went to the refrigerator and brought them a couple of sodas.

"There is one other possibility," Theo said as he popped open the can. "It could be that Rafael was one of the dudes involved in the sabotage and turned himself into a crispy critter in the process."

"Believe me, I'm aware of that."

"Do you think Bianca is?"

"Let her process what I told her. No need to rock her world any more than it's been rocked."

"Is the next move really to call the FBI?"

"I need to think this through. Right now Bianca's case is on hold until the criminal investigation is over, but at least we're still in court. The quickest way to get it tossed out for good is to put the idea in Barton-Hammill's head that Rafael was one of the saboteurs who blew up the rig."

"Fuck the FBI," said Theo. "We need to find out who opened that account and who deposited fifty grand, cash money. If you call the FBI, it all gets sucked into a black hole called national security. That'll be the end of Bianca's case, and we'll never know the truth."

Jack opened his soda. "I'm almost afraid to ask, but what would you do?"

"Let me go pay another visit to Mr. Jeffries."

"No," said Jack.

"Come on, dude. I know how to handle a pussy like Jeffries."

"No. Absolutely not."

"Do you want to know the truth or don't you?"

"I do," said Jack. "But right now, I'm feeling kind of tired, so I'm going below to take a nap. And while I have absolutely no control over your actions while I'm sleeping, I repeat: Whatever you do, Theo, do not go see Mr. Jeffries. Understood?"

Theo did a quick check beneath the table and said, "Damn, Swyteck, you may grow a set after all."

"Hilarious."

"Yes, boss. Understood."

53

Leonard Jeffries locked up the New Providence Bank and Trust Company at noon, the usual Saturday closing time. The bus dropped him two blocks from home. As the gravel road crunched beneath his plodding footfalls, only one thought was on his mind: secrets.

It was Jeffries' job to keep them. His clients relied on his discretion. Like all branch managers, Jeffries had attended the training lectures put on by the high-priced banking lawyers. The cardinal rule of banking—"know your customer"—had been drummed into his head. He thought he had done everything required to "know" Rafael Lopez. But that photograph that Swyteck had shown him looked nothing like the "Rafael Lopez" who had visited his branch, presented a Cuban passport, and opened the account.

This is going to be trouble.

A leafy tropical canopy blocked out the midday sun, but even in the shade he was sweating. Jeffries shooed the neighborhood chickens out of his front yard, cursing the birds for the fresh droppings on his porch. The door was locked. The housekeeper came every Saturday morning, and for once she'd remembered to lock up before leaving. Jeffries checked under the mat to collect the key he'd left for her, but it was missing. She'd done it again, gone home with the key in her pocket.

Stupid woman. He would have to change the lock. A neighbor had been robbed blind by a cleaning lady who had cut a duplicate key for her ex-con boyfriend.

Jeffries went inside. The living room was unusually dark for the afternoon. Two weeks earlier, he'd shuttered most of his windows in preparation for Hurricane Miguel. Thankfully, the storm had changed course and spared the Bahamas, only to whack Cuba and then swallow the Scarborough 8. Like any conscientious soul who had wasted a weekend nailing up plywood for a false alarm, Jeffries was leaving it up until the next storm came along, just to make it worth the effort.

Like a sauna in here.

Jeffries closed the door, but before his hand could reach the light switch, he was pummeled from behind. The force of the blow knocked the air from his lungs, and the weight of his attacker sent him hard to the floor.

"Don't move!"

Jeffries could barely breathe, let alone move. He was facedown on the carpet, at the mercy of someone much larger than he riding his kidneys. The huge hand that gripped the back of his neck felt powerful enough to crush his vertebrae at will. In a split second, the man hiding behind the door had stunned him into submission and taken complete control. The knife at Jeffries' throat sealed the deal.

"Don't make me use this," the man said.

Jeffries struggled to speak. "No need, mon. No need."

"You talk too much."

His mind raced. *Talk too much now, or talk too much at the bank?* As the manager for an offshore haven, he lived in fear of saying the wrong thing to the wrong person and pissing off clients. Or, worse, pissing off criminals.

"What did you tell Swyteck?"

His heart sank. That worst fear had been realized. This one was *very* pissed.

"Not a thing. I told him nothing."

The blade pressed harder against his neck.

"I know that's not true. I was watching. Swyteck went inside for twenty minutes and talked to one of your girls. He came out for two minutes, went back inside, and talked to you."

Jeffries didn't answer. Somewhere in the back of his mind, a voice cried out, begging him to resist. He ignored it, recognizing that his attacker had the upper hand in every way, from brute strength to the essential facts.

"I'll ask you again," the man said. "*What* did you tell him?"

"I—I thought Mr. Swyteck already knew. He is the lawyer for the widow. His name is on the access list."

"*I* put his name on the list, you dumbshit! He needed access to the box."

"Yes, then all is good. He opened the safe-deposit box."

"Did he take the bank record?"

"I don't know what he took, mon. I have no idea what was in the box. That's not my business. But as I say, all is good. He got into the box. No problem. No need for the knife, mon."

The grip tightened around the back of Jeffries' neck, the tip of the blade moved to his right earlobe, and the man spoke in a slow, deep voice. "I will cut you from ear to ear if you don't tell me exactly what you said to Swyteck."

"Okay, okay," he said, his voice shaking. "Let me think. I told him he had access to the account because he was the lawyer for the widow."

The tip of the blade probed deeper into his lobe, drawing a trickle of blood.

"What else?"

"That his client—that Bianca Lopez is the named beneficiary of the account."

The knife worked even deeper, as if to confirm that the banker had said too much. Panic was setting in, and it was telling Jeffries that it was just a matter of whether the man would cut him open here, on the living room floor, or take him to a place where the body might never be found. Jeffries groaned, more out of fear than pain, as the hot trickle of blood ran all the way to the corner of his mouth.

"What else did you tell him?" the man demanded.

"I don't remember. Really."

The blade twisted, and Jeffries grimaced in pain as the tip sliced through his earlobe and bore into the base of his jawbone.

"Tell me everything," the man said.

"The account holder," he said through clenched teeth. The pain was becoming unbearable.

"You told him the name of the account holder?"

"I thought he—Swyteck was on the access list." Jeffries could feel the rise in anger coursing right through the man's hold on his neck, and he braced himself for another twist of the knife.

"Did you tell him who made the cash deposit?"

"No. I didn't. I swear."

"That's good. See, I'm going to be paid a lot of money for that information."

"Excellent, I can help you with that," he said, desperate to find any reason to be kept alive.

"You probably could," the man said. "Problem is, I can't trust you anymore."

"You can trust me, mon!"

"If you give up that name, I lose a lot of money."

"You won't lose it," he said, his voice racing. "It was a cash deposit. We don't accept cash deposits at my branch. That deposit was made at the main banking center in Nassau."

"So you don't know who put the money in that account?"

"No. Truly, I don't. You have nothing to worry about. Nothing at all."

"You won't tell?"

"No, mon. No chance. How would I tell if I can't tell?"

"I couldn't agree more."

The blade entered below the jaw, and Jeffrie heard himself scream as six inches of cold stee slashed across his throat in one even motion, un leashing a crimson river.

54
.

Jack smelled burgers. Grilled burgers.

He actually had dozed off for a couple of hours after Theo left, and it was closer to dinnertime than lunch. Jack followed his nose through the salon, all the way to the back of the yacht. On the aft swim platform, at water level, he found Rick the grill master at work on the electric barbecue.

"Hungry?" asked Rick.

It smelled amazing. "I am now."

Jack climbed down a curved set of stairs to Rick's mini-oasis. The afternoon sun glistened on the polished chrome railings. A perfect breeze carried the grilling smoke away from the yacht and out over the harbor's deep-blue waters. On the deck above them, against a cloudless sky, a pair of jet skis begged for attention. For a moment, Jack imagined that he was alone with Andie, anchored near a remote Caribbean island, Jack handing her a chilled glass of champagne as she emerged from a swim in the crystal-clear waters, soon to lose her bikini.

Rick handed him a cold beer. "Where's Theo?"

Back to reality. "He went into town. He should have been back by now."

Rick flipped the burgers.

Jack drank his beer. "So when you do these yacht deliveries, you can use anything you want on the boat?"

"You can if you clean it up," said Rick. "That's your job, first mate."

I had to ask.

"How did things go at the bank?" asked Rick.

"Went okay," said Jack. He went to the rail, thinking. He didn't know Rick well, so he didn't want to share too many details. But Rick's take on certain things could be useful.

"Has Bianca ever been to the Bahamas?"

"Not that I know of," said Rick. "But I don't check her passport when she comes to work."

"Don't take this the wrong way, but how well do you really know Bianca?"

"Well enough, I guess. Better than most of my waitresses. She's been through a lot, so I guess you might say I've taken her under my wing. Why do you ask?"

Jack drank more of his beer. There was no indirect way to approach the subject with Rick, but he needed some peace of mind. He went for it.

"There's fifty thousand dollars in a numbered bank account at the New Providence Bank and Trust Company. It was a cash deposit made in Nassau. I need to find out who made it."

Rick stood over the burgers, spatula in hand, momentarily frozen. "You think it was Bianca?"

"No. But everyone from the FBI to Judge Carlyle is going to be asking some pointed questions in short order. I need to be able to rule out my client. The deposit was made less than three weeks before the Scarborough 8 exploded. September fifth."

"What day of the week is that?"

"Monday. It was Labor Day actually."

"Labor Day? Unless Bianca traveled by rocket ship on her lunch break, there's no way she made the deposit. That's one of my busiest days of the year. Every waitress I got works ten, twelve hours."

"That's what Bianca told me."

"Well, there you go. Now you've heard it from her boss, too. You want cheese on your burger?"

"Sure."

"Where would she get fifty thousand dollars, anyway?" asked Rick.

As a down payment for her husband's blowing up the Scarborough 8. Jack couldn't go there with Rick. His cell rang, giving him an out. It was Theo.

"What's up?"

"Not much," said Theo. "I'm over here at the highly impressive-sounding Royal Bahamas Police Force Headquarters."

"You're at the police station?"

"Yeah, it's on the east side of Nassau, on East Street North. I've been sitting here for over two hours. They finally let me make a phone call. I could probably use a lawyer."

"What happened?"

"Jeffries is dead. Cops seem to think I did it."

"Dead?" Jack sprang into defense mode. "Have you talked to the cops?"

"Nope. I'm sure that's why they kept me sitting here, thinking that I might."

"Good. Do not say a word until I get there. Don't talk to the cops, don't talk to the janitor in the hallway, don't talk to the guy standing next to you in the men's room. Don't talk to anyone. Do you hear me?"

"Yup."

"I'll be right there," said Jack. He hung up and put his phone away.

"Something wrong?" asked Rick.

Jack took a breath, wondering what the hell had made him think it was a good idea to send Theo off to visit Jeffries alone. "Nothing I can't handle," said Jack. "I hope."

55

.

"Bad case of déjà vu, ain't it, Jack?"

Jack was alone with Theo in a tiny, windowless room beside the holding cell at the Royal Bahamas Police Force Headquarters in Nassau. The reference to how they'd met—Theo accused of a murder he didn't commit—seemed apropos.

"Tell me what happened."

Jack was seated on one side of a table no larger than a school desk, notepad in front of him. Theo sat opposite him with hands clasped behind his head, relaxed in a way that only someone who had spent four years on death row could be relaxed in these circumstances. Behind Theo, hanging on the wall, directly above his head, was a framed photograph of a dozen jubilant young men with their caps on backward and enough bling around their necks to pass for gangbangers from Theo's old neighborhood. It was the police-force basketball team celebrating its fourth consecutive Caribbean Law Enforcement Championship.

"Bank was closed when I got there," said Theo.

"I spotted one of the assistants from the bank, the woman who helped you with the safe-deposit box. She was right next door in the salon, getting her nails done. I made up a little story of how I needed to see Jeffries, and she told me where he lived. Went to his house, knocked on the door, no one answered. I looked down and saw a little blood seeping out from under the door. I opened the door—"

"You opened the door?" said Jack, cringing.

"Yeah. I mean, what if the guy was hurt? Turns out he was dead on the floor. Throat slit wide open, blood all over. I called the cops. Here I am."

Jack was taking notes, getting Theo's every word but also jotting down his thoughts. *Time of death* was underlined, but another realization was foremost in his mind.

"We're back to where we were when we thought Josefina was dead."

"What do you mean?"

"The guy who kidnapped me in Cuba. The guy who attacked Bianca and controls Josefina. It's a safe bet that he's also the guy who killed Mr. Jeffries— probably for telling us too much about the numbered account. I've suspected it all along, but now we know for sure: we're up against someone who is willing to commit murder in order to get what he wants."

There was a knock at the door. Jack got up and answered it. Standing in the hallway was the police sergeant from the RBPF Central Detective Unit's Homicide Squad, the same detective who had checked Jack in at the station desk twenty minutes earlier. Beside him was a much bigger white guy whom Jack had never seen before.

"You got a visitor," said the sergeant.

The white guy flashed a badge. "Special Agent Michael Brunelli, FBI."

"FBI? In the Bahamas?"

"Obviously I'm out of my jurisdiction, so I can't come in unless you invite me. But I work with your wife."

Jack took that as a positive. He allowed Brunelli in, said good-bye to the detective, and closed the door. He didn't think it sounded too paranoid to ask, "Did the FBI follow me here?"

"No. The Bahamians ran Theo Knight through the FBI and Interpol database. His name—like yours—is linked to the criminal investigation into the Scarborough 8. Right now, there's not a higher priority at the Bureau. Got me here in under four hours, door to door."

Jack did a mental double take. "You said you work with Andie. Are you telling me that my wife is investigating the Scarborough 8?"

"Actually, she's my girlfriend."

"That's not really funny."

"I thought it was," said Theo.

"Anyway," said Brunelli. "I didn't come here to tell you what your wife is or isn't doing. Just be glad she's plugged in. If it weren't for her, you'd have Agent Linton here now busting your chops on behalf of the National Security Division. Instead, you got me."

"What does that mean, we 'got' you?"

"It means that even though you and Agent Linton seem to have gotten off on the wrong foot, hopefully you and I can help each other out."

"What are you proposing?"

"I've talked with the homicide detective. Theo Knight is the only suspect they have right now. So you are not going to walk out of this police station anytime soon. That is, unless you walk out in the custody of an FBI agent."

"I'm listening," said Jack. "What do you want from us?"

"Tell me everything. What you were doing here in the Bahamas. What you found at the bank. What Jeffries told you. All of it."

Theo scoffed. "Tell him to forget it, Jack. The Bahamians are gonna figure out I'm not their guy. If I have to spend a couple nights in jail, it ain't gonna kill me."

"Couple nights?" said Brunelli. "Where do you think you are, pal—the land of the free and the home of the brave? You know what the murder rate is in the Caribbean? Thirty in one hundred thousand. That's higher than any other region in the world. Not good for tourism. The local cops need to at least *look* like they're tough on violent crime. They are not going to let you go until they have a better suspect in custody."

Theo looked at Jack. "Is that true? Can they just keep me here?"

Jack didn't answer, which Brunelli seized upon.

"Jack doesn't know," he said, "which points out another problem. A good Bahamian criminal defense lawyer isn't cheap. And you'll need one ASAP. Unless you do the smart thing and just walk out the front door with me."

Jack considered it, then said, "Give us a minute."

"I'll be right outside," said Brunelli.

Jack waited for the agent to step out, but Theo was talking before Jack could get out a word. "Don't do it, Jack. We got burned already by Linton. Everything you told him, he used against you to crush Bianca's case. Don't get burned again. I don't care if this Brunelli guy is your wife's boyfriend."

"Will you please stop calling him Andie's boyfriend?"

"Sorry."

"My advice is that we should work with Brunelli," said Jack.

"Why?"

"Shit happens in the islands, Theo. As soon as the media gets hold of this, you'll be portrayed as a former gangbanger from Miami who got off Florida's death row on a mere technicality. There's going to be pressure to hold you, which will turn into pressure to charge you, which becomes pressure to convict you. If we have a chance to get the Bahamian police to release you from custody, we need to take it."

From the expression on Theo's face, Jack could tell that Theo was searching his mind for some way to disagree. He was silent, unable to find one.

Jack went to the door and opened it. "All right, Brunelli. Get us out of here."

56

—
.

Jack and Theo walked out of the Royal Bahamas Police headquarters at seven o'clock. Agent Brunelli went with them, step for step.

It had taken two hours to obtain the necessary approvals, which was lightning quick in the Bahamas on a Saturday evening. The team effort had been pretty effective, Jack and Agent Brunelli working their way up from the chief of the homicide squad to the assistant commissioner of crime management, and, finally, to the deputy commissioner and force internal inspector, who oversaw international policing and Interpol activities. There were conditions on the release. Theo could not leave the island, and the Royal Bahamas Police kept his passport. And Brunelli was to remain with him at all times, which Theo had no intention of making easy.

"What's your girlfriend up to tonight, Bruno?"

"It's Brunelli."

"And she's not his girlfriend," said Jack.

The car was a two-door compact, barely big enough for Jack alone, a total stretch for Jack *and* two men as big as Brunelli and Theo. Brunelli got behind the wheel, and as much as Jack would have preferred to ride shotgun, it was physically impossible for Theo to climb into the backseat. Jack yielded the passenger seat and squeezed in behind him.

"Where we headed, Brutus?" asked Theo.

"Brunelli."

"To the bank," said Jack.

Brunelli started the car and merged into traffic, clearly uncomfortable with the colonial holdover of left-sided driving. Jack expected some smart-ass remark from Theo about driving on the wrong side of the road, but it didn't come. He plugged the bank address into his iPhone GPS.

"Turn right in three blocks. New Providence Bank and Trust Company is on the left."

"Seriously?" said Theo. "We're going to the bank? I thought you were yanking my chain."

Jack had kept his part of the deal with Brunelli and told him about the bank account. Getting the royal police to sign off on Theo's conditional release had been a snap compared to getting a manager to open the bank on a Saturday night. FBI involvement had actually complicated matters, and keeping law enforcement out of it was the only way to make it happen without spooking the bank into shutting its doors for good.

"I'm going to find out who made the deposit," said Jack.

Brunelli parked across the street from the main banking center, which could not have looked more different from Jeffries' storefront branch. The three-story colonial-style building had textured walls of pink stucco, white fluted columns, and enormous front doors that made for a grand entrance. Towering royal palm trees, beautifully lighted, flanked the marble walkway. Jack felt like one of the circus clowns piling out of a packed VW Beetle, but the unlikely threesome finally squeezed out of Brunelli's tiny rental car. An elderly Bahamian gentleman was walking toward them on the sidewalk, about a half block away.

"That's gotta be Mr. Benson," said Jack. Benson was a barrister from Nassau, an expert on offshore banking whom Jack had found on the quick through his professional contacts in Miami. The best way to arrange an after-hours bank visit in Nassau was through a local lawyer who had a relationship with the bank.

"Does Benson know you have the FBI with you?" asked Theo.

"Of course not," said Jack. "Nor does he know that I'm with Theo Knight, the only suspect in the murder of the bank's branch manager. Let's keep it that way. I'll introduce you guys very briefly, first names only, no mention of the FBI, then you two can take a hike."

"Got it," said Brunelli.

Benson was a slow walker, showing his age, but finally he reached the group. He gave Jack his business card and shook hands.

"These are friends of mine," said Jack. "Michael and Theo."

"I didn't catch your last name," said Benson, offering his hand.

"Brunelli," said the agent.

So much for no surnames.

Theo said nothing, adhering to Jack's rule.

"And you are?" asked Benson.

"Me? Nobody," said Theo. "I'm here with Valerie Bertinelli."

"Brunelli."

"Sorry. Valerie Brunelli."

Benson shot a curious expression at Jack. "I think it's best if Mr. Swyteck and I go inside alone."

"That's the plan," said Jack. "Take a walk, men."

Brunelli led Theo away, and Jack overheard him muttering beneath his breath as they started down the sidewalk. "I swear I'm gonna freakin' smack you."

Get in line, thought Jack.

Jack crossed the street with Benson, who led the way up the marble stairs to the front entrance. Jack peered through the diamond-shaped window in the door. The brass chandeliers were on, revealing more Italian marble, rich walnut paneling, and museum-quality artwork. It was no stretch for Jack to imagine someone walking in with fifty thousand dollars in cash. A security guard emerged from the shadows and came to the door. A woman was with him, and she clearly recognized Benson through the glass.

"That's the bank manager," Benson told Jack. "Samantha Walters."

The guard opened the door, allowing Jack and his local counsel to enter. Benson and the manager were obviously friends, and they exchanged pleasantries about their families as Jack followed them across the bank lobby to the manager's office. Her desk was at one end of the spacious suite, but she led them to the oval conference table near the window. Walters graciously let Jack have the view of Nassau at night and, seated with her back to the window, she took the lead.

"I understand that you are interested in the identity of the customer who made the deposit into your client's account on the fifth of September. Do I have that correct, Mr. Swyteck?"

"Yes," said Jack. "I know this may sound unusual, but my client didn't know this account existed until after her husband died."

"That's not unusual at all in our line of work," said Walters. "But if I may ask: Why do you need to know who made the deposit?"

Jack had prepared for that very question.

"If the deposit was made by an American, I understand that we may have an FBAR issue."

FBAR—Foreign Bank Account Report—is an information form that American citizens must file with the U.S. Department of the Treasury if they hold more than ten thousand dollars in a foreign bank account.

Walters cleared her throat, then spoke. "Mr. Benson should be able to provide your client with more specific legal guidance. But let me offer two general thoughts. First, it doesn't matter who made the deposit. Your client is a U.S. citizen, and she is the beneficial owner of an account in excess of ten thousand dollars. Second—and I say this in strictest confidence—the filing of a Foreign Bank Account Report is an issue only if your client chooses to make it an issue. This bank does not hand over its clients to U.S. law-enforcement authorities for the mere failure to file an information report with the U.S. government."

"I appreciate that," said Jack. "Legalities aside, my client would sleep a lot better at night if she knew who made the deposit."

"Very well," said Walters. "We'll do the best we can."

"The best you can?" asked Jack. "You don't have a record of who made the deposit?"

"I'm afraid not," said Walters. With a jiggle of the mouse on the pad in front of her, the computer screen brightened, and a bank deposit slip came up on the LCD. She adjusted the monitor so Jack could have a clear view from the other side of the table. "As you can see, there is no signature line or other identifying marks on our deposit slips."

"The bank accepts deposits anonymously?" asked Jack.

"Yes, of course. It's a numbered account. The deposit is made when the account holder communicates his or her acceptance to the bank."

"So you can't provide me a name?"

"As I said: No."

Jack considered his options. "It may actually be more helpful to know what the person looks like. Would there be any surveillance video of the transaction that we can review?"

Walters nodded. "Since the deposit was made here, at our main facility, surveillance cameras would have captured a digital image of the lobby at various angles about every ten seconds."

"I would love to see that," said Jack.

"I thought you might," said Walters, "which is

why I asked my head of security to retrieve it before you arrived. Unfortunately, it seems that the data no longer exists."

"What happened to it?"

Walters didn't miss a beat, no sign of concern or embarrassment. "Frankly, we don't know."

Jack's lawyerly instincts were on alert, but he did his best not to react too strongly. "The deposit was made barely five weeks ago. You don't know what happened to last month's surveillance footage?"

"Under the bank's retention policy, surveillance data is kept for at least ninety days. We have located the data for the Saturday before and Tuesday after the Monday in question. But we have been unable to find the data for the specific date of interest to you."

"If your policy is to keep it for ninety days, it should be there. Can you check again, please?"

"Our search was quite thorough. It's gone."

Jack's instincts were churning. His gaze drifted back to the image of the deposit slip on the computer screen. "What about the actual hard copy of the deposit slip?"

"What about it?" asked Walters.

Jack had fingerprints in mind, but he didn't want to make the bankers think that *he* worked for the FBI. "Can my client have the hard copy?"

"We don't release original bank records to anyone," said Walters. "Not without a court order."

Jack glanced at Benson, trying to get the Bahamian barrister to weigh in on his behalf. "I don't want to make this adversarial," said Jack. "But if that's the way things are done, should we be seeking a court order?"

Benson was about to speak, but the bank manager interjected. "I think we can save you some time in that regard," said Walters.

"You'll give me the original?" asked Jack.

"No, no," she said. "What I mean to say is that getting a court order would be a complete waste of your time. The original deposit slip appears to have gone missing."

"Like the surveillance video," said Jack.

"Yes," said Walters. "Just like it."

Jack smelled an island rat. A Bahamian bank opens its doors on a Saturday night for the American lawyer of a widow who holds a measly fifty-thousand-dollar account. And all the bank manager could tell Jack was that the most crucial information had curiously or conveniently gone missing.

Benson rose. "Well, that about covers it," he said, shaking the banker's hand. "Thank you so much, Samantha. Mr. Swyteck and I very much appreciate the bank's courtesy."

"You are most welcome," said Walters, escorting the men from her office. "I don't suppose you and the missus would be interested in watching the members-only match tomorrow at Lucaya Cricket Club, would you?"

"Oh, yes," said Benson. "Love to, love to."

"Excellent," she said, showing them to the main exit. "Henry and I will pick you up at seven a.m. sharp. The bank's jet will have us in Grand Bahama by nine. There will be eight of us going. We'll make a day of it."

"Sounds delightful."

The security guard opened the door. Another round of handshakes.

"Mr. Swyteck, it was such a pleasure meeting you," said Walters, smiling. "And let me assure you that you are in very good hands with Mr. Benson."

"I would expect you to say no less," said Jack.

"And I'm so sorry that the bank could not be of more help to you," she said, still smiling as she directed him out the door.

"I'm sure you are," said Jack, his tone less than sincere. The door closed behind him. *I'm sure you are.*

57

Noori followed her taxi to LaGuardia Airport. From their first meeting in the back room of N.Y.C. Gadets, something about Viola had put him on alert. Their lunch at Spice Market had only heightened his suspicion. She was too eager to make a deal, but that was only half of it. Too often she spoke directly to Noori, which was rude to any elder. It was beyond rude to a Chinese elder like Long Wu, who was no mere figurehead and actually called the shots in the counterfeit business. No one would conduct business that way.

Unless her real interest was Noori.

The crowds were gone. Just a handful of cabs were outside the American Airlines terminal, dropping passengers for the few remaining flights that Saturday night. From the backseat of his taxi, Noori watched several cabs ahead of him at curbside check in. Viola had one carry-on over her shoulder, but her larger bag needed to be checked. Noori knew what was inside it. He'd been watching her for the past two hours, having followed her on the shopping spree. She didn't look pregnant to him, but she'd hit one baby shop after another, bags and bags of gifts crammed into a wheeled duffel bag that grew fatter with each visit to another store. By the time she'd hailed a cab for the airport, she was pushing the single-bag weight limit.

Still in his cab, Noori watched her shell out the additional fee for overweight baggage. The attendant handed her a claim ticket and boarding pass. She tipped him and went inside the terminal.

Noori got out of his taxi, let the driver go, and flagged the same baggage attendant. "Excuse me, sir?"

The attendant stopped.

Noori had no luggage. Just a twenty-dollar bill in hand. "That woman you just helped," said Noori. "I'm wondering where she's flying to."

The attendant hesitated only a moment, then took the twenty. "Miami. She's on the nine-ten flight."

"Thank you," said Noori.

Miami. A little curious. She'd told Long Wu that she lived in northern Virginia. But if she was buying counterfeits in bulk, tons came through the Panama Canal to the Port of Miami.

Noori walked to the taxi line for a ride back to Manhattan. A young couple was ahead of him.

"You want to split a cab to Midtown?" the man asked.

In a flash, the couple was gone, the wife dragging her husband out of the line to talk sense into him. "Split a cab? Really? This is *New York*, you idiot, not . . ."

Noori climbed into the next taxi.

"Hudson and Canal," he told the driver.

As the cab pulled away from the curb, he checked his smartphone. Several e-mails promised to make his penis larger, but the most recent one caught his attention. The subject line would have looked like spam to just about anyone else on the planet, but Noori knew better.

NR050527, it read. It was the account number from the New Providence Bank and Trust Company.

Noori opened the message. Just two sentences long:

One million by Monday. Or the attached goes viral.

Noori clicked on the attachment. The file opened, and a series of still images appeared on his screen. Six frames in total, each from a bank surveillance camera. The date and time were posted in the corner. They were from the fifth of September, a series of shots between 10:07 and 10:12 a.m. The images were a bit grainy, but they were clear enough. It was Noori entering the bank. Noori at the teller window. Noori filling out a deposit slip. Noori handing over an envelope. Noori stepping away from the teller window. Noori leaving the bank.

You son of a bitch.

He closed the attachment and tucked his phone away. "Turn around," he told the driver.

"What?"

"Turn around *now*," he said harshly, his anger misdirected. "Take me back to the airport."

58

.

Jack spent Sunday morning in the radiology department at South Miami Hospital. Andie had promised that they would do the first ultrasound together, and she'd held true to her word. Her phone call to Jack on Saturday night, telling him that she was in Miami, had come as a complete surprise. Jack got the first flight out of Nassau the next morning.

"Are you nervous?" he asked.

"A little," said Andie.

She was lying on the examination table, a warmed glob of clear gel resting on her exposed abdomen and upper pelvic area. The typical recommendation for women over the age of thirty-five was an ultrasound at eight weeks. Andie was at least seven, and she had no idea where her undercover assignment might lead her for week eight. She had a one-day window in Miami to get it done. Her ob-gyn was unavailable, but the hospital worked her in.

"Just relax," said the technician. "Nothing to worry about. The only thing you might feel is a little pressure on your bladder. It's full, right?"

"She's been drinking water for two hours," said Jack.

"Good. That will help the image." She placed the transducer on Andie's belly. "Here we go."

Jack watched the monitor, but the black-and-white image on the screen didn't look like much of anything to him. "What should we be looking for?"

"Everything's pretty tiny, so I'll point things out as we go along. I'll take measurements and get a more exact calculation of gestational age. At seven weeks there will be a heartbeat, so I'll get some video of that for you."

Andie squeezed Jack's hand. It made him smile.

The technician moved the transducer around Andie's belly. Jack kept his eyes on the screen.

"What are we looking at now?" asked Andie.

"That's your cervix," said the technician. "And there's the uterus."

"Where's our baby?"

The technician moved the transducer one way, then the other. "Let me get one little picture here," she said.

Jack still didn't know what he was seeing on the screen. "A picture of what?"

"Would you excuse me one minute?" said the technician.

"Where are you going?"

"I'll be right back."

She got up and left, closing the door behind her. Andie reached out and took Jack's hand. "She's acting weird," said Andie.

"I'm sure it's nothing."

"What if it's not 'nothing'?"

"Let's just wait and see."

The door opened. The technician had an older man with her.

"Hello, I'm Dr. Peters," he said.

"Is there something wrong?" asked Andie.

"Let me just have a look here," said the doctor. He studied the image on the screen, showing no expression. He applied the transducer to Andie's belly. Rather than the sweeping motions of the technician, his placement seemed more specific, almost surgical in its precision.

"Have you been experiencing any morning sickness?" he asked.

"I did," said Andie. "It stopped about ten days ago."

He put the transducer down and looked straight at Andie. He didn't have to say anything. It was in his eyes.

"I'm sorry," he said. "This pregnancy is not viable."

"What?"

"Are you sure?" asked Jack.

"There's no heartbeat," the doctor said. "There never was. Development stopped at five weeks."

"But . . . why?"

"There could be any number of reasons. It's nothing you did."

Jack could hear Andie catch her breath, as if all the oxygen had suddenly been sucked from the room.

"But I was . . . I was so sure I was pregnant. Just two days ago I was running to the bathroom, getting false alarms."

"Sometimes when you read the pregnancy books, you memorize what the symptoms are supposed to be, and you almost will yourself to feel them."

"No, it was real. I had to pee so bad."

"It's possible. That's the strange thing about silent miscarriage. Women sometimes continue to experience the symptoms of pregnancy. But the real indicator here was the end of your morning sickness."

Andie was silent, her gaze cast toward the blinking monitor.

The doctor rose. "Stay here as long as you need. But before you leave, stop at the front desk. We'll need to schedule a D and C."

"A what?" asked Jack.

"Dilation and curettage. It's a simple outpatient procedure to clean out the uterus. I am sorry." The doctor left the room.

The technician wiped the gel from Andie's belly. "We'll talk more in a minute," she said. "I'll give you two a little time alone."

The door closed.

Jack and Andie locked eyes, each staring at the other in disbelief. She sat up, and Jack sat next to her at the edge of the table.

"There are some tissues in my purse," she said. "Could you hand me one, please?"

"Sure."

He reached inside. He found the tissues, but something else caught his eye. He wasn't sure what made him pull it from Andie's purse, but he did. It was a little stuffed animal, a pink duck with the tag still on it. Dinosaur Hill.

"Her first toy," said Andie, her voice quaking.

"I'm so sorry, sweetheart."

"I saw this cute little shop in the East Village on Friday. I knew I shouldn't go in, but I did. I thought, Oh, you can buy just *one* thing. And then yesterday, like an idiot, I went shopping again. I was so sure we were having a baby girl. I bought all this stuff, blankets and blocks and—"

"It's okay, Andie. Everything is going to be o—"

Before he could get it out, Andie was in his arms, clinging to him, holding him tighter than she'd ever held him before. Jack wanted to say the right thing, but there was nothing to say.

In the four years he'd been in love with Andie Henning, Jack had known her to run down drug dealers in a dark alley at midnight. He'd seen the cuts and bruises on her body after an undercover assignment that she couldn't tell him anything about. He'd lain on the other side of their bed and listened to her talk on the telephone until three a.m., comforting a mother who'd lost a daughter to a serial killer. He'd seen a tear of joy in the corner of her eye on their wedding day, and he'd seen her choke up at movies. But this morning was a first.

It was the first time he'd seen Andie let go and cry. Really cry. Like a baby.

59
.

At two p.m. Jack was in the waiting room at the hospital's surgical center.

Andie's doctor had described the D and C as a fifteen-minute procedure. He'd left out at least three hours of waiting around. The prep was minimal, since she'd requested only local anesthesia, but Jack was getting zippo in the way of status updates from the nurse at the front desk. Since Andie's transfer to the surgical suite, Jack had been stuck sitting three chairs away from a hard-of-hearing old man who was "sick and tired of spill coverage," and who insisted on blasting *Family Feud* on the only television in the waiting room.

Survey says: Your time is up, old man.

"Sorry, I really need to change this," said Jack, as he switched to cable news. A wetland ecologist from the Everglades Foundation was being interviewed live from Islamorada, the turquoise waters of Florida Bay behind her.

"Most of Florida Bay is part of Everglades National Park," said the scientist, "and it contributes approximately one-point-one billion dollars to the Monroe County economy in terms of boating, bird watching, and recreational fishing. Scientifically speaking, the bay is an estuary, approximately one thousand square miles of shallows where freshwater from the Florida Everglades on the mainland flows into the sea. The next twenty-four hours will be critical in telling us how much oil we can expect to intrude north from the middle Keys into these estuaries, and how much is carried east into deeper waters."

From three chairs away, Jack felt an angry stare coming from the game-show addict. He glanced in the old man's direction, which triggered a snarky comment.

"You realize I'm missing the lightning round."

Jack's time in Key West and the Caribbean had left him out of touch with the mainland, but the old man was surprisingly typical. To anyone in the Keys, the spill was a nightmare, but to the average Joe in the next county, it was at most a nuisance. Jack supposed that when restaurants on South Beach started serving fresh Florida stone crabs with a side of brake fluid, people in Miami-Dade County might tune in.

The television interview continued. "There are folks who will call scientists like me Chicken Little, but this is an area that could be lost forever to future generations."

Future generations.

It reminded Jack why he was at the hospital, what he and Andie had lost.

Jack's cell rang. He tossed the TV remote to the

old man, told him to have at it, and walked outside to take the call. It was Theo, from Nassau.

"When are you coming back?" asked Theo.

It was about the last thing on Jack's mind. "Theo, I've only been gone six hours."

"I hate to sound needy, dude. But you were exactly right about how this murder was gonna play on the news here. My picture is on the front page of the *Nassau Guardian* right next to Jeffries. It's like we hit the lottery. Jeffries is the hundred-twenty-ninth murder this year, which breaks a freakin' record for the Bahamas, and it's only October. Everyone is making a huge deal out of this, saying how the Bahamas needs to get crime under control, how all these murders are killing tourism, no pun intended—that kind of thing."

"Can you e-mail me the story?"

"Just go online. Search 'Theo Knight, Royal Bahamas Police,' and"—he turned on his Bahamian accent—"'frightfully scary murderous scoundrel,' mon."

Jack massaged away the oncoming headache between his eyes. "Not good."

"Tell me about it. Even Bruschetta is wigged out."

It took Jack a moment to decode that one. "Is Brunelli with you?"

"Yeah, we're still at the motel. Right now the cops don't even know where I am. He's afraid if we go out, someone might call the police and I'll end up arrested."

"Has an arrest warrant been issued?"

"No. I don't think so. Honestly, I don't know."

"Let me talk to Brunelli."

"He's on his phone."

"Tell him to call me."

"Hey, hold on a second, I got another call."

"No, Theo, don't take it!"

Too late. Theo had him on hold, and Jack had an all-too-real fear that the call was from the Bahamian chief of police. A minute or so ticked away as Jack took a walk around the traffic circle outside the entrance to the surgical center. He had the phone to his ear, still waiting, when a nurse came outside to get him.

"You can see your wife now, Mr. Swyteck. She's just coming out of her anesthesia."

"Coming out? It was supposed to be local anesthesia."

"It ended up being more of a twilight."

"Is everything okay?"

"She's fine. A little groggy, but that's normal."

Jack followed the nurse inside, allowing Theo just a little more time to come back on the line. He was about to give up and disconnect when Theo suddenly returned, his voice racing.

"Dude, it was her again."

"Who?"

"Josefina."

Jack stopped cold, halfway across the lobby. The half-deaf old man clutched the TV remote and said, "Don't even think about changing the channel."

Jack spoke into his phone. "What does she want?"

"A million bucks, cash," said Theo. "First installment of the ten million. And she wants you to deliver it. In Cuba."

The nurse was holding the door open to the surgical suite. "Are you coming, Mr. Swyteck?"

"Are you gonna go, Jack?" asked Theo.

"It's time for the *Fami-leee Feud*!" the television blasted.

Jack told Theo he'd call him right back, tucked his phone away, and followed the nurse down the bright, sterile hallway.

"You don't happen to have any of that twilight anesthesia left over, do you?" he asked.

60

      ·

The post-op recovery room was a collection of patient bays separated by privacy curtains that hung from the ceiling. On any given weekday morning it might have been abuzz with surgeons, nurses, and a steady stream of patients wheeled in and out on gurneys. But not on a Sunday afternoon. For almost forty-five minutes, Andie was the only patient in the room, and Jack sat at her bedside until she shook off the effects of her twilight anesthesia. A nurse came by to ask how she was doing. Then she pulled Jack out of the bay to give him a little advice.

"There's an emergency C-section coming in here in about five minutes. You should probably keep the curtain closed."

"Understood," said Jack. "I hope it went okay."

"Perfect," the nurse said.

Jack returned to Andie, curtain closed. She was starting to look like herself, but it was clear that she didn't want to talk about the procedure, the miscarriage, or how she felt. At first, she didn't want to take any telephone calls, and Jack watched her let a call from Seattle—her mother—go to voice mail. The next call was different. It was an invitation to dive into work, a healing strategy that he had seen Andie use before. The call was from Agent Brunelli in the Bahamas.

"Hold on one second," she said into her phone. "Let me ask Jack to step out."

Jack gave her the required privacy and went to the other side of the empty recovery room. He was standing near the entrance, checking his phone for messages and passing time, when the double pneumatic doors opened. In came the new mother, flat on her back and unconscious, nurses' aides on either side of the gurney. Jack assumed that the young man bringing up the rear, eyes of confusion peering out from over a surgical mask, was the father.

"Congratulations," said Jack.

"Thanks," he said. "Twins!"

A wave of mixed emotions washed over Jack, and he wondered how long such feelings would linger. A week? A year? Until Andie got pregnant again? What if she couldn't get pregnant again?

Jack's phone vibrated with a text. It was from Andie: *Come back now.*

He went back to her bay on the other side of the room and closed the curtain.

"Does Brunelli know about the phone call Theo got?" asked Jack.

"Yes. Theo told him, and then he passed it on to our team leader."

"Which you can't say anything more about, of course. I know, I know."

"Actually, I can," said Andie.

"Andie, don't go breaking any rules for me."

"I'm not," she said. "We've reached a very strange intersection of our worlds where I would need to have this conversation if you weren't my husband. I'm not going to avoid having it because you *are* my husband."

Jack pulled up a chair. "Are you actually going to ask me to deliver some money?"

"Here's the situation, Jack. The man who kidnapped you knows enough about what happened to the Scarborough 8 to give us the exact sequence of alarms immediately prior to the explosion. He's credible, and if he gets his million dollars, he'll tell us who sabotaged the rig. I guess he thinks the more valuable information is *why* and *how* it happened, which he plans to milk for even more money. But for now we'll settle for *who*. Right now, the FBI has no bigger priority than that."

"But in addition to kidnapping me and Theo in Cuba, he just murdered a Bahamian banker. I know the FBI pays informants, but you can't pay a million dollars to a kidnapper and a murderer."

Andie didn't answer.

"Seriously," said Jack. "You *can't*. Right?"

"No," said Andie. "We can't. But we can pretend to do it."

"When you say 'we,' do you mean . . . me?"

"We know things about this man that you don't know. He's smart enough to insist that the money be delivered by someone he considers safe. Someone he will recognize immediately by sight, who he will know is not an undercover FBI agent. Someone who is an American civilian, whose safety the FBI won't take any chances with."

"Someone like me."

"Yes. Someone like you."

"Are you asking me to do this?"

"No. I'm conveying the FBI's offer to you."

"What kind of offer?"

"Brunelli is a very sharp guy. He's plugged himself in with the Bahamian homicide squad. The royal police are circling Theo like sharks. They need to make an arrest."

"Theo didn't kill Jeffries."

"I believe you. If you agree to let the FBI fly in a polygraph examiner, and if Theo passes the test, the Bureau will believe you, too."

"So what if the FBI believes me?" said Jack. "The royal police will want to give Theo their own polygraph, and I'll never agree to that."

"That's where the deal kicks in," said Andie. "The FBI will take Theo out of Nassau before the Bahamians can make an arrest. And once he's stateside, the Justice Department will oppose extradition."

"The Justice Department will give me that in writing?"

"Yes," said Andie. "If you keep the last part of the deal."

Jack knew exactly what she was saying. "If I deliver the money to Josefina."

"Yes," said Andie.

"Do you want me to do this?"

"If I told you I didn't, what would you say?"

"I wouldn't do it," said Jack.

"I thought so," said Andie. "That's why it's up to you."

"This is a decision we should make together," said Jack.

Andie's expression showed neither agreement nor disagreement. "The pressure is on the Bahamian police to make an arrest. Everyone from the Bahamas Ministry of Tourism to the Caribbean Association of Banks is beating the drum. Brunelli tells me that Theo will likely be arrested tomorrow morning. The charge is going to be first-degree murder. So ask yourself this question, Jack: Do I really want my wife to talk me out of this deal? Because that's what I'm going to do, if you let me."

Jack said nothing for a moment, the silence hanging between them. Finally he answered. "I think there's one more flight to Nassau tonight. Tell Brunelli I want to be there for the polygraph."

61
·

"Theo passed," said Brunelli.

Jack had expected no less. The polygraph examination was administered inside Theo's motel room in Nassau, and Jack had waited right outside the door. Step one—the easy part of Jack's deal with the FBI—was over. Or so Jack had thought, until the examiner invited Jack and Brunelli back into the room.

"I need to redo it," said the examiner. "It's not Mr. Knight's fault, but I have some reliability concerns."

"I don't understand," said Jack.

The examiner walked past the double beds to the desk, where his computerized eight-channel polygraph system was set up. Theo was seated in the chair, still connected to thoracic and abdominal respiratory sensors, a pulse and blood-pressure cuff around his arm, and galvanic skin sensors attached to his fingers.

"Let me explain something about polygraphs," said the examiner. "To get a reliable reading, the first thing I have to do is see how my indicators behave when the subject lies. I do this by asking a control question that I know the subject will answer untruthfully. For example, I might ask a religious person if he has ever thought about sex in church. He'll answer no, which is almost certainly a lie, and then I know how his lie registers on my instruments."

"I'm guessing Mr. Knight is not much of a churchgoer," said Brunelli.

"Shows how much you know, Biscotti."

"Brunelli."

"That's what I said."

"No, you called me—"

"Never mind!" said Jack. "What does all this have to do with the reliability of Theo's polygraph results?"

"I used a different control question for him," said the examiner. "Tough guys like Mr. Knight tend to lie about their sexual prowess. So I asked him: 'Have you ever had sex with two different sets of twins on the same night?' The 'twins' fantasy is a well-established male phenomenon, but two sets of twins in one night is over the top even for an X-rated movie. As I had predicted, however, Mr. Knight answered yes."

"So you caught him in a lie," said Jack. "What's the problem?"

"Now that I've gone back and looked more closely at the data, I suspect Mr. Knight wasn't lying."

Jack made a face. "Dude, I have to say the whole siblings in bed thing creeps me out."

"Y'all are full of shit," said Theo as he ripped

the Velcro fastener from his arm. "Lemme take this from the top and set things straight. First off, Bacci ball: my Uncle Cy has dragged me to the Greater Bethel AME Church of Overtown at least a thousand times. Second, Swyteck: let he who has celebrated without sin on the night of his release from death row cast the first 'creeps-me-out' stone. Third, the 'twins' thing ain't just a guy thing. If you don't believe me, come into my bar, mix three margaritas for any woman who read *Harry Potter* as a teenager, and then ask her if she ever thought about doing Fred and George Weasley."

The examiner paused, as if not quite sure how to respond. "In any event, the bottom line is that I can't give a clean certification without a reliable reading on my control question."

"Whoa," said Brunelli. "We don't have time to redo the test."

"Then no certification."

"Technically speaking," said Theo, "it was one set of twins before midnight, and the other set after midnight. So not the same night."

"There you go," said Brunelli.

"Liar, liar, pants on fire," said Jack.

"Certify the results," said Brunelli. "We're outta here."

Theo disconnected himself from the remaining instruments, and Brunelli whisked him and Jack out the door. The ridiculously compact rental car was parked right outside the motel entrance, and as they piled in, Jack would have sworn that it had actually shrunk since their ride to the New Providence Bank and Trust Company. Cramped inside,

Brunelli behind the wheel, Jack in the back with his knees to his chin, they sped away to the airport. A Cessna Caravan 675 was waiting for them on the lighted runway, its single engine humming. Brunelli handed out passports before they boarded. Jack and Theo were suddenly Bahamian citizens.

"Damn, I was hoping to be Swedish," said Theo.

Brunelli had finally learned to ignore him. "This is not an FBI aircraft or an FBI pilot," he said. "It's a private charter straight into Havana. Just follow my lead, and all will go smoothly."

The Caravan 675 was large enough for eight passengers, but the seating on this particular plane had been reconfigured to accommodate just four adults, two seats facing aft and two facing front, with a table mounted between them. It wasn't hard for a criminal defense lawyer to imagine a kingpin at the table counting his money while sampling long white lines of merchandise. Jack and Brunelli sat with their backs to the pilot, and Theo sat on the other side of the table, facing them. They were airborne by nine p.m., headed to José Martí International Airport. Jack peered out the window as the plane leveled off. With the cabin gone dark, the skies were a celestial light show, billions of bright stars on a pitch-black canvas far removed from city lights. Jack was searching for Orion when, for no apparent reason, the aircraft heaved, dipping sharply and then rising before leveling off again.

"By any chance, are we in the Devil's Triangle?" asked Jack.

"We're actually just leaving it," said Brunelli. "Cuba sits to the south-southwest of it."

Jack's gaze turned back to the stars, but Brunelli switched on the overhead light. It brought him back to earth, even if they were twelve thousand feet above the Caribbean. Brunelli laid a map of Havana on the table in front of Jack.

"We land at José Martí around eleven-thirty," he said, his finger on the map, giving directions as he spoke. "You and Theo will take a cab to Hotel Nacional in the Vedado district. Everything you two need for the drop will be delivered to your room before noon."

"Me *and* Theo? We're doing this together?"

"Yes," Brunelli said. "Not my idea, but I was over-ruled. We want this guy to believe that you came to Cuba without the FBI following you. It's just not believable that any sane human being would carry a million dollars in a duffel bag without someone to watch his back. That's Theo's role."

"Would be more believable if I was Swedish," said Theo.

"Deal with it," said Brunelli. "The drop is three p.m. at Coppelia's ice cream parlor."

"I know it well," said Jack. "Theo and I met Josefina there."

"That's one reason he chose it, no doubt. It's also a very public place, which is good from both your standpoint and his. It makes it virtually impossible for one side to ambush the other."

Jack glanced at Theo, the blink of the Cessna's wing-light reflecting in his eyes. "Just to be clear: the plan is for Theo and me to go there?"

"Yes. The guy knows both of you, knows that neither one of you works for the FBI, so he shouldn't have a problem with it. I can't get approval for you to tote a million bucks through Havana by yourself, even if you are being watched."

"We're using real money?"

"Yes. Of course there will be a GPS tracking chip in the bag and a microchip embedded in various bills."

"Where will you be?"

"You won't see me, but I will be shadowing you at all times. At various points along the way there will be other U.S. cooperatives keeping an eye on you."

"Will I be wired?"

"Yes. Earpiece and microphone, both so small no one will notice. The only voice you'll hear in the earpiece will be mine."

"Where's the mike?"

"You'll have several in your clothing and on the bag. But the microphones are not for any back and forth conversation between us. The only function of the mike is to pick up your conversation with Josefina."

"So I shouldn't respond to anything you tell me?"

"It's best for you to forget you even have a mike. Unless things break down and it becomes a matter of your personal safety."

Unless.

They sat quietly for a moment, the engine humming steadily as each seemed to contemplate the "unless" scenario.

"What if something does go wrong?" asked Jack. "What's the contingency plan?"

"I'm working on that," said Brunelli.

"Working on it? The drop is *tomorrow*."

"Hopefully by then I'll have things resolved to everyone's satisfaction. Right now, I'm not happy with what the Bureau is prepared to offer you. I want to do better for you. If nothing else, just for your wife's peace of mind."

"As it stands now, what's the contingency?"

Brunelli breathed in and out. "All international operations are complicated. This one especially. We're in Cuba, in the heart of downtown Havana. The FBI doesn't even have a legal attaché office here. I know it sounds crazy. We have legates in Iraq, Afghanistan, Pakistan, and Yemen, but none in Cuba. If something goes wrong, there's no relationship with local law enforcement. We can't exactly have a bunch of FBI agents popping out of the woodwork, guns drawn."

"I don't suppose *I'll* be armed," said Jack.

"No way."

"What if the shit really hits the fan and I'm arrested?"

"There's the rub," said Brunelli.

"Explain."

"It comes down to what I just said: we have absolutely no relationship with local law enforcement. If you are arrested by the Cubans, we can't guarantee your release."

" 'No guarantee' can mean different things," said Jack. "Are you saying you will fight like hell for my release but can't guarantee it? Or are you saying something else?"

"Fight like hell is what I'm pushing for."

"I'm asking where it stands now," said Jack.

"As of tonight, no one is willing to cause an inter-national incident over an American lawyer making a drop in downtown Havana."

For Jack, the proverbial lightbulb went on. "That's why you want Theo to go with me. If something goes wrong, you want this to look like anything but the FBI at work."

"No one is trying to trick you," said Brunelli. "The truth is, if you are detained, the effort to get you released from the Cubans won't be an FBI matter, or even an international law-enforcement matter. It will be about politics, completely behind the scenes. Your father's contacts in the White House would probably serve you better than any as-surances I could get from the FBI."

Jack hoped it wouldn't come to that. He had pur-posely kept his father out of the loop, insulating him from stress, ever since the trip to the emergency room.

"I'm not counting on political contacts if this blows up."

"Okay, but know this: publicly, the FBI will deny that it has anything to do with you."

"What if I say no deal?"

"My hands are tied, Jack. The only option is to turn this plane around and head back to Nassau."

"That's not much of an option."

"You got that right. The pressure on the Royal Bahamas Police to make an arrest in the Jeffries murder is huge, and right now the cops think Theo is their man. They have a sworn statement from one of the women at the bank saying that Theo came back looking for Jeffries and that she told him where Jeffries lived. Time of death is not the to-the-minute science that crime shows on TV would have people believe, so they have Theo at the scene roughly at the time of the murder. True, he's the one who called the cops, but he's not the first killer to try that ruse. And overlaying all of this is the fact that he's a former gangbanger from Miami who got away with murder once before, thanks to his smart lawyer, who happened to be the politically connected son of the governor of Florida."

"Politics had nothing to do with it," said Jack.

"I'm just telling you how it's playing out in Nassau," said Brunelli. "My guess is that Theo will be arrested tomorrow and spend at least the next four to six months in a Bahamian jail while they investigate the homicide. If the charges stick, he's looking at a year to eighteen months in jail before the case gets to trial. If he's convicted of first-degree murder . . . well, you're the criminal defense lawyer. You know the drill."

"Yeah, I know the drill."

Theo was looking at him from across the table. It had been a long time since Jack had seen him this serious, probably since they'd looked at each other through prison glass.

"You don't have to do this," said Theo.

"We'll stick to the plan."

"I mean it," said Theo. "You don't have to."

"I know I don't. I'm just playing the odds."

"What odds?"

"See, if we turn this plane around, we'll be flying

straight into the Devil's Triangle. Isn't that right, Bocelli?"

"Brunelli. Yes, that's right."

"There you go. It's safer to fly straight on through to Cuba. That's my decision. Just don't go thinking that I'm doing you any favors, Theo. You got that?"

Theo smiled and settled back into his seat. "Got it."

62

Noori woke at dawn. Ninety minutes of iso-
metrics prepared him for his day.

The morning exercise routine was something
that Noori had developed during his seven years at
Guantánamo, though in those days he had no idea
if it was morning, afternoon, or night. Camp 6 was
said to be reserved for "noncompliant" detainees,
but the alleged acts of "noncompliance," like the
alleged terrorist acts that had landed him and the
other Chinese Uighurs in Gitmo in the first place,
were never explained to Noori. Each detainee at
Camp 6 was confined to a small, windowless steel
cell with no access to natural light or air. Noori was
allowed no contact with fellow prisoners. Meals were
served through a slot in the door. Fluorescent lights
buzzed twenty-four hours a day, limiting sleep. He
was allocated fifteen sheets of toilet paper a day, but
because he used it to cover his eyes to help him to
sleep, his toilet paper—considered another comfort
item—was removed for "misuse." Even after his release, the Americans refused to acknowledge that he

was kept in solitary confinement, instead speaking in euphemisms of greater "privacy" and "single-occupancy cells."

Seven years.

Noori crossed his legs yoga style and breathed deep. He was trying to relax, pushing aside the anger inside him. But not all of it. A little anger was a good thing. It could get you through another day without sleep. It could get you through seven years of living hell.

It could put the world's largest oil rig on the bottom of the ocean.

Noori pushed himself up from the rug and walked to the window. Cheaper rooms had been available, but Noori had sprung for the top floor—not a perfect view of the harbor, but at least a glimpse of it in the distance. No matter the city, no matter the hotel, Noori always insisted on a view. Windowless rooms triggered bad memories and bizarre conduct that he couldn't explain, not even to his lawyer or his counselor.

Noori, why did you smear your feces on the walls of your cell?

I have no idea.

There had to be a reason.

I have no idea.

Noori opened the window and breathed in the morning air. Fresh air. It was something he no longer took for granted. Like the sun, the rain, or the stars at night. Even the unremarkable view of an old building across the street beat seven years of staring at the same four walls. Even the cracked and crumbling walls that hadn't been painted since Batista.

The walls in Havana were beautiful.

Sunday had been Noori's travel day. His route— New York to Miami, Miami to Kingston, Kingston to Havana—had been intentionally circuitous. He'd arrived in time to get a full night's sleep. Havana was coming to life, another workweek just beginning.

Noori, too, had work to do.

He grabbed a chair and went to the closet. It was the same room he and Long Wu always used for their trips to Havana. He climbed up on the chair and popped out one of the tiles in the false ceiling. He reached inside the crawl space, retrieved a metal strong box, and brought it to the bed. The key was on his ring. He unlocked the box and opened it. All was in order, just as he had left it.

One Russian Makarov PM semi-automatic pistol. One leather ankle holster. Three magazines of 9-millimeter ammunition, eight rounds each.

The Makarov PM had been in frontline service with the Soviet military for more than forty years, which meant that plenty were available on the black market in Cuba. Noori had purchased this one on his first trip to Havana, when Long Wu closed a deal for one million counterfeit handbags with a Russian billionaire who had suddenly stopped doing business out of Miami and had taken a serious liking to Cuba—which had no extradition treaty with the United States.

Noori lifted his pant leg, fastened the ankle holster, and secured the weapon. He checked himself in the full-length mirror on the bathroom door. No sign of a handgun beneath his khakis. He sat on the end of the unmade bed, thinking of the e-mail message that had prompted his trip to Havana: *One million by Monday. Or the attached goes viral.*

A million? Really?

True, Noori had promised him a million upon successful completion of the mission. True, also, that Noori's face was clearly recognizable in the surveillance video from the New Providence Bank and Trust Company. But none of that changed his mind: the fifty thousand dollars in seed money that he'd deposited in that account was plenty for a guy who earned $1,200 a year.

Not a penny more.

Noori's cell phone vibrated. There was another e-mail message with the same subject line: NR050527, the account number from the Bahamian bank. Noori opened the message and read it:

> I'm betting that the deposit slip has fingerprints. The original goes to the FBI after the bank surveillance photos go viral. Unless a wire transfer of $1 million hits the Bank of the West Indies (Cayman) Ltd., Account No. NR65430, by the end of business, Monday.

It was a new account, at a new bank, in a different country. The same offshore secrecy, a thousand miles away from the investigation by the Bahamian police into Mr. Jeffries' death and the Lopez account.

The e-mail had an attachment. Noori clicked to

open it. It was a photograph of the original deposit slip for the fifty thousand dollars. It had fallen into enemy hands—literally—as the hand that held it was visible in the photograph.

The eye tattoo, just below the wrist, wasn't staring straight at Noori. But it might as well have been.

Noori deleted the e-mail. He was angry, but he smiled. The demand that one million dollars hit the new Cayman bank account before the end of the day—with no mention of Noori's whereabouts—only confirmed that his trip to Cuba would come as a complete surprise to the greedy fool who was pushing his buttons. Noori rose from the bed and slipped the extra clips of ammunition into his pocket.

There would indeed be a "hit" before five o'clock.

Noori would make sure of it.

63

.

At noon on Monday, Jack heard a knock at the door.

A taxi ride from the airport had put Jack and Theo at the Hotel Nacional just after midnight, where they shared a double room. Heeding Brunelli's instructions, they'd ordered room service for breakfast, and they had yet to set foot outside their room, much less the hotel.

Jack checked through the peephole and opened the door. It was Brunelli. He had a small duffel bag in one hand and a stainless-steel briefcase in the other. Jack didn't do drug cases, but nary a criminal defense lawyer in Miami was unaware that the five-inch Zero Halliburton held exactly ten thousand one-hundred-dollar bills.

"Some ground rules," Brunelli said as he laid the duffel bag and the briefcase on the bed. "Number one: we are a serious law-enforcement operation from this point forward. That means no more 'Brunelli' jokes. It's not even a funny name."

"Agreed," said Theo. "Not like Venus Williams marrying Bruno Mars. Venus Mars. Now, that's a funny name. Brunelli? Not funny."

Brunelli was not amused, but Jack understood that humor was how his friend had remained sane on death row. Joking around was his natural reaction to stress. Theo could push things too far. Jack got that. But Jack had also seen the effects of prison on guys who'd never developed coping mechanisms. It wasn't pretty.

"We're going to stay completely focused from this point forward," said Jack. "No more goofing around. Isn't that right, Theo?"

He took Jack's cue. "If that's what Special Agent Brunelli wants, that's what Special Agent Brunelli gets."

"Thank you," said Brunelli. He popped open the briefcase. Jack's hunch about the cash had been correct. Benjamin Franklin was staring back at them, many times over.

"If it's not real, it sure looks it," said Jack.

"It's real," said Brunelli. "For your own safety, I'm not going to tell you which bills are embedded with a GPS tracking microchip."

He unzipped the duffel bag and emptied the contents onto the bed. There were two sets of clothing, one for Jack, the larger set for Theo.

"Guayaberas," said Brunelli. "Armored, but it's hard to tell. By Michael Cabrera, out of Bogotá. The president of Colombia loves these shirts."

Theo picked up the white one. "Very cool. And it's bulletproof?"

"To a point. Don't go out looking to get shot, but it will give you a chance to take a hit and make a run for it, at least up to a .38-caliber slug. Maybe a 9-mil, if not fired at close range. Beyond that . . . duck."

"And the jeans?" asked Jack, "also armored?"

"Yes. You'll be a lot warmer than you'd like to be, but not much we can do about that."

"Better hot than shot."

"Good line," said Brunelli. "I'll pass it along to Cabrera's marketing people. No need working up a sweat before you leave the hotel. Just put these on when you're ready to leave."

"What about the audio equipment?"

"All the electronics are sewn into the fabric. There's no switch or button to activate it. Once you're suited up, we'll be able to hear everything you say."

"Got it," said Jack.

Brunelli moved the cash to the duffel bag, explaining the move before Jack could ask why. "GPS tracking won't work through anodized aluminum," said Brunelli. "The bag also has backup microphones, in case the ones in your clothing fail. You don't have to keep the bag right on top of the table, but keep it nearby."

"What about my earpiece?"

Brunelli stepped closer and inserted it into Jack's ear canal. Jack checked in the mirror over the dresser. No sign of the earpiece.

"How's that feel?" asked Brunelli.

"Like there's something in my ear."

"You'll get used to it. We'll do an audio test before you head to the Coppelia to meet with Josefina."

"Speaking of, do I just go with the flow, or do you want me to follow some kind of script?"

Brunelli pulled a notepad from the briefcase. On it was a list of questions in the agent's handwriting. "I'm glad you asked," he said.

64
.

Jack left the Hotel Nacional de Cuba at 2:45 p.m. Theo was at his side, toting the cash-filled duffel bag.

Both the hotel and the Heladería Coppelia were in the Vedado district, one of Havana's most upscale and touristy areas. The blonde getting out of the taxi in front of the hotel was trying to pay in euros. The gay couple walking toward them, in the direction of the Malecón, were speaking Portuguese. Jack was two blocks from his hotel, almost halfway to the ice cream parlor, when he heard Brunelli's voice in his ear.

"Have you in sight. If you can hear me, tell Theo his fly is open."

It was a lame attempt at payback, but Jack did it.

"Your momma," said Theo.

"You'll have to do better than that, Brunelli," Jack said for the agent's benefit.

"Listen up," said Brunelli. "Make a left on Calle L and you're less than a block away. You won't hear from me again until we get a visual on Josefina. Good luck."

The old and decaying Hotel Victoria marked their turn at Calle L. To Jack's dismay, almost the entire city block ahead of them, all the way to the Facultad de Economía (business school) at the University of Havana, was without shade. He could almost see the mid-afternoon heat rising from the sidewalk. They'd only walked a quarter mile from the air-conditioned lobby of their hotel, and already Jack was sweating beneath his armored guayabera. It was nothing compared to Theo's soaking.

"Not sure about your 'better hot than shot' slogan," said Theo.

"Almost there."

Their previous walk to Coppelia had been from the south, but the building's flying-saucer design was instantly recognizable from any direction. The ice cream parlor was surrounded by a park, and the shade trees brought welcome relief. They were deep into the park, nearing the outdoor seating area for ice cream customers, when Jack's cell phone rang. It was 2:56 p.m. Four minutes before the scheduled meeting time with Josefina. Jack wasn't sure if he should take the call, but Brunelli cleared up the confusion.

"Answer it."

Jack stopped beneath a coconut palm tree and answered. It was Josefina.

"I didn't tell you to bring your friend," she said.

"You didn't say not to. Surely you didn't expect me to come alone carrying this kind of cargo."

"Okay, but change of plan," she said. "Meet at three-fifteen on the Malecón by Hotel Nacional."

The Malecón was the most famous esplanade in

Havana, stretching four miles along the waterfront, from the mouth of Havana Harbor in Old Havana to the Hotel Nacional in Vedado. Jack knew it.

"Okay," he said into the phone, but Josefina was already gone. Brunelli's voice was in his other ear. "Tell Theo what she said in a voice that I can hear. Don't stand there like you're talking to the FBI through a microphone."

He told Theo, but it was Brunelli who replied. "Go there. We're on it. Keep in mind that we have no way to find out where she's calling from. I don't have a team of techies to triangulate in Cuba."

Jack knew enough about police surveillance to understand Brunelli's limitations. It was impossible to get a location on a mobile phone with no technological access to the cell towers that relayed the calls.

"Let's go," he told Theo, but Brunelli got the last word:

"Jack, I'm green-lighting this change, but be careful with Josefina. I'm not as convinced as you are that she's an unwilling participant under this guy's thumb."

Jack heard him, but he didn't reply. They reversed course and started toward the Malecón.

Josefina tucked her phone into her pocket and stepped away from the window.

The business school for la Universidad de La Habana was directly across the street from the Coppelia, and the empty classroom on the fourth floor offered a clear view of the pavilion and surrounding park. The view was even better with binoculars, which her so-called friend Vivien was using to watch Jack and Theo.

"They're heading for the Malecón," said Vivien.

"Then I need to get going."

"Wait." Vivien laid the binoculars on the windowsill and dialed on her phone. Josefina could hear only one end of the conversation, the first minute of which was a recap. Then Vivien got to the point of her call.

"I'm almost positive Swyteck and his friend are being followed."

Josefina did a double take, but Vivien was the one with the binoculars. She still couldn't hear the other end of the conversation, but she assumed that the question in her own mind was also being put to Vivien: *Followed by whom?*

Vivien raised her binoculars and again peered out toward the park. "I think I saw Noori," she said into the telephone.

65

J ack and Theo waited at the Malecón until 4:15 p.m. There was no sign of Josefina.

"I don't think she's coming," said Theo.

Jack took a seat on the stone seawall, facing the esplanade. Josefina could not have chosen a more beautiful spot for the delivery of one million dollars. Behind him, waves splashed on the rocks below, a tropical breeze carrying in the salty warmth of Havana Bay. Rising above the rocky edges of a knoll—not quite an acropolis, but breathtakingly beautiful, nonetheless—sat the flagship Hotel Nacional de Cuba in all its eclectic combination of architectural styles. Despite a steady onslaught of camera-toting tourists, Jack and Theo had waited at the designated spot until 3:45, when Jack had started to wonder if there had been a miscommunication between him and Josefina. With Brunelli's blessing, Theo had stayed put while Jack went on a walk up and down the Malecón, searching. He'd gone west, all the way to a Madison Avenue–quality billboard that showcased photographs of U.S. Marines violently rounding up members of the Taliban and al-Qaeda, bold red letters proclaiming: FACISTAS— MADE IN THE U.S.A. And then he'd turned around and walked east, down to a colorful work of graffiti-art that someone had painted on a wall that faced out toward the United States, a cartoonish depiction of Uncle Sam growling and Che Guevara laughing. Its message read (in Spanish): MR. IMPERIALIST, WE DO NOT HAVE ANY FEAR OF YOU.

All told, Jack had probably covered a mile-long stretch of the esplanade. No Josefina.

"I think you may be right," said Jack.

"What do we do now?"

"I don't know. What do you think we should do?"

Theo shrugged. "You don't have change for ten thousand hundreds, do ya?"

Jack's phone vibrated. "Got a text," he said to Theo, but his narration was mostly for Brunelli's benefit, who was still monitoring them electronically. Jack checked the text more closely. "Not really a message," he said. "It's just a link to a website for *Cuba Times*. That's an online English-language newspaper about life in Cuba."

"Josefina's friend writes for it," said Theo.

"Open it," said Brunelli, his voice in Jack's earpiece.

Jack clicked on the link. Slowly, the page opened to the latest issue of *Cuba Times*.

"It's a story on the victims and survivors of the Scarborough 8 disaster," said Jack. "Written by Patricia Nuñez. That's a pen name for Josefina's friend, Vivien Delgado."

The image continued to build on Jack's screen. It was an indecipherable mess of pixels for nearly a full minute, but finally the photograph came into view. Five young men smiling for the camera on a sunny day. Each was wearing a hard hat and orange coveralls, a tangle of mud-stained hoses at their boots. They were leaning against the rail at the platform's edge, nothing but blue sky and ocean behind them. Jack recognized only one of them.

"It's a picture of Rafael with some of his coworkers on the Scarborough 8," Jack said.

Jack's phone vibrated again. He exited his browser to receive another text. This time there was a message, not just a link, which he read aloud for Brunelli's benefit: "'Look closely at his right hand.'"

Jack switched back to his browser screen. The photograph was still up. He zoomed in on Rafael's hand, which was draped over the shoulder of one of his buddies. He drew the image tighter and tighter—then froze.

"Rafael had a tattoo," he said.

Theo came closer, to look for himself. Jack described the tattoo for Brunelli. "Below the wrist, just above the thumb. It's an eye."

"You gotta be shittin' me!" said Theo, even though he could see it for himself.

"There's a caption beneath the photograph," said Jack, and then he read it:

"'Rafael Lopez (third from right) with four surviving coworkers. Lopez, whose mother was born in Mexico, prayed daily to Our Lady of Guadalupe for his safety. Many believe that Our Lady appeared to a humble Native American in 1531, leaving her image imprinted miraculously on a poor-quality cactus cloth, which should have deteriorated in two decades but has survived for nearly five centuries. The eyes of Our Lady are said to reveal much of what she saw in the sixteenth century, as well as messages to the faithful. While on the Scarborough 8, Rafael had one of the famous eyes tattooed onto his hand, so that Our Lady would keep him safe, watching over his every grasp of the rungs as he climbed high on the derrick.'"

Jack lowered his phone.

"Whoa," said Theo.

Jack turned around and looked out over the sea-wall, toward Havana Bay, toward the mile-deep ocean beyond.

"He's gotta be dead," he said in disbelief. "Doesn't he?"

66

The message crackled in Jack's ear at 6:00 p.m. "Let's call it," said Brunelli.

It was a three-minute walk from the Malecón back to the Hotel Nacional. Jack and Theo reached the veranda in time for cocktails, but not even Theo felt like imbibing. Brunelli met them in the lobby and took the duffel bag from Theo.

"Count it if you want, but it's all still there," said Theo.

"I'll trust you," said Brunelli. "Not that it matters. It's not real."

"You told me it was," said Jack.

"It was important for you to think it was. You're more convincing that way."

It made sense, but it made Jack wonder what else Brunelli had told him was false and for effect.

"Time to lose the James Bond clothes," said Theo. "I'm going up to the room."

Before Jack could say "me, too," Brunelli was pulling him aside. "We need a little postmortem, Swyteck."

Jack agreed and followed him to a quiet seating area just outside the hotel lobby. A two-foot green iguana scampered across the mosaic of Moorish tiles and into the bushes. Jack took the white wicker armchair. Brunelli sank into an overstuffed couch that almost seemed to swallow him whole.

"Why do you think she was a no-show?" asked Jack.

"Who knows? Maybe this was all a dry run. Maybe something spooked her."

"I don't think it was Theo," said Jack.

"I agree. But there's no way she saw me or my team, either."

"So what would have spooked her?"

Brunelli didn't answer. Jack watched his eyes and got a weird feeling. It was the same look he'd seen in Andie's eyes when she couldn't or wouldn't tell him something about one of her operations.

"You're not going to tell me, are you?" said Jack.

Brunelli pushed himself up from the sunken cushions and moved to the edge of the couch, bringing himself to eye level with Jack. "Let's talk about Theo. I have to take him back to Nassau."

Jack's response—something along the lines of what Brunelli could go do to himself—rose up and caught in his throat. Had Brunelli not been a friend of Andie's, Jack would have let it fly. He cleaned it up considerably.

"Sorry, but that's not the deal," said Jack.

"Those are my orders. My hands are tied."

"Then untie them."

"I can't. This is coming from Justice."

"By 'Justice' you mean the National Security Division?"

"Correct."

Jack leaned forward, looking him in the eye. "Here's what you tell the folks in NSD. Theo is in Cuba. You have no authority to arrest him here. You can't make him go anywhere or do anything. He's not going back to the Bahamas, period."

"That's not a wise posture," said Brunelli.

Jack sat back, thinking. "This is all about the photograph, isn't it. The tattoo on Rafael's hand."

"I can't discuss that."

"You don't really think he's alive, do you?"

He considered his response before answering. "Did you know that the only live video of the Deepwater Horizon explosion in 2010 was taken by some fishermen who were fishing near the rig?"

"What's your point?"

"It's not unusual for fishing boats to be hanging around oil rigs. Rafael could have been thrown into the ocean. Someone could have picked him up, transferred him to another boat, taken him to shore—who knows? It was a major catastrophe, total confusion."

"You know that didn't happen," said Jack. "Even if he survived the explosion, no fishing boats would have been near the Scarborough 8 in that storm."

"That's your opinion. But it really doesn't matter what you or I think, does it?"

"No. And apparently it doesn't matter what the truth is, either. Because NSD doesn't need the truth. All they need is a story. Now they have their story: Rafael Lopez blew up the Scarborough 8 and remains at large. Of course no one will ever find him, because he was incinerated. But that doesn't matter, because the Rafael Lopez story fits with some other agenda of the NSD. I don't know what that agenda is. You probably don't, either."

"You're reading way too much into this."

"Am I? You know, there's something I've always wondered about since the hearing where I cross-examined the vice president of Barton-Hammill about the alarm security. I wondered why the U.S. would allow state-of-the-art technology to be used on a Chinese rig."

"Safety," said Brunelli. "It was in everyone's interest that the rig operate safely."

"That's one explanation," said Jack. "But here's another: What if the alarm system was rigged in a way that allowed the U.S. to monitor everything that happened on the Scarborough 8 without the Chinese ever knowing it?"

"That makes no sense."

"The Scarborough 8 was the largest and most advanced oil rig in the world. It was built in China with over ninety percent Chinese parts and technology. Wouldn't the U.S. like to know every secret about every component on that rig?"

"Come on, Swyteck. You're saying that the Department of the Treasury granted an exemption to the trade embargo so that Barton-Hammill equipment could be put on the rig to spy on Chinese technology? *Really?*"

"The U.S. allowed a special exemption to the embargo, which it normally would never do. The U.S. handed over to the Chinese state-of-the-art technology, which it normally would never do. There had to be a compelling reason. What better reason is there than to allow the U.S. to monitor the activities of the Chinese, Russians, Venezuelans, and Cubans—not exactly our four closest friends—ninety miles from U.S. shores?"

"Seriously? You're accusing the U.S. government of blowing up the Scarborough 8?"

"Not at all," said Jack. "I'm saying that somebody from Barton-Hammill fucked up the electronics on the rig while spying from a remote location. That's what caused the alarm to malfunction in the storm. That's what caused the rig to explode. That's what the NSD is covering up."

Brunelli didn't answer.

"I know what you're thinking," said Jack. "I'll never prove it. And you're probably right. The National Security Division will take the position that Rafael is alive. The FBI's criminal investigation will drag on for three or four years and eventually back the NSD's position. Bianca's wrongful death lawsuit will go away for good; a widow can't sue for wrongful death if her husband isn't dead. That will leave no one in a U.S. courtroom to prove that Barton-Hammill caused the explosion. Eventually there will be an earthquake in California, a flood in the Midwest, a hurricane in the Carolinas, and everybody but the Conchs who are stuck cleaning up the mess from Marathon to Key West will forget about the oil spill. It all conveniently goes away."

Brunelli remained silent.

"I've said enough," said Jack, rising. "We'll fight that fight later. For now, you can't have Theo."

"I can't leave here without him."

"Then you'd better brush up on your Spanish.

Because you are way out of your jurisdiction. And Theo really likes it here."

Jack turned and headed back to the lobby. The elevator yawned open, and he rode it to the third floor. His anger was rising, much faster than the car. Brunelli was proving to be no more helpful than Agent Linton. Jack blamed himself. The pre-Andie Swyteck would never have been so trusting. At least on a subconscious level, the fact that he was married to an FBI agent had lulled him into an unhealthy level of comfort with the government. That wasn't how the "adversary system" worked.

Fool me once, shame on you . . .

Jack unlocked the door and entered his hotel room. The lights were on, and Theo's sweaty armored clothing was scattered on one of the beds. But the room was quiet.

"Theo?"

No response. The bathroom door was open, but Jack saw only a cockroach scurry across the floor. Jack checked the closet. Theo's clothes were gone. So was his overnight bag.

. . . fool me twice, shame on me.

Maybe Jack had been fooled again by the FBI. Theo had not.

"Damn it!" he said, angry only at himself. *Where the hell did you go, Theo?*

67

For the first time in his life, Theo walked right past a jazz bar without even the slightest temptation to go inside. He was on a mission.

He didn't trust Brunelli. Not for a minute did he believe that the FBI would keep its promise to resist his extradition to the Bahamas—not if he was the number-one suspect in the brutal murder of a Bahamian banker. He'd spent four years on Florida's death row for another man's crime; no way was he going to a Bahamian jail for a murder he didn't commit. Too many people had their own agendas. Theo had his own ideas about who had kidnapped Jack in Cuba, threatened Bianca in her trailer, and killed Jeffries in his living room. It was time to take matters into his own hands.

He stopped outside La Escuela de Boxeo. The long shadows on the sidewalk were disappearing as twilight turned into darkness. The light over the entrance flickered every few seconds with a bad electrical connection. Theo tried the door. It opened, and he went inside.

The hallway was dimly lit, but even in total darkness Theo could have simply followed his nose to the stale, smelly air of the training gym. All but one of the six boxing rings were empty. The lonely sound of one woman's punches echoed through the gym. Her trainer wore padded coaching mitts to absorb her blows. It was just the two of them, Josefina and Sicario, working late in the ring, as if nothing had happened. Theo would have something to say about that.

"Missed you today, girl," he called out.

Josefina stopped, her trainer lowered his punching mitts, and they watched Theo walk slowly toward them. He said nothing until he was almost to the ring.

"Something's not right here, Josefina." Theo stopped at the ropes, but his thinking aloud continued. "You train hard. You love boxing. Last time I saw you, we joked around, kept it light. But working in a bar makes me a pretty quick study on people. If there was one thing I knew about you when I left Cuba, it was this: money ain't what it's about."

She chewed her mouthpiece, silent.

"So I ask myself: What's in this for you?"

Sicario stepped in front of her, putting himself between Theo and his fighter. "Why don't you go ask yourself outside?"

"'Cuz here's my problem, dude. I can't think up a single reason why Josefina would *wanna* do this. So maybe the real question is, who could *make* her do something she doesn't wanna do? It has to be someone who's got the power to end her boxing career, to kill her dream. Someone who knows she wasn't really engaged to Rafael. Someone who could tell the Cuban government that she was part of Rafael's lie so he could get a job on the rig."

"That's pretty big talk," said Sicario.

"I'm a pretty big guy."

"We don't like talkers around here. Boxers only."

"You want to box?" asked Theo. "I'll box you."

Sicario laughed.

Josefina's mouth guard dropped into her glove, her voice filled with concern. "Sicario, don't. Your head."

"*My* head?" said Sicario, scoffing.

"Theo, just go away. He had to stop boxing because of his head."

"You're afraid he's going to hurt *me*?" said Sicario.

She was pleading with her trainer. "He's younger than you, and look at him. You can tell he grew up fighting. All he has to do is land one lucky punch to your head and—"

"Wear the headgear, if you want," said Theo. "I can still kick your Cuban boxing ass."

Sicario glared at him from inside the ring. Theo hadn't planned to pick a fight, but he'd picked one.

"Get us gloves, Josefina. This won't take long."

68

·

Jack followed his hunch and jumped into a taxi outside the Hotel Nacional.

"*La Escuela de Boxeo, Habana Centro*," Jack said, handing up a twenty. "Show me how fast this old Buick can go."

The driver didn't understand English, but he understood cash. The sixty-year-old Buick Special rumbled away from the car port, down the main driveway, and onto the Malecón. Traffic was moving along at about thirty miles per hour, top speed for many of the pre-Castro classics. Another twenty-dollar bill from Jack had the driver changing lanes and weaving between cars as if they were standing still. The cash incentives were working just fine— until they came upon a vehicle that actually was standing still. The smoldering shell of a vintage 1940s Ford pickup was blocking the right lane. The tourists strolling along the esplanade were moving faster than Jack's taxi.

"*Aquí está bueno*," said Jack, telling the driver to drop him off.

The brakes squealed, followed by a horrific grind from the transmission as the driver shifted into PARK. Jack jumped out of the backseat and ran the final three blocks. The light outside the school was still on—flickering, but on. Jack took a moment to catch his breath and then tried the door. It opened. Jack went inside. The front desk was unattended, but Jack remembered his way down the narrow hallway. The familiar sounds of boxing—footwork on canvas, gloves meeting, competitors sucking air—drew him into the gym. Then he stopped, taken aback. Theo was moving around the ring, squaring off against Josefina's trainer. Jack walked to the ropes and stood beside Josefina.

"Make your friend stop," she told Jack. She checked the clock on the wall, and when the second hand swept twelve, she rang the bell. The fighters broke. Sicario went to the far corner, and Josefina brought him a stool. Theo went to the opposite corner. Jack joined him.

"What do you think you're doing?" asked Jack.

Theo took a mouthful of water and spit in the bucket. "Rafael's dead. You know it. I know it. Sicario's our man. I'm gonna knock his ass out and rip those gloves off. We gonna see that same tattoo."

"He's a professional, you moron."

"*Was* a professional. He's old."

"Not *that* old. His hands are lethal." Jack shot a quick glance across the ring. Josefina was pleading with her trainer. "Josefina's over there right now, begging him not to kill you."

"She's beggin' cuz he should've hung up his gloves long before he did. All those punches left his skull like an eggshell. I'm gonna knock him out."

Jack cast another look to the opposite corner. Josefina gave up the pleading. She walked over to the bell and rang it. Round two. The fighters came out. Jack stayed right outside Theo's corner. Josefina came around the ring and stood beside him.

"Say something, would you? Sicario is not what he used to be. He's not quick, he's not strong. He's damaged."

Josefina's words hit Jack in a way that she couldn't have intended. They didn't describe at all the man who had overpowered him at Vivien's house.

Jack leaned into the rope and addressed himself to the fighters. "Don't see much point to this, men," he said in a voice loud enough to carry throughout the gym.

The boxers continued to move, sizing each other up, looking for an opening, but no punches had landed. Josefina's assessment seemed fair: Sicario was slow.

Jack tried again, speaking to Sicario. "Bianca has a right to know if her husband is alive."

Sicario tried a left hook, but it missed.

"He's dead," Josefina said, her voice loud enough only for Jack to hear.

Jack glanced in her direction, but her eyes were cast to the floor, refusing to meet his. Jack put the next question to Sicario, again in a loud voice.

"She has a right to know if he was involved in the explosion."

Theo ducked away from Sicario's wild right. Sicario regained his balance and shouted, "Guilty."

"Sicario!" Josefina shouted.

"He said he was going to do it."

"Sicario, no!"

Jack suddenly felt like the referee in another fight, one between Josefina and her trainer. "I want the truth," said Jack.

Sicario seemed energized, suddenly finding his long-lost rhythm as a fighter. He was clearly the aggressor, and he landed his first combination. Theo staggered backward but righted himself.

"You want to know the truth? I'll tell you the truth."

Theo wisely backed away, out of Sicario's reach.

"You don't know the truth!" said Josefina.

"I know what you told me. *That's* the truth."

"Sicario, stop!" shouted Josefina.

Sicario was breathing heavily. It was becoming an effort to talk, but he pushed through it. "Time for this shit to end, Josefina. Tell him. Tell him what Rafael told you."

Josefina grabbed the rope, ready to hop into the ring. "You don't know what you're talking about!"

"Tell him what Rafael said the last time you saw him."

Jack took a hard look at Josefina. She still had a hold of the rope, but her hands were shaking.

"Rafael told her everything," said Sicario.

"Stop!"

"He told her he was gonna do it."

Jack's eyes darted back and forth from the ring to the rope, from Sicario to Josefina.

Sicario suddenly found another gear as a fighter. He was on the attack, no longer measuring his opponent for the strategic combination. It was an adrenaline-driven surge that bore no resemblance to the former champion's patient and smooth style. This was pure anger, a recklessness that surely would have gotten him killed in a match with a skilled opponent. But Theo was a street fighter.

"Theo, get out of there!" Jack shouted.

Theo was back against the ropes. Sicario was right on him, hammering at his midsection.

"Just go down, Theo!"

The blows kept coming, but Sicario was tiring. The adrenaline rush could carry him only so far. It was like watching a car run out of gas, and the damage of too many blows and too many concussions in a career that had lasted way too long was evident. Sicario finally took a step back, putting a little space between himself and his human punching bag. It was enough space for Theo to unleash his bulging right arm with all the force he could muster. The punch caught Sicario between the eyes. His costly half-step away from his opponent became a backward stagger. Sicario was no longer a car out of gas. The stone had downed Goliath.

Sicario was on the canvas, out cold.

"Sicario!" Josefina shouted as she ran into the ring. She knelt at his side, put his head in her lap, and then screamed at Theo: "Why did you have to do this?"

"Jack told me to take him down."

"I told you to go down," said Jack.

Jack brought a cool, wet towel from the corner. Josefina applied it her trainer's forehead. He was breathing heavily but still unconscious.

"Take his gloves off," said Theo.

"Leave us alone," said Josefina.

Theo didn't back off. "I want to see the tattoo."

"He doesn't have a tattoo," said Josefina.

"I want to see."

Sicario was coming around and mumbled something to her in Spanish. Josefina glared at Theo as she untied Sicario's right glove. She pulled it off, then held up Sicario's hand for Theo to see. There was no tattoo. She untied the left, tossed the glove aside, and showed Theo his hand. No tattoo.

"You happy?" she asked.

Theo said nothing. Jack answered for them both. "No," he said. "Confused."

"He did it!" shouted Josefina. "Okay? Rafael did it. End of confusion."

"What?"

"Don't you get it, Jack? Rafael was so close to Key West, closer to the United States than to Cuba. He could practically see Bianca from the top of the derrick. Every other Cuban could leave Cuba under the new travel rules. But not Rafael. Not someone with a college degree and a wife who defected and who might never come back. He was ready to swim there."

"But, blowing up a rig?"

"They didn't *tell* him it would blow up. They *used* him. All Rafael wanted was some kind of emergency. Something that would get him and all the other workers evacuated to the closest dry land. Haven't you ever heard of wet foot/dry foot?"

Of course Jack had. It was the U.S. immigration policy that had produced those tragic images on television of Cuban refugees swimming toward shore until they could swim no more. It wasn't enough simply to reach U.S. waters. They had to get all the way to dry land to get asylum. Or else they were sent back to Cuba.

A noise cut through the gym, the unmistakable sound of the entrance door opening. It pulled a much-needed draft through an open window at the opposite end of the gym, cooling the ring for a moment, but the air went still again as the door closed with a thud. All eyes—even Sicario's—turned toward the dimly lit hallway. Footsteps echoed off the walls, and finally a man emerged from the shadows.

"Who are you?" Josefina asked in Spanish.

Noori didn't answer. He kept walking toward the ring.

Theo went toward him, stopping at the ropes. "She asked who you are."

Noori stopped outside the ring. "I'm looking for Rafael."

Sicario pushed himself up from the canvas. Josefina helped him to his feet, but he was still wobbly.

"Rafael is dead," said Sicario.

Jack was about to speak, but Noori pulled a gun from inside his jacket, which silenced everyone.

"So are you, liar," said Noori.

The gun was quickly aimed in Sicario's direction, the pop of a nine-millimeter round echoed through the gym, and Sicario dropped to the canvas for the last time. Josefina screamed and lunged at the shooter. Another deafening crack of gunfire cut through the gym, and Josefina fell forward and landed beside her trainer.

Jack went to her as Theo threw himself at Noori, but before Theo could make contact, Jack spotted something in the open window, and just as he realized what it was—an arm, a fist, a gun—he heard the pop of a revolver. Noori's head snapped back, and a hot spray of crimson showered the floor around him. It wasn't clear who had fired the shot from outside, but it was no amateur. Noori was dead before he hit the floor.

Jack rolled Josefina onto her back. Blood soaked through her shirt at the rib cage, just below the heart.

"Theo, get an ambulance!"

"How?"

"Run to a neighbor's house. Go!"

A trickle of blood ran from Josefina's mouth.

"You're going to be okay," said Jack.

"No, I'm not," she said, her voice barely a whisper.

"Just hang in there. An ambulance is coming."

She grimaced from the pain and grabbed Jack's hand. "Believe what I told you about Rafael," she said. "He thought if he played along, the rig would shut down. He just wanted to be with his wife. They needed someone on board the rig to mess with the alarm system. They used him."

"Who are *they*?" asked Jack.

Maybe she didn't hear him. Maybe she didn't know the answer. Or maybe she just had something more important to say.

"Funny thing is, I always did love Rafael," she said. "But there's something I want you to tell Bianca, because it's true: her Rafael never loved another woman." She smiled a little, fading. "He really was ready to swim to Key West. This wasn't his fault. It's just another love story."

Jack watched the life drain from those dark, mysterious eyes, and then her body went limp in his arms.

"Josefina?"

"Ambulance is coming!" Theo shouted as he rushed back into the gym. Brunelli was with him, and it was clear to Jack who had fired the shot from the dark side of the open window.

"I followed him here," Brunelli said, pointing with a nod toward Noori. "I was calling for backup when I heard the shots."

"Ten seconds sooner would have been nice."

Brunelli knelt down and checked Josefina's pulse. "She's gone," he said.

Jack didn't want to believe it.

"We have to leave her," said Brunelli.

"What?"

"An ambulance is on the way. And if I heard the first and second gunshots when I was outside this building, someone in the neighborhood probably heard them, too. They surely heard mine. The Cuban police will be here any minute. We have to go."

"We can't just leave," said Jack.

"They're all dead, Jack. We can't help them. We have to go. Now!"

Jack lowered Josefina's head gently to the floor. Brunelli jumped up into the ring, went to Sicario, and placed the pistol that he'd used to kill Noori in the boxer's open hand.

"This was a tragic love triangle," said Brunelli,

staging it, his gaze sweeping over all three bodies. "That's our story."

Jack kept Josefina's last words to himself. "More than you know," he said.

"Let's go!" said Brunelli.

"I'm not leaving," said Jack.

"Don't be stupid."

"I won't pretend that this is some love triangle gone wrong. I won't dishonor her like that. The truth is going to be told."

"Fine," said Brunelli. "Tell your client, tell the press, tell the world. But do it from Miami, and do it tomorrow—after Operation Black Horizon closes."

"Operation what?"

"Jack, we need to get you the fuck out of this country before you spend the rest of your life in a Cuban jail."

"What about Theo? He comes with me. He's not going back to the Bahamas."

"Understood. Your wife has the Bahamas covered. Right now. As we speak."

"Andie's in the Bahamas?"

"You'll see. Let our operation play out, and let's get out of here."

Jack checked with Theo—just a moment of eye contact—and they were in agreement.

"All right," said Jack. "We'll go."

Brunelli raced across the gym and down the hall, pushing the door open at a dead run. Jack could almost feel the hole in his heart as he and Theo followed the agent into the Cuban night.

69

Andie reached the marina in Nassau at nine p.m. She was focused on her mission, getting in role, but it was impossible not to take in the beauty of Albany Marina, so many yachts and so much luxury off South Bay. A half-moon hung above the palm trees. Running lights glowed on vessels across the harbor. A hundred-foot sailboat motored into a slip, its five-spreader mast so enormous that it needed a blinking red light to warn low-flying airplanes.

Backing up Andie were two international agents, legates from the U.S. embassy. It was a coordinated effort between the FBI and the Royal Bahamas Police Force. Andie and the legates were technically observers, lacking the authority to make an arrest on foreign soil. But the RBPF's execution of a Bahamian arrest warrant in connection with the murder of Leonard Jeffries was fully in keeping with the objectives of Operation Black Horizon. As of Monday morning, the RBPF had ruled out Theo Knight in the Jeffries murder. But they had completely lost track of their new suspect. A tip from Andie had steered them straight. Brunelli's team in Havana had tracked her to Nassau, where Andie picked up the trail. Vivien had led her straight to Albany Marina on South Bay, straight to the man who had murdered Jeffries—to the man who was Vivien's accomplice in a much bigger crime.

The FBI's efforts had earned Andie the favor of making one undercover contact with the suspects before the Bahamians moved in for their arrest. The RBPF moved into position in silence. Andie took a seat on the bench on the dock. Beside her was Long Wu, Noori's boss from N.Y.C. Gadets. His cooperation in this final phase of Operation Black Horizon would earn him immunity from prosecution on counterfeiting charges that could have landed him in prison for the rest of his life.

"Got a visual on the suspects," said Andie, her voice picked up by her wire. The FBI legates were out of sight, listening.

A dozen yachts rested side by side in long slips, each with the bow facing out, the stern backed up to the dock. From their seat on the wooden bench, Andie and Long Wu were looking directly at the stern of *Lucky Seven Seas*. Rick's delivery of the seventy-foot Johnson from Key West to Nassau had been a one-way proposition, and his contract to deliver the even larger *Lucky Seven Seas* to Havana would get him out of the Bahamas in style, and closer to the big payoff. The FBI could add the boat delivery, a violation of the U.S. trade embargo, to Rick's long list of crimes. According to Andie's intelligence, Rick had been making the trip for years.

It was how he and Vivien had hooked up and fallen into bed in the first place.

Andie waited for Rick and Vivien to draw even with her on the dock, then rose. "We need to talk, Rick," she said.

He and Vivien stopped before stepping onto the yacht. "Who are you?" asked Rick.

Long Wu stepped forward and delivered his only line. "This Noori's girlfriend," he said in broken English.

Andie took over. "Vivien, I'm sure you remember Dawut Noori's boss. You met on one of Long Wu's business trips to Havana."

"Yes, of course I remember," said Vivien.

Rick and Vivien exchanged glances. There was some obvious apprehensiveness on their part, but Andie sensed that she had gotten past the first credibility hurdle.

"Dawut is dead," said Andie.

She checked their reactions in the moonlight. There was none.

"I'm very sorry to hear that," said Vivien.

"We don't doubt your sincerity," said Andie. "I've seen the articles you wrote for the *Cuba Times* about Dawut and the other Uighurs detained at Guantá-namo."

"It was a gross violation of international law," said Vivien.

"You were one of the few journalists to point that out. And you are one of the few people who could understand Dawut's desire to get even with the country that held him in solitary confinement for seven years without a shred of evidence."

"I don't know anything about getting even," said Vivien.

"Really? From the tone of your articles in the *Cuba Times*, I would say you hate the United States more than Dawut did."

"Writing for the *Cuba Times* is not a crime."

"That's true."

"But Dawut had good reason to be angry," said Vivien. "I agree with that."

Andie nodded. "I tried to convince Dawut to put it all behind him. Now that he's dead, I know that I failed. That anger kept burning. He wanted big-time revenge. If the U.S. was going to detain him with no evidence that he was a terrorist, then, by God, he was going to be a terrorist. A major terrorist, one deserving of solitary confinement at Gitmo. I thought he was all talk when he said his plan was to blow up the Scarborough 8. Turns out, all he needed was one cooperative worker on the rig to pull off the plan."

Rick and Vivien stood mute.

Andie continued. "You found his man, Vivien. You found Rafael Lopez."

Neither of them responded. Finally, Vivien said, "I truly am sorry that Noori is dead."

"I don't care if you're sorry or not," said Andie. "This is business."

"What do you want from us?" asked Rick.

"I know Dawut paid you fifty thousand dollars. I know he owed you a lot more for getting Rafael to pull this off. I'm here to tell you that we're not going to pay you. You're not getting it from me, and you're not getting it from Long Wu."

"First of all," said Rick, "let's get things straight. Noori paid Rafael Lopez fifty thousand dollars."

"He didn't pay Rafael anything."

Andie held out her hand, illuminating it with a small flashlight. The tattoo above her thumb, just below the wrist, was identical to Rafael's. Andie noted their reaction, which they couldn't hide. But Rick still played it cool.

"A tattoo. So what?"

"The Eye of Our Lady," said Andie. "Temporary tattoo. Very high quality, but it washes off easily. Same thing they use in the movies. Same thing you used when you were pretending to be Rafael Lopez."

Rick didn't deny it. "What do you want from us?"

"My sources tell me that you have been very busy. Not only were you working Dawut to cough up what he promised to pay you. But you've also been working the feds to pay for information about the cause of the explosion. We want half."

Rick laughed.

"You think I'm joking?" asked Andie. "Dawut is dead. He can't be prosecuted for anything. You pay us half, or I go to the FBI and tell them who Dawut was working with."

"Tell them what?" said Rick, scoffing. "That Noori was working with Rafael Lopez? You have nothing on us."

"Rafael was your pawn," said Andie. "So was Josefina. You told them that the computer virus from Dawut would make the alarm malfunction in a storm. You didn't tell Rafael the rig would explode. You told him it would be crippled, floating without power at the mercy of the seas in a hurricane. The entire crew would be evacuated to the nearest shore, which was Key West. It was Rafael's ticket to be with his wife."

Vivien's expression went cold. The depth and breadth of Andie's knowledge clearly scared her.

"I'm right," said Andie. "I know I'm right."

"Maybe we can work something out," said Vivien.

"Shut up," said Rick. "She's bluffing."

"I'm not bluffing," said Andie, glancing at her tattoo. "You can buy Our Lady of Guadalupe temporary tattoos just about anywhere, but *The Eye* of Our Lady is pretty hard to find. Only a few online sources sell it. I happen to know that one of those websites shipped to you, Rick."

It wasn't a bluff; the FBI had it. Again, no denial from Rick.

Andie pressed further. "I also know that you made sure the bank employees saw the tattoo when you opened the accounts in Rafael's name at New Providence Bank and Trust. You made sure Jack Swyteck saw it after Vivien helped you kidnap him from her apartment. All this was to deflect attention from you, making it look like maybe Rafael Lopez—the man behind the explosion—was still alive. Most important, you made sure Dawut saw it, so when he came looking for the guy who was squeezing him for more money, he wouldn't think of you. Don't deny it. I got Dawut's phone after he died, and I saw the photograph that you e-mailed him—the one of the hand holding the deposit slip, just enough of the hand in the picture to show the tattoo."

Andie was sharing information that went way beyond her "girlfriend" undercover role, but she didn't care. At this point, she had them, and the look on their faces was worth it.

Rick turned and started to make a run for it, but he didn't get far. RBPF officers jumped out from their positions of hiding in the neighboring boats, guns drawn, trapping Rick and Vivien.

"Freeze!" the team of officers shouted.

The suspects stopped and raised their arms on command, but Vivien quickly cracked.

"This was Rick's idea!" she shouted. "I'm just a reporter."

"Shut up!" said Rick. "Noori paid Rafael. This was all Noori and Rafael."

"Rick forced me to do this," said Vivien. "This man's a monster."

"It was Rafael, you stupid bitch. Nobody but Noori and Rafael."

The RPBF officers cuffed Rick first, then Vivien. "You're under arrest for the murder of Mr. Jeffries," the Bahamian officer said. "And so are you, miss."

"What did I do? It was all him," said Vivien.

"All me, huh? Who was in Havana to collect the money?"

"You see?" Vivien shouted, imploring her arresting officer. "You see how he uses people just to keep from getting caught with his hands in the cookie jar? He's a monster, I tell you!"

Andie gave a little salute of appreciation to the Bahamian detective, then watched with satisfaction as the RPBF took them away. She could hear Vivien's shouting—*It's him! Not me!*—all the way to the end of the dock, until they finally disappeared into the police van in the parking lot.

Epilogue

T he news segments could have been written by Jack. All day, the "sad and tragic cause of the Scarborough 8 disaster" played out on American television. Jack watched one final report from the oil-tinged shores of Key West.

"It has nothing to do with the oil industry," the reporter said, as cleanup crews toiled behind her. "It has nothing to do with the trade embargo against Cuba, environmental terrorism by the left or right, or industrial sabotage by one corporate giant against another. This was the desperate act of a young man who wanted to get to America to be with the woman he loved. He sabotaged the Scarborough 8, thinking that because the rig was closer to Key West than to Cuba, all those aboard would be evacuated to the United States. Once there, he planned to claim asylum and be with the woman he loved. There was just one problem: his actions caused a massive explosion way beyond anything he imagined possible."

Jack turned it off. The Scarborough 8 was officially the worst oil spill in U.S. history.

And it was a love story.

He opened the French doors and stepped out onto the deck behind the house. Andie was sitting before her laptop in the shade of an umbrella, typing her final report on Operation Black Horizon. Their golden retriever, Max, lay at her feet, back from his doggie vacation at Mitzi's Boot Camp, which was originally to have coincided with Jack and Andie's honeymoon. He was sound asleep, no doubt exhausted from daily swims in the pool and racing in the fields with horses.

"I get most of this," said Jack. "But if Rafael was a derrick monkey, how did he get anywhere near the computerized alarm system?"

Andie looked up from her LCD. "You know I can't discuss my report."

"Surely the answer to my question is going to be public information."

She didn't argue. "Okay. Rafael was probably the most overqualified derrick monkey you'll ever see. He volunteered for it, but the degree he was working on from the university was in computer engineering. So he hung out with the other engineers and engineering students at meals or in the recreation room. He became their buddy, and they showed him around. He worked the friendships to get access."

"Why did he volunteer to be a derrick monkey?"

"So he could see to Key West. You have to remember, this was—"

"A love story," said Jack.

"A sad one."

"Makes me even sadder that Rafael only thought

he was seeing Key West. The Coast Guard expert that I brought into court said it was impossible to see that far, even from the top of the derrick."

"I'll bet what he actually saw was the Dry Tortugas. Fort Jefferson is pretty high above sea level at points."

Fort Jefferson. Jack could only shake his head at the irony. The old fort was where the doctor who set the broken leg of Abraham Lincoln's assassin had served his prison sentence.

"They should reopen it and lock up Vivien and Rick there."

"That would be too good," said Andie. "I'm told the Bahamas will seek the death penalty against Rick for the Jeffries murder. Vivien could get life as an accomplice, but hopefully we'll obtain extradition and the National Security Division will figure out a way to seek the death penalty under antiterrorism laws."

Jack wasn't in the mood for another death penalty debate with Andie. He changed the subject, if only slightly.

"I spoke to Bianca," he said.

"How did she take it?"

"Like you'd expect. Disgusted by Rick. Overwhelmed by how much Rafael wanted to be with her. Terrible feelings of guilt over the pain and disaster it caused. Not that the lawsuit matters anymore, but of course she knows her case is over. I wish I could have at least kept that fifty thousand bucks for her, but it's beyond a stretch to make a legal claim to an account that never really belonged to her or Rafael."

"Does she even have a job anymore?"

"Rick's Café is closed for now, but it won't take long to find a buyer for a bar on Duval Street. Funny thing, but the reason Theo went to Key West in the first place was to scout out the possibility of buying it with friends. Rumor had it that Rick was looking to sell before I even met him."

"In anticipation of a big fat Bahamian bank account, no doubt."

"I suppose. Oh, well. Maybe Theo and his friends will end up getting a steal on his bar."

"That would be something if Bianca ends up working for Theo."

Jack shook his head. "Sometimes I think life would be so much easier if we all just worked for Theo."

She caught his drift. "Okay, how much did you lose on this contingency-fee case?"

"Not sure. But it may pay off in referrals down the line."

"You mean from your friend Cassie in New York?"

"Believe it or not, Luis Candela. He has an oil client who allegedly bribed public officials in Ecuador and might be indicted under the Foreign Corrupt Practices Act. Said he'll probably be giving me a call."

"Great. Another case that you and I will see completely eye to eye on, I'm sure."

"Yeah. Candela's actually a decent guy. I think this could come through."

"But until then?"

Jack shrugged. "Until then, how do you feel about finishing our honeymoon at the Ritz Carlton on Key Biscayne?"

It was a full eight blocks from their house. "Sounds perfect."

There was silence between them. Then Andie reached over and took his hand. "You really okay?"

"Yeah. You?"

"I think so," she said with a sad smile. "Wish I could hit the rewind button and go back to our wedding day. But I can't."

Jack looked off toward the bay, thinking of Rafael gazing across the Florida Straits from atop the derrick. "Kind of the way Bianca feels, I would imagine."

"Yeah," said Andie. "I would imagine."

The memorial service at sea was on Friday afternoon. It was Bianca, Jack, Andie, and Theo.

The sun was shining brightly as Jack motored out their rented ski-boat from Key West. Twin outboard engines propelled them in a southwesterly direction for almost an hour. They were in international waters, no land in sight, when Jack cut the engine. Gentle waves slapped against the starboard side, a soothing sound.

"Take your time," Jack told Bianca.

She nodded and rose slowly. The boat was rocking, and it took her a moment to get her sea legs. Then she opened a book to read "El Cisne," an old poem by Elisa Monge.

Jack would have liked to follow it aurally, but Hispanic poetry wasn't easy for the minimally conversant. Bianca had printed out a rough English translation, which Jack shared with Andie and Theo. It lacked the power and rhythm of the native tongue, but against the backdrop of Bianca's reading of the Spanish original, even the printed translation approached poetry: "In the middle of the waters swayed / a handsome swan of snowy plumage / that sank his head into the foam / and with pleasure dipped it out again." Bianca read in a soft voice, stopping to collect herself as the woman in the poem returns to the lake and is unable to find her swan, and stopped once more, to choke back tears, when the woman discovers what has happened to him. A particularly long pause punctuated her struggle at the end: "Nevermore would the handsome, majestic swan / so proudly pass over the lake / nevermore would the rays of the silver moon / illuminate his graceful gliding."

When she finished, Bianca put down her book of poetry and went to the stern. Three wreaths rested side by side on the padded bench seat. With great care, she lifted the one in the middle with both hands. It was a mixture of colorful orchids and white butterfly jasmine (Mariposa Blanca), the official flower of Cuba. It was for Rafael. She walked to portside, whispered something that Jack couldn't hear—maybe *good-bye*, maybe *I love you*—and dropped it overboard.

She gripped the chrome rail tightly, her hands shaking.

Theo then rose, walked to the back of the boat, took another wreath, and dropped it over the side. It was for Josefina. Together, Jack and Andie dropped the third wreath for Sicario.

The water buoyed each of them, and the line of wreaths drifted away from their boat, a floral flotilla. Jack put his arm around Bianca, holding her close as they watched in silence. The wreaths were getting smaller, farther away, and then they all saw it.

When the wreaths had drifted about twenty yards from the boat, a gentle swell rose up, and the water flashed with ironic and ambivalent beauty. It surrounded all three memorials like a halo, framing them in an assortment of colors more brilliant than the blossoms that made up the wreaths, colors that set this solemn place apart from the deep-blue ocean around them. For an instant, it was like a rainbow floating on the ocean's surface.

It was the sheen of Cuban petroleum glistening in the Florida sun.

Acknowledgments

•

It's been twenty years since Jack Swyteck made his debut in *The Pardon*. I am forever grateful to Richard Pine, still my agent, who pitched Jack to HarperCollins, still my publisher. I didn't write that first Swyteck novel thinking it would become a series, so special thanks go to my editor, Carolyn Marino, who, after our fourth novel together, had the good sense to ask, "What ever happened to Jack?"

I do my own research, so the mistakes are all mine, but I'm grateful to many who shared their knowledge and expertise, including Rex Hamilton and his incredibly helpful friends at the Everglades Foundation; Gwen Keenan, director of Emergency Response, Office of Emergency Response, Florida Department of Environmental Protection; and Jacqueline Gonzalez-Touzet, for her insights into Cuba and, in particular, Cuban architecture.

I'm also grateful to Carolyn's editorial assistant, Amanda Bergeron, and to my volunteer beta readers, Janis Koch and Gloria Villa. They do much more than copyedit. They make me a better writer.

Congratulations to John and Samantha Murphy, who lent the name of John's father (Jim Murphy) to a character in *Black Horizon*. The generosity of the Murphy family at a "character auction" will benefit the children of St. Thomas Episcopal Parish School. The tradition of character auctions in Jack Swyteck novels started with *Beyond Suspicion* (Swyteck No. 2), and I'm happy to say that we've now raised over $50,000 for charity.

Finally, to Tiffany. Jack Swyteck came to life twenty years ago, and I feel like I did, too. Happy anniversary. I love you.

Read on for an excerpt from
James Grippando's

CANE AND ABE

Coming soon in hardcover
from Harper

Unbelievable was the word for her. Samantha Vine was unbelievably beautiful. It was unbelievable that she'd married me. Even more unbelievable that she was gone.

It was also pretty unbelievable that I'd fallen in love again and remarried. But resilience is more the rule than the exception, isn't it? People fall in love. People die. People somehow pick up the pieces and move on, accepting or not the soothing spiritual song that death is nothing more than a major change of address. But the most unbelievable thing about Samantha had nothing to do with us. Strictly speaking, it wasn't even about *her*. It was about her father. Luther Vine was once an African-American slave.

Bullshit, you say, and not because you think I'm just a crazy white guy trying to insinuate himself into black history through marriage. Or maybe that is part of your thinking. But mostly, it's the generational disconnect.

I totally get the skepticism. Slavery was outlawed in 1865 with the adoption of the Thirteenth Amendment to the U.S. Constitution. Samantha wasn't even conceived until then president Jimmy Carter pulled on a cardigan sweater in a chilly White House and asked all Americans to be like him, conserve energy, and turn down the thermostat to fifty-five degrees at night. All winter long, Luther and Carlotta Vine had crawled into bed and heated things up the old-fashioned way. The point is that racism persists, but Samantha was so far removed from the end of slavery as an institution that she had never known a U.S. Supreme Court without a black justice. She had no memory of the NFL without a starting black quarterback. She couldn't even name a hit song by Prince until he was officially the artist formerly known as Prince, and she wasn't old enough to party like it's 1999 until it actually was 1999.

So, back to that troublesome timeline. Even if Samantha's old man was literally an old man at her birth, it doesn't add up. In fact, it flies in the face of history. The last American slave died in 1971. Not one of Sylvester Magee's children was alive to see the headstone finally laid in his honor in Mississippi more than four decades after his death—coincidentally, the same year I lost my wife.

Samantha Vine, the daughter of a slave?

"No way," people tell me. "Not unless I'm missing something."

"You're missing something."

"What?"

"You don't know sugar."

"Fuck you, Abe. It's you who doesn't know shit."

"No," I say. "You don't know *sugar*."

I mean Big Sugar.

In the fall of 1941 a group of men traveled across the Deep South and visited the black part of towns like Memphis and Biloxi, offering "steady employment" to "colored farm workers" eighteen years or older. It didn't matter that Luther Vine was only sixteen. Nothing about the offer was legit. "Enjoy Florida Sunshine during the Winter Months," the ads promised, "while harvesting Sugar Cane on the plantations of the National Sugar Corporation." Luther wasn't stupid. Swinging a machete all day, cutting down twelve-foot stalks of sugarcane as thick as a man's wrist, and loading tons of cane onto a truck wasn't for college boys. "Any way you slice it," Luther often said, pun intended, "you're talkin' stoop labor." But the company promised good wages, as much as thirty dollars a week. Good living conditions, free rent, free meals, free transportation to Florida, free medical attention, and recreation were all part of the package. He signed up and got on the truck with the other recruits.

Their destination had been Clewiston, the "world's sweetest town," where thousands of acres of sugarcane butted up against the south shore of Lake Okeechobee in the Florida Everglades. The ride took two days. The men were fed twice, bologna and a slice of bread. Upon arrival, each recruit was handed a bill for eleven dollars—the cost of the "free" ride from Memphis. More charges quickly piled up. Seventy-five cents for a blanket. Fifty for a machete. Another thirty for a file to sharpen the blade. A dollar for a badge that identified a worker as a company employee. Fifty cents for water that wasn't too dirty to drink. Recruits were up to their eyeballs in debt before the first workday, which started with breakfast at 3:30 a.m. They were in the field by 4:30, broke for a short lunch, and cut more cane until dark. Wages for the first day were a dollar eighty, four bucks short of the amount promised. Superintendents patrolled the fields, armed with blackjacks and pistols, threatening anyone who wasn't working hard enough or who grumbled about wanting to go home. The best chance to escape was at night. After three weeks—twenty-one straight workdays, rain or shine, sunup to sundown—nine workers ran off from the barracks at the company camp. Luther was one of them. The plan was to hitchhike back to Memphis. They were arrested eighteen miles from Clewiston, fined forty dollars for "vagrancy," and returned to the field. The only way to pay off the fine was to cut more cane. Naively, Luther asked for permission to convert the fine to prison time, preferring jail. The superintendent cracked him with a blackjack and told him sure thing, as soon as he paid off what he owed the company, a debt that was getting bigger every day because he drank too much water in the field and needed medical attention for a snakebite.

There were enough runaways for word to trickle back home, and from there to the Department of Justice in Washington, D.C. Herbert Hoover himself approved the FBI's sixty-page investigative report. A federal grand jury in Florida indicted National Sugar and several employees for "conspiracy to violate the right and privilege of citizens to be free from slavery under the Thirteenth Amendment."

So, in my book, calling Luther Vine a former slave was no stretch, even if the indictment had technically been dismissed. "The grand jury was tainted," the sugar lawyers argued, "because there weren't any farmers on it." Right. And Timothy McVeigh should have complained about the lack of terrorists on the grand jury that indicted him for the Oklahoma City bombing.

Anyway, Samantha's father was coming up on his ninetieth birthday. The old man and I were still close, or as close as we could be. Luther was showing signs of dementia, and even though he had good days, he still told folks at the skilled nursing facility that his son-in-law was Abraham Lincoln. A stretch, to be sure, even if I was a tall white lawyer with four score and seven murder trials under my belt. I just went along with whatever Luther said. It only confused him to hear that I was senior trial counsel at the Office of the State Attorney for Miami-Dade County, the go-to guy in capital cases.

"I'm looking for FBI agent Victoria Santos," I said to the state trooper.

Her black-and-tan vehicle, beacons flashing, was one of six Florida Highway Patrol cars blocking the entrance to a mile-long bridge across the heart of the Everglades. The Tamiami Trail was the main route connecting east and west Florida below Lake Okeechobee, the second largest lake in the continental United States.

"And you are?" she asked.

"Abe Beckham, state attorney's office," I said as I flashed my badge.

It wasn't my job to visit every crime scene in Miami-Dade County, even when there was a possible homicide. But when the FBI was tracking a serial killer, it was critical for someone more senior from the state attorney's office to stay on top of the investigation. The chief assistant to the state attorney had personally asked me to follow up on the report of a body in the Everglades that had all the markings of a fifth victim in south Florida.

"That way," the trooper said, pointing toward a gathering of law enforcement agents beside the bridge. They were standing on the old two-lane stretch of highway that ran parallel to the new bridge, and which was no longer in use.

I thanked her, ducked under the yellow crime scene tape.

"Abe, hey, what's going on?"

I stopped at the sound of the familiar voice. It was the crime-beat reporter from *Action News*. We were two miles from the western frontier of urban sprawl, too far from downtown Miami to discern even the tallest skyscrapers, but I could see the microwave towers of media vans in the long line of traffic that stretched toward the morning sun. Helicopters were sure to follow. It wouldn't have surprised me to see a camera crew or two arrive by airboat—anything to be first.

"Nothing to say, Susan."

"Oh, come on, Abe."

Susan Brown had covered at least a dozen of my murder trials, and I usually gave her what I could.

But I truly had nothing. I turned and continued down the embankment.

The old road had undergone many improvements since Model Ts first rolled across it in 1928, and to many folks a new elevated bridge seemed a waste of money. But it was part of a multibillion-dollar Everglades restoration project, much of which was geared toward undoing the negative impact of the well-intended but catastrophic work of the Army Corps of Engineers in the twentieth century. Levees and canals built by the corps opened the sawgrass plains to sugarcane growers and other farmers, and roads like the 275-mile-long Tamiami Trail made the watery sloughs passable by motorists. The casualty in all the construction was the water flow essential for a healthy Everglades. The new bridge was raised on pilings, adjacent to the old road, to alleviate the damming effect.

I hopped from the embankment onto the old road but came up short. I was halfway up to my knees in muck.

"Ah, *shit*." It wasn't just the wet shoes and pant legs. It takes a thousand years of decomposition to create a foot of peat, and I'd just unleashed the rotten stink of nine hundred and ninety-nine.

"Let me help you out there, pardner," said one of the troopers. He tugged me by the arm, and the muck puckered like a suction cup as my foot emerged from the Everglades version of quicksand. I considered rinsing off the black mess in the standing water near a culvert, but the nine-foot alligator sunning itself on the bank changed my mind.

"Welcome to Shark Valley," said the trooper.

I assumed that it was just a name, that there weren't actually any sharks around, but I was none-theless glad to be on dry land. Not that there was much of anything dry around me. From the south-ern lip of Lake Okeechobee, tea-colored water flowed for a hundred miles, south to the tip of main-land Florida and west to the Gulf of Mexico, much as spilled milk spreads across the kitchen table. Covering these millions of watery acres, flat as a Kansas wheat field, were endless waves of sawgrass, a rare species of swamp sedge that has flourished for over four thousand years. This legendary "river of grass" divided the east coast of Florida from the west, an environmental marvel where visitors found exotic reptiles, manatees, and rainbow-colored tree snails, roseate spoonbills and ghost orchids, tower-ing royal palms and gumbo limbos. Here, biblical clouds of mosquitoes could blacken a white canoe within seconds, and oceans of stars filled a night sky untouched by city lights. There was no other place on earth like it. I rarely went there, except when passing through at sixty miles per hour on the drive to Naples.

Or, on a day like today, recovering a body.

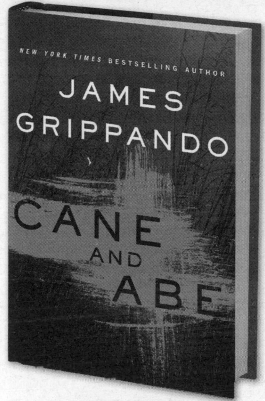